Just Desserts

Other Books by Patti Massman
(with Pamela Beck)

Fling

Rich Men, Single Women

Just Desserts

Patti Massman
and
Susan Rosser

. . . .

Crown Publishers, Inc.
New York

Published by Crown Publishers, Inc., 201 East 50th Street, New York, New York 10022. Member of the Crown Publishing Group.

CROWN is a trademark of Crown Publishers, Inc.

Manufactured in the United States of America

It has been said that a man at his desk is busy;
a woman at her desk is available.
To Brent and Michael Massman,
Julie, Jonathan, and Bob Rosser,
who understood that this isn't always true,
our love and gratitude.

. . . .

Acknowledgments

This story would not have been possible without the insightful, candid, and professional input from the following people: Angela Barton, Judi Bramlett, Adrienne Cantor, Barbara Federman, Dr. Susan Krevoy, Dr. Roger Lewis, Dr. Andrea Rich, Dr. Robert Rosser, Teri Schwartz, Hilarie Taub, and Linda Thomas.

For another kind of editorial input, we want to thank our parents— Anne and Eddie Schwartz, Ben and Thelma Maltz, and Ann Massman— who cried and laughed at all the right places.

A special thanks to our editors at Crown Publishers, Arlene Friedman and Jane Meara, who understood at every turn what we wanted to say and helped us say it better than we thought possible.

And to our agent, Harvey Klinger, who always returned every call and answered every question no matter what the hour. We're glad you believed in this project as much as we did.

Part One

Part One

Chapter

1

Some days, Diana Lowe thought, living in Encino was a poetic experience. The natural, unstructured beauty made overreacting seem normal in this bucolic suburb tucked away under the Santa Monica mountain range.

Encino. So quiet south of Ventura Boulevard in the old estate section where Diana lived that on a summer's day the loudest sound was the buzzing of bees or the crunching of dry brush under the hooves of the prancing deer that roamed the wilds only meters beyond her home and the other gated estates of the many famous business and entertainment-industry people who called the former Spanish land grant ranches and farms home.

They had discovered Encino's rustic charm, bought the multi-acred enclaves for a fraction of what the same homes behind gates would have cost in Beverly Hills, and turned the orange groves into tennis courts with striped canvas cabanas.

Encino. So quiet that at night the only sounds outside Diana's windows were those of coyotes howling over their kill and an occasional howl from one of the many rock stars who had turned the stables on their property into music rooms where they could bray the night away composing songs that would put gold and platinum records on their walls.

Encino. It was a quiet mixture of old and new—money, ideas, even trees.

Was it William Wordsworth or Robert Browning who wrote the words that expressed Diana Lowe's feelings so aptly on this perfect October afternoon? Which of the poets had felt "God's in his heaven, all's right with the world," as she was feeling now? Damn, if only she could sweep the name loose from among the other stored bits of information that had accumulated like so much dust over the years.

Let's see, she thought, driving now as though on autopilot, maybe it was Wordsworth. She was sure the lines had been written by an English poet. Nineteenth century.

Maybe it was Elizabeth Barrett Browning? Nah.

Diana had never liked Elizabeth Barrett Browning and never would have memorized any of her poetry, except for a good laugh.

Maybe it was Tennyson, she mused. If it was Browning or Wordsworth or Tennyson—no, definitely not Tennyson—had he been experiencing a fall day in England that could match one as glorious as this in Encino?

Diana felt so connected suddenly. She felt so tied to all the ages, to all the thoughts of all the ages, to all the writers who had the thoughts that were recorded and remembered down through the ages, that she forgot to watch for her street. So it was that when she came upon it suddenly, as though it had been drawn as an afterthought into a child's picture, she had to turn sharply to avoid a deep, jagged pothole or risk breaking an axle on her Mercedes station wagon.

Careening around the corner, Diana nearly barreled into a squirrel darting across the narrow road. She slammed on her brakes and screeched to a halt. She sat frozen for a second, her hands clutching the steering wheel while her eyes followed the oblivious squirrel's blithe path to the object of his intense attention—Christopher Berry, Diana's neighbor.

"Another close call," Chris yelled to Diana, looking at her with a bemused expression from where he knelt on the used-brick stoop in front of his ranch-style house. He held out a palm full of raisins, some of which the furry rodent brazenly grabbed. Chris stood up. The squirrel continued to munch away, seemingly undaunted by the imposing figure Chris made as he unfolded to his full height of six feet four and sauntered over to talk to Diana.

"One of these days I'm finally going to kill one of those rabid little beasts," Diana said with a shudder. "They always seem to pick *my* car to dart in front of."

"They trust Mercedes brakes, that's why," Chris said without a trace of irony in his expression. She had learned that comedy writers were like that; they could say outrageous things and never crack a smile.

"Oh, sure!"

"No, they do," he protested.

"Chris, really."

"They confide in me. We have serious talks about you Encino broads. You know that." Actually, until Chris had come to the Lowes' Fourth of July party earlier that year, he had managed to live on Live Oak Lane for years with none of the neighbors, including Diana, learning much about him except that he was a comedy writer who valued his privacy.

"You're a nut, do you know *that?*"

Chris nodded, revealing only the most minimal trace of sardonic delight in his large gray eyes as he glanced into the back of Diana's station wagon at the large number of grocery bags, then said, "What're you doing, getting ready to feed the entire U.S. Army?"

"Can you believe it?" she replied with a self-deprecatory laugh. "I went to Gelson's to get a few bags of M&M's for the cookies we're baking, and this is what I came out with."

"In my next life I'm going to come back as the owner of a supermarket in suburbia."

"I don't know what comes over me," she said, "but by the time I get to the checkout counter it's like I'm coming out of a coma and these items found their way into my basket all by themselves. Something odd comes over me. You know?" She went on without waiting for Chris to answer. "This time it was lasagna. I decided to make several casseroles for the freezer. I'll make an extra one for you and your girls."

Chris squinted from the shards of sunlight splintering the cottony clouds, creating a glare off the hood of Diana's white car. "Most men *lose* weight when their wives walk out on them," he said. "But I guess they don't have a Diana Lowe for a neighbor," he added with a warm grin. Diana not only cooked special meals for Chris and his daughters, she also was a veritable fount of useful everyday information for a man suddenly cast into the role of mother as well as father.

Chris pulled up his gray sweat shirt and patted his midsection. His abdomen looked flat to Diana, quite impressively muscular, in fact, but Chris said, "I'm still working off the extra two pounds I put on last week from the pork roast and potato pancakes you sent over."

Diana self-consciously glanced down at her oversize work shirt. She wanted to make sure its billowy fullness still covered her down to her thighs. Chris may have had two pounds of extra weight on him, but she had at least *forty*-two! Thank God it wasn't she who had been abandoned by her mate. Chris's body was a feast for women to drool over; he was a man who would always be desirable, while Diana didn't need anyone to remind her that she was overweight and on the wrong side of forty.

"That rat in a fur coat's waiting for you," Diana said. Indeed, the squirrel, his thick brush of a tail flicking, was trying to get into the jumbo box of raisins that Chris had brought outside with him.

"Waiting builds character," Chris intoned. "So, who are you baking cookies with this time?"

"My mother's in town," Diana explained. "When you come to pick up your lasagna, you can meet her," she added enthusiastically.

"I'm supposed to be working," Chris said, a frustrated look crossing his face. A few strands of his sandy blond hair fell across his high forehead from a sudden swirl of wind, and as he carelessly brushed them back with his hand, Diana thought he looked exactly like his famous father, Dwight Berry, the Academy Award–winning actor and heartthrob of his era. Like his father, Chris had strong, rugged features, with interesting imperfections that proved the whole was definitely more perfect than the sum of its parts.

"Are you procrastinating again?" Diana knew Chris's work pattern by now; he always took long strolls through the neighborhood or sat around feeding the neighborhood animals—tame ones as well as wild—when he couldn't write. Her two German shepherds, Romeo and Juliet, loved him.

"This time it's worse than writer's block!" he exclaimed, his thick brows coming together in a frown. "My new computer ate an entire chapter."

"You've got to be kidding," Diana replied.

"I wish I were. I pushed the key to save what I consider the best damn pages I've ever written, and the computer lit up and said 'thankyouverymuch,' then promptly swallowed my work for all eternity."

Chris was in the midst of a new project—he had taken an indeterminate leave of absence from his latest Emmy-winning television show to write a novel. He wanted to accomplish what every comedy writer dreams about doing—writing the great American tragedy. Two weeks after he started his preliminary outline, his wife had announced she was leaving him and their twin thirteen-year-old daughters to pursue a fantasy of her own—studying and photographing grizzly bears in Alaska.

"What could have caused your computer to do such a horrible thing?"

"A power surge."

"Well, I have just the antidote for power surges," Diana said, even though she didn't have the foggiest notion what power surges were.

He eyed her quizzically.

"Cookies!" she said, the corners of her wide-set green eyes crinkling with delight. "Hot, fresh Halloween cookies."

"You're something! How can I resist?"

"Well, resist for thirty minutes. They're not even baked yet."

Diana deposited two heavy grocery bags on the granite countertop in the kitchen. It was a speckled gray and black granite with a cool, rich beauty. Evidence of baking preparations covered most of the surface, but there was no sign of her mother. "I'm back," Diana shouted, then went out to the car and retrieved the rest of the groceries.

Diana walked between cupboards and pantry putting away her purchases. The pantry recently had been enlarged and now resembled a minimart. Its shelves were painted the same taupe as the walls in the kitchen, both coordinated with the newly bleached cabinets and hardwood floors.

In many ways, Diana's kitchen reflected the various stages of her married life. When she and her husband, Harvey, had bought their dream house fifteen years earlier, they had no money left to fix up the fifty-year-old place. Thus, they had lived for a time with the original linoleum floors and the cracked orange Formica countertops that reflected the taste of the first owners. After Harvey began to make substantial amounts of money as an oral surgeon, the first room that was redone was Diana's kitchen. They ripped out the old cabinets and put in new wood ones with fancy beveled trim. They replaced the linoleum floors with dark tongue-and-groove hardwood. They installed hunter green tiles with thick sienna grouting where the Formica countertops had been, and added a butcher-block work surface to the center island. Diana had spent months hunting for the perfect green and rose country print wallpaper and a round nineteenth-century American oak breakfast table with antique captain's chairs to complete the look. Diana had loved that kitchen, the dark, cozy if cluttered feeling suiting her to a tee. Last December, however, Harvey had announced that he wanted something different—something sleeker—in his life. Hence, the modern state-of-the-art ode to high-tech living that her kitchen had become.

Betty Miller, Diana's sixty-seven-year-old mother, plodded into the kitchen. She was twenty-four years older and at least twenty-five pounds heavier than her daughter, with streaks of gray in her brown hair, but like Diana, she was still pretty despite the double chin, the kimono arms, and the puffiness under her catlike green eyes. "I must be going through another change of life," she announced, dabbing a tissue at the beads of perspiration on her forehead.

"Is it hot in here?" Diana asked. A look of concern crossed her face when she saw how pale her mother had become in the short period of time Diana had been to the market. Ever since Diana's father had died of a coronary on the seventeenth tee of their country club eight years before, worrying about Betty's well-being had fallen onto Diana's shoulders.

Betty said, "Nah, I feel fine. See, it's passing."

"What's passing?"

"The dizziness. There, it's gone," Betty announced with a smile and a loud sigh of relief. "So, you got the candies?" she asked, already washing her hands at the oversize stainless-steel sink.

"Here they are." Diana laid the packages of M&M's on the counter. She put on her apron, which said "A woman's place is in the kitchen," and washed her hands, too. Soon she was busy rolling out a large ball of buttery dough her mother had prepared while she was out. "Oh, I almost forgot. That neighbor I've been telling you about—Chris Berry—is coming over in a few minutes for some cookies. He needs cheering up."

"I thought you told me he had dozens of starlets camped out on his doorstep waiting to cheer him up," Betty said.

"Mother, promise me . . . please . . . that you won't say anything like that to him when he gets here. You'll embarrass the life out of me."

Betty put the first batch of cookies in the oven before answering her daughter. "Can I at least ask him what JoJo Jenkins is really like?" JoJo Jenkins was the star of Chris's latest hit sitcom and one of the most beautiful television actresses in town. The local gossip rags had the "Texas beauty with a brain" linked romantically with Chris.

"I guess so," Diana said. "Just don't get too specific."

"You mean like, are her bazooms for real?"

"Yeah, like that!" Diana laughed.

The oven buzzer sounded a few minutes later. "Batch number one done," Betty announced cheerily, her button nose wrinkling up at the delicious aroma that now filled the kitchen.

"Smells like Halloween," Diana said. How she loved holidays. There were always so many foods to prepare, so many parties to give and to attend. The Lowe Halloween feast had become a favorite tradition of both adults and kids. Like most of her parties, this one had started out with a casual comment: "When you finish trick-or-treating, come on over for a bowl of chili." Everyone soon decided that Diana's chili was the best in Encino, maybe the best in the entire San Fernando Valley, and her desserts were decadent. Nobody, they all agreed, entertained with more ease or flair than Diana Lowe.

"Come see the goblin cookies. They came out great," Betty chirped, laying the baking sheets on a rack to cool. "Let's make more of those."

Diana eyed the baked goods critically. "The witches are fun, too, don't you think?" She poked at the bottoms of the cookies with a spatula, loosening them to prevent their sticking and breaking when cool enough to lift off. She removed one imperfect cookie from the sheet and nibbled at it absently.

In anticipation of Chris's arrival, Diana had left the front gate to her property open. Chris now strolled up the long driveway and let himself into the backyard through a second gate. Immediately, Romeo and Juliet bounded up to him. He fended them off deftly, managing to calm them down long enough to pull out two giant-size Milk-Bones from his sweat pants pocket. He threw them into the air for the shepherds to catch. With the bones securely in their mouths, the dogs loped happily to the far end of the property to enjoy their treat, leaving Chris to make his way to the back door unmolested.

"Honey, I'm home!" Chris sang out as he walked from the service porch toward the kitchen. "I'll be in for my cookies as soon as I finish opening the mail."

As soon as she heard him, Diana began to laugh. By this time Chris had entered the kitchen and could see that his parody of domestic bliss had entertained Diana, but it obviously had had a confusing effect on Diana's mother, for she merely stared at him with a puzzled expression.

Diana said, "Mother, he's always kidding. Chris, meet my mother, Betty Miller."

"Mrs. Miller, she's right. I am kidding. I always eat my cookies *before* opening the mail!"

Betty continued to stare at him.

Chris reached out and grabbed Betty's hand in a friendly gesture. Only Betty's hand was full of flour. "Oh, my word. Look at you!" she exclaimed.

"Hey, it's only a little flour," Chris said, slapping his hand against his thigh, leaving a white palm print behind.

"Now it's on your pants, too. Oh, dear."

"I don't care about these clothes. They're just some old rags I wear when I write."

"Do you really have five Emmys?" Betty blurted.

"No. Seven."

"My daughter told me how famous you are," Betty continued, ignoring Diana's warning glance.

"Not really," he said humbly. "But I sure am hungry."

Emmys Betty couldn't relate to; hunger, however, was a whole different story. Hunger she understood. As generous a hostess as her daughter, Betty flew into a frenzy of activity, racing between cupboard and refrigerator to get Chris a plate for the cookies and a glass for his milk.

"So tell me about yourself," Betty said, returning to her normal, garrulous self. She sat down next to Chris at the stone and glass table and placed an ice-cold glass of milk and several hot, buttery cookies in front of him. Before Chris could speak, she continued confidentially, "So how come a wife would run off to the wilds of Alaska and leave a gorgeous man like yourself?"

"Mother!" Diana exclaimed.

Chris chuckled. How like her mother Diana was, he thought—pretty, vivacious, open. "It's okay," Chris said. "To answer your question, Mrs. Miller—"

Interrupting him, Diana's mother said, "Oh, just call me Betty. All Diana's friends do."

"Well, then. Betty." He felled her with a grin that would have melted the hardest woman's heart. "To answer your question: my wife thought her dreams were as important as mine. I believe in dreams. Do you?"

"It all depends," Betty said. "I believe more in responsibility."

"But Marylou—my wife—wanted to prove to herself that she could live out her dreams. I couldn't stop her."

"But a woman leaving a husband and children, just like that?" Betty asked.

"I'm all for the institution of marriage. You know, for better or worse, till death do us part. But what can you do when your mate isn't?"

"That's a good question," Betty said, getting up to pour more milk for Chris.

"What do you think, Diana?" Chris asked.

"I think she was a fool to leave."

Chris picked up one of the cookies. It was shaped like a witch. "To Marylou," he said, devouring it in one bite.

"This damned indigestion!" Betty exclaimed, suddenly gripping the refrigerator door handle.

"Mom, sit down and stop doing so much." Diana looked at Chris with a worried expression. "I've been begging her for days to act like a guest and let me wait on her."

"Sit here," Chris ordered gently but firmly as he took Betty by the arm and nudged her into a seat at the table.

"I'll be fine," Betty said.

"You sure, Mom?"

"Of course I'm sure. It's that pastrami we had last night; I just know it. I should stop eating that stuff."

"I know what you mean, Betty," Chris said in a conspiratorial tone. "Every time I eat deli food, I'm sorry afterward. For me, it's the pickles."

Betty smiled gratefully at Chris. "Exactly. I eat that garbage. It tastes so good going down. Then afterward I suffer for two days waiting for that big belch to come and relieve the pressure."

"Mother! I don't believe the things you say sometimes."

Chris laughed. "Don't edit her, Diana. She's wonderful."

Betty's face suddenly became chalk white. Chris immediately said, "Maybe you ought to lie down."

"Yeah," she gasped. Betty heavily pushed herself up from the table. She inched around Chris, patted his hand, and said, "I think I will."

"Your mother's terrific," Chris said after Betty had left the kitchen. "I hope she's okay."

"She does suffer from indigestion. This time, though—" Diana began to say, but was interrupted by a resounding thud from the entry hall. "My God! What's that?" She ran out of the kitchen with Chris close behind.

They found Betty sprawled across the two bottom steps. She lay clutching her upper abdomen. "I can hardly breathe," she gasped.

Chris managed to pick up the rotund woman and carry her into the study where he settled her gently on the couch.

Diana sat on the floor next to her mother, wiping the perspiration off Betty's wan face with a tissue and tenderly pushing her hair off her damp forehead.

Chris phoned the fire department to request immediate assistance. After he hung up, he moved Diana aside and took Betty's pulse. It was fairly strong. "You're gonna be okay," he said reassuringly to Betty, whose eyes showed a mixture of pain and fear now.

"Are you sure?" Diana whispered.

"Yes," Chris said, although he wasn't sure at all. Still, his words calmed Diana. She resumed her place next to her mother, stroking Betty's arm.

Within a few minutes the sound of a siren could be heard.

Chris ushered the paramedics into the study. They went to work on

Betty immediately. After a few seconds, it seemed, they had her hooked
up to several machines and on her way out to the ambulance.

When Chris helped Diana climb into the back of the ambulance he
could feel her whole body quivering. He made a quick decision. He
climbed in, too. "I'm going with you," he said forcefully.

Chapter

2

Harvey Lowe pulled into the parking lot of Encino Grove Hospital, took a ticket from the machine, and drove around until he found a spot that was away from all the other parked cars. He hated the thought of someone carelessly scratching his gleaming new red Porsche 928. Before getting out, he placed a call from his car phone to his answering service, telling them he was going on his beeper for an hour. Then he glanced at himself in the rearview mirror, checking to see if his hair was perfectly combed. It was. He pulled the knot in his tie a little tighter. It was a black and gray Turnbull and Asser tie, chosen with great care to match his shirt. Very expensive. Very subtle. If Turnbull and Asser was good enough for Prince Charles, it was good enough for Harvey. The way the tie and shirt picked up the colors of his salt-and-pepper tweed suit appealed to his need for harmony and beauty.

He opened the door, its very heaviness making him feel like a million bucks, and swung his legs out. Before standing up he inspected his loafers for any imperfections in the shine. They were mink-oiled to mirror intensity, almost as gleaming as the paint job on his car. He flecked an errant piece of lint off the cuff of his pants, straightened the ribbing in his calf-high socks so each line would be perfectly perpendicular, then stood up.

He was five feet eight—five nine if you counted the extra inch the curls on the top of his head gave him. The curly hair had been Diana's idea after he had the hair transplant three years ago to relieve the creeping baldness that was turning his life into a veritable hell. Once he was fully recovered from the surgery, he had gone to her hairdresser, Steve, at Tressiers in Encino, for a permanent wave, resulting in tightly curled tresses that made him look younger than his forty-eight years.

Damn, he was irked, he thought as he marched purposefully through the lobby to the elevator of this small but efficient community hospital. Although he would never have admitted it to a living soul, he considered aging parents a time-consuming nuisance. At least Diana's father had had the decency to die quickly and spare them all the agonizing moments like the ones they were going through now with Betty. His own parents, thank God, were in good health, even though they were both much older than Betty. Best of all, they were living far away in Miami and called on Harvey's sister Heidi, who lived in New York, when they needed something.

It wasn't that he didn't care about his parents and Betty. He did. He had felt terrible when Diana called him with the news that she was at the emergency room with her mother, who quite possibly was suffering a coronary. He had told her he would be there as soon as he could break away from his office in Beverly Hills. Still, it had been several hours before he had finished seeing the last of his complicated oral surgery cases; he wanted—hell, he *needed*—to rest at home before dressing up in his new tuxedo for the Oral Surgery Center's fund-raiser, which he and Diana were scheduled to attend that night. This trauma with Betty was a glitch in an otherwise perfectly planned day. Harvey liked his life to proceed in an orderly fashion, with the minimum of surprises.

As he rode up to the coronary care unit in the elevator, he took out one of the three-by-five index cards he always carried in his inside jacket pocket so he wouldn't forget any thoughts that might cross his fertile mind, and jotted a few notes with his eighteen karat gold-nibbed Montblanc pen. He felt the eyes of a young candy striper on him as he wrote. She was short and blond. Quite pretty, in fact. Harvey felt young, virile. He smiled at her with puppy-brown eyes as he put away his pen and prepared to exit the elevator. "Have a nice day," he said to her in his most melodious voice as the doors closed behind him.

Harvey walked with a bounce in his step, proud of the fastidious image he projected, as he confidently approached the CCU nurses' station. "I'm Dr. Lowe," he announced to the nurse, then paused to let the heady effect of his presence permeate the atmosphere. Much to his dismay, she didn't seem impressed.

"Yes?" she said indifferently.

Harvey quickly explained who he was.

"They're all waiting to see Dr. Litsky in the visitors' lounge," she told him perfunctorily.

The minute Diana saw Harvey approaching the door to the waiting room, she jumped up from the Naugahyde couch and practically flung herself into his arms. She burst into tears. He held her dutifully for a few seconds, although her lack of control embarrassed him. "Now, now," he said, extricating himself from her stranglehold. He had to use all his willpower not to glance at his shoulder and automatically brush off any residue of her soggy assault.

"The doctor was here a few minutes ago. You just missed him, Harvey. Didn't he, Chris?" Diana blurted.

Harvey stepped back from his wife and glanced around the dreary cubicle of a room. He eyed Chris Berry. His first thought was that the guy ought to be ashamed of himself for going out in public looking like such a slob. They sure were different types, he and Chris. Harvey wouldn't have been caught dead in unpressed underwear, let alone baggy old sweat pants and a misshapen and faded sweat shirt. Even Chris's tennis shoes were frayed!

"Diana told me on the phone you were a help and a half today," Harvey said to Chris, extending his manicured hand to shake Chris's huge paw. Chris's hands were rough compared to his, Harvey noticed, a mild sense of disgust rising up in him.

Chris said, "Look, I was there. It was the least I could do."

"The doctor said Mom's EKG is okay, but he thinks she may have had a myocardial infarction," Diana recited. She opened her purse and took out a crumpled tissue and wiped her eyes and nose.

Harvey could barely look at his wife, she was so unkempt. Her naturally thick hair was askew and wild looking. Her makeup had become blotchy from intermittent bouts of crying. The stains her mascara left on her face only made her look heavier and older. At times like these Harvey seemed to see her anew, and he was jolted by the unbeautiful woman she had become. The pathetic reality of his marital situation seared through him like a white-hot pain, especially when he recalled how captivating Diana's looks had been when they first started dating. Her face had had heart-stopping molded curves, and her smooth, taut skin had begged to be petted. In fact, Harvey couldn't keep his hands off her all during their courtship. A sensual young man given to crumbling in the face of absolute beauty, Harvey couldn't help but feel cheated—tricked, almost—by Diana's immediate weight gain soon after their wedding. Only then had Diana admitted that she'd always had to battle extra weight, ballooning up then starving down for short, blissful spans of time. He had found her and fallen in love with her during one of her thin periods. How could he have known that it would only last for about twenty minutes?

They fought constantly about her diets; Harvey expected Diana to be on permanent vigil. She expected him to love and respect her despite her penchant to pork up. But he couldn't. Her lumps and bumps interfered with every aspect of their relationship. Frankly, her weight problem disgusted him, and her pathetic attempt to hide her rolls of fat under billowing blouses didn't work. It only made her look more like a two-ton Tilly in his estimation.

From the first, he would see other young women her age parade around in their skimpy bikinis and feel deprived, as though he had sent away for an expensive package that wasn't at all what the advertisement had said it would be. Over the years, Harvey had tried by his own example to goad his wife into dieting and slimming down, but lately she seemed to have given up even a shred of pretense of watching her caloric intake. Now her mother's illness only brought the potential horror of Diana's bleak future more into focus for Harvey.

"What about the lab results?" Harvey asked, a superior testiness creeping into his voice. "They will tell us what's really going on with her heart."

"They'll be out later tonight. That's what the doctor told me, anyway."

"What's the doctor's name?" Harvey asked Diana impatiently.

"Litsky. David Litsky. He was on call when the ambulance brought Mother in."

"Never heard of him," Harvey said.

"He seemed nice enough . . . competent," Diana said, looking over to Chris for confirmation.

"I agree," Chris said to Harvey.

"Okay. I'd better talk to him, though. We do have that black-tie party tonight."

"Oh, my God!" Diana cried. "I couldn't think of going now."

"Calm down," Harvey warned. "Let's see what Litsky has to say first. You don't even know if it was a heart attack."

"I don't care what he says, Harvey. I'm not leaving Mother's side."

Harvey heaved a sigh, turned on his substantial heels, and marched out of the waiting room.

The nursing supervisor paged Dr. Litsky for Harvey. Soon the two men were conferring in the doorway of the waiting room. Litsky said that Betty was doing nicely, resting comfortably now that she was on pain medication. "She's lucky she was brought in so swiftly," he said. "Personally, I do think she's had a heart attack, although a mild one."

"Would it be unthinkable for my wife and me to leave her tonight to attend a very important charity function?" Harvey asked.

Litsky thoughtfully rubbed his chin, which was covered with a day's growth of red stubble. "No, I should think not," he said. "She's stable."

Harvey eyed Diana triumphantly. "See, dear?" he said. "I think Mother would understand how important it is not to disappoint BeeBee Benedict, as she's the center's prime benefactor. We're sitting at her table, and you know this is the major event for the center this year."

Diana responded to Harvey's rationalizing with a contemptuous glare. "I know my mother would understand, Harvey. That's not the point. I don't want to leave her, not even for BeeBee Benedict and her mouthful of extractable teeth!"

"Do you expect me to go alone?" he asked, incredulous. "I need you with me."

"And what about what I need?" Diana turned away and found a seat on the other end of the couch from Chris. He eyed her sympathetically, a look not lost on Harvey.

"Then I guess I have no choice; I'll have to go alone," he said, ignoring her question. "How will you get home from here?" he asked.

"A cab? I don't know," she said shortly. "Have Todd pick me up when he gets home from football practice."

"You sure about this?" Harvey asked.

Diana nodded, looking beat and bedraggled.

"I'm going to say a few words to Mother," Harvey said in a subdued tone. "Then I'm off. I'll see you later."

He said a curt good-bye to Chris, then left them to enter the CCU for his five-minute visit.

An hour later, Diana insisted that Chris go home. "You've been a real help today," she said. "But you have your girls. They probably think you've been kidnapped. They need you, too."

"It's no problem," Chris said, "Consuelo's there to cook whatever greasy thing they want tonight."

"No, really. You can't do anything more here. I'll be fine. Todd'll want to see his grandmother anyway once he hears what happened. He'll take me home."

Chris stood up and stretched. He groaned. "I really am tired," he admitted. "Think I'll jog back home to wake up these old bones." Diana looked at him with a horrified expression. Jogging when tired was the last thing she'd ever think of doing! "It's only three miles," Chris said with a smile.

"Come on, then. I'll walk to the exit with you. I need some fresh air."

After thanking Chris profusely for all his emotional support, Diana wandered into the hospital gift shop to buy something to snack on until her sixteen-year-old son, Todd, arrived. Nothing held any fascination for her. At last she settled on two Snickers bars, her favorite candy. At least they had peanuts in them, a good source of protein, she rationalized. And they were the official candy bar of the athletes of the 1984 Olympics.

Chapter

3

As soon as Todd left for school the next morning, Diana took a quick shower, threw on a velour warm-up suit, then raced off to the hospital to be with her mother, whose heart attack had been confirmed by the lab tests.

At noon Diana went into the CCU to see her mother for the third time. Betty was anxious about the cardiac catheterization procedure she had just learned she would be undergoing later that day.

"It's nothing, Mother. Would I allow the doctors to hurt you?" Diana said with bravado.

"It really isn't all that terrible," one of the nurses chimed in as she fussed over Betty's I.V. line. "Everyone here has it done sooner or later."

"For my money, I'd prefer later," Betty said drolly.

Diana laughed. When her mother could joke, it meant everything would be okay. She squeezed Betty's hand. "I love you, Mom."

Betty squeezed back. Her grip was strong. "I'm gonna have pains more often." She smiled. "You haven't told me you loved me in years!"

Dr. Litsky walked into the CCU. Betty spied him. "How do I look?" she asked Diana. "He's cute. I like his red hair."

"Mother, he's no more than thirty-five years old!" Diana exclaimed with a laugh.

"So? I have to stop dreaming because I'm old? He has nice gentle hands."

"Here he comes. I'll tell him," Diana teased.

"Don't you dare embarrass a woman who's having a heart attack," Betty warned.

Diana leaned over and kissed her mother's cherubic face. "I'll see you when you get back from that procedure. Close your eyes and get some rest."

When she returned to the waiting room, it was empty. Grateful for the quiet and the extra space, Diana sprawled out on the uncomfortable brown Naugahyde couch, rested her head on the bunched-up velour jacket of her warm-up suit, and shut her eyes.

"Knock, knock, anybody home?" the familiar voice of her best friend, Carol Benton, rang out a few minutes later.

Diana opened her eyes. "Hi," she said, sitting up. "How did you know where to find me?" Diana had not yet told any of her friends about her mother's apparent heart attack.

"Chris Berry."

Carol owned the busiest travel agency in Encino, Eyeful Tours. Chris was one of her preferred clients.

"Where's he going now?" Diana asked.

"Nowhere. Marylou's coming in for Thanksgiving. He's footing the bill. She's got a real good thing going for her," Carol said in her husky cut-the-crap style. "He should just file for divorce and sever the cord."

"That's not what he wants, Carol. You know that. He hopes she'll come back and want to stay."

Carol flicked back her lion's mane of Farrah Fawcett hair with one of her thin hands and said, "Come on, doll, she's living with some hick mountain man in a hut in the wilds. This adventure of hers isn't all photos of grizzlies! Personally, I wouldn't take her back for all the tea in China."

"Then it's a good thing she's not married to you." Diana laughed. She noticed a brown bag bulging out of Carol's black patent leather satchel that doubled as purse and briefcase. "What's in the bag, goose?" she said with a grin.

"Before I tell you, how is your mother doing? Is it serious?"

"We don't know yet," Diana answered, her smile disappearing instantly. "A Doctor Williamson's going to do a cardiac catheterization on her later today."

"Sandy Williamson's husband. They're super people. Clients," Carol said matter-of-factly, as though the computer that was her brain was ticking off data. "Went to Paris last spring. Going on a cruise to the Aegean next summer with their boys."

"Sounds like he does a lot of these procedures," Diana said.

"Big bucks."

"Well, I hope 'Big Bucks' Williamson has good hands. He's going to thread a needle into Mom's heart." Diana shuddered. "Makes my stomach cramp up."

"Maybe this will help," Carol said sympathetically, opening up the brown bag with "Fromin's Deli" emblazoned on it, and removing two gargantuan roast beef sandwiches on kaiser rolls loaded with coleslaw and Russian dressing. "When I told Arnie who this was for and why, he went into the kitchen and made the sandwiches himself." Arnie was the crusty owner of Fromin's, the most popular deli in Encino.

"He's outdone himself," Diana marveled. There was enough roast beef in one half of the sandwich to fill up four more.

"Enjoy, doll," Carol said, handing one sandwich to Diana, and keeping one for herself.

Diana immediately took an impressive bite. Carol sat studying hers. "The more I look at this mountainous mass of meat, the less hungry I get. Can too much ever be too much?" she asked.

"Never!" Diana said with her mouth full of rare roast beef.

Diana continued to plow into her food. Carol took out at least half of her meat, claiming she would use it for her daughter's lunch for the entire week. Like a bird moving around until the nest was perfect, then settling down finally for a long siege, Carol at last was satisfied with her much diminished sandwich and opened her mouth to take the first bite.

"I thought you were starting a diet!" Harvey exclaimed, coming into the room and startling Carol as well as Diana.

"Give the poor woman a break, Harvey," Carol retorted. "She can diet after Betty gets out of this place."

Diana asked sheepishly, "What are you doing here in the middle of the day?"

"Mothers-in-law before mouths," Harvey answered. "I've canceled all my afternoon appointments."

Diana stopped chewing. "I'm so glad you're here, honey." It was amazing how a little gesture of kindness on Harvey's part could mitigate the pain his recent thoughtless and oftentimes rude behavior had caused her.

He smiled briefly, then said, "Carol, babe, you're looking great. Like that sweater."

Carol was wearing an ivory cashmere turtleneck sweater that hugged her long neck and complemented her peaches-and-cream complexion. The sweater was the same color as her wool gabardine trousers. She was the essence of stylish simplicity.

"Why don't you get an outfit like that?" Harvey asked Diana, who quickly finished off the first half of the sandwich.

Because they don't make clothes like that in tugboat sizes, she wanted to lash out. Forcing her voice to sound pleasant, she said instead, "Maybe I will. Once Mother gets out of here."

Harvey plunged on. "Look at her, Carol. Always wearing those unflattering oversize shirts."

Diana blushed crimson. She felt the acid in her stomach competing with the roast beef.

"I think Diana looks wonderful," Carol said loyally, glaring at Harvey.

"You don't have to go overboard with the compliments," Diana said to her friend. "I know I'm overweight. This is Harvey's perverse way of goading me into going on another diet."

"Well, look at what you're eating, for chrissakes!"

Diana looked down at the other half of her sandwich, which she had intended to enjoy thoroughly. "Here. You eat it," she said, thrusting it at him.

"I brought the sandwiches, Harvey," Carol said. "Don't blame Diana."

"I see you haven't even taken one bite, but my wife's already devoured half of hers!" He pushed Diana's extended hand away. "I don't want that. Jesus, Diana. Do we have to fight about your weight even here?"

Diana somehow felt disoriented. It wasn't she who had started the fight . . . or was it? He was so unpredictable lately, lashing out at her with no warning.

She took the offending half-sandwich, embarrassed to even look up at Carol, and sealed it inside its Styrofoam container. "Look," she said to Harvey, "I'm putting it in my purse. I'll take it home and give it to Todd. You happy now?"

She opened her purse under her husband's disapproving gaze. He happened to look downward, following the path of her hand, and he espied one of the Snickers bars Diana had bought the night before.

"Candy, too!" he exploded, his face bloating with fury. "That's it. I can't stand it anymore. Your mother has eaten herself right into a heart attack and faces sixty thousand dollars' worth of surgery, and you're going to end up just like her. I can't stay here another minute." He turned on his mink-oiled loafers and stormed out.

Carol looked shaken by his tirade. Diana was furious, but she was scared, too. Harvey had never shown such anger toward her in public before.

Without a word, she left Carol and rushed out after Harvey. She managed to squeeze into the elevator as the doors were closing. Since there were several other people in the elevator with them, they rode down in smoldering silence.

She followed him out, huffing and puffing, trying to keep up with his brisk pace across the parking lot to the far, deserted end where his gleaming red car was parked.

"Why are you doing this to me at a time like this?" she cried.

Harvey whirled around dramatically. "I've had it, Diana. I'm going to leave you unless you lose weight. I can't stand what you're doing to yourself."

Diana said, "What are you saying?"

"I'm sick of watching you fall apart," he said tiredly.

"I'll change."

"You've been on every diet known to man—and then some," he told her. "And you've been a failure on every one. Why should I believe you now? Huh?"

"I don't know," she answered. The tone of his voice was so odd—so devoid of love, so final—it scared her almost as much as her mother's illness frightened her. "Just give me another chance."

A week later, Diana sat in her internist's office. She had been poked and pummeled, had given blood samples and urine specimens. Uncharacteristically, she had even lost her temper when the nurse asked to weigh her in the hallway outside her exam room; she protested that she never, ever had to weigh herself at her gynecologist's office.

"Well, Mrs. Lowe," the nurse said, "we insist all our patients get weighed at *our* office."

Reluctantly, Diana stood on the scale waiting for the moment of ultimate embarrassment when the nurse would proclaim in a voice blaring, as though projected through a megaphone for everyone else to hear, that she weighed so much she had broken the scale.

Finally the ordeal of the exam was over. Diana waited for her internist to rush into his office, as he always did, to succinctly give her his diagnosis. She fully expected he would tell her that the shortness of breath that had caused her to make this appointment was nothing to worry about.

Instead Dr. Fernberg walked in slowly and sat down slowly and eyed her slowly.

She knew something was wrong. "How bad is it?" she finally got up enough nerve to squeak.

Fernberg sat on the edge of his swivel chair, his hands making a tepee shape on the desk blotter, his hooded eyes regarding her thoughtfully for what seemed like an interminable length of time. At last he said, "Diana, you're a physical wreck."

"I know that! But how am I?" she joked.

"Seriously, Diana. Your tests across the board are abnormal. Your blood pressure is one-sixty over ninety—that's terrible for someone your age. Your blood sugar is high. Your cholesterol is over three hundred; I insist my patients keep theirs under two hundred at all times." He eyed her as if to ask her if she had the right stuff to continue to be one of his patients.

She smiled meekly, hopefully, at him. He continued to look grim.

"And your triglycerides—they measure the amount of fat in your body—are way off the charts, too. Diana . . . Diana, that's why you're out of breath. It's not merely your mother's situation that is causing stress. Honey, it's your health we're talking about now. You're not only overweight—"

"Dr. Fernberg, I've been starving myself on a diet for the past week. And you know what happened? I *gained* three pounds!"

"I'm not surprised," he said matter-of-factly.

Taken aback, Diana said, "You're not?"

"How many diets have you been on over the years?"

"You name it, I've been on it. I've tried the Stillman Diet, the Scarsdale Diet, Diet Center, Nutri/System, Jenny Craig, the Beverly Hills Diet, the French Pill Diet. Why, once Harvey even had me on the Drinking Man's Diet."

"Just as I thought," Fernberg said. "No fad diets, no crash diets, ever work. You know why?"

"I suppose that's because once I went off the diet, I went back to eating my old way and put the weight back on."

"That's true. The majority of those diets weren't constructed for long-term use. If you were to stay on them for any length of time, Diana, you could become so sick they'd have to bring you in to see me on a stretcher. Some of these plans are basically so unhealthful, so unbalanced nutritionally, that the end result of them is not only illness but more fat on your body."

"What?"

"Without going into it in great detail, let me just say that what you lose in the beginning on those fad diets is mostly water weight. You get on the scale after two weeks and you think you're thinner because the scale says you're thinner. Actually, the scale is our worst enemy."

"Don't I know *that!*" Diana moaned. "But I have to lose weight," she added, a desperate look in her eyes.

"That brings me back to your test results. Look, Diana," he said, rubbing the bridge of his nose, which had red marks on it from his glasses. "I think you need to work on your health first, your weight second. If you are willing to trust me, I will prescribe a new regimen for you. It may seem strange at first, but it will help lower your cholesterol and quite possibly your sugar and triglycerides, too."

"Of course I trust you," Diana said forcefully.

"Then I want you to stop counting calories from this day forward and count grams of fat instead."

Diana looked at her doctor as though he had suddenly started speaking ancient Greek to her. "I don't get it," she said.

"It's very simple, really. Every gram of fat has nine calories. Therefore, I want you to multiply the number of grams of fat by nine. Then divide that number by the total number of calories in that portion of food. If the fat content exceeds thirty percent of the total number of calories, you can't eat it."

"Dr. Fernberg, I'm embarrassed to admit this, but I am closely related to the lower primates when it comes to math. In other words, I'm a retard. I don't understand one word of what you just said."

Dr. Fernberg chuckled as he took out a sheet of paper and his fountain pen. "For example," he said, "let's take a can of Mrs. Parducci's split pea soup."

Diana's mouth began to water. She loved Mrs. Parducci's pea soup—with bacon.

"The Mrs. Parducci's brand has one hundred forty calories and six grams of fat." He wrote those numbers down on the paper.

"So far so good," Diana said.

He smiled at her enthusiastic attitude and continued writing slowly. He underlined the important points with bold strokes. "Okay so far?" He eyed Diana.

She winked at him. "I'm still with you."

"I knew you could do this," he said happily. "Next, you must calculate what percentage the fat is of the total number of calories."

Diana saw him calculate, then write a total of thirty-eight percent. She smiled broadly. "Hey, I understand this. I really do!"

"Now according to our rule, that percentage is above the percentage of fat allowable, so you can't eat this brand of pea soup. But if you're a clever shopper and you like pea soup, I'll bet you can find a brand that has little or no fat in it. That brand you can buy—and eat. Without guilt!"

"Without guilt," Diana repeated under her breath. "I haven't put anything in my mouth in years that hasn't made me feel guilty."

"Well, a new day has dawned for you, Diana. Now remember, this is not a diet. This is your new way of life. Count fats, not calories. Make that your mantra, if you will. There are more things you can eat than you thought imaginable. I want to see you back here in two months."

"No diet, no guilt. I feel guilty already," she murmured as she left his office.

Chapter

. . . .

4

What a day this has been, Diana thought, fumbling with her key in the dark, then letting herself in through the service porch door. She was spent from the ordeal of her doctor's appointment as well as from the emotional roller coaster she'd been on with her mother, who was scheduled for quintuple bypass surgery in a little more than four hours. Betty had been medicated early that evening, but the drug hadn't sedated her right away. Diana had spent most of the afternoon and night at her mother's bedside. When Betty finally fell into a drug-induced stupor at around 2:00 A.M., Diana had changed her mind about staying the night at the hospital, deciding to get several hours of sleep in her own bed rather than camp out in the cramped waiting room.

Dragging her body into the kitchen, Diana poured herself a glass of orange juice. While she stood sipping the frothy juice, she heard faint sounds of the television coming from the family room separated from the kitchen by plantation shutters. She opened one of the slatted partitions. The den was dark except for eerie shadows cast by the television screen.

Diana saw Harvey sitting on the L-shaped leather couch, clad only in his underwear. He was engrossed in the movie on the screen and didn't notice that she was there. As she observed him undisturbed, his enthusiasm for the movie suddenly made her flash back to a vision of the first time she had met him as he was walking with a friend of hers on their college campus. Harvey had been student body vice president and a BMOC. Diana couldn't believe that he would even give her the time of day, let alone ask her out. His boundless charm and boyish good looks— impish brown eyes, small nose, and deeply cleft chin—had made him a much sought after date by all of Diana's crowd. Diana was struck now by the realization that the softer Harvey of her youth was rarely visible these days. He had been replaced by an acerbic, critical man. He had become self-absorbed, strident, impressed by material possessions over the years, as if he had invented a new persona for himself and his family, but only he knew how to wear it properly. Diana felt confused by Harvey lately; it was almost as though her husband's success as a dentist and the power that had come with having money and assistants to carry out his every order had reshaped him, had changed his very genetic structure, hardening him and even making his features more brittle, less forgiving.

What was it that had made him look so like his old approachable self again? she wondered. She switched her gaze to the television screen and saw a graphic sex scene from a triple-X rated movie being played out between two women—one a Eurasian, the other an auburn-haired beauty —and a golden-haired man, all three moaning in apparent ecstasy.

Diana glanced at Harvey again. Then at the screen. Then Harvey. She was too stunned to speak out, for with each groan of pleasure uttered by the entangled trio, Harvey's own breathing became more labored. When he could no longer contain his excitement, he sought the bulge between his legs, which had surged up beyond the elastic confines of his black bikini briefs.

With a minimum of movement, Harvey deftly pulled down his underwear and began to stroke himself. Slowly at first, more quickly as his sexual tension mounted, he assaulted his erection with both hands, his eyes never wavering from the screen.

Diana waited. And watched. Part of her mind heaved with rage, another part was overwhelmed by a tidal wave of loneliness.

At the moment of Harvey's climax, which he timed with impressive precision to the sultry screams of the Eurasian vamp, Diana found her voice. "I'm home," she sputtered.

Harvey's hands froze mid-spasm. He tried to pull up his underpants and turn to look at her at the same time he reached for the remote control to turn off the set. If she hadn't been so furious, Diana might have laughed.

"I thought you were staying at the hospital with your mother!" he said much too loudly.

Diana stood stone still and eyed him for a long moment. Then without saying a word, she slammed the partition shut.

She rushed upstairs, still seeing the expression of ecstasy on her husband's face in her mind. She had not seen such a rapt look in years. She couldn't recall the last time Harvey had caressed her with real passion. And she had stopped trying to arouse him. In fact, they hadn't made love in months.

Damn him, she thought miserably as she flung on her oldest flannel nightgown and quickly buried herself to the top of her head under the blanket. Memories of her earlier love life came rushing in on her. On their honeymoon they had made love so often that neither of them could sit comfortably at the end of their ten-day trip to Tahiti. He had wanted her hands, only hers, on him in those days. Although the frequency of their lovemaking had dwindled over the years, they had continued to share moments of intense desire and there had always seemed to be a mutual attraction. Or maybe not. She wasn't sure anymore. Yes. She was sure. Harvey had wanted her once.

She recalled the time they had been in Bermuda, staying at a golf resort. A friend had given them a joint of marijuana to take on the trip, promising them that it would enhance their enjoyment of the sexual act. Skeptical, they had smoked part of it anyway just before dinner one night in their room. Feeling no effects at first, they had gone to the dining room and drunk most of a bottle of champagne. All at once, Diana's perceptions had altered. She claimed she could hear the guitarist's music coming in through the back of her head. Harvey said he had never tasted such good food before in his life. Diana thought that was hilarious. Harvey thought her laugh was sexy. They had practically mauled each other through their second course and three desserts apiece. They became even more giggly.

And daring.

Choosing to meander back to their bungalow across the pitch-black golf course instead of taking the path, they stopped several times to kiss. These were drug-induced kisses, soul kisses, where Harvey's tongue and hers did acrobatic maneuvers. Their kissing progressed. Harvey pulled down Diana's sundress, which had been held up only by an elastic ruffle around her shoulders. He took her breasts in his mouth, teasing her nipples, pressing his face into her cleavage.

He pulled down her panties, almost roughly flinging them a few yards away. He fell to his knees and tongued her clitoris. Inflamed beyond belief, Diana pulled at Harvey's hair, moaning. He stood up and she tore off his shirt, flinging it in the general direction of her panties and shoes.

Diana had the urge to run. Harvey chased her. A bank of clouds blew across the moon. Shrouded in darkness now, Diana stopped, letting him find her. After he almost tackled her, they fell laughing to the velvety grass. Diana lay on her back, Harvey poised above her. He lifted her legs and placed them around his neck. He plunged into her, and she felt sensations deep inside her vagina that she had never felt before. Her orgasm was forceful and long.

Afterward, he had lain on top of her, not wanting to let the moment go, murmuring words of love. When at last they uncoupled, they couldn't find their clothes. Laughing like lunatics, they collected palm fronds to cover their nakedness, and barely missed being spotted as they sneaked into their beachfront bungalow.

In the morning when they went to play golf there was a notice posted in the clubhouse stating that "a woman's sundress, etc., and a man's sport shirt and pants, etc." had been recovered on the tenth fairway and could be claimed in the clubhouse Lost and Found. They howled about the "et ceteras," but they were too embarrassed to retrieve their belongings.

Now, as Diana tossed and turned, planning what she would say when her contrite husband crawled into bed next to her, she realized that their golf course sex-capade had taken place almost eight years ago! Where had the time flown? And more important, why had their passion died? No immediate answers popped into her weary mind. Diana finally fell into a fitful sleep when it became clear to her that Harvey was not going to follow her upstairs tonight and plead for her to forgive him for saving the best of himself for . . . himself.

The next afternoon Diana moved through her neighborhood super-market at a snail's pace, happy to have this diversion from her problems with her mother and Harvey. Normally, combing the aisles of Gelson's Market was a wonderfully mindless activity for Diana. Today, however, her mind never dipped into its usual semicomatose state but remained fully vigilant, fully alert. She scrutinized the label of every item, studying its contents.

"Hi, doll," Carol Benton called out, startling Diana in the crackers aisle. Diana held a box of Nelson's Nibbles in one hand and a mini-calculator in the other. "I didn't expect you to get out of the hospital today. How'd it go for Betty?"

"Seven hours under the knife, can you believe it?" Diana said with a grimace. "Just as I was about to tear my hair out with worry, they wheeled her past the waiting room door." Diana shuddered at the unpleasant memory. "I thought she looked like death warmed over, but the surgeon said she came through it like a trouper. By the way, thanks for the incredible basket of flowers. The nurses said they'll water it until my mother gets out of the Intensive Care Unit."

"How long will that be?"

"Barring any complications, a few days. Harvey thinks her weight could be a problem."

"Since when is Harvey a heart specialist?"

"You know Harvey, Carol. If he can point out my mother's or my weight to us, he'll do it."

"You two still going at it?"

Diana thought about the scene with Harvey in front of the television the previous night, and a second scene early in the morning when they had had a dilly of an argument about his apathy toward Diana physically. Somehow he had turned the incident around and made her out to be the culprit who had wronged him. "Things could be a whole lot better," Diana sighed. "And now there's another problem."

"What now?" Carol asked.

"My doctor says I have to take care of my health before I even think of going on another diet. That's why I'm marketing with this silly thing." She pointed to the credit card–size calculator.

Carol looked at her blankly.

"I'm counting grams of fat. You see, I have to stop counting calories and make sure my fat intake is less than thirty percent of the total calories of the food I eat."

Carol clearly was stumped and said, "You and your cockamamy discoveries."

"It's simple, really."

"Yeah, like the Beverly Hills Diet. 'I only eat fruit,' you said. I thought you were going to die from the diarrhea it caused."

Diana chortled. "Yeah, I remember. I can't even look at a pineapple anymore without my mouth puckering up and my bowels going into an instant uproar."

"And remember how simple the liquid diet started out? Until we all went to Hawaii and you had to lug along three extra suitcases filled with yucky protein drinks."

"Well, this diet is different. It isn't even a diet. It's a new way of life."

"Sure it is," Carol said skeptically. "All I can say is that it goes to prove one thing—if you search hard enough and long enough, you're bound to find a doctor who'll tell you what you want to hear."

Diana looked stricken and said, "Are you trying to tell me that I don't really want to lose weight, so I'm searching around for someone who'll tell me to stay fat?"

"I'm not saying anything. Hey, I've got to run. I have a client coming to the office at four o'clock. Bye," Carol said, blowing an air kiss past Diana's cheek. "Oh, and happy counting."

Diana returned her attention to the box she was holding. She read that these tiny harmless-looking crackers were made with a dreaded vegetable shortening composed of partially hydrogenated oils. She recalled Dr. Fernberg warning her off of anything hydrogenated. These oils were really hardened fats and one of the worst things a person could ingest.

But Todd loved these little round crackers. To buy or not to buy? That was the question. She used to think they were cute; now she saw Nelson's Nibbles as lethal.

Farther down the crackers aisle, however, she found several products that were acceptable. Feeling powerful and in control of her own destiny, Diana jauntily moved into the cereal section where she stashed a dozen fat-free cereals into her cart.

Ever more elated by her discoveries, Diana plunged eagerly into the soups. Hooray! The treasure hunt Fernberg had created for her had a happy ending—she discovered Anderson's split pea soup, which had no fat at all! Diana quickly cleared the shelf.

On to the breads. Much to her delight, Diana found that most breads had little or no fat. She smiled all the while as she loaded a second cart with bagels, buns, sourdough rolls, and assorted loaves. Without butter or margarine she figured she could scarf down several pieces of bread a day. She stopped for a second as the thought of Harvey's reaction to seeing her devouring huge rolls passed like a dark cloud across her mind.

In the condiment section she loaded up on several types of mustard. Mustard, she decided, was like a wild card—it could be anything she wanted it to be. For the present, mustard was going to become a substitute for mayonnaise.

Her spirits plummeted again amid the salad dressings. Diana, old girl, she thought, seeing that most of her creamy favorites were taboo, you're going to have to make your own dressings from now on. Visions of concocting vinegary delights—some of the new vinegars on the market were seasoned with whole forests growing in the bottles—and combining them with her mustards lifted her spirits. She even began salivating at the thought of using mustard with honey for days when her sweet tooth acted up.

Spurred on by an irrational hope that she might discover a low-fat dessert, she stopped and examined the label on a tofu-based non-dairy dessert. This one had to be a winner, Diana was certain. How could she go wrong with tofu and non-dairy, with the label screaming out that it was cholesterol free? She was horrified when she read the small print and found that more than fifty-six percent of its calories came from fat. She did her computations four times just to be certain her calculator hadn't suddenly broken. It hadn't.

Keep on trucking.

Potatoes. "They're all starch," she heard Harvey's voice ringing derisively in her ears. So what, so what, so what? Diana kept thinking. Fernberg had called her early in the afternoon at the hospital to see how her mother had come through surgery, and as he started to hang up, he blurted, "Potatoes."

"What?" Diana had asked.

"I forgot to tell you that you can eat all the starch you want, potatoes included. Without butter, of course."

Of course. Potatoes without butter? He told her to be inventive.

She read the labels of all the steak and barbecue sauces and found that most of them were perfectly okay to eat. Potatoes topped with chives and steak sauce. Sounds good, she thought. Maybe not as good as sour cream, but it would do. Potatoes with barbecue sauce. Potatoes with spaghetti sauce. Why not? How about potatoes with spaghetti? Live dangerously. She was getting punchy.

What is this? Butter Buds? She sought out the manager to ask if this product was any good. He promptly assured Diana that it was a wonderful alternative to butter for the consumer who required a fat-free product.

"You're looking at her," she said, and promptly slam-dunked five boxes into the fourth cart of this epic shopping expedition.

She raced through the fruits and vegetables, buying everything in sight, including the once forbidden high-calorie bananas. She could hardly wait until breakfast tomorrow. She drooled over the vision of cereal with sliced bananas on top. Maybe she'd have breakfast tonight.

By the time Diana wandered over to the cheese section of the market, more than two hours had elapsed.

"I can't believe you're still here," Carol exclaimed. She had returned to buy a Brie wedge to serve at a small dinner party she was hosting that night. She had forgotten it on her first, rushed visit.

"Oh, hi," Diana said, appearing distracted and weighted down after hours of doing mathematical calculations.

"Are you writing a book?" Carol joked, laughing at the pages of notes about the hundreds of foods Diana was charting.

"Carol, you wouldn't believe how much fat sneaks into our daily diet," Diana exclaimed. "Why, did you know that most cheese is over ninety percent fat?"

Carol shrugged and said, "I always buy that low-fat product for myself."

"That's just the point!" Diana nearly shouted. "The manufacturers are wily. Their advertisements fool us into believing that these new products are low in fat. Well!" Diana grabbed a package from the refrigerated display and waved it in front of Carol's nose. "This may be lower than the regular cheese, but it's still over fifty percent fat." She quickly did the calculation and showed it to Carol, who shrugged. "It really frosts me to think that I believed them and bought this stuff."

"Calm down. You'll have a stroke."

"I can't calm down. Don't you see? All these years I was loading low-cal cream cheese on my toast and bagels. It may not be ninety percent fat like regular cream cheese, but it is still *seventy-nine percent* fat. It makes me sick!"

Carol shook her head and regarded Diana with an expression of bemused skepticism. "Diana, you're always this manic when you start one of your new schemes. You'll get over this one just like all the rest. In some ways, I understand Harvey's frustration with you. What is this," she asked, "your tenth full cart of food?"

Diana grinned sheepishly. "No. Only my fourth."

"Doll, go home and rest. Your mother's going to need you."

"You really think all this is stupid?"

"I don't know. Honest. What I do know is that if I don't get home with this Brie, my guests will be sitting there staring at one another without me!" She wheeled around and, with her characteristic dramatic flair, left Diana standing in her wake.

At last, after three hours plus, Diana went to the checkout counter. As she awaited her turn, she picked through several of the promotional items that lined the table next to her. Among them was another of Diana's favorites, granola bars. Too tired to think by now, Diana automatically threw two boxes into the cart. Suddenly she remembered her mission and retrieved one of the boxes of health-food cookies, which were advertised as low in cholesterol and high in protein. An expert now, she quickly scanned the ingredient chart. Jesus, as Harvey always said, these healthful snacks were more than forty percent fat.

What was the world coming to? Diana wondered as she put both boxes back on the display table. Here was another manufacturer proclaiming the health value of a product when it clearly wasn't healthful at all.

There obviously was a gross difference between fat and cholesterol, a difference she would never confuse again. She wondered if all consumers were as easily duped as she had been prior to her visit to Dr. Fernberg. She suspected most people were.

She looked around and noticed all the fatty foods people in the market were buying. She felt like shouting out to the whole world what she had discovered in just one visit to the market, but she knew she'd probably be arrested if she did that. She couldn't afford to spend time in jail right now, she decided; her mother needed her. Well, then, she'd just have to hold her excitement inside until she got home and could share the news with her family.

It was already dusk by the time Diana left the market. It was dark by the time she reached her street, a little more than two miles away. Seven years ago Diana had filed a petition to get two streetlights for Live Oak Lane, claiming it was dangerous for the neighborhood children without them. After a long, acrimonious struggle, she had succeeded. There was one light at the cul-de-sac near her house and a second one at the far end of the block next to Chris Berry's house. Never once in seven years had she regretted the presence of those lights—until this night.

As she sped up her street the lamp that illuminated the Berrys' driveway and front yard beamed down on Chris, who was leaning against his car. Although it was quite cold, he was barefoot and clad only in a terrycloth robe. Even if Diana had tried to avert her eyes, she could not have helped noticing that Chris's hair was darkly damp, that he was nearly naked, and he was entwined in an intimate embrace with none other than JoJo Jenkins.

Without realizing that she was slowing down to a near crawl, Diana came almost to a total stop in front of Chris's driveway. Suddenly feeling quite conspicuous, she gunned the engine, distracting Chris. When he saw her, he yelled for Diana to stop. Mortified, but not knowing why, Diana sped past without so much as a wave of her hand.

She heard the phone ringing as she carried in the first of the many bags of groceries. "Todd!" she yelled. "Either answer the damn phone or go out to the car and bring in some of these bags."

Todd appeared around the corner. He resembled his father more and more, possessing the same shape of eyes and head, with the same deep cleft in his still hairless chin. He stood munching on a Sonora chip and acted as though he had suddenly gone deaf. "I didn't hear the phone," he said defensively as it continued to ring.

"It could be the hospital," Diana replied angrily, rushing into the kitchen to answer it herself.

"Why didn't you stop?" Chris said the minute she picked up the receiver. "I wanted you to meet JoJo Jenkins."

"How nice," Diana said, forcing a pleasantness into her voice that she didn't feel toward him right now.

"How's Betty doing?" he asked. "She's been on my mind."

Chris's concern made Diana suddenly feel stupid for being irritable with him. Chris was her friend; he had a right to kiss anyone he wanted—even JoJo Jenkins. "Mom's a trouper, Chris. She went through hell today, but the doctor said she's going to pull through it."

"When can I visit?"

"For now only the immediate family can see her. But it's really sweet of you to ask."

"I'm a sweet guy," he replied with a chuckle.

"I know. But you still have to wait until she's out of the hospital."

"I may be gone by then."

"Gone? Where?"

"Hawaii."

"That sounds terrific. For how long?"

Chris said, "Months. It's an offer I may not be able to refuse."

Todd had actually brought in the rest of the groceries and was putting them away. With every passing second, however, he was beginning to realize that his favorite junk foods were not going to emerge, and his face took on an increasingly menacing scowl.

Diana noticed this while trying to carry on her conversation with Chris. "You mean a work offer?"

"The best offer I've had in years, really. A dramatic series this time, about the women who served in the Vietnam War. But I don't know. It's a lot to consider. Missy and Meg would have to enroll in school over there. I think I need a mother's advice, Diana. What would you do?"

"Children hate change. It's a tough one, Chris. But you're the adult. You have to do what's best for you. Kids are more pliable than you think. They adapt."

Todd looked at Diana with murder in his eyes.

She looked away.

Chris said, "I guess I could be dragging them off to worse places than Hawaii."

Diana agreed. She then listened intently while Chris briefly described the new project to her. His excitement was uncontainable.

"As much as I'll miss you," she said sincerely when he had finished, "I think you'd be a fool to pass this up."

"Mom," Todd whined, unable to wait quietly a minute longer.

"Look, Chris, I have to go. My son's being a royal pest." She glared at Todd, who glared right back. "I'm sorry."

"Hey, don't be sorry. You've just solved all my life's problems."

Diana hung up. "Okay, young man," she snapped at her son, "what seems to be *your* problem?"

Todd flew into a rage that equaled any Harvey had had recently, berating his mother for buying nothing edible. "Where's my Nelson's Nibbles?" he yelled. "And my ice cream? And the double-cream Penguin Cookies? There's not even one lousy bag of Sonora chips," he shrieked, showing his mother that the bag in his hand had only a dozen or so chips left in it.

"That's enough!"

"But—"

"Just calm down!" Diana was forced to bellow over her son's bleating. "Look, Todd, the stuff you're used to eating isn't good for you. It's filled with a killer called F-A-T!"

Diana rushed into the pantry and pulled out boxes of macaroni and cheese, cans of chili, cookies, cake mixes, crackers—foods on which her family had existed for years. "Just read these labels," she pled. He refused. "Okay, then, I'll read them for you." She went through every one—chapter and verse—to prove that she was right. Then with considerable fanfare, she emptied each and every one, throwing the contents down the drain. Todd stood by looking as though his entire world had caved in around him.

Harvey had come in from the study at the tail end of Diana's whirling dervish act. "What's this about counting grams of fat instead of calories?" he said.

Diana turned to face her husband. "I'm glad you heard," she replied. "Dr. Fernberg wants me to get my health in order before putting me on any new diet. He says I have to stop counting calories."

"Wonderful!" Harvey spat sarcastically. "And I have to pay his outrageous bills?"

"Harvey, listen. He says I can eat anything that contains less than thirty percent of its total calories in fat." She quickly told him how the formula worked.

"That's it!" Harvey bellowed. "I won't stand for this nonsense. What kind of doctor has Fernberg turned into? Huh? Has he lost his mind? Look at you! Can't he see you need a strict diet, not a calculator?"

Diana cried out, "Stop berating me. I'm sick, Harvey. You have to let me try this."

"I do?" he taunted. "We'll see about that."

"Don't threaten me again."

"Oh, so I'm supposed to sit back while you stuff your face with anything you want just because it's no more than thirty percent fat?"

"Yes," Diana replied, mustering up all the dignity she possessed.

Todd had disappeared into the pantry. Now he walked out carrying two bags of bite-size candy bars. "At least she didn't throw away these," Todd said to his father.

"Let me see those," Harvey ordered. He grabbed one out of Todd's hand and inspected the package containing snack-size Snickers bars. "It says here these candies have eighty calories and six grams of fat." He walked to the kitchen desk and found a piece of paper and a pencil. He made a few quick calculations, then turned to face Diana. "These contain more than sixty-seven percent fat."

Diana blanched.

Harvey smiled victoriously at his wife. "Are you telling me you're never going to eat your favorite of all favorite candies again?"

Diana swallowed. "Yes," she squeaked. "That's exactly what I'm telling you."

"I don't believe you!"

"Hey," Todd exclaimed. "I just did the Three Amigos bars, and they only have twenty-two percent fat in them."

"Let me see those," Diana said, grabbing the bag away from Todd before Harvey could.

Diana studied the nutritional breakdown. She took her calculator out of her purse and did the calculations. Sure enough, there was only twenty-two percent fat in one eighty-calorie bite-size Three Amigos bar. "Jupiter Candy Company has a winner!" Diana exclaimed. "Their candy has three times less fat than the same-size Snickers." M&M-Mars Candy Company, eat your heart out, she thought. You've just lost one of your best customers. If she had any self-doubt about her willpower before, there was none now—a Snickers would never again pass her lips!

"Todd, leave the room. I want to speak to your mother—alone."

Todd warily eyed his father, then fled.

Diana stood holding the bag of Three Amigos.

"Give those to me," Harvey said.

"No."

"Diana, this is stupid. You know as well as I do that candy is not acceptable. Don't be a fool. Give them to me. Now." He held out his hand like a father waiting to catch a toddler who had tottered while trying to take those first dangerous steps.

"No. Fernberg said—"

"Fuck Fernberg and his quackery!" Harvey ranted.

Diana held her ground. "These are less than thirty percent fat."

"Then you do plan to eat them?"

Diana looked thoughtfully past Harvey for a long second. Suddenly she made eye contact with him as something close to a smile creased her face. "Yes. That's *exactly* what I plan to do," she said. With that, Diana turned her back on Harvey and, with a proud toss of her head, walked out of the kitchen.

Diana's newfound assertiveness did not sit well with Harvey. Over the next several weeks, his behavior became even cooler and more aloof. Diana tried in every way to smooth things over, especially since her mother was recuperating at the house and she knew he was upset about her presence.

Betty's inability to follow her doctor's orders enraged him. He found her smoking in her room one day after she had promised the doctor she would never touch another cigarette. Then she cajoled Todd into running out to buy her Bavarian whipping cream for her coffee, and when Harvey saw her filling half her cup with it, he stormed out of the house. Later he explained to a frantic Diana that since he couldn't control his mother-in-law, and since he certainly wouldn't think of asking her to leave, he had decided it would be best if he worked longer hours and spent as little time at home as possible.

Diana was torn between her love for her mother and her loyalty to her husband. Perhaps that was why she reacted so violently when she returned from the market a few mornings later to be greeted by the odor of cooked bacon.

Betty was finally up and about, but this return to her old form was just too much for Diana. She found her mother wrapped loosely in her bathrobe. With her still considerable bulk spilling over the kitchen chair, she reminded Diana of the *Star Wars* fatso, Jabba the Hut. Shamelessly, Betty dunked a buttery croissant into a cup of coffee enriched with the Bavarian whipping cream that she had promised to throw away. With her free hand she picked at a piece of sugar-cured bacon. The sight of such unadulterated self-indulgence sent Diana into a Shakespearean rage. Lear's finest diatribes paled in the face of Diana's ranting. Spewing stored-up frustration like an erupting volcano, Diana covered her mother with an unending flow of molten invective. Betty seemed impervious to Diana's harangue as she sat in determined silence.

"Say something!" Diana ordered her finally.

Betty put down her cup. She picked up a second slice of bacon and bit into it. She chewed. She swallowed. She stared at her daughter.

Diana finally groaned and said, "Do you know what I'm thinking?"

"You've been yelling at me nonstop without coming up for air. Don't you think I already know what you're thinking?"

"No! What I'm *really* thinking!"

"Okay," Betty said, her mouth pursed grimly. "What?"

"I'm picturing you in the hospital with all those tubes stuck into you, with bleeding incisions, with your breath short and ragged. I'm hearing you cry out to me, begging me to hold you. I'm remembering you couldn't cough to clear your lungs because it hurt too badly. How you kept vomiting. How . . . Oh, God, don't you get it yet? I don't want you to die."

"Shouldn't that be up to me?"

"Don't you care if you live?"

"You want the truth?"

"Of course I do."

"Ever since your father died . . ." Betty's voice trailed off. Tears filled her eyes. She blinked them away, then defiantly shoved another piece of bacon into her mouth and chewed it with purpose. She put down her napkin and, with her dimpled hands braced on the table for support, pushed her body up out of the chair and walked slowly out of the kitchen.

Diana sat stunned, unable to move for several minutes. Her stomach churned. She felt physically ill. Her mother didn't care if she lived or died. She was clearly out of control, killing herself slowly with food.

Diana found Betty sitting on the edge of her bed crying softly. She looked so forlorn—almost *small*. Diana began to cry, too. "Ah, Mom. Can you forgive me?" she said at last. She sat down and put her arm around her mother's shoulders.

Betty produced a tissue from the sleeve of her bathrobe and wiped away the tears. "What's to forgive? Just leave me alone about my eating."

And so Diana backed off, even though Harvey wanted her to get tougher. Still, their truce was not an easy one. Everything seemed forced between her and her mother. They tiptoed around the edges of every conversation now like people afraid to awaken a sleeping monster. It made

Diana wonder about her relationship with her mother. Of what had it consisted? Where was it headed? There would be no more floury hours in the kitchen together baking cookies, cakes, and pies. No more long phone calls to discuss which recipes really were best for creamy chicken tetrazzini or rich beef Stroganoff.

Why had food become their common denominator? Diana puzzled over that one, coming up with no certain answers. Had they talked about anything else in years? Probably just the kids. Sometimes Harvey's business successes. Not much else. Weight had become a taboo subject now, as had happiness, love, and loneliness, the kind that came from losing a husband who had doted on Betty unwaveringly every day of their long marriage. Food had indeed become a calm harbor, a safe place to anchor in a sea of generational differences. The farther Diana rowed away from the kitchen now, the farther away from her mother she seemed to be sailing as well.

Diana ached at the thought that, like people who were ill prepared for a change in the weather, she and her mother no longer had the right instruments with which to navigate out of a storm toward each other.

I'm adrift, Diana thought to herself often in the days after she and her mother had fought and reconciled. Fleetingly, she longed to recapture that childlike closeness with Betty, to sail back into the arms that had always anchored her in the past. Who was it who had said "You can't go home again?"

And it didn't help that Harvey was making every moment harder on her.

Oddly, Diana's oasis of warmth and friendship was Chris. He visited her mother every day for three weeks, even though he was busy preparing to leave for Hawaii. He cheered up Betty and Diana with stories about his work and his father's illustrious days as a screen star.

But soon even he deserted her. In fact, Chris and her mother left town on the same day. Diana was going to miss them both terribly. Her mother would always be welcome, though she had become a time-consuming and frustrating intrusion into her tension-filled marriage. And Chris. Well. He was just Chris, and the thought of him not being around for the next year—maybe not ever again—made Diana feel as though an empty space already had been left in the place where her smiles were born.

All during that first day after Chris and her mother departed, Diana struggled against a growing sense of loneliness.

Keeping busy, she spent hours cleaning her mother's room. She was astonished to find even more forbidden goodies that Betty had stashed and forgotten in every nook and drawer. Seeing anew the evidence of her mother's self-destructive behavior, Diana decided that Harvey did have his insights. She planned to forgive him for his heavy-handed manner with her mother. She planned to forgive him for *all* his hurtful behavior lately, including the mortifying snub when he had decided it was more fun to play with himself than to play with her.

As the day faded from bright November sunlight to an early, chilling twilight, Diana dressed for an evening out, taking special care in applying a subtle moss green eye shadow to highlight her eyes and a rust-colored blusher to accent her cheekbones and make them appear suntanned even in November.

As always, Harvey's preferences were on her mind as she took out one dress after another, discarding each choice after trying it on and seeing herself in the mirror through her husband's critical eyes. At last she found a dress stuck in a far corner of her closet. She hadn't worn it in eons, but it was one Harvey had loved. In fact, he had bought it for her. She had agreed with him then that the rich wine Merino wool sheath looked good on her, and now as she turned to inspect herself in the mirror, she believed it still did. She accented it with a diamond butterfly pin that had been Harvey's mother's engagement present to Diana.

The jeweled pin was Estelle Lowe's fondest memory of Florence, Italy. Forget Michelangelo's *David!* The only art Harvey's mother cared about was the kind she could buy and wear. Well, Diana was wearing the Lowe family's idea of art, and she knew her husband would be pleased.

As she awaited the cab that would take her across the canyon into Beverly Hills where she was to meet Harvey and some business friends for dinner, she felt optimistic again and hoped that her life was going to get back on track. Eagerly she laid out mental plans about what she and Harvey could do to put the romance back in their marriage.

Chapter

. . . .

5

Harvey sat at the bar in the Grill on the Alley in the heart of Beverly Hills, jotting notes to himself on his three-by-five index cards while awaiting the arrival of Diana and the couple who would join them for dinner. As he sipped a Beefeater martini on the rocks, he glanced around and decided, as he did every time he ate here, that he loved this restaurant. Its dark wooded masculine ambience appealed to his preference for studied decorum and proportion. To him it was the essence of an unpretentious eating establishment with an old urban flair. It virtually screamed understatement with its traditional black and white square-tiled floor, its simple green leather booths, and stark white tablecloths. The menu was a chic combination of sophisticated Continental cuisine and down-home Americana, with choices ranging from liver and onions and apple pie à la mode to pasta with pesto.

Harvey had arrived at six-thirty, a half hour before the others were due to meet him. He wanted to relax, have a drink, and plan his strategy for winning Mark Rifkin's complete confidence. Mark was the only other oral surgeon on the elite west side of Los Angeles whose practice rivaled Harvey's in size. Rifkin had gone into practice a year after Harvey had, both of them joining older men who were established already. Harvey's partner had retired five years ago. Harvey had not taken in anyone to replace him, but had decided to go it alone for a time and keep all that extra income for himself. Then five months ago, Rifkin's partner had died suddenly. Harvey had immediately begun to think of what a coup it would be if he could get Rifkin to hitch up with him. Together they would virtually corner the oral surgery market in that part of town.

Harvey and Mark had met for several lunches and a couple of breakfasts to see if they could get something going professionally. They had agreed in principle to proceed with preliminary plans to merge their practices. Harvey had been seeing nothing but dollar signs for a week now. Tonight was their first social get-together. Mark felt it was crucial that the wives get along, too, if this was to be a successful enterprise. Harvey had said he agreed wholeheartedly with this idea, although he really didn't agree at all. Who the fuck cared if the wives liked each other?

Harvey put his three-by-five cards into his jacket pocket and ordered a second martini. As he waited for it, he glanced down at his pants. They were new, bought last week at Polo on Rodeo Drive, a few blocks from the Grill. He patted the crease of the gray flannel pleated-front pants, kicking out his foot so the cuff would lie correctly against his gray, black, and burgundy Argyle socks. He noticed how good those socks looked with his cordovan alligator loafer-pumps, which rode lower on his arch than regular loafers, allowing more of the sock to show. A good choice, he decided; the burgundy in the socks was picked up again in his tie and in a faint thread woven into the fabric of his tweed English-cut hunting jacket with a patch of buttery suede on one shoulder.

He had learned from his mother that in choosing the right clothes he would project an image of success. She had convinced her impressionable son over the years that his own father, had he listened to her counsel and dressed the way she told him to, would have been able to bridge the gap that separated mere accountants like him from the money managers who called themselves investment counselors and got to hobnob with the upper crust.

"Looking spiffy," the restaurant's owner said, coming up behind Harvey, who was about to take a sip from his drink. He had not seen Bob Spivak enter the bar area from a door next to the entrance.

Harvey turned around on his seat. "Thanks," he said, beaming as he shook Bob's hand. Harvey liked being singled out by the proprietors of the restaurants he frequented. Especially "in" establishments like the Grill. Recognition pumped him up, made him feel six feet tall. "Important dinner tonight."

Bob nodded and looked past Harvey, waving at someone else he knew. Bob was a local boy who knew many people on both sides of the hill. Harvey had met him when their sons were on the same Little League team. Harvey would always love Todd just that much more for having given his father the opportunity to get to know a man who one day could give him a better table in a restaurant. "Where's your better half?" Bob inquired, turning his attention back to Harvey for a moment.

Harvey's first instinct was to protest that *he* was the better half by far, but instead he said, "Diana'll be along shortly. Look, would you save that booth up front for us?"

Harvey pointed to the one he wanted. If there was a number-one table in this place, that was it. He wanted to impress the Rifkins, who undoubtedly would know instantly that he had clout. "We're having dinner with the Rifkins. You know them?"

"Rifkin? Sounds familiar."

"Great oral surgeon. Practices near here. Wife's a writer," Harvey explained.

"I think she's been in here a couple of times. Alison Rifkin, right?" Harvey nodded.

"Now I remember. Wrote a best-seller. She's a real knockout."

As he spoke, Diana emerged from the vestibule. Harvey took one look at his wife and felt an overwhelming disappointment well up inside him. She was no knockout, that was for sure. All he could see was how her wool sheath accentuated her wide hips. Embarrassed by her size, Harvey was certain Bob must be seeing her the same way he was, so he was surprised when Bob encircled Diana in his arms and gave her such a warm welcome. In the miasma of his mind, where he stored trivial information, Harvey refused to accept that it had been Diana who had become really good buddies with Bob, not him. It had been Diana and her love for food that had cemented a warm relationship with Bob, for during the arduous months before the unveiling of the restaurant, when Bob was involved in the creation of the menu, he had turned to Diana for advice.

Harvey stood up and pecked his wife's cheek after Bob released her from his grip.

"The Rifkins aren't here yet?" she asked.

Harvey glanced at his gold tank watch, leaving his French cuff pulled back long enough for Bob Spivak to see that it was the latest model from Cartier. "They're due in fifteen minutes. Sit down."

Diana nodded and sat at the bar next to Harvey. Bob made his excuses and left them to tend to Steve Martin, a regular customer.

"You're not really having alcohol, are you?" Harvey asked just as Diana was about to place her order with the bartender. Alcohol was fattening, and Harvey always became annoyed when Diana had a cocktail and took in all those "silent" calories.

"Dr. Fernberg didn't say I couldn't, you know," she protested mildly.

Harvey's eyes narrowed and a scowl crossed his face, leaving two long ridges where his eyebrows met. "Well, you know what I think of Fernberg!"

"Okay, sweetheart, I'll just have a Perrier with lemon, lime, and two Sweet'n Lows."

"Fine." Harvey placed the order for Diana.

They sipped their drinks while Diana chattered on about her mother's departure for her home in Palm Desert via a Palm Springs limousine service, and how lonely Diana had felt the rest of the day. He nodded, although he was secretly ecstatic that his mother-in-law was finally gone.

The Rifkins arrived none too soon—Diana's voice had become a drone, painful for Harvey to endure.

Mark and Alison Rifkin were a stunning couple. He was tall with broad shoulders. He moved in a nonchalant manner that made women's heads turn in admiration. It didn't hurt, either, that he had thick burnished-copper hair and piercing blue eyes.

Alison Rifkin was petite but shapely, with large breasts and a narrow waist. She wore an electric blue V-necked cashmere sweater that tantalizingly showed off her cleavage, and a tight black leather skirt that gave Harvey fits because it hugged her high, round ass in such a tempting fashion. Around her tiny waist was a wide black belt that made Diana look like a 747 in comparison. Alison was a woman who could get away with flash: her black stockings had sexy seams up the back, and her stiletto heels gave her the look of a hooker who was reserved for the man who could pay a thousand bucks an hour for her services. Even her hair, a jet black mass of curls, seemed vibrant in a young, devil-may-care, almost rebellious way. It set off her white, white skin. She even had sexy ears, with huge silver earrings dangling from the lobes. While Harvey noted that her nose had a bump at the bridge, he liked the way it turned up jauntily at the narrow tip. Her sable brown eyes were fringed with the thickest spiderweb lashes he had ever seen, and her full lips were painted a juicy, luminous cherry red. She knew how to use that mouth, too, for its fullest impact, pursing her lips, licking them ever so slightly again and again while she talked so that Harvey could barely concentrate on their first bits of superficial conversation.

As far as Harvey was concerned, Diana certainly seemed to be doing everything in her power to ruin his chances of forging a social union to go along with his much-desired professional liaison with Mark Rifkin. In fact, she started to unravel the delicately woven fabric of their relationship the moment they all began to discuss the various specialties of the house.

"The liver and onions is my favorite," Harvey told Mark and Alison.

Diana, with her big mouth, jumped right in and said, "If I'm not mistaken, liver is about seventy-nine percent fat."

"So what?" Harvey replied, unable to mask his annoyance. He felt Alison's huge brown fringy-lashed eyes rest on him for a second. "Not everyone at this table has to worry about high cholesterol," he said with a short laugh, looking directly at Alison.

Alison avoided his gaze and directed her comment to Diana. "I heard the former surgeon general say that all Americans should eat less fat."

"That's right," Diana replied in that enthusiastic voice that irritated Harvey to no end. "I'm on a low-fat—almost no-fat—program myself."

"Really? Tell me about it. I'm always looking for a new diet," Alison said, smiling warmly at Diana.

"Well, it's not a diet. It's a regimen to help lower my cholesterol, and then I'm going on a diet." She smiled and added, "Anything under thirty percent fat I can have."

"Is it some sort of restrictive Pritikin thing?"

"Oh, no! It's my own thing. Why, I can even eat this bread." She started to pick up a thick, fluffy slice of warmed sourdough bread with a flaky crust, but Harvey firmly, with that same forced smile still pasted across his face, removed it from her hand and put it back in the basket in the center of the table.

Diana blushed the same wine color as her dress. Alison turned her head as though trying to summon the waiter for another drink. Mark stared at Harvey. An uncomfortable silence permeated the air around them.

"Everyone knows that bread is a no-no," Harvey said with a self-conscious chuckle.

Diana wouldn't let the subject die. "That's not exactly correct, dear," she said. "According to my doctor, starch is not the enemy; fat is." She paused to pat Harvey's hand. He had to fight off the urge to pull away from her. "But since my husband worries so much about my weight, I guess I don't need to eat any bread."

Harvey held out the basket for Alison to take a piece. She started to take a slice, then declined.

The waiter approached the table to take their dinner order. Harvey defiantly requested the liver and onions with mashed potatoes and gravy. When Diana placed her order, Harvey felt like murdering her, for she spent a good two minutes dictating exactly how she wanted her pasta and fish prepared.

Harvey envied Mark. *His* little joy of a wife obviously knew better than to rock the boat on such a momentously important evening for both men. She thoughtfully told the waiter she wanted the same boring dinner as Diana, even though Harvey suspected that if party pooper Diana hadn't been there, Alison probably would have chosen a steak and fries.

Once the ordeal of ordering was over, the conversation switched into overdrive and began to purr along nicely. Everyone seemed to get along. The women sat quietly listening to the men talk about their oral surgery practices. Harvey's spirits soared and, with them, his hope for a profitable union between him and Mark.

During dinner, however, Diana spoke out again before Harvey had the presence of mind to kick her under the table. Why couldn't the woman keep her mouth shut and let Alison enjoy a few lousy teaspoons of Parmesan cheese on her pasta, for God's sake? Who cared—except Diana —if it contained seventy percent fat?

When the women went to the ladies' room, Harvey apologized to Mark for Diana's obsessive behavior. Mark told him he and Alison were both enjoying getting to know her. Sure, Harvey thought ruefully—enjoying her about as much as they'd enjoy a pit full of vipers.

"Mark, we're having Mexican food for dinner tomorrow," Alison exclaimed when she and Diana returned from the ladies' room. "Diana just gave me the most scrumptious recipe for low-fat burritos—with frijoles."

"Isn't my wife great?" Mark said. "Always ready to jump in and try something new."

Alison turned to look up adoringly into her husband's face. Harvey noticed her seductively rub Mark's arm. From the moment they had sat down, she hadn't kept her hands off him, it seemed to Harvey. He could just imagine what her slim-ankled foot must be doing under the table. Most likely she was rubbing his leg—and other places—with toes painted the same tawdry color red as her fingernails. And here he was, saddled with dowdy Diana dressed in an unfashionable sheath and on the verge of total physical collapse, like her mother. If this deal fell through, he would only have Diana to blame.

For dessert Harvey ordered cheesecake, Mark ordered a hot fudge sundae, and Diana and Alison—who now was following Diana's lead on every course—ordered fresh fruit.

When the waiter deposited their desserts in front of them, Alison thought she spied a speck of red strawberry amid the blueberries and raspberries. "Oh, I can't eat this," she told the waiter before he could escape. "I'm deathly allergic to strawberries."

"You mean even one?" he asked deferentially.

Diana took the glass goblet from Alison and pushed the fruit around with a spoon until the offending piece of strawberry was clearly visible. "Here it is," she proclaimed.

"I'm so allergic," Alison said, "that if a strawberry so much as touches another thing I put in my mouth, I break out in disgusting welts that take days to disappear." She shuddered, her huge silver earrings swinging sexily.

"Please bring the lady another goblet of fruit—without the strawberries," Harvey ordered gallantly.

"But I will have a teeny bit of whipped cream." Alison smiled with an adorable tilt of her curly head.

Harvey decided she had the kind of thick, naturally curly hair that was perfect for an affair. She could submerge herself in a Jacuzzi or make love in a shower, quickly towel-dry her hair afterward, then go home without anyone suspecting what she'd been up to.

"I think I'll have a little whipped cream, too," Diana said, breaking into Harvey's fantasy and ruining it.

"No, she won't," he told the waiter with another forced smile. "She's only kidding."

Diana looked sheepish. "He's right. I don't need it. And it is all fat. God, bad habits are hard to break."

"You're serious about this stuff, aren't you?" Alison said.

Diana looked thoughtful for a moment, then replied, "I suppose it's no different than your allergy to strawberries. I guess in some ways," she added, looking as if she had been struck by a bolt of lightning, "I'm allergic to fats. Putting them into my system has made me fat over the years, and now they're actually making me physically sick—the way strawberries affect you."

"That's typical of my wife's attempts at scientific thinking. Really, Diana, that's ridiculous!" Harvey said, feeling as though Diana's comments somehow diminished him in the Rifkins' eyes.

The evening ended with a round of pleasant good-byes, but Harvey fell into a brooding, rigid silence as soon as he and Diana sped off in his car.

"Say something!" Diana pleaded finally.

"What can I say?" he whined, tacking an audible sigh onto the end of the sentence.

"Why does everything I do bother you so?" Diana's voice sounded strained, like a rubber band stretched so taut it was about to snap.

"Because . . . you're stupid?" he said, as though it were a rhetorical question. "Because you're a drag?" He snarled. "Because you make me seem like less, never *more!* Who needs you, anyway?"

"Is that all?" Diana said with a tinge of gallows humor in her voice.

Harvey turned his head to look at her and almost drove off the road. "See what you make me do?" he shrieked. "Everything bad in my life is *your* fault."

Diana sat silent now.

Harvey drove home with a vengeance, hunkering over his steering wheel and taking the turns of Benedict Canyon at breakneck speed.

Later, as he tore into their cul-de-sac, Diana noticed one lone light on at Chris's house. A sense of desolation washed over her when she remembered he was gone. How could it be, she wondered, that she was sitting next to another living, breathing human being—her *husband*—and yet she felt so alone, as if she had been marooned on a deserted island with no hope of rescue?

She wished her mother were still staying with her. Had Betty still been there, Diana could have barged in and talked with her for a few minutes before mounting those stairs that led to the barren desert that her bed had become. Why had she thought earlier in the day that she could make Harvey love her the way he once had?

Maybe she would call her daughter. Jessica would be certain to be up at this hour. No, she didn't want to risk sounding sad on the phone. Jessica had had too many sad calls from home lately concerning her beloved grandmother. This was supposed to be a happy time in her life: first year of college, new friends, a whole exciting world of knowledge. No matter how bad Diana felt, she was determined that her daughter should have fun and not be burdened with fleeting domestic problems.

And she certainly couldn't talk to her son—even if he had been awake—for Todd was at that stage where he was an impossible mixture of gruff tough guy and soft little boy, and growing more out of reach for her every day.

As she entered her dressing room, Diana realized with a pleasant start that she had mounted the stairs without feeling winded. That was the first time in weeks! She wondered if it was the psychological release she was feeling as a result of her mother finally going home or if the improvement really had a physical basis, as her doctor had suggested it might.

While she hung up her dress, Harvey wandered into his part of the dressing room to put his clothes away. He had not spoken to her since their last bitter exchange in the car awhile ago.

As Diana brushed past him on the way to the bathroom to wash off her makeup, she caught a glimpse of herself in the mirror on the door. "Do you think I look a little thinner?" she asked hesitantly.

Harvey finished hanging his jacket on a specially marked hanger that would code it to all the shirts, ties, pants, and shoes of similar pattern and color in his closet. He turned and gave Diana a once-over. "How could you possibly think you were losing weight on that ridiculous diet? Bread. Candy. If you'd weigh yourself even once in a blue moon you'd know you're as fat as always," he said with the same disgust in his voice she imagined a judge would use when pronouncing the death sentence on a cop killer.

Diana's eyes clouded over with disappointment as she rushed past Harvey into the bathroom and stopped in front of the scale. She stood staring at it, as though it were daring her to get on. A few seconds passed, and so did her resolve to see if she had gotten thinner. She turned to view herself in the full-length bathroom mirror and decided unhappily that Harvey probably was right. Feeling lower than ever, she threw on a Lanz nightgown, thinking she didn't need to look sexy for Harvey tonight—or any other night, for that matter.

She slipped into bed and turned on her side. Harvey followed soon after, quickly dousing his light. There was a silence between them as wide as the Grand Canyon. She couldn't take it any longer.

She turned to face him, trying to discern his features in the dark. She brushed his forearm tenderly with her nails. That used to turn him on. Now he instantly pulled away. "This can't go on!" she said angrily, sitting up and turning on the bedside lamp.

Harvey turned over heavily, leaning on one elbow. "What can't go on?"

"Us! Like this! You're rude to me in public. Always angry at me. We don't talk. Not even in bed."

Harvey sat up and rubbed his eyes. Some of his curls were mashed down on one side already. Diana had an urge to tell him, for she knew how he hated for his hair to be uneven. Instead, she continued to stare at him impassively, her arms crossed over her chest. He glanced at the clock; it was after midnight. "Can't this wait until morning? I have a lot of patients tomorrow." He always tried to evade messy arguments with that excuse.

"No, it can't," she said with as little emotion as she could, although she felt like screaming. "Something is terribly wrong, wrong with this marriage. With us."

Harvey took a deep breath, then exhaled. "I agree," he said finally.

Diana eyed him, alarm suddenly spreading through her. He had the same tone of finality in his voice that he'd had in the parking lot of the hospital when he had told her to lose weight or he would leave her.

"Look, Diana," he said as though struggling for air. "I always thought I believed in marriage. But lately . . . I don't know. Lately, I've begun to think maybe, for some people, it just doesn't work."

"What are you trying to tell me?" Diana said, beginning to shiver from a cold wind that was billowing up from inside her heart.

"Look . . . what I'm trying to say is that I may love you, but I'm not *in* love with you. Not anymore."

"Since when?" she asked.

"Since . . . since a long time, actually. I don't know exactly when, but a long time."

"Are we talking years? Months? Minutes?" she implored.

"Stop this. It's so unfair to you," he said. "Maybe we should think about . . . separating."

"I don't believe this is happening to me," Diana cried, tears forming at the corners of her eyes, turning them a fetching blue-green, a color that had always in the past brought Harvey to his senses. Tonight he didn't seem to notice.

"I warned you not to start talking tonight," he said.

Diana said, "What difference does it make—tonight, tomorrow? Would you feel different tomorrow? Because if you would, then let's forget I brought this up."

Harvey got out of bed and began pacing the spacious bedroom, stopping to lean pensively against the gray marble mantel of the fireplace for a few seconds, then starting to pace again. "It's too late to turn back," he said during one of the lulls in his pacing. "Maybe I should move out."

"Don't do this to us, Harvey. Please. You're just under pressure now. Mother's heart attack, the surgery . . . tonight trying to impress those people."

"Can't you face up to the truth?"

"And what is the truth?"

"You're fat, you're boring, you have no control over yourself, you have silly notions—like you're allergic to fat the same way another person is allergic to fruit or nuts. Well, I'm sick of being married to a . . . a Looney Tune. I suggest we think about a divorce."

Diana couldn't believe she was really part of this horrible scene. This happened to other people, not to her. All marriages had rocky points, but you got over them. Didn't you? She buried herself under her blankets, shivering until her teeth began to chatter. "Come back to bed," she implored. "You'll feel better in the morning."

Chapter

· ·

6

The misery did not fade with the first light of day. Nor did it disappear at breakfast, when Diana and Harvey sat with Todd and didn't say one word to each other.

Todd left for school with a sullen expression on his face. Looking drained, Harvey left soon after for work. Diana sat in the kitchen, unable to move, then after an hour, forced her weary body up and into some clothes. She knew she should get out of the house, but she didn't have the energy. She sat listening to KABC Talk Radio. Some psychologist gave a few pointers on living to those who called in for his advice. She dialed the number a few times but hung up when she heard the receptionist's voice.

Diana began to cry finally, and sat all afternoon with the television droning, providing background noises for her loud sobs.

When Todd returned home for dinner, he found the house dark and the breakfast dishes still unwashed. He discovered his mother curled up on the sofa in the family room, swaddled in an old plaid wool blanket, her eyes puffy and red from crying. Alarmed, he asked Diana if his grandmother was all right.

Diana took one look at her son and began to sob again, managing to get out that Betty was fine, but that she was falling apart. "Dad doesn't love me. He wants a divorce," she squeaked.

"It's just a fight," Todd said unemotionally.

"Not this time," Diana replied.

Todd studied his mother for a few seconds, then lashed out, "I don't blame Dad. All you do is cook and eat dumb food, and today you didn't even do the dishes."

With that, he turned and stormed out of the house, not even telling Diana where he was going. She was too stunned, too broken up, too weak, to follow him out.

It was after eight when Harvey drove into the garage.

The minute Diana heard him, she raced upstairs to fix her makeup.

She found him mixing a stiff drink in the family room. "You look awful," he said.

Her eyes were red-rimmed, probably permanently so, and no amount of mascara was going to hide what she'd gone through all day. "Oh, I'm okay," she lied, feeling on the verge of another crying jag. "I didn't fix dinner."

"Let's go out," he suggested. His voice sounded strained, foreign to her.

"Oh, I couldn't," she protested. "I'll cook something here."

"I want to go out," he insisted.

They went to a local café and saw at least five couples they knew. Trying to pretend nothing between them had changed was the hardest thing she'd ever had to do in her entire life.

"So, do you feel better?" she finally got up enough nerve to ask.

Harvey regarded Diana for a few seconds. His eyes looked sad even though he had something akin to a smile pasted across his lips. "I feel the same as last night," he said quietly. "Nothing's different."

"Oh." Diana wanted to shrink and disappear. She needed to be home, near her tissues, not sitting in a neighborhood bistro, pretending to be happy.

"I want you to think of me as a friend," he told her later, as they climbed into bed.

"I want a husband," she cried. "I have all the friends I need!"

"Don't start," he warned.

"How can you do this to me? I don't want to date. I don't want to be a single. I'm a couple person, Harvey. Please . . ."

He shut off his light and turned away from her.

For the next two days there was a tentative détente between them. When he was home, Harvey behaved like a zombie. Diana trod on egg-

shells, her self-confidence undermined. All she could think about was trying to satisfy Harvey's every whim. He wanted none of it.

"Stop pretending we're happy," he finally said. "It's so phony."

"But I want to please you."

"You can't."

Soon after that exchange, she discovered Todd crying in his room.
She went in, sat arm in arm with her son on the edge of his bed, and cried
with him. The tension in the house had finally gotten to him, too.

"I don't want my life to change," Todd sobbed.

"It won't," Diana promised without much enthusiasm.

"I can't take much more of this," she told Harvey later that night.

"Neither can I," he admitted.

"I'll die if you leave," she threatened.

"No, you won't."

The next day Diana spent hours on the phone calling all his old
buddies. "Talk to him," she pleaded. "We've been together too long for
this craziness to undo our marriage."

"I see you've been lobbying in your own behalf," Harvey accused her
when he got home after ten without giving her an explanation for his
tardiness. "Stop it!"

"Okay," she said meekly, hating herself for being such a coward. "I
love you, Harvey. That's what made me call all those people.

"But I don't love you," he said with an exasperated note in his voice.
"Can't you accept that?"

"No."

"Diana, I want a divorce. I'll be generous."

"I don't want to be another statistic! I don't want to be a divorced
woman."

"I can't take much more of this."

The next afternoon Diana dressed up and drove into Beverly Hills.
She surprised Harvey at his office just as he and his assistant, Laurie Lewis,
were leaving to go to lunch. He became livid when he saw Diana walk
through the door.

He berated her loudly in his private office for barging in on him. She
reminded him that she had always shown up unannounced. Things were
different then, he retorted. She was so upset she picked up a dental magazine and threw it at him, barely missing his face. He grabbed her arm and
twisted it.

"Ouch!" she shrieked. "Now we'll add physical abuse to everything
else."

"I don't want to hurt you," he said, retreating across the room to keep a safe distance between them. "Just go. Just . . . get out. Now."

Mortified, Diana slunk past Harvey's dental assistant and left.

She called Carol the minute she got home, sobbing hysterically. Carol left work and spent the rest of the afternoon consoling Diana. Nothing helped. Every time it looked as though Diana had finished crying, she would start up again.

Carol finally left her after seven, even though Todd had called to say he was spending the night with a friend and Harvey had phoned with a lame excuse about a "meeting."

After ten, Diana heard Harvey's car careen up the long drive. She was too drained emotionally to move off the den couch. She heard him greet their two dogs. It broke her heart to think that they, too, were losing their master, just as she and her kids were losing a husband and father. She was in tears by the time Harvey wandered into the family room.

"You look like death warmed over," he said.

"I know," she replied. "I'm never at my best when my husband says he wants a divorce."

"Stop with your stupid jokes," he warned. He stood at the doorway, as if he were afraid of being contaminated by her if he came too close.

"You used to like my stupid jokes," she reminded him. She blew her nose loudly. He winced.

"I've come back to pack a few things. I rented an apartment."

"Oh, my God! No!" she cried.

"You knew it was only a matter of time," he said sadly.

"Harvey, don't do this to us. Tell me what to say, what to do, and I'll do it."

He shook his head and abruptly left her staring at the space he had just occupied.

He returned awhile later after depositing several suitcases in his car. He stood hesitantly in the doorway and said, "I'm really, really sorry it has to be this way."

Diana couldn't look up at him.

"I love this house. The kids. The dogs. Some part of me even still loves you." Diana looked up finally to see that real tears were streaming down Harvey's face. He was human after all. An irrational hope surged through her.

"Then don't go," she begged. "We can go to a marriage counselor. Talk this through."

"I've talked enough. I have to act now," he said, wiping the back of his hand across his eyes. "I have to find out if there is something more in this life for me."

With that, Harvey turned and left her once again. She heard the faint sound of the car door slamming, of the dogs' nails on the brick drive as they raced him to the electric gate, and of her own heart beating. She was surprised to feel the thu-thump, for she felt as if she had died.

Once she realized she would go on breathing, go on living, Diana was overcome by an uncontrollable need to eat. She got up from the couch, wrapped the wool blanket around her like a serape, and stormed the kitchen looking for food. Not only was she starved from not eating all day, but her usual response to stress and all things unpleasant was to stuff herself—preferably with sweets.

She searched the pantry. There were no sweets to be unearthed there, not so much as a measly stale cookie. She emptied the freezer in the kitchen, looking for a Mrs. Smith's peach pie. It was gone, probably eaten by her mother while she was recuperating.

Diana moved on to the refrigerator. Nothing there, either.

In the garage, which looked so empty without Harvey's car parked in it, she opened the door of the deep freezer and searched for the pecan torte from L.A. Desserts that she had been saving since last Christmas for a special occasion—such as this one. Lord have mercy, the box was there! She opened it. Damn, her mother had gotten to that, too! The torte was gone. Not even one little crumb remained for her to savor.

Behind several frozen dinners that she kept in the freezer for an emergency, she spied a familiar container. Häagen-Dazs. Ice cream. Chocolate chocolate chip. Her favorite by far. So rich. So creamy. With those delicious chunks of dark chocolate to nibble on while the creamy goodness of the ice cream coated the roof of her mouth.

She held the container close to her chest, the way a mother might hold an infant to protect it. She rushed back into the kitchen and found the biggest cooking spoon in the drawer. She tugged off the frayed cardboard top of the carton. Ohmygod, a full container of ice cream looked back at her. Her eyes grew round, and excitement filled them. She took the spoon and plunged it deep, deep into the container, making sure that it would reemerge loaded with that chocolaty goodness.

Suddenly she stared at the ice cream. A smile began to spread across her face. A real smile that lit up her eyes. She felt like someone who had stepped outside of her body and could watch herself from some other place as the spoon neared her mouth. Then something odd began to happen. Her hand couldn't move any closer. She watched her hand lead her body across the room to the sink. She watched the other hand turn on the hot water and let it run over the spoon, which held the biggest glob of ice cream she had ever planned to eat in one bite. She watched the ice cream trickle through the hot water and wash in a brownish goo down the sink. You're doing it, she thought, amazed by the strength of the conviction that infused her.

You not only don't want to eat this ice cream, she told herself. You *can't* eat it! You and Alison Rifkin. You're both allergic, and just as dainty Alison with a twenty-inch waist wouldn't think of putting a strawberry—a harmless strawberry that you could eat a million of—past her lips, you can no longer think of putting ice cream or any other fatty food past *your* lips. Not even when you're sad . . . or angry or happy. Never again. You're allergic to fat, so you won't eat it. You're allergic to fat, so you can't eat it. She started saying this out loud, in rhythm with the swirl of the remaining ice cream as it washed down the drain.

When it was all gone, she smiled. Maybe Harvey was right. Maybe her logic was flawed. Maybe she was a Looney Tune. But her reasoning worked for her. She had actually thrown away that ice cream because she wanted to. Nobody else cared whether she ate it or not; she could eat a hundred pints of ice cream or ten thousand french fries or five million Big Macs. No one cared. Harvey's hand was not going to appear ever again out of nowhere to stop her from eating things. She was on her own with this struggle. And deep inside her a warmth started to spread outward because she knew—she *knew*—she had won the first big battle. Flawed logic or not, she knew that she could break the cycle of her habits with the belief that she would no sooner hurt her body with fats than Alison Rifkin would hurt hers with strawberries. And that victory would bolster her resolve for many battles to come.

Chapter

7

Before Harvey had bolted out of her life, Diana would have bet anyone it wasn't possible for a person to decompose while still alive. One month into her separation, she knew now it could happen.

The smallest decisions loomed above her like demons, making her feel more and more insecure. She had lost all sense of herself. Even something as insignificant as deciding which room to sit in had become an agonizing, time-consuming event.

Grooming herself, on the other hand, an activity that used to devour a good chunk of her time, now was completed in a thoughtless minute. Simply, she no longer cared. This morning, Diana merely scooped up the clothes she had left in a little cloth mess on the floor in her closet the night before and threw them on, then quickly left her dressing room without giving another thought to the sweat suit she had worn every day for over a week.

She sat down before her dressing room mirror, ran a brush through her hair, and pulled it back severely, anchoring it at the nape of her neck with a tortoiseshell barrette. Harvey had hated her hair that way, claiming it made her face look like a full moon. More disturbing to her now, Diana noted her hair had lost most of its usual brilliant shine. God, even my hair is sad, she thought, mentally adding this new development to the altar of her Shrine to the Vilification of Harvey. She knelt before this imaginary shrine every night when she couldn't sleep, and again every morning when she glanced into the mirror and realized she had become nearly unrecognizable even to herself. Dispensing with all pretenses at looking presentable, she knew with increasing conviction that her unpainted, pain-etched face was the outward mirror of the desperate feeling of desertion that raged within her. Sunken, sallow cheeks, bereft of the glow makeup used to give them, and deep dark circles scorched into bags under perpetually bloodshot eyes suited her dismal state of mind.

As ready as she would ever be for yet another self-inflicted lonely day, Diana straightened her side of the bed, then wandered downstairs. Unable to concentrate on anything remotely cerebral—even the gossip column of the newspaper was too much for her lately—she rambled instead through the rooms of her silent house, sipping a cup of tea while straightening unmussed pillows on couches and flicking invisible motes of dust off perfectly clean furniture. She settled at last in front of the television and stared with glazed eyes at the screen, her mind racing back over the major event of the morning.

Her kids had left before seven in a chauffeured stretch limousine Harvey had rented to take them to the airport for their flight to Denver. It was two days before Christmas, and for the first time in her life, Diana was going to be alone on this holiday. Todd and Jessica had accepted an invitation to spend their two-week vacation skiing in Vail with their father.

"No, you should go," Diana had argued halfheartedly with them several weeks ago when Harvey had first posed the idea. They were afraid of hurting their mother by abandoning her during the holidays, but how could she deny them their fun?

Although she loved to vacation in the mountains, she never had been a skiing enthusiast. She liked the bundled-up winter ambience of ski resorts, the romantic inns with stone hearths and roaring fires. She loved the mulled wine, the hot buttered rum, and the bubbling pots of cheese fondue she had spent hours concocting while Harvey skied, returning to her rosy-cheeked and feeling virile. But the bulky ski outfits always had made her feel as huge as a lumbering polar bear. They were noisy clothes, too, treated with waterproof materials that made her crazy because she could hear her thighs rub together when she walked. No. It was better this way. Harvey and the two kids together. Diana alone. Anger shot through her like tiny painful electrodes embedded under her nails.

How could Harvey have done this to her? Oh, she could imagine him showing off on the slopes in his expensive name-brand outfits, new European skis, and state-of-the-art boots. Showing off—on an easy run. She hoped Harvey fell, caught his tips and tumbled head over skis down the mountain, became embedded up to his eyeballs in powder. No. Better yet, he should fall on his ass in front of the crowded lodge at high noon—on perfectly flat terrain, looking like an uncoordinated jerk. Or he could break his leg—and his neck—with a group of nubile, sexy, long-legged girls looking on, mocking him.

The vision of Harvey in pain and with a monumentally bruised ego helped. Diana took several deep breaths, exhaling slowly, the way she had been instructed to do years ago in Lamaze class. Was getting rid of rage supposed to be as gut-wrenching as giving birth?

She got up and walked aimlessly into the kitchen. She brewed herself a fresh pot of coffee. It was only eleven. She decided to rearrange her pots and pans.

Carol Benton rescued Diana from herself for an hour at lunchtime. In her usual breezy manner, she barged in unannounced to borrow one of Diana's many ornate punch bowls for the eggnog party she and her husband, Billy, were hosting the next evening, Christmas Eve. "It seems so odd to be giving you this," Diana said, a scowl crossing her brow as she handed Carol her best cut-crystal bowl.

"I know," Carol replied sympathetically. She pressed her lips together and shook her head. "Giving up your traditional parties one by one . . . that must be tough for you. First Halloween because of Betty. And now Christmas."

Diana stood staring past Carol as though reliving in her mind all the good times.

Carol said, "What time did Todd and Jessica leave?"

"What? Oh, before seven. I don't want to talk about that," Diana warned.

Carol pantomimed zipping her mouth shut, then followed her nose over to the delicious aroma of cinnamon coffee and poured herself a cup.

"Stay for lunch," Diana said, an urgent pleading tone creeping into her voice, when Carol took her last sip and washed out her coffee mug.

Carol glanced at her watch. "I only have a few minutes," she said apologetically. "The office is crazy this week. And I'm really starving myself these days. I'm surviving on coffee."

"I'll make one of my nonfat specials for you," Diana said enthusiastically, ignoring Carol's excuses. She began her preparations while Carol took the punch bowl out to the car.

"Do you realize that the only time I hear any happiness in your voice is when you're talking about your food?" Carol commented with a laugh when she returned to find Diana whipping up a salad made with white meat of tuna mixed with spicy mustard instead of mayonnaise. Diana put a scoop on a sourdough bun.

"Here," she said. "Enjoy."

Carol looked queasy. "How do you expect me to eat all of that and still lose three pounds by tomorrow?" she lamented. "If my stomach bulges out even one inch, it'll ruin the look of the dress."

Diana shrugged.

Carol prattled on, "This hostess gown's incredibly slinky, even for me. Red jersey with bugle bead trim. It clings in all the places I need to get thinner!"

"Then I'll eat half of yours, too." Diana unceremoniously took part of Carol's sandwich and placed it on her plate. "Happy now?"

A look of anguish filled Carol's eyes. "You've got to get out of this house."

"Why?"

"Because all you do is . . . if you start to socialize, maybe you'll eat less," Carol sputtered, abandoning any pretense at diplomacy.

Between bites Diana mumbled, "I'm only eating a sandwich."

"But your weight—"

"Oh, screw my weight. I don't have anybody to be thin for! Besides, I can have every single thing in this sandwich, Carol."

"But such a big bun?"

"Calm down! I'm following my rules. In fact, I eat less than thirty percent fat most of the time."

"Well, I worry about you."

"Then stop worrying." Diana raised her sweat shirt to let Carol get a peak at her midriff. "See? I only have two rolls of blubber now instead of three. I noticed that yesterday."

"You mean you're losing weight?"

"Maybe." Doubt suddenly crept into Diana's voice as she said, "You didn't notice?"

"How could I? I haven't seen you wear anything but these same damned baggy sweats."

"I don't have anyone to impress."

"Impress yourself. Go out and live it up, doll, and charge it to that bastard Harvey."

"One less roll of fat isn't a good enough reason to celebrate," Diana said. "Frankly, I can't think of any reason to go out, except to the market occasionally."

"That's just it! You . . . of all people . . . not going to the market at least five times a week? Everyone's talking, Diana! You can't become a . . . a . . . hermit. Please, don't let Harvey do this to you."

"It's not his fault, really." She forced a weak smile.

"Oh, doll, don't start on that line again. It is too his fault! You've been a perfect wife . . . a perfect everything . . ."

As though talking to herself, Diana continued, "He warned me . . . begged me to change. God, he used to love me so much." Diana walked to the freezer and opened it. "When we were first married, Harvey couldn't keep his hands off me." She let out a small, sad laugh and took two miniature Three Amigos bars out of the freezer. "Honestly, Carol, he used to wear himself out thinking up romantic things to do for me . . . for us to do together. All I had to do was stay thin. No big deal. Right? Wrong! I failed, not him."

"That's no reason for him to leave you."

"I'll admit he's hard to please. But he's always been that way. Besides, he hates fatness. Especially on me, or our kids. He says we're a reflection on him. Want one?" she asked, offering Carol one of the candy bars.

"None for me," Carol said, waving off Diana's offer. She watched Diana chew the candy. "I was hoping maybe . . . perhaps . . . you might have stopped eating those as a result of this ordeal," Carol said. "Cindy Wilton lost tons of weight after she got separated."

Diana finished her candy, eyed the second one, then put it back in the freezer untouched. "I guess I'm just who I am. At least I'm still following Dr. Fernberg's orders. I haven't touched a drop of ice cream, and that's amazing for me. It's like I'm allergic to fats."

Carol regarded Diana skeptically.

"Well, at least I'm not winded anymore."

"That's great! Do you want to start going to the gym with me?" Carol asked hopefully.

"Nah."

"You have to have some physical activity."

"I do. I cry five times a day."

Carol chuckled. "That's not the kind of sustained exercise I had in mind for you. You need to think about yourself more."

"To tell you the truth, I don't really care what happens to me. I mean, I wouldn't commit suicide or anything, but if I were in a plane crash I wouldn't care if I died," Diana admitted as she followed Carol outside to her car.

Carol whirled around and looked at Diana, aghast. "Don't talk that

* * *

Diana awoke with a start out of a sound sleep. Nodding off on the couch in the family room with the television blaring was a common occurrence these days. Todd usually woke her up to remind her to go to bed. After a few disoriented seconds, she remembered there was no Todd. She was alone. She glanced at her watch. It was after midnight and every light in the house still burned brightly. Wrapping the plaid wool blanket around her hunched shoulders, Diana padded from room to room downstairs flipping off switches. She hesitated a moment, then decided to leave on every outside beacon.

She petted Romeo and Juliet, letting them jump all over her for a few minutes. "It's just you and me, guys," she whispered to them, feeling morose again as she planted kisses on the tops of their heads. When she shut the gate to the side yard where the two dogs slept at night, Diana felt so vulnerable that she almost took them in with her.

Overwhelmed by the silence that greeted her inside the darkened house, Diana turned on all the lights she had just shut off. For good measure, she rechecked every door to make certain each was securely locked.

Ready at last to put the final barricade between herself and any unwanted intruders, she mounted the stairs to her bedroom, where she locked the double doors, then pressed the numbers to activate the security system. Even pushing the numbers brought tears to her eyes tonight. The combination was Harvey's birthday: 12, 23, 41.

Diana lay in her bed, bundled under her comforter. Still, she shivered. Nothing offered the human warmth she ached to have engulf her. Her mind raced wildly across memory landscapes, chasing away any possibility of sleep.

Harvey's birthday.

She vividly recalled the first one they had spent together, although it was more than twenty years ago. "I don't know what to buy for you," she had said to him. His birthday and Christmas were only two days apart. She had wanted to make a grand gesture for her beau of six months.

"There is something special that I want," he had whispered into her ear in his car where they were necking high above the city on a deserted lovers' lane.

Now in her lonely bed Diana could even bring back the smell of his after-shave lotion, a woody scent. "What?" she had murmured.

"You."

The word had brushed across her face like a summer's breeze: You, I want you, Diana . . . you.

way! A lot of people love you. Care about you." She hugged L
of them in tears now. "You know, you do feel a bit thinner."

"I do?" Diana pulled back and laughed through her tears
not kidding me, are you?"

"I never joke about fat!"

Diana sniffled. "I don't even have any tissues on me."

"Here." Carol grabbed two out of her purse and handed (
Diana. "Please say you'll come to my party tomorrow night."

"Ah, the real reason for your unexpected visit comes out at 1
Diana said.

"It wouldn't be the same without you."

"It won't be the same anyway. I'm the one who always gave t.
party . . . with Harvey." She wiped her nose. "Let's not talk about it 1
I'll start to cry again. Sometimes these crying jags remind me of timed
release capsules: they come over me at regular intervals."

"Maybe if you went out and bought yourself a really neat new outfit
you'd feel better. Maybe then you'd get more excited about my party . . .
and about the single men I've invited especially to meet you."

"Oh, God, you didn't! Men. Who'd want me, anyway? I'm at gravi-
ty's whim. I'm expecting my waist to fall down around my ankles any day
now."

"Stop it this minute!"

"No, really. Look at the bags under my eyes. And these wrinkles
around my mouth. I'm no prize package, you know."

"You are, too!" Carol protested. "With a few dabs of makeup, you'll
be back to your old gorgeous self. I hate the way you demean yourself
lately."

"What am I going to do?" Diana murmured suddenly. "I feel so
awful. So alone."

"Diana, I've got an idea. Come to my house. Stay with us for the
next few days."

"God, no. That would be worse. Everybody laughing and happy. I
mean, I have to be here." Diana sucked in her breath and exhaled in a
sigh. "I'll be all right," she insisted. "You'd better go or you won't get your
million errands done."

"You sure? I'll stay if—"

"No! I'm sure. I'm okay. Honest."

As soon as Carol left, however, another fit of despondency hit Diana
like a big black steel wrecking ball coming suddenly out of a cloudless sky.

It left her reeling. She spent the remainder of the afternoon and part
of the evening in tears.

How could she resist him? She was nineteen. A virgin. Breathlessly, she had asked, "When?"

With his characteristic enthusiasm, Harvey had made all the plans. Her girlfriends thought she was the luckiest girl in the world. So did she. She loved the way he took over. His need to control had seemed appropriate then. They had spent the night at the Bel Air Hotel. Hidden away behind lush flowering foliage and ponds dotted with lilies and graceful swans, the hotel was much too expensive but perfect for the importance of the event. Although the night had been her gift to him, he wouldn't let her pay, though he had let her buy the expensive French wine he had chosen, which was waiting for them in a silver ice bucket on a stand in their flower-scented room.

She had been nervous. Oh, how nervous. Harvey had led her through the evening, though, guiding her to the moment of their first coupling with a steady stream of compliments. "You're the most beautiful girl I've ever known," he had said again and again. She had seen the look of delight and astonishment in his eyes once he had disrobed her and bared every part of her to his intense scrutiny. She had writhed under the spell of his loving words and his feverish caresses. He had laced her nipples with wine and licked off the wetness.

Even now, as she lay in her cold bed alone, her hands roaming over the breasts he had once loved, she could rekindle some of the doused fire that had blazed that night. He couldn't get enough of her. They had made urgent, cat-scratching love.

Such a grand passion they had shared. Diana had accepted as fact that no two people on earth could ever have loved as wildly—or as deeply —as they had that night. It had been the celebration of Harvey's birthday as well as the celebration of the birth of their eternal commitment to each other.

What had gone wrong?

She tossed onto her side and stared into the darkness. Was it really her weight that tore them apart? Was she a different person when she was thin? She didn't think so. How could his happiness be founded on the size of her thighs? Could she have been devoted all these years to someone so superficial? Or was he merely using her fat as an excuse to avoid looking at problems more difficult to pinpoint? She had suspected that Harvey was at his core basically unhappy, unsatisfied. Was she just the projection of his own dissatisfaction? She had made so many excuses for his inability to find contentment over the years—refusing to acknowledge it, wishing it away like sweeping dirt under a rug.

She looked at the clock. It was two-thirty in the morning. She tried to remember what it felt like to be happy. She couldn't. All she knew now was this overwhelming loneliness, a sadness so penetrating she could taste it.

She hoped Harvey was as lonely in his bed in Vail.

Why did he have to torture her this way? She hated being alone. She hated him.

She needed the sound of a familiar heart beating beside her. His heart. Why wasn't he here with her now? He had even robbed her of the warmth of her children.

Diana got up and threw on her bathrobe. She turned off the alarm and raced downstairs and out to the side yard. "Come on, kids," she whispered to her slumbering dogs. "You get to sleep with me tonight."

Fully awake now, and excited to be inside, Romeo and Juliet bounded into walls and each other on their way up the stairs to Diana's room.

"This is a mistake," she said lovingly as soon as she had locked her door again and reset the alarm. The two dogs were frisky and unrestrained in their glee, leaping onto and off of her bed. She was sorry Harvey had insisted they remain "outside" pets, untrained to the ways of their bedroom.

"Down!" she commanded. They regarded Diana with blank dog expressions and proceeded to pull at one of her throw pillows. "Stop that this instant!" she yelled, startling them.

She pointed her finger down at the floor. Romeo obeyed this command and immediately lay at Diana's feet. He began to lick her bare toes. Juliet decided this looked like fun, too, so she lay down and began to nibble at the bottom of Diana's nightgown.

Diana caressed their wet noses gently, and they quieted down. "Okay, now. Let's try to get some sleep." She put Juliet, then Romeo, on Harvey's side of the king-size bed, then quickly climbed into her side and shut off the light.

A few quiet minutes passed with Diana lying surrounded by doggie breath and damp fur. Suddenly Romeo inched his way to the top of the bed and practically straddled Diana's head, nearly covering her face with his body. She tried to calmly but firmly nudge the dog away.

Probably sensing a change in Diana's body language, Juliet decided to jump off the bed and burrow into a pile of pillows across the room. Soon Romeo leapt off of Diana's head and bounded over to see what was going on.

"This isn't going to work," Diana groaned. "Let's go, kids," she sighed, tugging a reluctant Romeo and Juliet out of her room by their collars and depositing them back in their yard, where they promptly curled up in the same contented, sleepy-time positions Diana had found them in earlier.

Her bed smelled like dog, and her pillow and blanket had hair all over them. It made her sneeze. She was getting more forlorn and miserable by the second. She needed human warmth. She had never wanted to be uncoupled. "I like being married," she had cried to Harvey when he said it would be good for her to experience singlehood again. "I like having you in bed with me every night."

She reached across to Harvey's pillow. She pulled it against her chest and stomach, pretending it was her husband. An ache that began in her heart and spread through her body wouldn't go away.

In tears now, Diana got up again and walked around in circles, needing to keep moving or she would scream.

Desperate to attach herself to something, anything, that reminded her of happier times, she wandered into her closet to get the comforter Harvey and she had abandoned when they sold their queen-size bed. She never had been able to part with that spotted rag of a blanket; both kids had been conceived on it.

Suddenly Diana stopped at the door and looked back. The closet seemed protective, as though its very smallness could wrap itself around her. She stepped well within its confines, closed the door, and shut off the light before making a nest for herself on the floor. She tightly bundled the ragged comforter around her like a baby being swaddled. She lay rigid and shaking, despite the familiar cocoon wrapping of her happier past. I must be going crazy, was Diana's last teary thought before she fell asleep.

Chapter

. . . .

8

The corridor of Dr. Feinberg's office suite seemed like Grand Central Station to Diana, with nurses and patients bustling between examining rooms and the dreaded scale on which she was about to be weighed. Diana sighed resignedly and slipped out of her shoes. "I can't watch," she blurted nervously when she stepped onto the scale and saw the weighted metal immediately dip to the bottom before the nurse could calibrate it for her exact weight.

The nurse clucked and said, "Now, now."

Diana was certain she heard "You're a cow!" She wanted to take a peek and see if the secret suspicion she had been harboring for several weeks now that she had in fact lost a few pounds was correct, but she couldn't do it; she just stood rigidly on the cold metal platform with her eyes scrunched shut. It seemed to take the nurse an eternity to set the weights to her satisfaction. "Getting weighed is more painful than having a root canal without an anesthetic!" Diana admitted to the nurse who finally was telling her she could step down.

"Well, I don't know why you feel that way, Diana. You've lost nineteen and a quarter pounds since your checkup in November," the nurse said in a businesslike voice.

Diana's eyes grew wide in disbelief. When that extra roll of fat around her midriff had melted away during the Christmas holidays she had suspected she might have gone down five, maybe six, pounds. But nineteen and a quarter? Never. You had to struggle to lose that much weight. You certainly didn't do it while eating, and enjoying, three satisfying meals a day! "Are you sure?"

The nurse said, "Of course I'm sure."

Diana flung her arms around the woman, who had no chance to escape. "I love you!" Diana exclaimed with a laugh. "You're fabulous!" she shrieked as everybody in the hallway turned to stare at her.

Clearly flustered by Diana's outburst, the nurse sputtered, "Wait a minute. I didn't do anything. You did. You're the one who lost nineteen pounds."

"And a quarter," Diana muttered. "I did!" Tears of excitement and happiness filled her eyes. "Could I ask you a favor?"

"Sure," said the nurse, straightening her hair where Diana had mussed it.

"Could I get weighed again?"

The nurse eyed Diana the way she might an escaped asylum inmate. "If you want."

Diana stepped eagerly back onto the scale. She watched as the nurse moved the weights, then reset them. Her heart skipped several elated beats as she waited for the lever to balance perfectly in the middle at her new, lower weight. "This is so wonderful," she exclaimed, insisting the nurse set the scale three more times.

When Dr. Fernberg came into the room to examine her, Diana experienced yet another boost to her flagging self-esteem. He effusively complimented her on her progress in changing her life-style, pronouncing her to be in much better physical shape than she was three months ago. She nearly floated through the rest of the exam, even the hard part, when she had to tell Fernberg about her separation from Harvey.

Harvey.

Oh, how Diana wanted to share her good news with him. She could picture the astonished look on his face when she phoned him. She suddenly felt smug, sure of herself again. She had a better idea than calling him: she'd drive right to his office.

She put her old velour warm-up suit back on, finally willing to believe that her clothes were really as baggy as they had been feeling. But her elation ebbed the moment she saw herself in the mirror. She still had dark circles under her eyes, and she was wearing no makeup. Nineteen and a quarter pounds or not, she couldn't face Harvey looking this way.

* * *

Diana pointed her car in the direction of the Oak Valley Mall. She let her mind roam with carefree abandon across the fields of her new eating habits: I eat Three Amigos candy bars and I've lost almost twenty pounds; I eat toast with honey, jam, or even apple butter and I've lost almost twenty pounds; I eat pasta with zesty red sauce and I've lost almost twenty pounds; I eat thick sandwiches and I've lost almost twenty pounds —I *eat* and I *lose!*

Harvey?

She *could* be the woman he wanted her to be.

Different.

Slim.

Diana experienced anew the euphoria that had eluded her for the past months. She noticed how blue the February sky was after a night of rain, the azure color contrasting startlingly with the snowcapped mountains in the distance and with the towering trees in varying shades of green that lined the route. Leaving her window open a crack, she enjoyed the cool winter breeze that blew through her hair, and she reveled in the fresh aroma of wet grass.

Diana swung her car into the crowded Oak Valley Mall lot and immediately found a parking space. Surely this was an omen that her life was about to take a turn for the better.

With a sense of purpose, Diana marched directly to her favorite store, the only one where she had been able to find clothes to fit her in the past few years—the Now Woman, catering to ladies size 14 and up. It was a pricey boutique whose designs were based on the concept of maternity clothes, made to stretch in the stomach, waist, and derriere.

Diana stopped in front of the display window to see if any of the outfits caught her fancy. Usually she spied several ensembles she had to have before she even walked into the store. Today nothing seemed right for her. Maybe I don't belong here anymore, Diana thought.

She turned her back on the Now Woman and walked the twenty yards into Saks Fifth Avenue.

Diana took the escalator up to the Designer Salon.

"May I help you?" a saleslady asked her.

Diana eyed the tall, reedy woman. No one who worked in the Now Woman was thin. "Just looking," Diana said.

"Well, if you see anything you want to try on, let me know and I'll help you. My name is June." She smiled warmly at Diana.

Diana browsed through the Giorgio Armanis, Ralph Laurens, Anne Kleins, and she was in heaven. Loaded down with several selections, she found June and asked to be shown to a fitting room. "I'll be back in a minute," June said, leaving Diana alone to face her new body in a three-way mirror.

She tried on the Polo outfit and beamed at her reflection. Although it fit perfectly, she decided she didn't really like it enough to buy it. In years past, Diana had bought many outfits not because she loved them but because they were the only ones that fit her.

She reacted the same way to a very expensive Giorgio Armani pants ensemble in black wool crepe. It's nice, she thought, but I have other choices. *Choices!*

Diana slipped into the size 14 Anne Klein suit. She had saved it for last, having already decided she loved the beige and black tiny-print blazer and matching skirt. She couldn't believe it; the skirt was actually too big! God, she *loved* Anne Klein. She felt like kissing the skirt. "Could you get me a twelve in this?" she asked June proudly when the saleslady returned to see if she needed anything. She felt like kissing June, too, when the woman didn't laugh in her face for requesting something so absurd as a smaller size.

"We didn't have a twelve," June said when she returned to the dressing room, hurriedly adding, "but I brought you this." She held up for Diana's approval one of the most stunning outfits Diana had seen in some time. It didn't look like anything she owned. The skirt and turtleneck sweater were made of the softest violet wool, bordering on gray, with little flecks of lemon yellow patterned into it. The jacket was a nubby yellow and violet-gray herringbone mohair, with raglan sleeves and stylish shoulder pads that accentuated the elongated Eisenhower cut, which was hip length instead of hugging the waist.

"Escada," June intoned. "Came in only this morning."

Harvey loved Escada clothes. Every time Carol Benton wore one of these expensive German-crafted outfits, he had commented on how wonderfully they were tailored.

"I'll try it on," Diana said, taking the hangers from June.

"I swear it's you," June said as though the two of them were old buddies.

Diana nodded, somewhat impatient now to be left alone.

June, obviously sensing this, departed quickly, closing the door behind her.

Diana slipped into the sweater. She eyed herself in the mirror approvingly. She loved the way the little flecks of yellow among the purplish-gray coordinated with the bold weave of the jacket. The material felt dreamy against her skin. She rubbed her hands seductively up and down the arms. Harvey'll go nuts over this sweater, she thought.

She stepped into the skirt. The sweater bloused perfectly over the waistband, leaving no unsightly bulges. She wasn't silly enough to fool herself into believing all her bulges were gone, but some of them had disappeared, and now she could admit that she looked better from every angle. She ran her hands sensuously over her hips—the way Harvey used to caress her. Suddenly she could picture a scene unfolding between them later. He would be in his private office and she would saunter in, wearing this incredible outfit. He would look up from the desk with a startled expression, which would turn to one of delight.

She made a half turn in the dressing room and took the jacket off the hanger. As she put it on, she tried to decide if she made more of a fashion statement wearing it or if it would be sexier draped over her shoulders in a cavalier attitude. Of course Harvey would jump up from his chair and rush over to her, grab her by the shoulders and look deep into her eyes. He would tell her how beautiful she looked, how different . . . how slim. Then he would take off the jacket. Yes, she would wear it around her shoulders so he could slip it off easily. He would fling it onto the couch and notice the wonderful violet and yellow plaid lining before being unable to restrain himself from kissing her.

Maybe, just maybe, Harvey would lift up her sweater and caress her breasts, undo her bra and let the silky gray satin undergarment—which she now planned to buy as soon as she paid for the Escada outfit—fall to the floor. Her nipples would peak and darken under his touch. She and Harvey would sink to the floor and make love with her new skirt up around her waist, for they would be too passionate to take any more time to disrobe. Diana stood imagining this scene, a wetness growing between her legs as she could almost feel Harvey enter her, filling her up, moving slowly, then with more urgency—

"How are we doing in there?" June's voice lilted through the slatted door.

Diana turned crimson as she was transported instantly back from her reverie to the reality of the Saks Fifth Avenue dressing room. She flung open the door. "What do you think?" she asked tentatively, no longer the sure-of-herself femme fatale of her imaginings.

"Just like I said: it's you!" June beamed proudly.

"It's more than I ever spend on clothes," Diana admitted with a gulp awhile later as she signed the charge slip. To go along with the skirt, sweater, and jacket, June had convinced Diana she needed a matching silk handkerchief to stuff into the breast pocket. Diana knew she was laying out a small fortune, but she decided with only a tiny surge of guilt that this was an investment in her future!

Practically bouncing on the balls of her feet, Diana stopped in the lingerie department where she bought new gray silk underwear bordered with alençon lace and a pair of ice gray stockings. In a dressing room she changed into the sexy underwear and her new outfit, putting her old things into a bag to be thrown away for good when she got home.

"This is so exciting," the lingerie saleslady said when Diana told her why she was wearing all of her purchases. "If I'd have done something like that maybe I'd have still been married today," she sighed.

"Who can ever know?" Diana murmured.

"Well, at least you've lost all that weight. My Lord, almost twenty pounds."

"I was on this regimen for my health, and by mistake almost, the pounds literally melted off of me. I've been eating bread up the kazoo, pasta, baked potatoes, all those starchy things most diets tell you to stay away from. I figured out that these foods in and of themselves were not the culprit in my life. The fats were, so I tell myself I'm allergic to fats."

"I'm a skinny minnie," the saleslady said to Diana with a laugh, "but I'm gonna try out this diet, too. Never know when your arteries are clogging up. Cash or charge?"

"Charge," Diana said. She dug into her purse for her wallet and hit a round object. "Oh," she murmured, taking out a roll of film that needed to be developed. "What floor is the PhotoMat on?"

"Don't know. A trip?" the saleslady asked.

"My children's trip. Over Christmas. My son keeps insisting he'll get them developed, but you know how sixteen-year-old boys are. Forgetful. This film hasn't budged off the kitchen counter in two months!"

She stuck the roll of film in her jacket pocket and then signed the charge slip.

After buying a new pair of gray suede pumps and a purse to match, Diana stopped in the cosmetics department. She didn't want to double back home to put on makeup; it would be easier to buy something right here and now.

Diana headed over to the Prescriptives area where several salespeople were available. While inspecting some lavender-toned eye shadows, she was accosted by the makeup artist.

"Do you ever use yellow?" he asked in a high-pitched nasal voice. "It would look stunning with that fabulous outfit you have on."

"Why, uh—" Diana sputtered. In a million years, Diana never would have thought of wearing yellow above her eyes.

"Now, don't say no," he chided her gently. "Not only would it go great with your suit, but it would be so fabulous with your eye color."

"Yellow?"

"We could blend it with some of this purple . . . or charcoal. And . . . here, let me show you," he said, speaking very quickly, almost overwhelming Diana. He culled out a few odd shades of shadow. "In fact, why don't you let me do your entire face? We're doing complimentary demonstrations today."

"I was just on my way—"

"It'll only take fifteen or twenty minutes. I happen to be free and I'd love to work on your eyes," he cooed. "They're dreamy."

Diana blushed. "Well—"

"Oh, do it," he urged.

Diana glanced at her watch. It was only one-fifteen. Maybe Harvey was still at lunch, and she would have to wait for him to return. That would be awkward. "Could I come back in three minutes?" she asked. "I might as well drop some film off at the PhotoMat. Do you know where it is?"

"Second floor. I'll be waiting for you," he said.

Diana deposited the film and raced back. She had more energy in each step now than she'd had in her whole body for months.

The makeup artist was waiting for her as promised. Before she knew what had hit her, Diana was ensconced on a high chair with a cotton bib protecting her new sweater.

As he worked, the makeup artist prattled on about Diana's beautiful eyes and skin, although he scolded her for letting a certain dryness invade her pores.

He convinced Diana she needed all new products, including an anti-aging cream, herb masques, lip moisturizers, eye gels, eyeliners, lipsticks, blushes, glosses, makeup bases, and a variety of eye shadows to match the colors in her new outfit.

Five hundred dollars and thirty-five minutes later, she stood up and moaned, "I think I need my hair done now."

"Let me call the salon upstairs and get you an appointment with Raphael—he's the new José Eber," he chirped.

At last Diana was completely ready. From her nails to the last-minute waxing of her legs, to her hairdo and makeup and clothes, she was ready to claim her man.

It had cost her nearly three thousand dollars.

Five people were ahead of her in line when she went to collect her photos. All of them seemed to take an eternity checking and rechecking their packages. By the time Diana paid for her pictures, she was in too much of a hurry to look through them. It was already after three o'clock.

She raced another Mercedes out of the lot and made her left turn into traffic like an Indy driver. She sped along side streets and made several short turns, avoiding part of the Ventura Boulevard traffic. She cruised onto the freeway and began her drive toward her destiny, elated every time she caught a glimpse of herself in the rearview mirror.

At the bend of the Ventura Freeway, where it melded into the San Diego Freeway, Diana hit a snarl of traffic. She turned on her radio to the all-news station. Within a few seconds she learned that a three-car accident with injury in Sepulveda Pass was the culprit. Cars were backed up for miles, spilling onto three freeways.

She settled in for a long ride. She put on an oldies music station, opened her sun roof, and let the cool air wash over her. When the traffic came to a total halt, Diana decided to look through Todd's photos. The first photo was of Todd and Jessica in front of Harvey's fancy Century City condominium the morning they had departed for Vail.

The next few pictures were of Todd and Harvey at the airport. They were mugging and generally acting silly. Diana felt cheated suddenly, but forced the feeling down.

The traffic inched along. Diana drove and sang loudly to an ancient Connie Francis song, "Who's Sorry Now?"

Getting impatient, Diana decided to get off the freeway and take surface streets. At this rate Harvey would be long gone from work before she ever got there. She maneuvered onto the shoulder of the road and made her way to the Van Nuys off-ramp. It seemed that everyone had the same idea, for now Diana was stuck in off-ramp traffic that was even worse than the freeway tie-up.

With nothing to do but try to keep calm, she picked up the photos again. The next one was taken at the Denver airport. It was of Harvey, Todd, and a woman. Diana glanced at it without recognition at first. Then she realized the woman was Harvey's assistant, Laurie. What a coincidence, Diana thought initially, wondering why the kids hadn't mentioned running into her.

The next picture was of Harvey and Laurie, both smiling. Diana experienced a string of sickening realizations as she quickly thumbed through the rest of the pictures, only to find that Laurie was in most of them. No wonder Todd didn't ask me to get his film developed for him, she thought as the truth hit her full force: this woman—this *assistant*—had been living with *her* children and *her* husband for two weeks!

Diana fought back a sudden urge to vomit. Sitting sickened in her car, a captive of Los Angeles traffic, she didn't know what to do. She felt like screaming. She felt like running from the car, leaving it and her life behind her. How could Harvey have taken a girlfriend along on a vacation with *her* children? She felt betrayed, too, by Todd and Jessica. They had known all these weeks that their father was involved with a woman and had not told her.

What a fool she'd been. She should have known Harvey was having an affair the very minute he had said, "I love you but I'm not *in love* with you." How could she have been so ingenuous to assume that he would be waiting for her to reappear in his life and that when she did, he would take one look at her—almost twenty pounds and three thousand dollars lighter —and enfold her in his arms and love her the way she wanted him to?

This was not about fat at all. This was about lust—Harvey's for another woman!

Tears began to course down her face. Rivulets of black mascara mingled with yellow and gray shadows and liners to make a sorry pattern on her artificially bronzed cheeks. She didn't even try to keep the soiled tears from falling onto her new clothes.

Part Two

Part Two

Chapter

. . . .

9

"Eyeful Tours," Diana said pleasantly into the phone for the hundredth time that day. "May I help you?"

"Carol Benton, please," the caller said, then added, "Wait. Is this . . . Diana, is that you?"

"Chris!" Diana exclaimed excitedly.

"Diana, it is you. Damn, am I glad you're there." He paused a beat, then blurted, "What are you doing there answering the phone?"

"I'm working here now."

"You're kidding," Chris said. "I'm calling to find you and you're there."

"To find me? Are you back in town?"

"Nah. Still slaving away in Hawaii. But I need a little favor," Chris explained. "My house in Encino is flooded. At least the service porch and kitchen are, and God knows what else by now. Consuelo's useless in a crisis."

"Of course I'll help. Don't worry."

"I knew I could count on you. But I'm shocked that you're working. You've destroyed my fantasy—the last living full-time housewife has bitten the dust."

Diana cleared her throat. "Chris, are you sitting down?"

"Should I be?" he asked.

"Harvey and I are separated."

"What!" Chris exclaimed. "When?"

"Right before Thanksgiving."

"Are you okay?"

"Better. But I was a real mess."

"I wish you had called me."

"I couldn't talk about it," Diana said. "You wouldn't believe what's been going on. At least working has been a distraction."

"So you're a working lady. Huh!"

"It's only a part-time job. Carol felt sorry for me," Diana said.

"Why? Isn't Harvey paying your expenses?" Chris asked.

"At first he was Mr. Generosity. Guilty conscience, I suppose. Then I found out he was having an affair—with his dental assistant. So I changed all the locks on the doors. You should have seen the look on his face when he tried to get in to get some of his things. 'This isn't your house anymore,' I told him. 'If you want to come in, you'll have to get my permission.' Now he's not so magnanimous."

"Whew! How're your kids taking all of this?"

"Jessica's okay, I guess. She calls from school and says she's fine. Todd and I hardly speak. He's turned into a little Harvey. That's tough on me. But I'm surviving. Aren't you glad you called?" Diana said with a laugh.

"Actually, I am. And I want to hear everything, but I have to get back to the set. A storm's coming in. We've got to shoot this scene before it starts pouring. I'll call you at home tonight."

"Great!" Diana said, suddenly feeling happier than she had in weeks.

At midnight Los Angeles time, Chris phoned. Before he could get in more than a hello, Diana told him she had solved his flooding problems with two quick phone calls. All was quiet for the moment on the California front. Sounding tired, Chris apologized for calling her so late, explaining that he had just finished work. He sounded more stressed out than he had earlier, but he refused to burden her with what he called the boring details until she told him all about her situation.

Diana dispensed with Harvey in a few acerbic comments. However, when Chris began to prod her about her troubled relationship with her son, Diana's attempt to sound strong crumbled.

Her heart still ached at the thought of how she had driven home that afternoon after discovering Harvey had a mistress and, like a lunatic, had confronted Todd in his room where he was at his desk studying. She could still see the way his fingers had gripped the pencil tighter and tighter; she could still hear the pointed tip snap from the pressure he had put on it before he swung around in his swivel chair and faced his screaming mother with tears in his eyes. He had sat there silently, the tears welling up and spilling down his cheeks, listening to her rant and accuse him of betraying her by not telling her about Harvey's sordid love affair.

"No wonder you didn't want me to develop that film!" she had spat, throwing the package of pictures at him, hitting him squarely in the chest. She could still see the way he had winced, but he had remained mute. "Say something!" she had screamed.

"What's there to say?" he had finally whispered. "Dad likes her."

"Dad likes her? He *likes* her! Is that all you can say?" she shrieked. Diana had crossed the room on wobbly legs and had begun to shake her son by the shoulders. He'd sat like a rag doll, flopping around under her grip, passively enduring her tirade—her insanity.

Still possessed by the demons of jealousy, betrayal, and humiliation, Diana had stormed out of his room and spent the next half hour on the phone screaming at Jessica much the same way.

Unlike her brother, Jessica had interrupted Diana finally, calming her mother down as she explained that Laurie had stayed in another condo in their complex at Vail, and while Laurie did seem to be extremely "friendly" with Harvey, he had been cool about his behavior toward her in deference to his children's feelings. Jessica insisted that her father had not admitted his "deep" affection for Laurie until a month ago.

Still hurting from this latest slap of reality, but quieted for the moment by Jessica's rational voice, Diana had hung up and immediately gone to find Todd to tell him she was sorry for overreacting. Todd had fled the house.

Harvey had phoned later that night to inform a frantic Diana that Todd had moved in with him. Even after Diana told Harvey why she had lost control over her emotions, he still insisted it was *her* anger that drove their unhappy son away.

She came away from that and subsequent conversations with her estranged husband always feeling as if she were the villain—never Harvey. And she knew that he never tried to assuage the rift between her and her son. If anything, he fueled it.

For over three weeks, Todd had refused to talk to Diana. Harvey had remained her only link to the boy, and he had made life hell for Diana with his smug insistence that Todd loved living there as much as Harvey loved having him. Despite Harvey's toys—a fully equipped weight room to rival any health club, a water-bed in the guest room, and an eight thousand dollar THX sound system to enhance his television—Todd eventually moved back home. He seemed more sullen than ever to Diana, but he refused to discuss his feelings with her. Nor would he tell her why he had wanted to return home.

In fact, Diana told Chris, Todd barely talked to anyone anymore. "He's walled off emotionally," she admitted sadly, "and it's all my fault."

"Welcome to the guilty parents' club," Chris said, telling her his own tale of woe about his daughters' troubles adjusting to their Hawaiian school. He said his girls had accused him of being an ogre for making them move to paradise.

"Harvey's taking my kids on another fancy trip—to Mexico—for Easter break," Diana said. "Laurie's going, too."

"The twins are shipping out to Alaska to visit Marylou."

"So we're both going to be alone for the Easter holiday."

"Yeah." He paused, then said, "Hey, you don't have to be, you know."

"I hate singles bars," she joked.

"I had something more like Diamond Head and blue lagoons in mind," he said. "Spend Easter with a pal, Diana. Come be with me."

Diana hesitated.

His enthusiasm for the "plan"—as he immediately dubbed her proposed visit—dented the emotional barrier Diana had been building up between herself and the rest of the world, and she finally agreed.

Diana pedaled furiously on the stationary bike Harvey had left behind when he moved out. She had recently learned from Todd that Harvey didn't need it anymore; he had bought a new three thousand dollar model that simulated the experience of riding in the Tour de France.

At first she thought of the old bike as the enemy, daring her to get on it and fail, as she always had with any physical endeavor. Then one night when she was suffering a particularly acute bout of insomnia, she had—out of desperation for something to pass the time away—ridden the bike on zero tension. After only five minutes of exercise she was panting so heavily that her tongue became numb and she had to get off. But a miracle had occurred once her heart stopped thudding wildly in her chest. Stumbling back to bed, her legs feeling limp as overcooked spaghetti, Diana had fallen instantly into a blissfully dreamless sleep. As days of riding turned into weeks, Diana learned that the more she sweated, the better she slept. Slowly she had worked up to an hour a night. The bike had paid another big dividend, too: Diana noticed that her thighs and stomach were firming up faster than they had been when she merely followed her eating regimen but was sedentary.

Tonight Diana only half listened to the guests on "The Tonight Show," which blasted out at her over the whir of the bike's mechanism. Her mind was really elsewhere, dreamily musing about her trip to Honolulu next week. She wondered what Chris would say when he saw her, for although he had phoned her several more times to gab away the kinks of his grueling days on the set, she had never mentioned one word to him about her tremendous weight loss—over twenty-seven pounds now—nor had she hinted that the result of his calls had been her decision to buy sexier clothes that she thought he would like.

With Carol egging her on—admitting she was getting a vicarious thrill out of the possibility that Chris Berry had a romance with Diana on his mind—Diana had made liberal use of her charge cards at every store, resulting in an impressive wardrobe of size 10 resort clothes. Diana lovingly glanced at her many stylish purchases, which she had laid out all around her bedroom like a decorator showing off fabrics: vibrant double front pleat shorts and slacks in solid key lime green, tangerine, and navy, coordinated with unstructured warm-weather blazers, sweaters, and tank tops in snazzy Italian Duomo and Uffizi patterns; three plunging-backed one-piece bathing suits in splash patterns of hot pink, canary yellow, and black with matching cover-ups; several pairs of Italian sandals; five sundresses, three of which were strictly daytime fun pieces and two of which were sexy strapless numbers perfect for a romantic dinner à deux; and a hoard of soft, silky lingerie, which she fantasized Chris would slowly take off of her before they made wild love on the secluded beach that fronted his rented Diamond Head villa.

A *People* magazine advertisement flashed across Diana's television screen and caught her attention. "Look for these stars inside next week's *People*," a voice said as a montage of famous people's faces cascaded into view. Among them was a photograph of Chris standing next to a swimming pool with Barbie Mallory, the twenty-year-old sex-kitten star of his new dramatic series. Chris was staring down at Barbie's breasts, which were clearly visible through a drenched and clinging blouse. Barbie was looking up at Chris like a lovesick puppy.

Diana had to get that magazine.

She immediately shut off the bike, ran into her closet, and threw on a sweat suit over her shorts and T-shirt. She quickly rubbed the perspiration off her face with a hand towel and grabbed her purse with the speed of someone fleeing a house on fire.

She drove well past the posted speed limit down a nearly deserted

Ventura Boulevard, her mind filled with jumbled thoughts, all of which were incoherent. She arrived at the curbside magazine stand as it was about to close. "Do you have the new *People* magazine?" Diana asked the old man who ran the stand.

"Over there," he mumbled, pointing in the general direction of the porno magazines.

Sidestepping *Hustler* and a slew of other girlie magazines, Diana eventually located several two-week-old *People* magazines. Frustrated, she retreated to her car. She sat for a few seconds to collect her thoughts. This is stupid, she thought. Go home.

Instead, like a woman possessed, Diana drove farther away from her house to an all-night newsstand on the corner of Ventura and Van Nuys. "Where's *People* magazine?" she barked at the proprietor.

Without looking up from the racing sheet he was studying, he pointed wordlessly to the far end of the stand.

Diana found last week's magazines. Dejectedly, she walked back toward her car.

"You didn't find them?" the man shouted after her.

Turning around, Diana said, "They were the wrong week."

"Oh, you want next week's. We just got them in. Can you wait a minute?"

"Sure," Diana said.

The man used a knife to cut the thick twine that bound the bundle of magazines. "This is it," Diana said. She paid for one and hurried to the quiet of her car. She thumbed through the magazine and found the picture of Chris and Barbie Mallory that she had seen on her television screen earlier. Her heart sank.

When she got home, she made it no farther than the kitchen before she stopped and opened the magazine again to the Star Tracks page she had dog-eared in the car. There it was—The Picture. It hadn't gone away, nor had the look of longing in Chris's face disappeared as he gazed down at Barbie. Why did Diana's life always have to be shattered by pictures— first of Harvey and Laurie, now of Chris and Barbie Mallory? She reread for the tenth time the damning caption: "The latest coup in Chris Berry's life, it seems, isn't landing the Vietnam War series 'Where's Charlie?' but capturing the heart of his young, young female star." Diana felt more miserable each time she looked at the picture. She felt like punching herself in the mouth for being so off base about the import of Chris's calls and about his invitation to visit. He had said all along that they were pals. Pals. That's all they ever would be.

"You're a fool, Diana Lowe," she said aloud, slamming the magazine shut.

She got up and threw it into her trash compacter. While she listened to the satisfying sound of Chris's photo being crushed, she found a bag of marshmallows in the pantry. Taking the entire bag of fat-free treats with her, Diana mounted the stairs to her room. Sitting on the edge of her bed, she laid out the marshmallows in the shape of the letter C and slowly ate each one, rehashing in her mind every conversation she and Chris had had recently. Sadly, she realized he had never so much as hinted that they were anything but friends.

She lumbered into her closet and removed her sweat suit. She turned and inspected her body from every angle in Harvey's three-way mirror, trying to imagine what Chris would think if he saw her. Her mind went blank.

Diana got back on the bike and rode it for another hour and a half, forcing herself to concentrate on a boring late late movie. Falling into bed after two, she lay there spinning one elaborate, convoluted scenario after another—stories she could tell Chris about why she couldn't come to Honolulu after all. Unfortunately there were holes in each story big enough to drive a Mack truck through. At last it came to her: an excuse so simple that it had eluded her until now—her mother. Betty really needs me, she would tell Chris. I have to be with her in Palm Desert for Easter. How could he argue with that? If he did, she began to fantasize, then maybe . . .

But he didn't.

He accepted her feeble excuse with words that oozed disappointment. Diana thrived for days afterward on those words. Then doubt began to play tricks with her mind. Had Chris really meant what he said? Or was he merely being nice to a lonely neighbor? He was an award-winning writer who knew better than most how to turn a phrase. Yet he had sounded so sincere. Could he have faked how he sounded? Of course he couldn't. Of course he could . . . couldn't . . . could. Driving herself crazy, Diana vacillated like a young lover plucking daisy petals until finally the sincere regret in his voice disappeared from her memory bank entirely.

All she was left with, as she drove down to the desert to spend the holiday with her mother, were empty words, a stunning resort wardrobe, and a jumbo bottle of Hawaiian Tropic lotion with number 30 sunscreen to remind her of what she had given up.

Chapter

10

Harvey's emotional alarm blared the second he noticed the look of
disappointment that clouded Laurie's eyes when the bellhop showed them
their room at the Pierre Marques in Acapulco. This hotel was one of two
that constituted the exclusive beachfront Princess Resorts complex. Only
someone had forgotten to tell Harvey that the Pierre Marques was the
poor relation!

"Pet," Laurie whined as she made a cursory inspection of the drably
decorated room and its equally drab, and cramped, bathroom. Not even a
pleasant view of the tropical gardens with a glimpse of ocean could mitigate her displeasure. What he had promised her would be a luxurious,
sophisticated, romantic hideaway—a hotel fashioned out of what once had
been the private estate of an American robber baron—turned out to be
nothing more than a showy lobby fanning out to a jumble of worn-down
rooms.

Still, Laurie might have been grateful, Harvey thought fleetingly. For
although the Pierre Marques was no longer a five-star hotel, it certainly
beat Rosarita Beach where she used to vacation, in a fucking camper, in
her pre-Harvey days.

"I'll call down and get us moved to a better room," he said to Laurie in an apologetic tone, sorry he had let the bellhop go with such a big tip before getting this problem with their accommodations settled.

Harvey had hardly finished dialing when there was a rap on the door. Laurie hurried to open it.

"We're going for a walk," Jessica said with her usual enthusiastic smile. Harvey always marveled at the way his daughter seemed at home instantly in any new locale. She was the essence of adaptability. She had already shed several layers of the clothing she had worn on the plane and now appeared ready for an afternoon in the Mexican sun. If she were only ten pounds thinner, she'd be perfect, Harvey thought.

"Want to come?" she asked Laurie and Harvey. "You can unpack later."

Harvey smiled at her. Jessica knew he always unpacked before doing anything else on a vacation.

"Yeah," Todd said, walking in behind Jessica. "I want to check out the pool."

"You go," Harvey said. "I'll have everything all cleared up by the time you return. *Sí. Un momento, por favor,*" he said suddenly into the phone. He motioned for Laurie to go with his kids. She kissed him quickly, then was gone, leaving behind a scent of Giorgio perfume and the memory of her shapely legs poured into a pair of French jeans.

The thought wafted through Harvey's mind: "I'd do anything for you, babe, anything . . ."

"*Sí*, English," Harvey said. "Yes. These rooms . . . I'm certain my travel agent could not have booked us into this type of accommodation." Harvey had switched to a Century City travel agency; Carol's angry response to his new life was too much for him to handle. Now he was sorry he had acted in such haste, for the hotel's manager assured Harvey that these were indeed the rooms his agent had booked. Carol would have known better. "These are your best rooms? Well, then. A suite perhaps? No, only one." The kids could stay in their present room. "No, it doesn't matter if the suite is nearby." He didn't like the idea that they were in adjoining rooms anyway; Laurie was definitely a screamer when she climaxed.

"I'd do anything for you, babe, anything . . ."

The manager phoned back a few minutes later. He told Harvey he was sorry, but the suite he thought was going to become available was not going to be released after all. Perhaps in a few days . . .

Harvey sat glumly on the edge of the bed. Laurie was not going to be pleased. He glanced at his watch. She had been gone seventeen minutes. Harvey missed her already.

He got up and began to unpack his clothes. Harvey was as meticulous in a hotel room as he was at home. Shirts, socks, pants, trunks—everything went into the closet or drawers in order according to color.

Laurie returned alone twenty-eight minutes later, exactly. Todd and Jessica were still exploring, she told him.

She was flushed from the walk and perhaps from the humid Mexican heat. He loved the rosy hue that infused her chest and crept upward, and he stopped hanging up his clothes to come over and kiss the nape of her neck where some of her silky blond curls lay damply.

She wriggled out of his clinch. "Pet, we're moving," she gushed. "To the Princess. You should see it. The lobby's spectacular. They're expecting us right now."

Harvey appeared at a loss. Not even Diana would presume to change his plans without permission.

"I know it's very, very, *very* expensive, darling, but it's a to-die-over hotel. They only had suites left, but they're fabulous. And your kids' suite—"

"The kids, too?"

"Just come and see it, pet."

She nuzzled up to Harvey, opening his ecru linen shirt and making little tangles out of his chest hair with her fingers before planting a wet kiss on his left nipple.

He slipped his hand down her jeans. She wasn't wearing any underwear. She leaned into him and let him inch his hand between her legs. She was already wet. Ready.

"Okay," he said huskily. "But just to look."

Half an hour later the bellhop returned to remove their luggage for the transfer to the newer, noisier, more bustling, and much, much more expensive Princess Hotel.

Yet, Harvey told himself, the look of rapture on Laurie's face as they rode up to their penthouse suite with ocean and mountain views was worth any price he had to pay.

And his kids' room wasn't adjoining theirs; it was on an entirely different floor of the hotel.

"I'd do anything for you, babe, anything . . ."

Still, as he unpacked for the second time in less than two hours, Harvey had to fight down a twinge of anger. Or was it the feeling that the situation was out of his control? Or was it that he suspected he was being used? Or was it that Laurie was not exactly what she had seemed a few months ago when she was his lowly—and grateful—dental assistant?

There were so many things about her that made him wonder how "real" she was. Her fingernails, for instance. He had marveled over their long, perfect shape for months before she laughingly confessed that they were molded out of acrylic. Her own, she said, were bitten down to the quick.

Then there were the hairline scars beneath her armpits. He had noticed them soon after he became intimate with her. When he had questioned her about them, she proudly admitted to him that she had had breast implants two years before. He had been shocked, for her breasts felt so soft, so real.

And he told himself it didn't bother him that much to learn that her naturally curly blond hair turned out to be permed—and bleached.

Not that he cared, he told her with a laugh one night, but what else about her was fake? Laurie promptly popped out one of her contact lenses, which was a stunning blue, and let him in on her little secret: her natural eye color was an unremarkable brown.

But that was it. At least her uptilted nose, flat stomach, shapely legs, and perfect ass were real.

And most important, Laurie's lust for Harvey was real. Of that he was certain. She said she couldn't get enough of him. And he had never been so turned on sexually by any other woman. They made love in every way; nothing was too kinky for Laurie. And they made love everywhere— at work while patients lay recovering from oral surgery, in airplane bathrooms, in the backseats of limos, and even on the beach in broad daylight. The woman was shameless.

And her skin was so creamy white and smooth and taut that he physically ached when he couldn't reach out and touch her. And the folds of her cunt hugged him so tightly.

"I'd do anything for you, babe, anything . . ."

Still. He *could* say no to her. He wasn't a total fool for love. He had some pride.

Then why did he get so aggravated during the ensuing days when Todd and Jessica chided him with the refrain: "Whatever Laurie wants, Laurie gets"?

How could mere children possibly understand what the sight and feel of her did to him?

Why, if it hadn't been for the heart-stopping, erection-producing vision of her in that Brazilian dental floss bikini, which gave a full and quite delicious view of her entire ass, a view that had every man in all of Mexico panting with envy, Harvey might have been able to mean it when he had said no to her outrageous request to acquire some trinkets in the jewelry store in the hotel shopping arcade.

"This place is a tourist trap," he whispered to her knowingly when she dragged him one morning after brunch into the store to show him a lapis, diamond, and gold-nugget necklace with matching bracelet.

"Harvey," she whined, "I like this."

"I don't."

"But *I* do!"

He took her by the arm and propelled her out of the store. "Don't do that again," he warned.

"Do what?" She genuinely seemed perplexed.

"Insist that I buy you something when I say no."

"Okay," she said, falling into a sullen pout.

Harvey's heart lurched; she sure knew how to make him feel like a first-class heel.

They returned to the pool, where she refused to talk to him. Harvey tried to read a book. All he could do, however, was watch the other men watching Laurie strut around the pool.

His kids came by to tell him they had eaten lunch even though it was not on the modified American plan he had opted for to save a few bucks. He warned them not to make that mistake again if they valued their lives.

"But we were hungry, Dad," Todd said defensively.

"Then eat more breakfast tomorrow." Breakfast was part of the plan, as was dinner.

"I'll throw up if I have to do that," Jessica complained.

Harvey looked at her disdainfully. "Good. You could stand to lose a few pounds."

"That's disgusting, Daddy," Jessica hissed, two spots of anger flushing her cheeks.

"Okay. Okay," Todd said. "We're going parasailing. We just wanted you to know where we were."

"Not that you'd care anyway," Jessica said sarcastically, turning her head to see where Laurie was.

"I care. Especially since parasailing sounds expensive. Is it part of our package?"

"No," Todd said quietly.

"Then play tennis."

"We already played tennis," Jessica simpered. "I have a blood blister on the bottom of my foot to prove it. Not that—"

"You'd care," Harvey finished the sentence for her. "I care."

"Then let us go parasailing. It's our vacation."

"How much does it cost?"

"About twenty-five thousand pesos each. I think." Todd looked to his sister for confirmation.

She shrugged.

"Why don't you two take up competitive sand castle building or something else that's free?" Harvey suggested.

"Oh, Daddy, don't be stupid," Jessica replied with a laugh.

"I'm serious. It's sand castles or tennis. And that's all I'm going to say on the subject."

"But—"

"No buts, either of you!"

Todd and Jessica slunk away.

At least Harvey felt better, more in control—of something.

Then he noticed Laurie. She was sitting at the far end of the pool near the waterfall that cascaded over the swim-up bar. For some time she had been talking much too animatedly to an Arnold Schwarzenegger look-alike, a sun-bronzed muscle-bound kid who had no business leering at her the way he was.

Harvey was instantly galvanized into action, although he remembered to square his shoulders and suck in his gut before he sauntered over to intervene. "Hi!" he said.

Laurie looked up at Harvey as though all of his hair transplant plugs had suddenly fallen out. "Oh, hi."

Mr. Muscles flexed, then flashed a full set of snow-white bonded teeth as he said with studied annoyance, "Can we help you?"

"She's with me."

The hunk looked stunned and asked Laurie, "You really with him?"

Laurie shrugged and stood up. "I'm famished. Let's have lunch," she said to Harvey.

"I'd do anything for you, babe, anything . . ."

"And would you like to try parasailing, too?" he asked. "I hear it's a thrill a minute."

She was no thrill a minute that night, however, refusing even to touch him. She said his breath still smelled of the jalapeño peppers in his hamburger at lunch and it turned her off.

The next morning he played nine holes of golf alone while Laurie took an aerobics class. Then he stopped in at the jewelry store just to look. He left twenty minutes later not only with the necklace and bracelet but with a pair of earrings to complete the set.

Back in the suite, Harvey excitedly took off his clothes and wandered into the bathroom where he slapped on the combination of four designer after-shave colognes that Laurie liked. He dabbed the concoction everywhere, taking extra care not to miss all those secret places she loved to explore.

Smells were so important. Diana had never enjoyed the various new aromas he had tried to inject into their relationship over the years. I like the old one, she always said. She was so passé.

Diana. Now there was a bitch who sure knew how to spend his money lately. She had some nerve. Why, she was practically camping out at Saks Fifth Avenue if the bills he'd been getting were any indication.

Women. Always spending. Spending, spending, spending. What did they think he was? A fucking money machine?

A sex machine maybe.

He slipped into bed, eagerly anticipating Laurie's X-rated thank-you.

He reached over and patted the present, which he had placed on her pillow, wrapped in a fancy box. He fondled himself absently as he looked around the suite. Laurie's presence filled all the spaces. Her new luggage, her new clothes—most of them gifts from other tourist-trap arcade stores —were strewn everywhere.

Harvey let his suddenly limp penis slip out of his grasp. He closed his eyes and felt for a brief instant as though the walls were closing in on him.

He took a deep breath and held it. Something had to give.

The more Laurie spent, the angrier he got with Diana.

At last the answer came to him.

Harvey exhaled loudly.

He'd show her who was boss.

Chapter
. . . .

11

" 'Contrary to your normal and customary life-style and behavior prior to your separation from Harvey Lowe, apparently you are now using the probable dissolution as an excuse to run up exorbitant sums on your personal charge cards,' " Peter Webb, Diana's attorney, read from an incendiary letter she had received earlier in the week from Harvey's attorney.

Webb, a trim, scholarly-looking man in his late forties, glanced over his reading glasses at Diana. "Are you okay?" he asked.

Despite the chic image she presented in her Escada suit, she looked emotionally drained. Reeling. How could she be okay after living through the traumatic events of the last few days?

First there had been the mortifying experience at Neiman-Marcus in Beverly Hills where she had gone to browse in the hope of finding a birthday present for Jessica, who was due back from Acapulco at the end of the week.

This must be my lucky day, she thought, when after no more than five minutes in the store she had come upon a cable knit sweater in the Young Attitudes section. It screamed Jessica, Diana decided, for it was a loose and sloppy weave—one size fits all—exactly the way her casual daughter liked to wear her clothes these days. And the design was a rainbow of vibrant colors on a stark white background, which would complement Jessica's rosy complexion.

"I'll take it," Diana had said to the saleslady, who told her she was delighted to wait on such a decisive customer. Diana gave the woman her charge card because she had no more than fifty dollars in her personal checking account. "And could you gift-wrap it, please?"

The woman began to write up the sales slip and asked almost as an afterthought, "What about the skirt that goes with it?"

"I do love it," Diana said, "but the sweater is already over a hundred dollars."

The woman nodded and finished writing up the sales slip. When she entered the amount in the register with Diana's charge number, she said, "Something must be wrong. Do you have a new card?"

"No. Why?" Diana had asked.

"The computer's rejecting this one."

"There must be a mistake," Diana answered confidently.

"Let me try it again," the saleslady offered. "In fact, I'll call it in."

When the woman hung up the phone she eyed Diana strangely. "It seems this card has been canceled."

"I don't understand," Diana said defensively, feeling flushed suddenly.

"Do you have any other cards—Visa, Master, American Express?"

"Oh, of course," Diana said. "All of them." She dug through her wallet and handed the woman her gold Amex card.

That had been canceled, too.

Diana had begun to feel a growing mixture of emotions, with a decided emphasis on embarrassment and rage, as one by one she learned that all of her credit cards had been canceled.

That had been only the beginning. Within twenty-four hours she had received by certified mail Harvey's threatening letter, written by an attorney. The tone of the letter had felt like a slap across her face; it had stung her as much then as it did now, although Peter Webb was reading it without any emotion.

Even in his droning monotone, Diana could hardly listen to the bitter words he uttered: " 'It is now apparent that since the date of your separation, you have incurred charges for clothes in sums that rival the annual budget of certain Third World nations.' " Webb took off his glasses and gazed at Diana. "Well!"

She stared wordlessly back at him.

"Diana, is there any truth to these accusations?"

Diana seethed under a thin veneer of calmness. She adjusted her skirt and leaned forward in the tufted leather armchair. "Mr. Webb," she said at last, "I've lost thirty pounds recently. I needed some new clothes, and I had to buy my daughter a birthday gift. Is that a crime?"

Webb got up from the swivel chair behind his oak partner's desk and walked thoughtfully over to the picture window that spanned an entire wall of his spacious tenth floor office suite. Behind him on this smog-free day was a crystal-clear view of the San Fernando Valley all the way to the Angeles National Forest foothills. On any other day Diana might have enjoyed the beauty of the vast lowlands rising up into verdant foothills and sharp ridges; today nothing could calm her conflicting emotions.

Webb strolled back to consult the notes on his desk. "Now, you've told me that your husband left you in November of last year."

"That's correct," Diana responded.

"And he's been paying all your expenses?"

"Yes." Diana hesitated. "Well, not exactly. Remember I told you about changing the locks on the doors of my house?" Webb nodded. "Well, after I did that, Harvey cut back the flow of money a bit. I've been making up some of the difference by working part-time for a friend of mine who owns a travel agency. It was okay—until he canceled all my cards. Can he do that?"

"He's under no legal obligation to you at all," Webb explained softly. Diana noticed that he had kind eyes with little laugh wrinkles at the outer corners. In fact, everything about Webb's demeanor seemed to contradict the reputation he had of going for the jugular on behalf of his clients, ninety-eight percent of whom were women. "Are you aware that you are at the mercy of your husband's largess?"

"I guess I thought he would just go on . . . you know, giving me what I need."

"You must understand, Diana, until the court orders him to pay you, he can cut off funds whenever he feels like it. In fact, all the money he's been giving you would be considered a gift by the court."

"A *gift?* It's my money, too. Isn't it?"

"Let me put it to you plainly and simply: he who controls the checkbook has all the power. Are you authorized to sign on any of his accounts?"

"Let me think. . . ." she said, her voice trailing off. "Maybe one. Then again, maybe not. Oh, I don't know. It's never come up, you know. He's always given me a check to deposit in my household account at the beginning of every month."

"What about savings accounts, stock market accounts, money market funds?"

Clearly frustrated now, Diana said, "I've always let him take care of everything. Don't you see, I never even stopped to consider all this. I just assumed . . . I feel like a child. So stupid."

"Diana, you're not alone. I encounter situations like yours every day. 'Trust me, darling, and sign here,' the husband always says. And, like you, the wife does."

"What does all this mean?" Diana asked.

"The letter?" Diana nodded. Webb said, "It's clearly a tactical maneuver. Your husband obviously has decided to force you to take legal action."

She stared at him with a puzzled look.

"As long as the money he's giving you is considered a gift, you're not a tax deduction. In fact, you cost him money. Your husband's attorney undoubtedly has advised him to cut off all support to impel you to file for dissolution and to get an order to show cause."

"I cost him money? Do you know how much *he* spends each month?" Diana said with a bitter laugh.

"That's immaterial. He's probably been told that he may be paying you more each month than he has to. The court goes by financial income guidelines, period. If you file for dissolution, he can claim your financial support as a tax deduction and force you to pay income taxes on it as well."

"I really don't understand anything about him lately. I've given him no reason whatsoever to treat me like this. I'm at my wits' end. I only want what's fair."

"Of course you do," he said sympathetically.

"Don't I own half of everything?"

"In fact you do. But it will take time to sort it all out."

"I don't believe this!" Diana exclaimed.

Webb sat down at his desk and waited until Diana looked calmer before speaking again. At last he asked, "Is Harvey still sending you a household account check at the beginning of each month?"

"Yes, but I haven't gotten one yet this month. He's been out of town with my children." Diana stopped, and a look of panic spread across her face. "Wait. You're not insinuating—"

"I'm afraid you may be in for a rude shock," Webb informed her with a frown. "I'd be willing to bet your husband has no intention of making this month's payment or any other from now on."

Diana pressed her hands into her aching temples and said, "I thought
. . . I trusted . . . I never expected a war."

Battle lines were quickly drawn. Each day brought another bloody
wound.

As her attorney had predicted, Harvey stopped all flow of funds to
Diana.

She had no recourse but to go to court and file for dissolution and an
order to show cause, but satisfaction wasn't to be won quickly. It would
take several weeks at least for the case to be heard.

Diana was wild with anxiety over her increasingly precarious financial
situation; her state of mind fluctuated between paralyzing depression and
abject terror.

One night a few weeks into her ordeal she was filling out yet another
complicated form to get a bank credit card, staring at the space that asked
for her annual income and beginning to feel defeated even before sending
the application off. In fact, the whole process of trying to get new cards in
her own name had made her realize that when she had become a Mrs. she
had given up any claim to her own identity. It was as though Diana, as a
separate entity, had ceased to exist. At the height of her frustration with
these forms and the implied threat of rejection, Todd wandered in unsus-
pectingly to ask for a hundred dollars so he could buy himself the latest
craze in tennis shoes.

She instantly lashed out at him. "You're so spoiled. Every time I turn
around, you want a new pair of tennis shoes, even though your old ones
are perfectly good."

"You buy *yourself* everything you want. Dad told me that's why
you're in this mess."

"Oh, did he, now?"

"Yeah, he did," Todd said bluntly.

"And did he tell you he spends more than I ever have?"

"Well, he's earned the right to spend that money, Mom. He's the
one who worked for it."

"Just get out of here. Get out of my sight," she shrieked, too emotionally ragged to think clearly enough to defend herself against Harvey's
blatant attempts to make her children think less of her.

"Fine," he screamed at her. "I'll get Dad to buy them for me." He
turned and stormed out of her room.

She cried all night after that, hating herself for having to say no every
time Todd wanted something new. She hated knowing that he could go to
his father, who always said yes with his generous use of half of her money,

which she couldn't touch. Oh, how she hated Harvey for reducing their relationship to dollars and cents.

The intensity of her emotions overwhelmed her. She didn't know she could hate this much and still breathe.

Not even her mother could come to Diana's rescue. Although Betty had plenty of money to spare, Diana adamantly refused to tell her anything about this dire turn of events for fear of exacerbating her precarious state of health.

"I'll give you a full-time job," Carol offered when Diana confessed how bad things had become.

"You can't. My attorney has advised me not to work any more until my case has been heard. He says it could look to the court as if I'm able to support myself. He says I have to play hardball, too. It's looking pretty grim, Carol. I go to the market and stare at the cans of cat food. It's all I'll be able to afford soon."

Carol smacked her open palm against her forehead and said teasingly, "Not another new diet!"

"You're terrible," Diana said. "Have some faith I'm still religious about following my regimen. In fact, I've lost another five pounds."

"I thought you looked thinner. Let me see," Carol said, insisting Diana drop her pants right in her kitchen. "My God, look at you! You have no cellulite left in your thighs," she exclaimed.

Diana giggled and pulled up her jeans. "I'm telling you, the fat just keeps melting off of me. I'm starting to wonder if I'll ever stop losing on this program."

"Bite your tongue!" Carol said. "You know you can never be too rich or too thin."

"Well, at least I may achieve the thin part. Who would have thunk it?" Diana said with a laugh.

"I have to hand it to you, doll. I never thought you'd be able to stay on your low-fat program, let alone lose weight, while going through all this shit. Especially when I saw you scarfing down all those Three Amigos bars."

"I told you sugar's not the enemy, fat is."

"Maybe I should try eating your way," Carol mused. "No matter how much I starve myself these days, my thighs still are starting to look like cottage cheese."

"So do it. I have to admit, it's been easy eating my new way. It's become my way of life. You know something, Carol? My diet is the one constant in a sea of change."

"Maybe the worst will be over soon," Carol offered hopefully.

Diana crossed her fingers.

But it did no good. There was more to follow.

And Peter Webb brought it to her one afternoon when he phoned to tell her he had good news and bad news. Which did she want first?

"The good news," she said.

"Your hearing date's been set. You'll have some money soon."

The bad news was that a property title search had revealed that the posh Century City condo, which Harvey supposedly was leasing, had actually been purchased as his sole and separate property one month before he left Diana.

"I thought he was using part of your half of the community property and trying to hide it from you," Webb said. "Unfortunately your husband claims that he has had an account into which he has been putting profits from investments he made prior to your marriage."

"That's not possible!" Diana exclaimed. "He was a student. *I* had to work."

"Don't give up hope. The burden's on him to prove his allegations. I'm going to put the best forensic accountant in town on your case. When we get through scrutinizing Harvey's records, he'll wish he never heard the word 'divorce.' "

Chapter

. . . .

12

"Oh, what a tangled web we weave, when first we practice to deceive!" That quote sure fit Harvey's predicament, Diana thought, for when confronted with the information that Peter Webb had unearthed about his secret bank account and its dubious origins, Harvey was forced to admit that the ruse had been his overly aggressive attorney's idea of "creative bookkeeping." With egg on his face, Harvey finally backed down and made a reasonable financial-support offer that would return Diana to some semblance of her former life-style.

"I propose a toast," Carol said, raising her glass of champagne avec framboises. "To science."

Diana took off her sunglasses and eyed her best friend with a bemused expression.

"Wait." Carol smiled. "I'm serious." She gently tapped her glass against Diana's and said, "To science. If we can put one man on the moon, why not all of them?"

"My thoughts exactly," Diana said with a laugh.

Diana picked at the clump of raspberries at the bottom of her champagne glass. "Life can be so sweet sometimes," she murmured, gazing out at the low, rolling surf breaking a few yards in front of them.

She and Carol reclined on a blanket in front of the Bentons' Malibu Colony hideaway, a small, charming Victorian cottage once owned by a famous chanteuse. The minute Carol's husband Billy had taken her out to see the lavender and yellow clapboard structure, she had fallen in love with it. They had purchased it completely furnished. Both inside and out, the cottage was a perfect example of nineteenth-century Americana, and although it looked like an old maid aunt sandwiched as it was between an Art Deco redo and a concrete, glass, and steel contemporary, Carol didn't mind. It was good enough for her to spend a rare quiet weekend there with Billy, and even less frequently with their three busy teenagers.

Diana held out her emptied champagne flute. Carol immediately refilled it from a bottle of Louis Roederer Cristal that she had brought to the beach from Billy's prized wine cellar at home in Encino. She then twisted the amber-colored bottle back into the antique silver bucket that sat in the sand.

"Want some more berries, too?" Carol asked.

"Sure, why not?"

Carol scooped the raspberries into Diana's glass and put a few more into hers, too. "Where is that man?" she said, turning to see if there was any sign of her husband.

Diana checked her watch. "It's only two-fifteen. Why are you so anxious?"

"It's just that he said he'd be here," Carol said cryptically.

"Such wifely concern's not like you," Diana replied.

Carol and Billy had been married for twenty-two years, and over a hilly course of ups and downs in their relationship they had developed a healthy respect for each other's space.

Carol traveled constantly for her agency, and Billy put together vast real estate deals for foreign investors and himself that kept him in the fast lane, too. Yet he and Carol always saved some time to connect with each other.

"We may do our own thing, but just once I wish he'd get someplace on time," Carol said.

Diana pulled her sunglasses down to the tip of her nose and squinted suspiciously at Carol over the top of them. She said, "Billy's not planning to show up here with that pathetic surgeon you fixed me up with last week, is he?"

"God, no," Carol said with a chuckle. "Billy's learned his lesson. I still can't believe that jerk spent the whole evening trying to find out if you played around while you were married."

"Well, he did. I've never met anyone quite so blatantly horny. Only after I assured him I was the closest thing to a nun he was ever going to meet did he relax. I mean, really. The truth is he was only interviewing me as a sexual prospect. That man's fear of disease is pathological! He could have saved his breath, though. I wouldn't go to bed with him if he were the last man on earth. If he's what's out there, Carol, I don't think I'm ever going to enjoy dating."

"Don't worry, doll, you'll find someone terrific. Just give it time." Carol paused, then said, "There's always Chris Berry. He's certainly not afraid of women."

Diana blushed.

"Have you talked to him lately?" Carol asked.

"He called last week to chat. But I wasn't in any mood to be nice. I think I hurt his feelings."

"That's wonderful," Carol chided. "The greatest catch this side of the Rockies and you cut him dead."

"What difference does it make? His taste in women doesn't exactly include my type."

Carol tsked and shook her head as though to say Diana was a hopeless case, then glanced impatiently over her shoulder toward her house again.

"What's with you?" Diana asked. "Is Billy out on the boat all by himself or something?"

Diana knew that if Carol had one phobia, it was that her husband was going to go out on his boat alone, do something stupid, and fall overboard.

Carol said, "He's not sailing today. He's buying another toy—a two-person catamaran this time."

"Then relax," Diana insisted. "How often do you get to spend a whole day at the beach like a lady of leisure?"

"You're right." Carol refilled her champagne flute and sat sipping her drink and gazing dreamily out at the water. "What a day."

"I know," Diana replied. It was one of those early June afternoons, overcast but unusually hot, with a faint odor of salt and seaweed permeating the air, the kind of day Diana loved because the beach wasn't as peopled as it was in the height of summer.

They lay soaking up the muted rays of the sun, both silent now, lost in private thoughts.

"Do you know who said, 'it's only yourself that you find at the sea'?" Diana asked awhile later.

"e. e. cummings," Billy Benton III answered in his resounding baritone voice. "I'm surprised the only brilliant English major I know, besides myself, would have forgotten that," he added with a laugh.

He had come up behind Carol and Diana, who hadn't heard his approach. He stood there with his faded old ripped jeans rolled up, his thick muscular legs spread apart to balance better in the sand. He pushed his aviator sunglasses up on his forehead, and Diana was taken by Billy's huge hazel eyes, which were usually not quite so visible behind his sunglasses or the regular glasses he wore at all other times.

Carol tied her bikini straps and stood up. "Diana's got more on her mind these days than poets," she said, throwing her arms around Billy's ample waist and planting a warm kiss on his lips. He patted her ass affectionately. "I thought you'd never get here," she said.

"I couldn't decide on the sail color for the Hobie Cat. I kept thinking Brian would like red; then I remembered that Jenny loves blue. I don't even know what color Erin likes."

"Yellow's her favorite color—this month," Carol said with a laugh.

"It doesn't matter. I finally decided on one of those multicolored jobs. That way everyone's happy."

Diana sat up and adjusted her swimsuit. Although she had lost almost all of her weight—nearly forty pounds—she still felt self-conscious about her body in such skimpy apparel.

"Stand up and let me look at you," Billy insisted. He was forever astounded, he repeatedly told Diana, at her physical transformation over the past few months.

Diana stood up shyly.

"Go on, turn around and let me see all of you," Billy continued. "Hot damn, you are looking terrific."

Diana beamed.

"I can't wait to tell Harvey the next time I talk to him."

"Don't bother," Diana said, the pleased look fading from her face. "The kids have told him I'm much thinner. He couldn't care less, since he's found the bimbo of his dreams."

"You have it over her any way you cut it, Diana. In fact," Billy said, eyeing his wife with a smile, "Carol better watch out, or—"

"Or I may just trade you in for a younger quarterback," Carol interrupted. Billy had been a star football player in college, but over the years the muscles he once proudly showed off had softened considerably. Happily for Billy, Carol never inflicted her preoccupation with dieting on him; she really didn't seem to care if the man she loved carried extra baggage around his waist.

"She sure knows how to hurt a guy," he said to Diana with a wink. "I need some loving. Come here and give me a kiss," he ordered Diana in that gruff yet friendly way of his.

Diana hugged him and brushed her lips across his cheek.

She sat down next to Carol on the blanket again while Billy continued to loom above them, casually digging his bare toes into the warm sand.

He smiled impishly down at the two women. "So what have you girls been talking about?" he asked.

Diana sensed he had something up his sleeve. He was incapable of keeping a straight face when there was a surprise in the air.

"Billy, sit down and shut up," Carol ordered in a friendly tone.

He plopped down in the sand next to Carol and continued to grin like the cat that ate the canary.

"Okay, what are the two of you up to?" Diana asked.

"Just look at that face," Carol said. "Billy, you are worse than a baby, I swear. He can't wait to tell you."

"Tell me what?"

"Can I tell her now?" Billy implored his wife.

"No, I want to."

"Now who's acting like a baby?" Billy kidded.

"Tell me *what?*" Diana exclaimed.

Carol grabbed Diana's hand and squeezed it excitedly. "You know that complimentary trip the Palace Hotel in Saint Moritz gave me and Billy for ten days next month?"

"Of course. Haven't I been green with envy ever since you told me you were going?"

"Well, be green no more, Diana," Billy said.

"What do you mean?"

"*You're* going with me instead of Billy," Carol blurted enthusiastically.

Diana looked stunned. "Why?" she sputtered.

"Billy met that boat-racing guy—you know, Dennis Conner—in San Diego last week. The one who won the America's Cup. They hit it off, and Dennis invited Billy to go with him on a race to Ensenada. It's the same week as our Switzerland trip. Naturally Billy wants to dump his old lady for the macho adventure of his life. He came up with the absolutely brilliant idea that I take you instead. Just think what delicious damage we could do in Europe!"

"Oh, I couldn't—"

"Don't say 'couldn't afford it,' " Carol interrupted. "This entire ten-day trip is free—gratis."

"For you. I mean, you do so much business with the hotels," Diana said.

"And if I bring you to share my room, it's no different than if I bring Billy."

"Well, a little different, honey," Billy said with a lusty laugh.

"He's right. Change the date. Why would you want to be there with me?"

"Because Billy doesn't love Europe. Because you deserve a rest. Because you've earned the right to some fun after all the shit that bastard Harvey's pulled on you lately. You're going."

"You might as well accept it, Diana. When Carol uses that tone of voice you're doomed."

"But—"

"But nothing. Your kids aren't going to be around all summer anyway," Carol rushed on.

"Well, that's true," Diana said. Jessica had decided to stay in Berkeley for summer school, and Todd was going on a six-week teen tour of the United States. "Switzerland," Diana murmured. "I can hardly believe this."

"You better believe it, doll. All you need is a toothbrush and some hiking boots."

"And one more thing," Diana said sardonically, opening her beach purse to take out her sweetest possession. "You can't leave home without it," she recited with a laugh as she showed off her new American Express card. "It may not be gold like Harvey's," she said, "but it's all mine."

Chapter

. . . .

13

Diana stared out the dining car window of the private Swiss Rhaeto railway line at the continually changing sights.

When she had started this last leg of her journey, she had viewed somber castles, brightly painted quaint farmhouses, almost toylike railway stations. Later she had seen enchanting mountain villages, and now as the train steadily chugged higher and closer to her final destination, Saint Moritz, there was an almost mystical vision of the mountains beginning to show themselves in precipitous ravines, and the excitement of seeing surging streams and towering rock formations.

Inside the dining car, where she was imbibing white wine and finishing a five-course lunch, Diana was surrounded by another kind of beauty, for the designer of this particular train had re-created down to the last detail the elegant style of the early 1930s. Diana's table was covered with a starched white linen cloth. The silverware shouted substantiality by its very heaviness. The richly paneled walls of pure mahogany and even the delicate china plates and serving dishes evoked an air of upper-class gentility.

Although Diana experienced moments of pure joy from the scenery, from the ambience of the dining car, even from something as simple as the sweet taste of the wine she was drinking, she couldn't stave off the rolling waves of anxiety, relentless and unsympathetic, that kept coming at her.

At these moments Diana felt like a rudderless boat bobbing on a troubled sea, at the mercy of the tides and other uncontrollable, sometimes perverse, forces that could take her wherever they wanted.

After all, wasn't this trip merely the absurd conclusion to a capricious series of events? One minute she had been embroiled in a bloody battle with Harvey over money, wondering where her next house payment was coming from. The next minute, it seemed to Diana, Billy Benton had blithely given her his ticket so she could travel with Carol to one of the most exciting resort towns in the world.

Then presto, her life had abruptly changed again.

As it turned out, a mere two days before Carol and Diana's scheduled departure, Billy had wrenched his lower back while working on his yacht. By that evening, he was in great pain and unable to walk. His plans to sail with Dennis Conner had to be canceled. In fact, Billy's orthopedist prescribed complete bed rest in the hospital where he could be totally immobilized. Billy harbored an irrational fear of hospitals; he put up such a fuss that his doctor finally gave in, but only after extracting Carol's promise to watch over her husband at home. She had no recourse but to stay with him and play Florence Nightingale.

Diana had agreed that Billy's health was infinitely more important than a jaunt to Europe. She had immediately suggested they cancel or at least postpone their trip.

Carol said it would be criminal to pass up a free five-star vacation. And as much as she wanted to postpone it, she couldn't. Her travel schedule for the next six months was an intricate meshing of interlocking parts —moving one would have destroyed all her careful planning.

She insisted Diana go anyway. Diana balked. "Everything's arranged," Carol assured her reluctant friend. "I've even called Andrea Badrutt, the owner of the Palace Hotel, and he's waiting for you with open arms. All you have to do is get on the plane and remember to get off in Zurich. The train will be waiting right at the airport. Your luggage will be transferred automatically. Believe me, it's as simple as one-two-three."

"But you know how bad I am in math," Diana joked, trying not to acknowledge the panicky feelings that were rising up in her. She tried picturing herself hiking in the Alps alone. She couldn't. Eating alone. She couldn't. Even shopping alone didn't appeal to her. "I can't possibly go without you," she protested.

"Of course you can," Carol had insisted.

"But, alone?"

"Yes. Diana, you're a capable woman. And you need a change of scenery."

Well, now Diana was alone. And the scenery sure was different. But as she glanced at all the passengers sitting in twos, threes, and fours at the other tables—most of them laughing and chattering happily in a variety of languages—Diana wondered, as she had intermittently since she boarded the plane in Los Angeles, how in the hell she was going to get through the next ten days all by herself.

As luck would have it, the weather turned foul and the train made its final ascent into Saint Moritz in a driving rain.

The sky was an ominous blackish gray when Diana disembarked, and she stood feeling bewildered and lost for a minute as she surveyed the bustling station.

The downpour chilled her and gave her goose bumps. She buttoned her raincoat up to her neck; she was glad she had decided to wear a lamb's wool skirt and matching sweater for the plane and train rides instead of a cotton summer suit.

She hadn't expected such a sudden change in the weather, nor had she expected the train station to be so plain and unimpressive. Carol's voice echoed in Diana's brain. "It's the people who make Saint Moritz what it is," Carol had counseled her, "and all the natural beauty, of course."

The Palace limousine driver awaited Diana at the baggage claim area. He was easy to spot among the other drivers, for he wore a black chauffeur's cap with the name of the hotel emblazoned across the front in gold lettering. A squarely built man with a broad face, prominent nose, and bumpy skin, he looked unapproachable, but he responded warmly to Diana's introduction and spoke impeccable English. He said he hoped she had had a good trip up the mountain, and he assured her that the storm was an ephemeral one and the "champagne climate," for which this part of Switzerland was so famous, would surely return by the next day.

With a porter lugging Diana's valises behind them, the driver led the way outside to the car. The limousine was a long ebony Rolls-Royce, one of the most impressive she had ever seen. While the porter loaded the trunk, the driver held a big black umbrella above Diana's head as she stepped into the backseat.

"Would you care for the use of one of our blankets?" he inquired. "It's not a long ride, but it is frightfully damp today."

He immediately produced a burgundy and heather mohair blanket, which Diana let him lay gently across her lap, allowing a portion of it to cascade down to cover her bare legs.

She settled back for the ride to the Palace. Despite a persistent residue of gnawing anxiety, she allowed the beginnings of a feeling of being a princess to seep into her consciousness.

Almost before she got comfortable, however, the driver turned onto a semicircular driveway, cut the engine in front of an unimpressive hotel entrance, and escorted her through a revolving door guarded by a discreetly nodding attendant dressed in burgundy livery.

Diana's sensible one-inch heels click-clacked on the black and white tile floor, then lost all sound as she stepped onto an antique Persian rug for the final few steps to the registration desk.

A family of Arabs in flowing robes and turbans was registering. Their many requirements seemed to be taking up the resources of every available concierge, although one of them did acknowledge Diana long enough to take her name and tell her she would be attended to shortly.

Moments later a wiry, sporty-looking man in gray flannel slacks, a turtleneck sweater, and a houndstooth blazer emerged from one of the doors that flanked the registration table. As he approached Diana, she noticed that he walked with a decided limp and used a cane.

"You must be Diana Lowe," the man said when he reached her side.

She was pleased. "Why, yes. And you must be . . ."

"Andrea Badrutt. At your service," he replied, clicking his heels and extending his free hand to shake hers. He had an amused twinkle in his eyes, nice even features, and a full head of silvery hair. Diana thought he was at least in his late sixties. "We've been expecting you. I must apologize for the wait, but sometimes it cannot be helped," he explained, his Swiss-German accent quite strong.

"Oh, I don't mind. I've been enjoying the scenery," she said, pointing to a Harry Winston jewelry display case.

"We try to please our guests in every way," Badrutt bantered. "Even the most difficult ones." He nodded discreetly toward the registration desk where the Arabs had finally been placated and were following one of the concierges through a grand set of double doors.

"They insisted upon staying in the Gunther Sachs apartment in the tower," he confided. "But Gunther doesn't ever let it."

"Gunther Sachs?" Diana asked. She felt an anxiety attack coming on. How would she survive in this rarefied atmosphere if she didn't even know who the players were?

"I'm sorry. Among his many claims to fame, my dear, Gunther Sachs was once the lucky husband of Brigitte Bardot."

Diana said with mock recognition, "Oh! *That* Gunther Sachs."

"The Palace has had many fabled guests. I could tell you stories for hours. Your charming friend Carol has always been one of my best audiences." He clucked and said, "A pity she couldn't come with you."

"I know," Diana said. "Traveling alone is a first for me."

"Yes. Carol has told me all the details. I and my hotel are at your beck and call," he offered gallantly. "And now I think you must be tired. Let me have Dieter get you settled." Badrutt made his polite departure.

Within a few minutes Diana was being led into the grand lobby of the Palace through double doors guarded by two attendants also dressed in the hotel's burgundy livery.

Moved by the Gothic grandeur of the soaring vaulted ceilings and the enormous paintings, Diana was struck by a sensation of having entered a cathedral rather than the central public room of a ski lodge.

"Here we are, madame," the attendant said when they reached Diana's room on the *bel étage*. Carol had instructed her to change to that floor if for some reason they mistakenly put her someplace else. It was the best location in the hotel, Carol had told her, with knockout views.

The view was spectacular, although somewhat muted by the rain. The attendant tied back the rich damask drapes and parted the Swiss lace curtains to reveal a vast panorama of lake and, beyond that, the sharp rise of the mountains, most of which were shrouded in low hanging clouds. He exhorted her to be sure to peek out first thing in the morning; if the storm had passed by then she was in for a treat, for the peaks were still covered with snow.

Diana tipped the porter generously, and before he left he said that anything Diana needed, Badrutt's Palace could provide.

How about a man? she thought fleetingly, then chased the thought away.

"You're alone in Switzerland," Diana murmured aloud as she hung up her outfits in one of the four capacious wardrobes.

After unpacking, she wandered into the bathroom. It was nearly as large as her bedroom at home.

Sipping a glass of the purest cold water drawn straight from the tap, she meandered back into the spacious bedroom. She kicked off her shoes and enjoyed the sensation of the velvety rose carpet tickling the aching balls of her feet.

Diana was exhausted from the long trip, and the twin beds looked inviting. The headboards and footboards, of painted white wood with gilt trim, matched the French provincial wardrobes and gave the impression of being both homey and regal. She sat down on one of the beds and sank into the poofed goose-down comforter. Its pristine white lace and satin cover matched the silk bedspread and the white linen sheets and pillow-cases, which felt softer than silk.

Diana lay down and stretched. In a minute she began to doze, half awake, half dreaming.

She wondered what Harvey was doing now. Probably humping Laurie in his private office. God, he would have loved this posh hotel. He would have beamed for days if Andrea Badrutt had greeted him the way he had greeted Diana. Carol had assured her that if the grand old gentleman did meet her upon her arrival she should feel special, since he did that only for important guests and old friends.

Eat your heart out, Harvey Lowe, Diana mused as she dipped further into a somnolent state. You've got the bimbette of your dreams, and I've got a beautiful room with a balcony and a stunning view of the lake—all alone in Saint Moritz. . . .

The shrill ring of the telephone awoke Diana. It was the concierge calling to tell her that Monsieur Badrutt had taken the liberty of making a nine o'clock dinner reservation for one at The Restaurant, the hotel's fanciest dining room.

Diana mumbled a thank-you and hung up. She lay unmoving for a few minutes, still feeling disoriented from her nap. At last fully awake, she glanced at her watch and was surprised to see that she had been asleep for only half an hour. In some ways she wished she had slept right through dinner. Maybe she could sleep through all of her meals.

Maybe she could sleep right through this whole vacation.

She picked up the phone to call the concierge to tell him she wouldn't need the reservation for one after all.

Don't be a fool, she heard Carol's voice taunting her. Just go out there and wow 'em, doll.

She cradled the receiver. She picked it up. She put it down.

There was only one way to get past this fear.

With her Baedeker's guidebook to Switzerland in hand, Diana closed the door to her room and made her way downstairs to take tea.

The lobby was abuzz with people. "It's the rain," the maître d' explained to her when she commented on the crowded room. "In the summer it's usually quieter at this hour, except when it rains or snows."

"Snows?" Diana questioned.

"Once or twice in the summer we get snow. This is a mountain resort, after all, isn't it? Here's a nice place for madame to sit." He bowed and left Diana at a small table for two close enough to a forty-foot-high bay window to allow her to appreciate what was visible through the down-pour of the view of the lake and mountains.

As she had the first time she walked through this space, Diana mar-veled at the immensity of the lobby and its towering Gothic ceiling with vaults made of varying shades of wood. More impressive still were the walk-in-size stone fireplaces, all ablaze now to warm the damp air.

A waiter, wheeling a cart, approached her. On it were china plates and cups, a Georgian silver tea set, ornate silverware even heavier than what she had used on the train, and a wide selection of teas and cakes.

After making her choices and settling back in her chair, she sipped the tea and nibbled a flaky biscuit with marmalade, pretending to be engrossed in her guidebook when in fact she was really more interested in the three people at the table next to her—one startlingly attractive woman and two attentive men. The woman spoke with an upper-class English accent and seemed to be the center of the men's attention. Diana couldn't tell how old the woman was, but her attitude seemed young as she threw her head back to laugh heartily. Her hair, the color of India ink, was stylishly moussed, cropped severely at the jawline, and teased up at the forehead in several artful turns. She had on a fuchsia turtleneck sweater that matched her lipstick, and a multicolored Hermès scarf that complemented the sweater. She wore it tied loosely around her shoulders.

Diana had a better view of one man who leaned forward as though he didn't want to miss a word the dynamic woman said. He was a dapper older man with an angular face, ruddy cheeks, gray hair parted and combed to perfection, and a pencil-thin mustache. He wore a short loden jacket, typically Bavarian, and Diana was certain he would also wear a quaint Alpine hat with a brushy feather perched in the band.

The man on the woman's other side Diana found most intriguing, for he was the stereotypical Latin lover. Young, with a look of ennui pasted across his face when the other man spoke, he came to life only when the woman directed a comment his way. Lucky her, Diana thought, for he was a beautiful specimen of masculine sex appeal with his slick black hair, small straight nose, firm jaw, and athletic build. He looked to Diana as though he had stepped right out of the "What's Happening in Europe" pages of *Town and Country*.

Despite the muted but persistent hum of voices that surrounded her, Diana was easily able to eavesdrop on their free-flowing conversation with-out being at all obvious.

The woman was a hummingbird conversationalist, easily flitting from one subject to another: plans for a party, an upcoming tennis tournament at the hotel, a Sotheby auction and several music festival events in that other posh Swiss resort, Gstaad.

Occasionally Diana heard only a piece of a sentence, as one or another of them lowered his voice. She had to fight off the urge to lean closer so as not to miss a word.

As the group rose to depart, Diana overheard the woman suggesting they all meet at the hotel's Renaissance Bar for a drink at nine before going in for dinner.

Diana made a mental note: the Renaissance Bar before dinner. Sounded good. She would have liked that—but not alone.

The next day brought brilliant sunshine, as predicted by the hotel's chauffeur. He had failed, however, to prepare Diana for the delicious, fresh earthy smell of water evaporating off of leaves and bark, or the awe-inspiring vision of flowers of every color and description that greeted her as the funicular deposited her and other hikers at mid-mountain Corviglia.

On this first hiking expedition, Diana was anxious to see the sights and eat a casual picnic lunch along the route back to Saint Moritz.

Even though she looked totally American, outfitted as she was in jeans, sneakers, and a colorful sweat shirt, instead of a dirndl or lederhosen, Diana still felt a spiritual bonding with her surroundings as she stood on the edge of the world. Like Maria Von Trapp in *The Sound of Music*, she turned and saw in every direction snow-capped mountains leading down to lush green pastures dotted with farmhouses and chalets painted the way she remembered them in storybooks.

Here she could be alone and be happy.

And she was.

Setting out with a bounce in her step, Diana stuck to the well-marked path, deviating occasionally to appreciate the stands of pine and patches of sunflowers, daisies, and other wildflowers that were just as beautiful but which she could not identify by name.

At the halfway point of her mapped-out hike, she stopped to eat the lunch the Palace had packed for her.

For the first time in weeks she felt truly content as she reclined on her elbows for a while and inhaled the healthful mountain air.

Occasionally other hikers passed by. She waved to them with a smile and a nod. They waved back. A couple of them even said a few words to her, sometimes in languages she didn't understand. It didn't matter, for she sensed that everyone was feeling the same oneness with nature she was experiencing and this was their common language. It made her feel more connected, yet freer than she had in a long time.

A bee buzzed around her head, then flew into a field of daisies. She stood up and took the same route, plucking one of the flowers and tucking it behind her ear. Not even on vacations to Hawaii had Diana ever worn a flower in her hair. Harvey had thought it was corny. Somehow it seemed like the right thing to do here.

Resuming her tiring trek down the steep incline, which was an expert ski run in winter, Diana was filled with the tranquilizing effect of her surroundings. How ironic, she thought, that it was the Swiss who had invented Valium and given it to the world. It was a shame they couldn't just bottle their environment, for in the months of stress that Harvey had caused, Diana had never felt this relaxed after taking one of those little yellow pills.

"Why, halloo," Dierdre Nieuwirth warbled in her lilting English accent, intercepting Diana at the last crossroad before the final descent into Saint Moritz. "So we meet again. Care for some company?"

Dierdre was the stunning Englishwoman Diana had noticed the day before at tea. Andrea Badrutt had introduced them that night at dinner, for he had been standing at Dierdre's table talking to her and her consorts when Diana passed by on her way out.

"I'd love that," Diana replied, furtively snatching the flower from behind her ear and tucking it into the pocket of her jeans. "I'm surprised to find you out here alone."

"Ah, but this is what I live for," Dierdre replied in a theatrical voice. "An hour or two with nature. It revives one's soul, don't you agree?"

"Why, yes."

The two women fell into step. "What do you think of our lovely little town?" Dierdre inquired after they had walked in silence for some time. They were only a few meters away from the hotel, approaching it from the lake side.

The view of the back of the Palace was as grand as the front was simple. The hotel seemed to rise out of the water like a turreted medieval castle.

"All of this makes me speechless," Diana confessed. "Words cannot describe how uplifted yet tranquil I feel after only one day."

A bit of breeze stirred the air. Dierdre wound her immense scarf around her neck with her long, expressive fingers. Everything she did exuded drama, Diana decided, captivated by this tall, ageless beauty who made even a simple pleated skirt, wool sweater ensemble, and sensible suede walking shoes seem chic.

"Have you time for a nip?" Dierdre inquired suddenly as they entered the pool area of the hotel.

The pool, which could be used indoors as well as outdoors, looked out over the lake and the green hills and mountains down which Diana had just hiked. A waterfall cascading into one end of the pool added to the soothing ambience with its constant roar, for it drowned out the noise of the many children who frolicked in the shallow end, with their nannies and, in some cases, with their stylishly dressed and coiffed mothers looking on.

Dierdre chose a table just inside the open glass partition out of the glare of the late afternoon sun. A waiter approached immediately and fawned over this woman whom he knew by name.

She ordered one of her favorite regional wines, insisting Diana share it with her, although Diana did decline an invitation to join her in an order of risotto di carne di maiale, saying she was still too full from her picnic lunch to eat again so soon.

"You must come here often," Diana said as they waited to be served. "Everyone seems to know you."

"Oh, everyone does," Dierdre replied matter-of-factly. "I have wintered in Saint Moritz all my life, you see. I'm English, but I was born in Switzerland. I don't usually vacation here in summer, though," Dierdre said.

"Oh?"

"I have a summer home in Sardinia. This summer, however, I'm redoing my chalet."

"Is it near here?"

"Oh, yes, quite. In Suvretta, a few kilometers away. My home is next door to the Shah of Iran's place."

"Oh."

"And both are close to Christina Onassis's chalet. But of course they're both dead. The houses just sit there unused. Pity. Such a waste of beautiful furniture." Dierdre laughed gaily at her own tasteless joke.

Diana joined in, a spontaneous response to this woman whom she found so enchanting—and different.

"My, my! Fritzie was right," Dierdre said out of the blue, felling Diana with the intensity of her appraising stare. "You do have astonishing green eyes. They are especially exquisite when you laugh. You should remember to laugh always."

Diana blushed and asked, "Who's Fritzie?"

"Fritz Konenberg, the gray-haired gentleman with the little mustache who was seated next to me at dinner. Everybody calls him Fritzie. He has a passion for women with beautiful eyes. He absolutely insists you come to dinner with us tonight."

So that was why Dierdre Nieuwirth had stopped her on the hiking path. Obviously, Diana thought, this was a game to her—playing go-between.

"You will come, won't you?"

If Diana had thought of Herr Konenberg at all, it would have been to fix him up with her mother! If any of Dierdre's group had piqued her interest, it was the Latin heartthrob, Pedro Samaranche, who turned out to be a jet-setting, Brazilian tennis pro.

"I'm in the throes of a rather unpleasant divorce," Diana explained.

"How unfortunate."

"It's nice of you to invite me, but I don't think I'm up to it," Diana said diplomatically.

Dierdre persisted. "Oh, Fritzie is harmless. Quite charming, actually. A brilliant man. Witty. Wealthy as Croesus—no, wealthier. Men of his caliber are quite a catch at any age. There are women in every corner of the globe who would be quite thrilled to know of his interest in them."

"I'm flattered. But I'm definitely not in the mood."

"Oh, nonsense. One cannot be in Saint Moritz and not be in the mood."

Diana hesitated, and before she could say anything, Dierdre rushed on, "Fritzie has the Midas touch, it seems."

"Oh?"

"Yes. His family owned all the printing presses in Germany before the war. They printed newspapers, even made all the theater tickets, transportation tickets. Got out two steps before Hitler. He's a Jew, you see."

"He *is* a lucky man, then, to have escaped," Diana said.

"Yes, he certainly is. Had to start all over. Today he has real estate in every part of the world. And people everywhere court his company."

"He does sound exceptional."

"I'm quite certain you will find him amusing. But I won't kid you, Diana. Once Fritzie makes up his mind he wants something, he is relentless. And he was so taken with your eyes."

"What if I wear sunglasses?" Diana said with a laugh.

Dierdre chuckled. "Oh, yes. That would be good."

"What about you, Dierdre? Are you married?" Diana asked.

"Actually, I'm a widow. My darling husband died five years ago. A pity. After two brief mismatches, I finally landed the perfect man for me." Dierdre frowned for a brief instant, then seemed to will a smile back into her eyes.

"I'm so sorry," Diana said.

"Yes, well. I've learned to get along nicely by myself. You see, dear, there really is a vast difference between being alone and being lonely."

Diana nodded, thinking back to how lonely she had felt with Harvey those last few months before he left her.

"Do you know Texas?" Dierdre asked suddenly, switching topics again in her stream-of-consciousness style.

Diana was learning to flow with the current. "I've been to Dallas/ Fort Worth Airport once to change planes," she said with a smile. "Why?"

"Oh, nothing really. Well. My only daughter, by my first husband, lives in Dallas. Quite a place, Dallas. Don't like it much, actually. Too many women wearing ball gowns with cowboy boots."

Diana laughed. Dierdre's madcap view of life appealed to her.

"Haven't seen Penelope in almost three years. She'd be about your age. She's thirty-five."

"I'm forty-three," Diana admitted.

"Well. You certainly don't look it. I'm sixty-two myself," Dierdre said proudly as she finished off the last of her risotto. "And never been under a plastic surgeon's knife."

Diana was stunned. Dierdre didn't look more than fifty, if that. Except for a few fatigue lines around her almond-shaped brown eyes, her skin and figure were those of a young woman.

Diana gushed, "You're incredible. Really."

"I shall share my secret of youth with you, Diana." She leaned forward and whispered, "The secret is never to worry about what you can't change."

"I worry about everything lately," Diana admitted.

Dierdre eyed her sympathetically and patted her hand. "Well, you must put an end to that sort of behavior. It causes wrinkles and leads to an early grave," she said, noticing the time. "Oh, my word! I had no idea it was so late. I have a massage scheduled in two minutes."

"Now, that sounds wonderful," Diana sighed. She already was beginning to feel her leg muscles tightening up from the arduous walk down the mountain.

"I have a massage every day when I'm here," Dierdre said. "Stefan is divine. Why don't you come with me into the health club and we'll see if you can get an appointment after mine?"

"Do they have a woman—a masseuse?" Diana asked shyly. "I've never had a masseur before."

"No. Only Stefan."

* * *

"Is madame ready?" the masseur asked Diana, who had been whiling away the waiting period writing "wish you were here" postcards to everyone she knew, except Harvey. "I'm Stefan," he said quietly in a charming Eastern European accent.

Beyond the accent, Diana saw a shock of thick ash blond hair that brushed the very top of his suntanned shoulders, fjord blue eyes, a sensual mouth, and a physique that looked like the prototype for Michelangelo's *David*.

As she followed him into his little work space, she couldn't help but notice his high, firm rear outlined clearly through a pair of thin white cotton pants held up by a drawstring, and his well-defined back and arm muscles, which rippled in a tight-fitting white ribbed tank top.

While he explained his massage method, Diana noticed the room was quite austere. There was only one small chart of the human anatomy and its pressure points mounted on the wall near the door, a massage table in the middle of the space, and a card table with bottles of oils and a cassette player on it in the corner.

"Are you used to massage?" he asked her at the end of his well-rehearsed spiel.

"Oh, yes. I like it deep and hard." Suddenly she blushed, hoping his English was either good enough to understand the intent of her response or bad enough not to get the unintentional innuendo.

"Fine." He smiled, picking up a towel off the massage table and handing it to Diana to exchange for her terry-cloth wrap. "I'll turn around while you change," he said.

When he turned back, Diana was already lying on her back on the table, having done her best to cover her torso with the scanty towel.

"So, then. Is there some hurt I should know?"

"Only that this was my first real day of hiking. I just came down the mountain and there's not a spot on me that doesn't ache already," she said, beginning to feel less awkward about this attractive masseur touching her body, for his manner was congenial yet in every way thoroughly professional.

He replied, "I'll do the best I can. It's a shame I have only a half hour."

He dimmed the lights, turned on a cassette of soothing classical music, and placed moist cotton pads on her eyelids.

Stefan started with the aching arches of her feet, massaging one at a time. Then he slid his oiled fingers between her toes, manipulating them until it felt as though he were easing out all the tension in her body. A half hour of attention on her feet alone would have been worth the price of the massage, Diana thought.

He was good. *Real* good. In fact, he had the strongest yet gentlest fingers she'd ever experienced. In all the years she'd been having massages, she never realized what she had missed in not having one by a man.

"Am I hurting you?" he asked awhile later, kneading deeper as he moved up her legs, past her calves, toward her inner thighs.

"Oh, no. It feels wonderful," Diana murmured drowsily.

He folded the towel aside to expose her hip. "You have wonderful tan," he said.

Diana had gotten quite dark from her five-day stay at Carol's beach house, plus a few extra Sundays lounging around her pool at home. She had a tan line that was startling in its contrast. "Thank you," she replied.

"Quite lovely," he murmured.

Diana adjusted the moist pads on her closed eyes. "I feel so relaxed."

Stefan didn't say anything after that, allowing Diana to lie there without having to carry on a conversation. Her thoughts flew in a million directions at the same time. She felt herself flowing into an increasingly sybaritic state. Let it go, Diana, she thought. Let it all go.

Much too quickly, the half-hour session was over.

The next day Diana decided on a shorter walk and a longer massage.

"An hour is always preferable," Stefan told Diana with a smile when he turned back to face her before she had finished adjusting her towel. She was certain he had seen most of her body. Somehow the idea of hiding parts of herself from him seemed unnecessary. The thought made her feel light-headed, daring—the way she felt after drinking a cocktail on an empty stomach.

She lay on her back, her eyes shut under moistened pads, the soothing classical music flowing over and around her, under and into her, as he began his routine with her feet once again.

"I never realized how tiring hiking *down* a mountain could be," Diana explained, telling him briefly about the walk she had taken in the morning and early afternoon.

"I make you feel good," he promised. His choice of words in English was pleasantly limited, Diana decided with an inward smile.

She felt as though she knew the rhythm his hands would play out on her body. Knead, circle, pull. Knead, circle, pull.

With her eyes shut, she relived the blond vision of Stefan walking out to get her today at the table where she sat near the pool. His bright white smile. The recognition of a faint cleft in his chin, which she hadn't noticed before. A sudden tensing of his forearm muscles. His broad fingers pointing out to her the workout area of the club. The tapping of his clogs on a section of the floor that was uncarpeted. His tanned toes peeking out from the bottom of his white pants.

Circle, knead.

He had a wonderfully rhythmic quality in his massaging, like a powerful yet graceful dancer.

Wouldn't it be wonderful to have this rhythm extended into sex? Diana thought for a flash.

The thought was gone just as instantaneously.

Her mind wandered, reliving moments of the previous night. "You not only have a beautiful face and a lovely figure," Fritzie had told her at dinner, "but with your refreshing openness and wonderful sense of humor you could have any man in this room. Including me," he had added with a cute little tilt of his head.

She had put him off with charm and a million questions about his life and his group of friends. He filled her in on everyone, taking special care to warn her away from Pedro Samaranche, who, Diana decided, drank much too much champagne but was still sexy, drunk or sober.

Diana wasn't at all surprised to learn that Pedro belonged to Dierdre —"heart and soul," as Fritzie had described the liaison. "She makes no bones about her preferences," he confided with a twinkle in his eyes. "Dierdre loves her automobiles *very* old and her men *very* young."

Diana had laughed, a bubbling-up of pure delight. Fritzie said he loved the way her eyes sparkled when she was happy. He had a way of making a pass seem like a charming, innocent compliment. By the end of the evening, he had told Diana he wanted to take up all her time while she was in Saint Moritz.

Well, she had replied coquettishly above the din of the music playing in the hotel's popular disco, perhaps *some* of her time. And it had been quite odd, Diana thought now as she lay in the massage room listening to Handel's *Water Music*, that when she had told Fritzie that, a vision of Stefan, of all people, had filled her mind and she could almost have recreated from memory the delicious feeling of his hands on her inner thighs, where they were now.

Is he taking more time today in this area of my body than he did yesterday? she wondered suddenly, denying the stirring emotions his touch was creating in her. Of course he is, dummy, Diana admonished herself, you're here for an extra half hour. Everything is getting more attention today.

But later that night, after a pleasant, uncomplicated dinner with Fritzie and a real estate developer friend of his from Marbella, Diana lay

in bed alone remembering Stefan's practiced touch. She decided she
wasn't just imagining things; he *had* spent more time on her inner thighs
than on any other place on her body. But moments before she fell into a
deep sleep, she changed her mind again.

So it was that on the third afternoon in Stefan's private music-filled
cubicle, Diana took even more time arranging herself and her skimpy
towel on the table.

Stefan looked and didn't say anything.

But when he reached Diana's inner thighs his movements slowed.
And slowed some more. A new, languid rhythm reached out to her.

His fingers moved millimeters past her bikini line, she was certain.

What if he touches me? she thought. A moment of trepidation
washed over her. Did she want that?

Anything you might need, Badrutt's Palace can offer, Diana remembered the porter telling her only a few days ago. How about a man? Diana
had thought then. Now she was thinking, How about *this* man?

That night Diana dreamed she was in Hawaii with Carol, Fritzie, and
Dierdre. They all wore flowers in their hair except Diana. She refused,
saying it was a silly thing to do. But out of thin air, it seemed, Stefan
floated into the picture. He was wearing his white cotton tank top and a
pair of the briefest bikini swim trunks, similar to those worn by the many
men who lounged around the Palace Hotel pool every afternoon. Then
Diana was walking on the beach alone with Stefan; they weren't in Hawaii
any longer, but on the shore of the lake that bordered Badrutt's hotel.
"Why don't you wear flowers in your hair?" he asked her in that interesting European accent of his that charmed Diana so. "It's silly," she replied,
although she said it more like a question than a statement. "No, no," he
assured her and instantly put his hand into her jeans pocket. She felt hot
and excited. What else would he do? She spread her legs, ready for his
hand to break through the confines of her pocket and begin a warm search
for . . . Instead he pulled his hand out and in it was the daisy she had
tucked into her pocket self-consciously the day she had met Dierdre on
the hiking trail. It still looked fresh and smelled like a rose. "I'm putting
this in your hair because you are beautiful," he told her, his ice blue eyes
shining as he looked down at her. He tenderly wove strands of her hair
around the flower's stem. She felt awkward and self-conscious, for her hair
turned curly suddenly and didn't seem like the hair on her head. Then he
flew up the mountain, and she followed him to the patch of daisies she
had discovered on her first walk. He plucked hundreds of them and wove
them through her hair. He turned her into a natural work of art. Then he

laid her down on a bed that suddenly appeared in the midst of the field of
flowers and . . .

She had thought of nothing but her massage appointment all morning. Not even a visit to Dierdre's impressive chalet could shake her out of
her state of heightened anticipation. Dierdre had noted that Diana
seemed preoccupied, like a woman in love. Was it Fritzie who was on
Diana's mind? Someone else she'd met on her own?

Diana had smiled, remaining outwardly calm in her denials.

Not even Stefan could tell how nervous she was when she lay down
on her back on the massage table that afternoon and waited for him to
turn up the music and dim the lights. He doesn't know, she thought,
relieved. It occurred to her that perhaps she could passively dictate the
rules.

She let her legs lie in a more relaxed position, a little farther apart
than they had been on the previous days.

Stefan at last worked his way up to her inner thighs. Had he become
quieter? More intense?

One thigh. Then the other. Diana gulped when she felt his little
finger ever so slightly brush against her pubic hair, the sensation almost
lost among the firmer rhythm of the rest of his warmly oiled fingers
making their circular motion farther down.

There. He did it again.

Almost imperceptibly, her legs inched farther apart.

What fingers he had. Soft, hard. Slippery. Curling warmly around
her body in ever widening motions.

Closer to her labia. Almost touching. Flickering toward . . . closer.

Diana tried not to swallow. The sound would have been deafening,
she was sure.

The sexual tension in the room was almost palpable. It's up to you,
Diana, she thought. But did she really want this to go any further?

She could have a fling with eager Fritzie instead. Wealthier-than-
Croesus Fritzie. He could give her the world. Diamonds. Emeralds. Ru-
bies. Pearls.

Then there was Stefan. Ah. The wild abandon of youth. The promise
of physical delight in the rhythm of his hands. All over her body—everywhere.

Fritzie?

Stefan?

Was that his erection pressing into her arm? She dared not move.

Oh, how she ached to experience him. On her. Over her. Under her. In her!

But she couldn't ask. *Wouldn't* ask. Was it possible, Diana wondered —hoped—as she lay so outwardly still yet so agitated and ready in her mind, to *will* Stefan to make love to her without ever moving a muscle?

Chapter

. . . .

14

Although his eyes never wavered from the unfamiliar bends in the winding road, Chris Berry still managed to push the buttons on his car radio until he found the country music station he wanted. "Hey, listen to this," he said to Carol Benton who sat next to him. "This song's one of my favorites," he explained.

Without warning, Chris's voice suddenly filled the entire car with a perfect twangy aping of the popular warbling of Randy Travis.

Carol applauded and said, "I didn't know you were a country music buff."

"I've always been a country boy at heart. And now that I'm going to maybe own my own ranch—"

"Now, don't get excited before you've even seen the damn place," Billy Benton shouted from the back of the car.

Carol twisted in her seat to check on Billy's position. He was sprawled out on an air mattress with a back rest set up in the rear of Chris's four-wheel-drive Jeep Wagoneer.

Of course, Billy wasn't even supposed to be out of bed, let alone riding in a car in Malibu Canyon to view a piece of property—forty acres that had once belonged to a star of the silent screen. But time was of the essence, Chris had explained on the phone when he called to ask for Billy's counsel. Billy was the only real estate investor whose opinion Chris trusted.

The property presently was owned by a friend of a friend—a struggling director who needed cash fast. Since Chris had come into town for only a couple of days to preview the two-hour opening episode of his new series for the studio and network executives, the offer was a now-or-never proposition.

Billy was so eager to get out of the house for a few hours he would have said yes to watching grass grow. He insisted he'd be happy to advise Chris.

Now as they bumped along the narrow entrance road to the ranch, each rut brought with it a mild yelp from Billy who was trying to change his position to better see the terrain.

"It's very dusty here," Carol said as she stepped out of the car after Chris parked it. She lifted her eyebrows doubtfully as she glanced around, then down at her white tennis shoes and whiter-than-white jeans.

"It's the country, for chrissakes," Billy told her. "When I said wear jeans, I didn't mean prissy white ones. What did you expect—Tara before the Civil War?"

Carol ignored her husband. He'd become predictably grouchy from the cabin fever caused by his forced imprisonment in his bedroom, and they had been at each other's throats for days now.

"Help me out of here," Billy insisted, trying unsuccessfully to sit up.

Chris rushed to his assistance, gingerly easing him out over the tailgate of the car.

Billy grunted as he tried to straighten up. He made a tragicomical sight, for he was bent over, with part of the corset the doctor insisted he wear around his gut for support showing through his T-shirt.

Carol stepped over some errant sagebrush and wedged herself under Billy so he could throw his arm around her shoulders for support when he walked.

"There," he announced, trying to hide the grimace that was threatening to take over his face. "This will be fine." He took two steps and in his shuffling gait inadvertently kicked up a cloud of dust, which settled nicely onto Carol's white shoes and pants.

The property had a certain rugged beauty. From the bluffs one could gaze out over acres of shrubs and groves of trees broken by a shimmering lake with the lacy branches of more trees hanging low enough over one end to brush the water whenever the hot, dry summer breeze picked up.

"The guy who owns this property now doesn't live here. He leases it to movie companies for use as a location site," Chris explained to Carol, who seemed more interested in the odd color brown the dirt and dust were turning her white clothes and shoes.

"How interesting," she said absently, picking a few bramble thorns out of her pant leg.

"But he's not doing so well since they canceled the series that was shot here, and I'm not sure I'd be any more successful getting new business than he has been," Chris continued, almost talking to himself now.

"You shouldn't buy this piece of land with income in mind anyway," Billy said.

"I know. But if it turns out I'm not the ranch type and I decide to sell, how many lots do you think I could get out of it?"

Billy stopped walking, bending over slightly farther with his hands on his hips. "I studied the plot plan last night. The way I see it, you could probably get ten lots out of the forty acres. But that's not your problem."

"What is?"

"The covenants and restrictions are written so you can't subdivide here."

Chris became subdued. He looked disappointed as they walked a few more yards to a sitting area abutting a dock that led into the lake. An unfinished stone house was perched on a building pad that jutted out above the dock.

"I think I'm gonna lie down in the shade for a while," Billy announced suddenly, "and pretend I'm Huck Finn."

"He likes to think he grew up on a farm," Carol said.

"Yeah, like me," Chris smiled. "A farm in the middle of Bel Air. Maybe that's why I think this would be so great. I picture the twins on horses, me rowing a little boat around the lake. And all of us living happily ever after in that *casa* not so *grande* up there. Stupid stuff like that. But I sure don't want to spend almost five million dollars and, if I don't like it, wind up with a white elephant."

"My thoughts exactly," Billy said. "Personally I don't think this place is such a great investment," he added with a groan as he tried to lower himself into a prone position.

Both Chris and Carol helped Billy lie down on the dock. He dangled one hand in the water and finally looked comfortable. He insisted Chris and his wife leave him alone and explore the rest of the property.

Chris and Carol worked their way carefully up to the bluffs. At the summit, they stood quietly for a few minutes, lost in thought and the view.

Carol broke the friendly silence first. "I can't believe I'm standing here among the tumbleweed with you instead of climbing down the Alps among the edelweiss with Diana."

"Life does work in funny ways, doesn't it?" Chris replied softly.

"You would not have believed how Diana carried on the day I took her to the airport. I practically had to push her kicking and screaming onto the plane."

"Sure." Chris laughed, turning to begin their descent to the dock.

Carol followed, calling out, "I swear you'd have thought she was being sent to a gas chamber instead of to Saint Moritz."

"Why?"

"She was petrified at the thought of traveling alone."

"Really? I wouldn't have thought she would be the type to need company."

"Hey, we all need company."

Chris stopped at the base of the rock incline to help Carol down the last steep jump. He held her hand and although she landed evenly, the pressure of her feet on the loose earth created another little dust cloud, which settled on the last vestiges of white on her shoes and pants.

"And you need some clean clothes." He stood staring at Carol and began to laugh. "Real country folk, you are!"

"I should be in Europe basking in the alpine sun, guzzling champagne with my lonely friend."

"You underestimate her," Chris said.

"Like hell I do. Nobody knows Diana better than I do."

"I guess I always saw her mothering everybody. So capable, you know. She seemed so self-sufficient."

"That's where you pegged her wrong. She depended on that asshole husband of hers for everything but cooking. Now she's out there on her own. It's been rough."

"You two talking about Diana?" Billy asked as they approached him in the middle of their discussion.

"Who else?" Carol said with a grin.

Chris helped Billy up. He let Billy lean on him for the short walk back to the car.

"Have you seen Diana lately?" Billy asked Chris.

"Not since I left for Hawaii back—when was it?—God, November."

"He's in for a surprise, isn't he, honey?" Carol said.

"Oh?" Chris said.

"Man, she has changed so much you won't recognize her," Billy said. "Her figure is even better than—" He stopped and eyed Carol. "Well, almost as good as my wife's."

"No!" Chris exclaimed with a whistle. "I find that hard to imagine."

"Well, close your eyes and think of the centerfold of *Hustler*," Billy said. "That thick head of hair longer than she's worn it in years; her green eyes more noticeable because her face is thinner, you know, with those great angles; legs up to here"—he pointed to his neck—"and a pair of tits—"

"Billy, really," Carol interrupted with a laugh. "You'd think my husband was her press agent or something."

"I can't believe she's not in town," Chris said. "I wanted to see her. Talk to her."

"Then call her," Carol ordered. "She really does look amazingly good."

"But is she happy?" Chris asked.

"Ah, that's another story," Billy shouted from where he reclined again in the back of the Wagoneer.

"Billy's right. I really worry about her emotional state."

Chris became quiet, visions of Diana slim and suffering wafting through his mind. "I wish things would turn around for her so she'd be happy," Chris uttered.

"Me, too," Carol replied. "I get so sad every time I picture her sitting in her luxurious hotel room doing nothing. She told me point-blank she didn't think she could go hiking all alone. And she's too self-conscious to sit around the pool in those abbreviated bikinis all the European jet-set women wear. And I sure can't picture her going alone to those jumping discos at night. What a waste. In some ways, I'm sorry I pushed her into this trip."

"You can't blame yourself if she's unhappy," Chris said quietly.

"I guess you're right," Carol sighed, "but frankly, I don't think Diana was ready for Saint Moritz."

Chapter

15

Stefan adjusted the towel that had covered Diana's torso so that her chest and stomach were exposed. I can't believe this is happening to me, she thought when he began to massage the sides of her breasts.

He hadn't touched her in this area before today.

"Is this good for you?" he asked.

Oh, yes! she wanted to shout. Instead, she said in a thick, breathy voice, "Uh-huh."

I can't believe this is happening to me, Diana thought again when suddenly he cupped one entire breast and she could feel his oiled fingers graze her nipple, which instantly became taut.

"Is this all right?" he asked. He removed the cotton pads from her eyelids so she could see as well as feel what he was doing. She opened her eyes and stared at him, hesitating before responding. Did she want this to happen? "Yes," she said simply. "Yes."

He leaned against her; she could feel his penis pushing into her arm as he worked his way back down her belly, his hands making ever-widening circular motions until he reached the towel, which he had draped across her pubic area.

Without moving his hands off her belly, he brushed the towel to the floor. She lay exposed under his gaze, unembarrassed, wanting him to look at her.

"You have such beautiful body," he murmured, his hands gently prodding her legs farther apart, probing until his fingers found her hidden nub of flesh.

She closed her eyes.

"Look at me," he said.

Her eyelids fluttered open. She fixed her stare on his face—his blue, blue eyes—as his hands slowly transported her into that arena of pure pleasure.

Over the sound of the cassette music, Diana could hear the woman who made the massage appointments outside their cubicle in the hall talking to a customer. She could hear the weights on the exercise equipment being lifted, then clanging down.

"Aaah," she murmured, all extraneous sounds fading out of her consciousness, for every one of her senses was suddenly centered on his fingers, which brought her to an orgasm that transcended pleasure and pain.

She had to make a small fist of her hand and stuff it between her lips to stave off a crescendo of moans as she quivered under his touch.

When he felt her relax, he leaned close and whispered into her ear, "Roll over." Willingly she turned onto her stomach.

Stefan walked from the side of the table to the end, where her arms were stretched out above her head, her hands close enough now to reach out and touch him. She didn't know if she should be aggressive, so she wasn't. She didn't move.

And he didn't ask anything of her for himself. He just seemed engrossed in Diana's pleasure, as he silently continued his sensual journey from her shoulders down her spine. He massaged her buttocks and slid his hand between them, finding her clitoris from that erotically different angle.

She came again, and again, the orgasms like waves rolling over her in what seemed to be a never-ending succession.

When he pulled his hand away for a moment, she grabbed it and licked his fingers. She could smell her own odors on him mingled with the fragrance of the oils he used. "I liked that," she admitted.

"Me, too," he said, bending farther over her to kiss the nape of her neck.

Stepping back, he opened his fly. "Please," he said, putting her hands around his semierect penis.

I can't believe this is happening, Diana thought yet again, as both of them, his hands on hers, stroked him until he was hard. She realized he was uncircumcised, which made this an even more exotic first for her. Touching him this way aroused her again. She wanted to bring him to a climax, but he stopped her because their time together was drawing to a close.

She sat up and Stefan kissed her. His mouth covered hers; his lips were soft, and she loved the gentle pressure of his tongue seeking hers.

"No harm done?" he asked, as their last private seconds together ticked away.

Diana saw that he looked worried now, almost scared. He suddenly seemed younger, vulnerable. She touched his shoulder. "No harm done," she reassured him.

That night Diana had an erotic dream. Although the details were lost to her, the orgasm that accompanied the dream woke her up. She lay in bed for hours unable to sleep, her thoughts filled with images of Stefan.

"You have a beautiful body," she recalled him telling her that day. Now with her own hands she traced the outlines of her breasts, then marveled at the narrowness of her hips, the firmness of her legs, the flatness of her stomach.

Feeling sensuous and still aroused from her dream and the memories of her amorous afternoon, she imitated Stefan's expert touch and brought herself to another intense orgasm.

The next morning Diana dallied on her veranda, dreamily taking in the sight and smell of the many potted plants and flowers the Swiss seemed to think were a necessity of life. The various scents of the roses, azaleas, dahlias, and honeysuckle mingled with the delicious aroma of her breakfast of strong coffee, melon, and wild strawberries.

A rap on the door brought her inside. It was a porter delivering a handwritten note from Dierdre Nieuwirth. She and Fritzie were inviting her and Pedro to spend the afternoon with them in Zurich. They would return to Saint Moritz around six in the evening.

Diana called Dierdre to decline the offer. She said she preferred a day to do nothing, for she confessed that Dierdre and her entourage had worn her out with their evening of partying the night before. They had dined at the Hayloft, and followed the food and wine with a few hilarious hours of bowling at Chesa Veglia, a popular haunt for tourists and locals, which was situated near the Palace. Diana had been enthralled by how easily Europeans put their old buildings to use for new purposes, for the Chesa Veglia— built in 1658 and still retaining most of its ancient charm—now served as the home of several popular restaurants and discos as well as the bowling alley.

Although it was partly true that the late night revelry had tired her, the real reason for her refusal was that Diana didn't want to forgo even one appointment with Stefan. He had become the focus of all her energy, the high point in her day around which all else was constructed.

As bizarre as the whole affair with Stefan seemed to her, she could not deny the purity, the utter simplicity of it. He gave pleasure. She took it.

As she awaited Stefan in her usual seat at a table in the poolside café, she looked around at the male guests who might have interested her before Stefan and realized happily that none of them could tempt her now. He had saved her from having to date, from being set up for possible rejection, from the sort of entanglement that necessitated conversation, getting to know each other, making commitments.

As wonderful as Dierdre and Fritzie were—they had welcomed her into their set with open arms, included her in their many chichi activities at night—theirs was a world to which she had no long-term aspirations to belong. She felt the pressure of having to be gay, witty, and "on" all the time for those people who expected to be entertained.

As wild and outrageous as this affair with Stefan seemed, as consumingly erotic and naughty as it was, she was comfortable with the knowledge that it existed apart from anything that might be termed "real."

"Is madame ready?" Stefan asked as he did every day when he came to get her at the snack bar where she sipped a glass of wine.

His casual question held a different import for her now. She stood up and nodded. He smiled. She could feel the new, unspoken intimacy between them.

She lay on the massage table, trying not to feel impatient as he seemed to take an extraordinarily long time on her feet, then her calves, then her thighs. Had she misread the smile, the between-the-lines meaning of his words? Was yesterday a one-time aberration?

She was already wet when he finally slid his fingers into her, and she came almost instantly, stifling a moan with the towel so no one outside the cubicle would suspect what was going on inside.

"Spread legs more," he whispered, walking to the foot of the table, leaning over to put his face between her thighs, while caressing her breasts with his hands.

The same tongue that had probed so gently in her mouth now made her writhe as he licked her, teased her with little pointed jabs.

Stefan brought her to another, another, and yet another orgasm with his mouth.

Clearly all boundaries between them had been irrevocably crossed. He pulled off his shirt and stepped out of his pants.

Diana loved the sight of his naked body. Every part of him was sculpted, muscular, but not overly so.

He started to mount her.

Suddenly reality hit her full force. "Do you have a condom?" Diana whispered.

Poised above her, he hesitated, looking down into her eyes. "No."

"Then I cannot . . . we can't—"

"I understand," he said gently, easing himself off of Diana. Without rancor, he finished her massage in the nude.

"Tomorrow?" he asked.

"Tomorrow," Diana murmured, feeling deliciously spent.

My life is in that massage room, Diana admitted to herself. Everything else is simply passing time until that hour with Stefan.

Even while her love affair progressed with him day after day, she kept replaying in her mind the first moment he finally entered her. He had put two small pillows under her buttocks, then spread her wide with his hands and slowly, millimeter by millimeter, filled her. It had been so many months since she had been with a man. It was even better than she had fantasized. She had never felt more alive than in that room with her young lover.

Still, she realized happily, her passionate trysts with Stefan released in her the ability to experience the rest of Saint Moritz boldly. Every sight, every smell, every sound, every texture, was richer and more real to her because of the emotional release and the healing effects on her psyche of her secret affair.

She didn't tell him she was leaving until the day before her departure.

They lay together on the massage table after having made love, touching each other for the last time.

He told her finally, in an intimate whisper, a little bit about his life in Yugoslavia. He had lived as a boy on the Dalmatian coast, learned his trade there in the resort area of Dubrovnik. He was married, had a young daughter. Diana was surprised to find out he was only twenty-four years old.

He wanted to know how old she was. "Old enough to appreciate you," she said, kissing his shoulder.

Diana already had decided that she would never ask Stefan any of the questions that filled her mind when she wasn't with him, about why he had taken the chance of losing his job over her, for she instinctively felt his responses would of necessity be forced flattery. Later she realized with a pleasant start that it didn't really matter anyway; she didn't want to know.

They had happened. Period. Her time with Stefan was an isolated, almost existential experience; it had liberated her. She would never go back to being the old Diana. For that she was thankful.

"Will you return next summer?" he asked, a pleading note in his voice. "I must know you again."

"Perhaps," she said, meaning it then.

But after she had boarded the plane in Zurich and had sat in the window seat watching Switzerland disappear from view as the pilot fixed his course for America, Diana knew she would not be able to "bring back the hour of splendor in the grass," nor did she want to.

Stefan, she decided, had given her a precious gift: her renewed sexuality. With Harvey, Diana ultimately had been made to feel ashamed of her body and completely unworthy of a male's intense erotic interest. Stefan had told her in hushed tones over and over again how much of a woman she was, how exciting she was. She saw for herself how capable she was of making him cry out with pleasure.

It occurred to Diana suddenly that she had always felt that if she got thinner, got smarter, got . . . got more of everything, *then* maybe Harvey would respond to her, would love her again as he had seemed to love her long ago.

Yet in Saint Moritz Diana discovered that not only Stefan couldn't keep his professional distance, but Fritz Konenberg—a man swamped by the attention of women all over the world—had said in no uncertain terms that if she gave him any encouraging sign, he would pursue her to the ends of the universe.

As her plane winged its way across the Atlantic Ocean, Diana realized that nothing she could have done would have made Harvey love her more, made him interested in her for herself alone.

She could never have been enough of anything to please him.

Somehow that revelation made her feel even freer than she had in Saint Moritz. The failure of her marriage, she realized with such a jolt she almost said it aloud to the sleeping woman in the seat next to her, was not her fault.

You are who you are, Diana, she kept telling herself—capable of sticking to a diet, bright and witty enough to enchant one of the wealthiest bachelors in the world, sexy enough to enthrall a masseur who works with bodies more beautiful than yours every day of his life.

Diana Lowe, she thought, you're pretty damned great!

Chapter

16

"What do you have in here—rocks?" Carol joked as she lugged the larger of Diana's two suitcases to the car.

"Rocks? No. Memories," Diana said with a little self-conscious laugh. "I'm loaded down with them."

"Oh?" Carol said, eyeing Diana with a questioning look. She hoisted the suitcase and thunked it down with a groan inside the trunk. " 'Loaded down with memories,' she says. Of what, pray tell?"

"It was a nice trip. What am I saying? It was a *great* trip! The best ever! I'm indebted to you, Carol, more than you know." Diana blushed as she tried to avoid Carol's eyes.

Carol's expression changed from absolute blankness to one akin to a dark room all at once flooded with bright light. "What happened in Saint Moritz?" she asked with more intensity.

Diana bent over to fuss with the wheels on her smaller suitcase, still avoiding the question.

"Diana, look at me."

Diana glanced up, eyed Carol with a silly grin, but said nothing. She seemed to take forever placing the second valise in the trunk.

It was a humid summer afternoon in Los Angeles, and Diana was dressed too warmly; it had been cold and rainy in Saint Moritz when her train departed, ironically like the day she had arrived. Her face glistened now with perspiration. Was it merely from the heat? Giving up her precious secret, she suddenly realized, was going to be more difficult than she had thought. But why? she wondered fleetingly as she wiped beads of perspiration off her brow with the back of her hand, still saying nothing. Stalling.

"Oh, my God! I understand now," Carol exclaimed. "You went and got laid. And you can't say it. That's *it*, doll, isn't it?"

Diana slammed down the trunk lid, then walked slowly to the passenger side of the car and stood looking over the top at her friend. "Uh-huh," she admitted at last, her face suddenly awash with a look of utter delight. "I did have sort of a . . . a little fling." Diana blushed crimson.

"I knew you looked different the minute I saw you get off that plane! There is this . . . this—"

"This *what?*" Diana interrupted impatiently.

"*Glow*. There is this glow about you. Even the way you walk is subtly different. Sort of a hey-look-at-me strut." Carol smiled at Diana and shook her head. "I can't believe it. You've been screwing your brains out and you didn't even call to tell me!"

"Ssh!" Diana laughed, looking around to see if anyone of the multitude near them had heard Carol's loud comment.

"Okay, then. Get in the car," Carol whispered conspiratorially. "We'll lock all the doors and roll up the windows. I won't be able to take another breath until I hear everything. And I mean *everything!*"

After a few false starts in the car on the way home, followed by a big tumbler of gin with a splash of tonic that Carol mixed for her in the Lowes' bar, Diana loosened up and rose to the task.

She finally satisfied Carol's prurient curiosity with a hitherto hidden talent for providing graphic and deliciously romantic descriptions of each sexual encounter she'd had with her magnificent Eastern European lover.

When she had finished her tale, however, Diana had a moment of misgiving about having told Carol. "What happened sounds sleazy, doesn't it?"

"Why would you think *that?*" Carol asked, surprised.

"Oh, I don't know." Diana hesitated, thinking. "Yes, I do know. I decided on the plane home that I would never tell anyone about Stefan. Not even you." A faraway look entered Diana's eyes. "Being with him was so special, so romantic, so . . . perfectly pure that I was afraid putting the experience into words would demean what we shared and make it appear slimy, common, when it wasn't."

"Diana, look at my face. Do you see someone judging you?"

Diana shrugged. "I guess not."

"You *guess* not! You better believe I'm jealous as hell. What woman with even one normal brain cell wouldn't love to have a man give her pleasure in the way you just experienced it? Shit, if I had special-ordered an affair for you, I couldn't have done any better than you managed to do for yourself. I'm proud of you, Diana. Real proud. Don't ever think that Stefan was a sleazy moment in your life."

"But it was just sex."

"So what's wrong with that?"

"*Great* sex," Diana embellished with a laugh.

"And that's exactly what you needed at that time. Affairs of the heart can come later."

"That's what I realized, too," Diana said. "But . . . oh, I don't know. I guess I was worried that if I told anyone what I did, it would be misunderstood."

"Believe me, doll, I understand."

"You aren't lying, are you?"

"Christ, sometimes your insecurities make me want to scream! Of course I'm not lying. Unless," she said with a leer, "there's something *really* kinky you haven't told me."

After Diana assured Carol that there was nothing more to tell, they followed the Stefan chapter with a gossip chaser. Carol simply refused to go home until Diana filled her in about her friend Badrutt, after which she wanted to hear every last detail about Dierdre, Fritzie, and the rest of the Saint Moritz cast of jet-setting characters.

Five hours later, when Carol finally left, Diana was hoarse, bleary-eyed, and too tired to unpack.

Diana stripped, letting her clothes lie where they fell on the floor of her closet; she stumbled into bed, not even bothering to put on a nightgown. With her kids still away, she had no reason to cover up. For the first time since Harvey left her, Diana was enjoying the experience of being completely alone in her house.

After waking at dawn to the sound of squirrels scurrying across her roof, their scratching nails competing with the chirps of baby birds thriving in a nest atop the chimney of her bedroom fireplace, Diana couldn't fall back to sleep.

She got up and dressed casually in running shorts, a tank top, and sneakers.

Still reveling in the afterglow of her vacation, she took a brisk three-mile walk through her neighborhood with Romeo and Juliet, breathing in the fresh air that had yet to be polluted by a day's worth of car exhaust fumes, returning forty-five minutes later to the delicious aroma of coffee, freshly brewed in her automatic coffee maker. She poured herself a mug and sipped it slowly as she sat at the kitchen table. Since her newspaper delivery had been canceled for two weeks, she had no excuse to put off tackling the foot-high stack of mail that had accumulated in the ten days she was away. As she methodically went through each piece, she came upon an envelope bearing Harvey's new home address.

She opened it, wondering wryly if it was an invitation to a housewarming.

It wasn't.

Inside was a memo, written in Harvey's neat script in bold black Montblanc ink. "Diana," it said, "I regret to inform you that our main investment—the R. K. Wilder Building—has gone bad. The tenant has filed Chapter Eleven."

She read the papers that accompanied the memo. The bottom line was that the other investors and Harvey and Diana were going to have a serious negative cash flow. The building, which had provided an income of ten thousand dollars a month for each of them, was now going to cost them over fifteen thousand dollars each month. They would have to come up with the mortgage payments out of pocket on this multimillion dollar investment.

She phoned Harvey at work.

She hadn't heard his voice in months. He sounded like an intimate stranger, speaking to her about their life together as though he were a disinterested third party. He explained that because of the financial bind this investment was putting him in, he would have to reduce her monthly payments until further notice.

"But, Harvey—" she replied, not believing that he was being truthful.

"No 'buts,' Diana."

"You can't ask me to live on nothing. You don't."

"I'm not asking you to live on nothing. And furthermore, everything costs me twice as much now. I'm supporting two households, and your expenses far exceed mine, whatever you may think." He sighed so loudly Diana thought she could have heard it all the way across town without a phone to connect them.

"I find that hard to believe," she spat.

"I don't want to fight with you, Diana. Facts are facts. All I'm saying is that this investment was ours together. We have to pay the penalties *together*. Maybe we should think about putting the house on the market."

"You're not selling *my* house!" she screamed, then slammed the phone down.

The minute she hung up, she phoned Peter Webb. "Can he make me sell the house?" she asked.

"If you need X number of dollars to live on and he can't provide that much because of legitimate business reversals, then you may have to sell the house. Or you may have to get a full-time job."

"Or kill myself!" Diana lamented.

"Or kill Harvey for his insurance money," Webb joked.

"That's the best idea I've heard since I arrived home." She looked at her watch and saw that she hadn't been back from Europe twenty-four hours yet and already she felt as though she had never been away, never had a break in the continuing nightmare she was being forced to endure since Harvey had left her.

"Don't get despondent," Webb said. "You're strong, Diana. Resilient. We'll think of some way to salvage the house, if it can be done. And if you'll send me the memo and the other documents about this investment, I'll look into it for you."

"Okay," Diana said meekly.

"Things could be worse," Webb said.

And they were.

Betty called to welcome Diana back from Europe and to say hello from Chicago, where she was staying for a few weeks with her brother and sister-in-law. "By the way," she said almost as an afterthought, "I had to go to the hospital in Chicago for dizzy spells." Diana's heart sank to her stomach as her mother told her the doctors there did some tests and told Betty they thought perhaps two of her heart grafts had collapsed, but she could do just fine with the remaining three that were okay. "Things could be worse," Betty said just before she hung up.

And they were.

A special delivery letter arrived from the IRS. A 1983 real estate tax shelter in which Harvey, with Diana, had invested had been ruled to be a fraud. The Lowes owed the U.S. government over one hundred thousand dollars in back taxes, which had to be paid immediately or the interest penalties would continue to accrue.

"Don't say 'Things could be worse,'" Diana warned her attorney when he took her frantic call and she spilled out her ever-growing tale of woe. Peter Webb remained noncommittal about the possible financial reverses, and he did little to calm her frayed nerves.

"I think I need Billy," Diana said to Carol, whom she phoned the minute she had said good-bye to Webb.

"After that steamy tale of sex among the masseurs you told me last night, I don't think you'll need another man for a year!" Carol replied with a lusty laugh.

"Carol, I'm serious," Diana said. "I'm about to have a nervous breakdown."

"What happened?" Carol asked.

Diana briefly related the series of phone calls and letters she had gotten over the course of the morning. She said she needed Billy's expert advice.

"I'll find him and get back to you," Carol promised.

Fifteen agonizing minutes later, Carol called Diana to say she could meet with Billy at four o'clock at the Gold Grill, a popular eatery in Los Encinos Plaza. Billy had financially backed the place two years before for the proprietor, Ted Gold.

Diana arrived a few minutes early and found a parking space under the only shade tree left at the far end of the open-air shopping plaza. Killing time, she stopped to admire one of the many Encino landmark oaks, a seven-hundred-year-old tree that commanded respect; its massive three-foot-thick trunk and never-ending network of branches extended out like a leafy umbrella over the center of the two-story Mission-style mall with its traditional red-tiled roof. Having chosen the longest path to the restaurant, Diana passed a dim sum café, two beauty shops, a facial and body-waxing salon, and several upscale clothing stores. She noted that the breezy pastel summer cottons already had been replaced in the display windows by wools and corduroys in fall colors.

It was still too much like an oven outside to consider heavy fabrics. The summer weather in the Valley stayed hot and dry morning, noon, and night and didn't begin to turn cool until the beginning of November. Besides, Diana thought, trying not to feel sorry for herself, she couldn't even afford to *think* about new clothes now.

A gust of sere wind playfully lifted the hem of her gauzy white spaghetti-strap sundress, revealing most of her tanned legs. She brushed the skirt down against her knees and walked the last few yards to the Gold Grill.

The restaurant closed after lunch and didn't reopen until six o'clock, but Diana pushed open the unlocked glass and pickled-wood door and walked inside anyway.

The interior was cool and inviting, decorated in popular Southwest contemporary—stark white stucco walls, chairs and banquettes in pastel

Indian-blanket prints, bleached wood stools with rush seats facing a beveled stone counter, and dwarf cacti in little clay pots gracing each table.

The kitchen was in full view behind the counter. Two chefs were chopping fresh vegetables and marinating chicken and meat for the evening rush of loyal patrons. They glanced up briefly at Diana and returned her smile without missing a beat.

Outside on the patio, Billy sat at a round wood table. Although the day was still hot, the patio was shaded by a buff canvas canopy. He was deep in conversation with Ted Gold and a young woman Diana didn't know.

The second he heard Diana's sandals on the terra-cotta tile, he interrupted Ted, jumped up from his chair, and enveloped her in a warm embrace.

After introducing her to Susan St. John and reintroducing her to Ted Gold, who admitted he hadn't recognized the new Diana, Billy took her to another table across the patio where they could confer privately.

Diana's chair was near a low hedge. On the other side of it a manmade brook, its banks mossy and crowded with multicolored day lilies, bubbled on its carefully designed course through the woodsy mall. Normally Diana loved sitting outside at this restaurant to eat while listening to the soothing babble of the water. Today, however, the only soothing sound she wanted to hear was Billy's voice telling her she wasn't going to have to sell her house.

"Carol told me briefly what happened, but why don't you start from scratch?" Billy urged.

Instead, Diana handed him a sheaf of papers that she had brought with her.

Billy studied them, then looked up.

"Are we going to be ruined?"

"Let's look at this rationally, Diana."

"I'm not rational about anything regarding Harvey and money these days," she moaned.

"I know," he said quietly. "But try. Harvey may have tried to put one over on you with that condo purchase, but in this real estate fraud he was the one who got duped. The general partner is a certifiable crook. But that won't help you with the IRS. Everyone who invested will have to pay back taxes and interest. Harvey's going to have to fork over one hundred thousand big ones. That's a fact."

"But—"

"Wait. Hear me out. The other fact is that for several years Harvey had the use of all that money he didn't have to pay in taxes, and since I'm one of his primary advisers, I know he invested that money well. Harvey can afford to pay back the government without it wiping you out. It's a one-time setback."

"So I can stop driving myself crazy over that fiasco?"

"Right. Which leads me to the R. K. Wilder affair. Interestingly enough, there was an article in the *Wall Street Journal* a few days ago about the tenant filing for bankruptcy. At least you're dealing with a New York Stock Exchange Company and not some fly-by-night business."

"I didn't even know that," Diana admitted.

"And because of that, you've got a couple of major U.S. suppliers and a Japanese consortium standing in the wings looking at the possibility of taking the company over. If that happens, Diana, you could wind up with a stronger tenant than you have now." He took a breath, then said, "Didn't Harvey explain any of this to you? He and I have been talking about it for weeks now."

"No," Diana answered, "and when he suggested I sell the house, I hung up on him."

Billy laughed. "Carol would have done the same thing."

"It's so frustrating when you've never been in control of any of the finances and then suddenly you're supposed to know everything, understand everything—which I don't. And worse, I feel as though I'm at Harvey's mercy and I don't trust him anymore. It all makes me feel so tired . . . and so insecure," Diana lamented.

"You can't let it get you down. We'll come up with some way to supplement the money Harvey gives you. Let me think about it." He squeezed her hand and added, "You do know that Carol and I are here for you no matter what?"

"Are you kidding? If it weren't for you guys, I don't know what my life would be like."

"It might be like Susan St. John's," Billy said. "She's been trying to make it on her own, and she's not doing so well. In fact, we were brainstorming when you got here. Let's go join them. Misery loves company, as they say."

"Thanks, but I think I'll just go home. I've been enough of an interruption for one day."

"I'm not going to let you slink off and hide in that house of yours and feel sorry for yourself. Come on, Diana, you may be able to help Susan. You always have such great ideas."

Billy took Diana's arm as though she might run away and escorted her to Susan and Ted's table.

"I have that place over there." Susan, a pixielike young woman in her early twenties, pointed to a narrow storefront with the name Hard Bodies lettered on the plate-glass window. It was situated on the other side of the path from Gold's Grill. "It's an exercise studio."

"You are in incredible shape," Diana said, noting Susan's well-defined arms and shoulders, wondering how she might look in an outfit like Susan's—Day-Glo green and black spandex tank top and matching knee-length pants. "When did you open for business?"

"Six months ago. I used to give private instruction in people's homes. That's how I met Ted."

"I persuaded her to open up a studio here," Ted said.

"But since she hit the boulevard, business hasn't increased as fast as she and Ted thought it would," Billy explained. "Ted asked me if I could come up with some angle to help Susan get things moving."

"It's not that I don't have a clientele," Susan said somewhat defensively. "I do. It's just that the rent is so high that it's been hard to get big enough fast enough to keep my head above water."

Diana nodded politely, although she still felt too edgy despite Billy's comforting counsel to sit and listen to someone else's monetary problems today. She wanted to tell Billy she had to leave, but she didn't see how she could do that without sounding rude and ungrateful.

"She's tried all the usual advertising gimmicks that don't cost an arm and a leg," Ted told Diana.

Susan sighed and smiled at Ted. "But that hasn't done the trick either."

"I see," Diana replied, noticing the intimate glance Susan cast Ted's way. That look, along with Ted's protective fawning over Susan, flashed "love affair" loud and clear.

"When you got here, we were tossing around the possibility of her subleasing part of the store to someone who sells workout clothes and accessories," Billy explained.

That led to a detailed—and for Diana an agonizingly long—discussion of the sublease rules of the shopping center. While they talked, Diana sipped a glass of iced tea that Ted had poured for her from a pitcher on their table. She felt the first grumblings of hunger and realized she had forgotten to eat once the succession of calls and letters began early in the morning. Reaching into her purse, she found a Three Amigos bar and pulled it out. She opened the wrapper and apologized for eating in front of them, explaining that she was famished.

"Hey, you can have something from our kitchen," Ted said. "A little salad. Some cold chicken. Don't ruin that good diet you've been on with candy."

"Don't bother, Ted. I would rather have this," Diana said firmly.

"Wouldn't all of us," Susan said. "But have salad instead. You don't want to put on pounds now."

"I won't," Diana told her confidently, breaking off half of the small bar and popping it into her mouth. "There's less fat in one of these than in a tablespoon of Ted's *diet* ranch dressing."

"She eats those little motherfuckers all the time," Billy said proudly. "I used to grab them out of her hand, but I finally stopped. You can't knock success. I mean, this little lady has lost over forty pounds eating candy!"

"Really?" Susan looked skeptical. "Tell me how you managed *that* miracle."

In an instant the conversation veered away from Susan's business problems as Diana launched into an impassioned speech about fats and health and weight loss.

Billy sat watching her, listening to Diana. He beamed like a parent whose child stumbles about at home but once on stage gives a flawless, graceful performance. Without intervening, Billy let Ted and Susan, both caught up in Diana's enthusiasm, flood her with a series of wide-ranging questions, all of which Diana handled with ease.

"Here we are talking about my diet," Diana finally said after almost an hour had passed, "when Susan needs Billy's help—and so do I."

"I think you just helped yourself—and Susan," Billy said quietly, sitting back in his chair with one finger tapping his lip.

All three of them turned to eye him.

Billy sat forward and smiled. "Ted, you can help, too."

"How?" Ted asked.

"I've been thinking."

"So what else is new?" Ted laughed.

Billy suddenly became all business. "Look, your restaurant is closed from three-thirty until six. Would you consider giving Susan and Diana carte blanche to use the grill and the counter for one and a half of those hours?"

"I might," Ted said. "Yeah, I guess I could manage that."

"Okay. Now," Billy said, his speech speeding up as his ideas flowed out. "As an adjunct to her series of exercise classes, Susan advertises a new, revolutionary way to eat without guilt. When people sign up, for a nominal additional cost they get a cooking demonstration in the most popular new Encino restaurant and a lecture from Diana Lowe about how to shop, cook, and eat in a low-fat but *fun* way. What do you think?"

"I don't know," Diana said, taken aback by Billy's innovative plan.

"Diana, you need money." Billy looked at her, then at Susan and Ted. "Diana needs a job and an income; Susan needs more clients and a gimmick. Diana is her gimmick. Ted's restaurant is the instrument through which all of your needs can be satisfied. And there you have it!" He smiled, sat back, and folded his hands across his belly.

"I like it," Susan announced, looking hopefully at Diana.

"I would get paid for the cooking demonstrations and lectures?" Diana asked, eyeing Billy.

"Right," Billy replied, looking quite pleased with himself.

"You know," Susan gushed, "if this idea takes off, there's no reason why Ted couldn't let us use this place in the early mornings, too. My seven-o'clock ladies would jump at any new diet idea; they're all fanatics!"

"She's already taking over my entire restaurant," Ted exclaimed.

"That's women for you," Billy said. "You give them six inches, they want nine."

"Or ten," added Susan with a mischievous grin.

Diana flashed on a vision of Stefan, erect and ready to enter her. She blushed as she said, "Or eleven!"

Part Three

Part Three

Chapter

17

Diana had been so engrossed in her research that she only now realized her reading glasses were beginning to press heavily on her nose. She took them off and rubbed away the pain as she perused the collection of data she had amassed in the hours she had been going through the card catalogs and staring at microfiche files in the UCLA Biomedical Research Library. Eyestrain and blurry vision notwithstanding, she remained energized by her work. Browsing through research libraries and bookstores all over town had replaced window shopping and feeling sorry for herself in the two months since she had burst onto the Encino scene with her cooking classes and lecture series.

She practically lived at the Biomed Library now that Dr. Fernberg had joined Diana in her undertaking and had steered her toward a mountain of seminal research in the field. Last month during her checkup, where she learned she had lost yet another ten pounds—for a grand total of fifty pounds in less than a year—Diana had told Fernberg about her new career. She had also mentioned that several of the people in her classes had made appointments to see her privately; they were anxious to work out, with her assistance, individualized plans that would lead to permanent weight loss. Realizing that by using herself as a guinea pig,

Diana had stumbled upon a unique interpretation for the application of sound scientific facts, Fernberg offered to widen her base by letting her counsel his overweight and weight-conscious patients. He would charge them a flat fee for the program, out of which he would pay Diana a percentage for lecturing to them and giving them recipes.

After a nervous, somewhat tentative beginning, Diana now had ten private clients, fifty of Dr. Fernberg's patients, and four full classes of eager dieters at the Gold Grill.

While standing in line awaiting her turn to ask the librarian to locate books and articles that were not available in the open stacks, Diana noticed a woman creating quite a stir. She stood out from the students and other research types in her persimmon miniskirt, matching jacket with enormous padded shoulders, and a wild silk blouse unbuttoned enough to reveal much of her ample bosom as she bent over to stuff some papers into a lizard-skin briefcase. Seemingly unaware of the sideways glances she was getting from every man and most of the women in the room, the femme fatale walked pertly toward the exit, her large earrings swaying with each step, and the heels of her knee-high suede and lizard boots clacking on the floor. Intrigued, Diana watched the woman and suddenly realized that this person was none other than Alison Rifkin, the writer and wife of Mark Rifkin, whom she had met months ago. She dashed to intercept Alison at the exit. "Hi," Diana said brightly.

Alison stopped and smiled, a friendly reflex, but Diana could see from the blank stare that entered Alison's eyes, that she didn't know who Diana was.

"Diana Lowe," she said, still not used to old acquaintances not recognizing her new face and body. Today Diana had poured that new body into narrow cords and a sweater tucked in to show off a silver belt and her tiny waist. Since Alison and she had met, Diana also had had her hair cut and streaked. It was now just above shoulder-length, naturally wavy, and parted on the side leaving a few provocative strands to fall over her forehead.

"My God! I can't believe it's you," Alison blurted loudly, drawing annoyed looks from the serious studiers sitting nearby.

Diana smiled and motioned that they should walk outside. "I forget what a shock it is for people who haven't seen me lately," Diana explained once they were in the bustling hospital corridor.

"I never would have known it was you," Alison said. "You look entirely different."

"It is amazing, isn't it?" Diana said proudly. "That low-fat diet that I thought *wasn't* a diet—turned out to be the best diet I've ever been on."

"That low-fat regimen you told me about did *this* for you?"

Diana nodded.

Alison said, "You know, I wanted to call you after I made those delicious burritos, but when Mark told me you and Harvey had separated, I felt funny about it. I never know what to say."

"I know," Diana said. "I never know what to say, either. And it probably was even harder with Mark and Harvey not becoming partners after all."

"I guess it was partly that, too."

"Mark not wanting the partnership somehow became *my* fault," Diana said with a frown. "Harvey told me it was probably because I talked too much that night when we had dinner at the Grill on the Alley."

Alison's face registered surprise. "Diana, I don't like to get in the middle of separations—you never know when a couple might get back together—but for whatever it's worth," she said, "I want you to know that Mark and I both thought you were delightful. So don't ever blame yourself for what didn't happen between my husband and Harvey."

"Thanks, Alison," Diana said with a grateful smile. "I'm relieved to know that."

"But tell me about you. What are you doing here?"

"Research," Diana said, laughing at the obvious. "My dieting has expanded into teaching classes about the low-fat way of life. I also have private clients who come to my house. What are you doing here?"

"I'm doing research, too—for a character in my new novel. I have to make her die after a lengthy illness and still look gorgeous and healthy," Alison sighed. "It's not easy finding the right disease. I've been at it all day. I was about to take a walk through Westwood to unaddle my brain. Want to join me?"

Five minutes later Alison and Diana were strolling away from the UCLA campus into the heart of Westwood Village.

They passed movie theaters, casual and funky restaurants that catered to the college crowd, bookshops, and store windows artfully displaying a wide array of youthful clothes.

"You want some frozen yogurt?" Alison asked as they neared Penguins. "Theirs is the best. I get it every time I come into Westwood. Can you eat yogurt?"

"Sure. The nonfat. Sounds good to me, in fact."

Each of them bought a small cup of nonfat yogurt. Diana topped hers with assorted fresh fruit; Alison didn't because there were strawberries in the mixture.

"I'm allergic to strawberries," Alison said.

"I know," Diana replied.

"You do?"

"Don't you remember? That night at the restaurant? Dessert?"

"Oh, I forgot about that."

"Well, it was your strawberry allergy that helped me stick to my diet."

"You're kidding!" Alison exclaimed.

"I'm not. Remember I said that maybe I was allergic to fats the same way you're allergic to strawberries?"

"Not really," Alison admitted. "I think I had one glass of wine too many that night. I don't recall much except Harvey snatching the bread out of your hand right after we were seated, and the burrito recipe you wrote down for me."

They continued their stroll back toward the library, eating and talking about Harvey and about Diana's diet. "In many ways," Diana admitted, "I'm totally indebted to you for giving me the psychological hook to keep me focused on the reason why I can't put high-fat foods into my body. In fact, my entire lecture series is entitled 'Allergic to Fat.' My clients all love it!"

Alison excitedly said she was delighted to have unwittingly given Diana the basis for her eating plan.

"Even my skinny friends have jumped on the bandwagon and are eating my way," Diana said, "now that I have less cellulite on my entire body than they have on one thigh!"

"That does it!" Alison exclaimed. "Sign me up this minute."

They discussed possible times, but since nothing seemed to fit into Alison's cramped schedule Diana invited her to attend an evening lecture she was giving the following week at Stony Ridge Academy, a private high school for girls in Hancock Park. A mother of one of the students had taken Diana's class at the Gold Grill and had thought the teenage girls should hear Diana's inspirational message. "I'm going to discuss everything you'll need to know to get started on the regimen," Diana told Alison.

After leaving Alison, who could only assure her that she would at least try to be there, Diana returned to the library and settled in for another long siege, wishing the hard wooden chair were padded, but all thoughts of discomfort soon were lost amid the excitement of discovery and the reaffirmation of her theories.

Furiously writing notes on a legal pad, Diana's hand flew across the lined yellow pages, filling one up after another. More and more, she realized, all the latest research was pointing to the same conclusion: the fat you eat today is the fat you wear tomorrow, and counting calories is not the answer to permanent weight loss; counting fats is.

What excited Diana even more was that in all her research she did not find one plan as easy as hers to follow, or as easy as hers to stay on—and definitely none of them was as much fun.

Hancock Park had once been one of the most exclusive neighborhoods in all of Los Angeles. Its glory days had begun in the 1920s and extended into the 1950s. The mansions, one grander than the next, that graced broad, tree-lined streets had been inhabited by the crème de la crème of Los Angeles society whose children attended many of the private schools in the area.

In the late 1950s and the 1960s, this exclusive neighborhood began to decline in popularity as Beverly Hills, Bel Air, and Pacific Palisades beckoned from the west. Then all the areas around Hancock Park deteriorated until the once uppity enclave became an odd island of luxurious dwellings surrounded by a sea of poverty.

For a time the future of the local private schools had looked grim. Then in the late 1970s, with the influx of foreign money pushing the prices of homes on the west side up into the stratosphere, young families with a yen for a mansion rediscovered Hancock Park. That resurgence alone would not have turned the tide for private schools like Stony Ridge. What finally brought students back in droves for good were the contentious years of the public schools' busing crisis.

In the 1980s, however, with its financial future finally secure, Stony Ridge Academy had to contend with the same problems the neighborhood public schools faced: drugs, drinking, and unwanted pregnancies. And lately another problem had reared its ugly head at Stony Ridge: eating disorders. More teenage girls at this private school seemed to suffer from bulimia, anorexia nervosa, and just plain bad nutritional habits that led to a lifetime of weight problems, than from any of the other social diseases.

A nutritional counseling program for Stony Ridge Academy girls had been in the works for months, but nothing had been finalized when Nancy Gumbel, one of Diana's first students at the Gold Grill, suggested to the headmistress that Diana Lowe would be the perfect person to speak to the student body.

Since the Gumbel Family Foundation had endowed the school's new sports complex, the headmistress was inclined to agree with anything Nancy Gumbel proposed. "By all means," the headmistress had said, "invite her."

The big night had finally arrived.

Now, as Diana set up her visual aids on an easel in the auditorium, which had been the ballroom of the turn-of-the-century mansion that had become the central building of Stony Ridge, she noticed that nearly every one of the 150 seats was taken already. Nancy Gumbel had warned her to expect a large turnout, but this was going to be the biggest group Diana had faced thus far in her short career.

She felt the first stirrings of anxiety in the pit of her stomach as she always did before a lecture; today was doubly hard, however, for she wasn't at all certain how a group of overprivileged teenagers would respond to her.

"I made it," Alison Rifkin huffed, coming up behind Diana and tapping her on the back.

Diana turned to face her new friend. She was surprised to see Alison dressed more conservatively than usual in a demure shell-colored linen suit and bone leather pumps, with a simple Chanel shoulder bag. "I'm so thrilled you're here," Diana said with a smile. "I saved you a seat up front." She pointed to an unoccupied folding chair. "Come on, I'll introduce you to the headmistress and to Nancy Gumbel and her daughter, Sean. Nancy's the program chairwoman."

After a few minutes of superficial chitchat, the headmistress—a large, impeccably dressed woman in the Barbara Bush mold—excused herself from the clique and walked to the center of the room. She rapped a baton on the lectern and called the gathering to order, droning on for five minutes about the pressing social reasons that had prompted this event. She sheepishly apologized for the fattening selection of cookies and muffins the mothers had made to be served afterward on the veranda. She then spent another five minutes extolling Diana's virtues in a rambling introduction.

"Thank you for all those compliments, Mrs. Fields. I'm going to do my best to live up to them."

Diana paused and looked out over the audience, drawing them in with her direct eye contact, then said, "I used to look like this." She dramatically turned over a blank sheet of paper on the easel to reveal a blown-up portrait of herself taken one month before Dr. Fernberg had put her on the low-fat regimen.

She expected loud "ohmygods" whenever she showed this photograph to one of her classes, and she got them in spades tonight.

"I was fifty pounds heavier less than one year ago," she said when the murmurs died down. "I was desperate to lose weight, but I didn't know how. I had been on so many diets over the years; none of them worked for me. I tried starving myself and even that didn't work. In fact, I gained weight."

Diana paused, then said, "Worse still, I was beginning to feel short of breath after something as simple as walking up a flight of stairs. So I went to my doctor to find out why. He did a lot of tests. Then he sat me down and told me that all my years of abusing my body with one fad diet after another had brought me to the sorry state I was in—fat and unhealthy.

"He wanted me to promise to stop dieting immediately." Diana hesitated, then went on, "But I panicked and said I couldn't do that; for personal reasons I was under intense pressure to get thin quickly. My doctor was very convincing, however. He scared me so about my health that he finally persuaded me to at least try his way. After a few weeks of not dieting, the strangest thing occurred—I started to lose tons of weight. How it happened is what I want to share with all of you tonight."

Diana flipped the blowup of herself over the top of the easel. Now the audience sat staring at a picture of a mouth-watering wedge of chocolate cake next to a carrot.

"How many of you would eat a piece of chocolate cake if you were on a diet?" Diana asked. No hands went up.

"Well, then, how many of you dieters would opt for the carrot?" The response was unanimous.

"You're right. That choice was easy. How about"—she flipped the page to show the next picture—"one slice of low-fat American cheese versus two slices of thick, crusty bread. Which would be acceptable for a dieter to eat? The cheese"—she paused—"or the bread?" Almost the entire audience chose the cheese.

Without commenting further, she said, "Now, how about popcorn?" She turned to an illustration of a box of popcorn and a box of Cracker Jacks. "How many of you would automatically reject the Cracker Jacks in favor of popcorn when you go to a movie or a ball game?" The audience responded unanimously in favor of the popcorn.

Diana quickly moved on with a nod. The next illustrations gave the audience a choice between two frozen dinners: Weight Worriers southern-fried chicken patty and vegetable medley and Milton's fried chicken. Although the girls groaned in disgust over both choices, the majority voted for Weight Worriers, assuming that any diet meal would have to be better for them than a non-diet frozen dinner.

Finally Diana revealed a blowup of a miniature Three Amigos candy bar and an airplane size packet of cholesterol-free, coconut oil-free peanuts. The audience agreed the peanuts would be better for them.

"Thank you for being so enthusiastic in your responses," Diana said.

"But let's pause a moment and consider a few things. You made your choices based on the foods you've been conditioned to think of as fattening. But I'm going to ask you to de-condition yourselves and do what my doctor asked me to do: stop thinking about diets and food the old-fashioned way; start counting fats, not calories. He laid down a thirty percent rule: no more than thirty percent of the total calories of any food I chose to eat could come from fats. In the case of the carrot versus the chocolate cake, it's obvious that a carrot, like all vegetables and fruits, has no fat while the cake is filled with it. The other examples, however, present some tricky choices.

"Bread versus cheese. How often have I seen my daughter and her friends rummage through the refrigerator looking for a snack and come up with cheese? I used to satisfy my midafternoon hunger pangs with cheese, too. Yet all of us would do ourselves a favor if we ate one or two pieces of bread and forgot about the cheese. Most breads have very little fat—some have none at all—but most cheese is loaded with fat—sometimes as much as ninety percent. Even Parmesan cheese is seventy percent fat. And in the low-fat cheese that you voted for in overwhelming numbers, almost fifty percent of the calories come from fats.

" 'So what?' you say. 'It's calories, not percentages of fats, that really make a difference in weight loss and control.' Tell that to the dimples in your thighs! For that's what cellulite is—pockets of fat. The joke about the woman who says that instead of eating ice cream, she might as well just rub it directly on her thighs is not far off the mark. The latest research shows that the fat you eat today is the fat you wear tomorrow. Fat is not broken down and digested like carbohydrates and proteins. Fat goes right to fat cells and is almost instantly stored.

"So that brings us to Cracker Jacks versus popcorn. Popcorn is touted as a nutritious low-calorie food. And it can be—if it's air-popped without oil and butter. But most of the popcorn we eat at the movies and at ball games and the microwave brands with health claims blazing out at you in big bold letters are not healthful. According to the Center for Science in the Public Interest, except for air-popped corn, most packaged brands have so much grease, you might as well be eating potato chips, which average sixty percent of their calories from fat. The microwave corns average fifty-six percent fat, and the same goes for movie theater popcorn.

"On the other hand, the prize in a box of Cracker Jacks isn't just a useless toy; it is the knowledge that you're consuming only thirteen percent of the total calories from fat!

"Are you beginning to get the picture?" Diana paused, then said, "As consumers we are often duped by those who want us to buy their products." Diana waited to let this thought sink in, then continued, "It is important for all of you to be aware of that. But how can you maintain this vigil on your own? It's easy." She turned another page to show a blowup of the backs of the frozen dinner boxes, revealing the nutritional information data with the calories and grams of fat highlighted.

Diana pointed out that the non-diet chicken dinner had 460 calories and 13 grams of fat—in other words, only 25 percent of its calories came from fat. The diet chicken patty and vegetable medley had 260 calories and 15 grams of fat—over 50 percent of its calories, therefore, came from fat!

"Ladies, personally I wouldn't recommend either of these dinners," Diana said, "but what I'm trying to show you here is that while the Milton's dinner is higher in calories, the Weight Worriers dinner is higher in fat. Research shows that diets high in fat, even when they are low in calories, do not produce the dramatic and permanent weight loss people get when they cut down on fats.

"So let me ask you again: which would you choose, the no-cholesterol nuts or the chocolate candy?" The audience looked stumped. "What if I tell you the nuts have ninety calories and seven grams of fat and the Three Amigos bar has eighty calories and two grams of fat? Off the top of your heads, which do you think contains a lower percentage of fats?"

The girls in the audience shouted out, "The candy!"

Diana beamed. "That's right. Without even calculating the exact percentage of fat to total calories, you can tell that if the nuts have seven grams of fat and the candy only two, and their total calories are almost the same, the candy has less fat in it."

Diana turned to the next page on her easel to reveal a mathematical formula for figuring out the exact percentage of fat in a food.

Before Diana could go on, she noticed one anxious young girl waving her hand frantically. "Yes?" Diana said, acknowledging her.

The girl stood up and said indignantly, "How can you say that candy is better for us than nuts?"

Diana smiled. She had been confronted in this manner before. She said pleasantly, "I'm glad you brought that up. I will be discussing proteins, which nuts contain, versus carbohydrates and fats later, but we can clear up a myth about sugar right now and perhaps free ourselves from being captives of our cravings. The main objection to sugar is that it is pure calories without much nutritional benefit, but sugar by itself does not cause weight gain. Researchers such as Adam Drewnowski of the University of Michigan have shown that we have to look out for the fat that usually accompanies sweets, because the combined effect of their calories may be more fattening than sugar alone. Drewnowski also showed that we can indulge our sweet tooth safely as long as our diet is low in fat. Sugar does not, therefore, make us fat. Fat makes us fat. Fat is the culprit, not sugar. Does that answer your question?" Diana asked.

The girl said a meek yes, which could barely be heard above the excited buzzing of the audience, then took her seat. When the noise died down, Diana continued.

"Now I'm going to give you the cornerstone of my regimen: Every gram of fat has nine calories while every gram of carbohydrate and protein has only four calories—that is, fat has more than twice as many calories per gram as does protein or carbohydrate. If I just ate the same portions of food but switched from fats to proteins and carbohydrates, I would be taking in two times fewer calories.

"If you remember only one thing out of this lecture, please remember this fact: every gram of fat has nine calories.

"Therefore, every gram of fat must be multiplied by nine. Take the nuts, for instance, which contain seven grams of fat." She turned back toward the easel and flipped to a printed formula:

"Now, to get the percentage of fat, you have to divide the total calories into sixty-three." She turned the page to illustrate the next step:

"To get the exact percentage you now multiply by one hundred to remove the decimal point."

"As you can see, that is how I came up with the fact that seventy percent of the total calories of that little bag of peanuts comes from fat."

She went through the same calculations with the Three Amigos bar, which had eighty calories but only two grams of fat.

"These calculations don't lie. And neither does my body. In less than one year I have lost fifty pounds by eating nothing with a fat content exceeding thirty percent. The most wonderful part of this regimen is that the weight lost is fat, not muscle. I have gone from a size sixteen to a size six. I have never felt better, and I've become a wiser consumer over the past year."

Diana then went into the definition of "fat" and compared it to the often-used word "cholesterol," showing that the terms were not interchangeable, showing further that low-cholesterol or cholesterol-free products are not necessarily free of fat.

"Remember," she said with enthusiasm, "it is fat, not cholesterol, that makes you fat."

Then she segued into the arena of proteins, defining the term for her spellbound audience, ending with, "Unless we're pregnant and eating for two, we don't need to consume megadoses of proteins to stay perfectly fit."

This naturally led into a discussion of carbohydrates. Diana told the girls and their mothers that the latest research showed that if we all want to become as fit as long-distance runners, we should eat the way they eat: seventy percent of our diet coming from complex carbohydrates such as potatoes, bread, grains, and beans; twenty percent from protein; and only ten percent from fats.

"Isn't our life span like a long-distance race? Aren't we all merely the sum total of whatever we fuel our bodies with?"

Diana then capsulized several of the diets in vogue today. "What they don't provide, and what my regimen does provide," she said, "is a way to control your own destiny. Those diets—the ones that do battle on the airwaves, advertising for your money and devotion—ask you to give up your self-control in return for a quick weight-loss scheme using their food, their pills, their thoughts. The minute you lose a few pounds and finish their plan, their food, their pills, the weight comes back on, because your mind-set hasn't been altered one iota. Researchers have shown that no one can keep weight permanently off without first changing his or her mental outlook.

"About the only thing that gets permanently thinner on one of these diets is your wallet," Diana joked to resounding applause.

"Don't I know what that sense of failure feels like," Diana moaned. "You lose a lot of weight and in a few months it's right back on you. And maybe a few extra pounds to boot. Girls, you must understand *why* that happens, why it will happen every time you starve or purge yourselves."

Diana succinctly explained the body's basal metabolism and how it functioned. She clearly outlined why it slowed down and burned fewer calories when the body was in a starvation mode; how it stopped functioning efficiently after a crash diet, how people destroyed any chance of permanent weight loss by using a diet that was extreme, like most fad and crash diets.

"So what's so great about my diet? you ask. What's so different about my regimen? you want to know." Diana turned her charts back to the picture of herself fifty pounds heavier.

"It works," she said simply but proudly. "You know why it works? I'll tell you. It works because it is *not* a diet. My regimen is exactly what the doctor ordered—a total change in attitude, a complete alteration in your approach to eating. Recall that I started my nondiet diet when my doctor told me to stop dieting altogether, to stop counting calories. I began my regimen to get healthy. I learned that my body became over-fat long before I became overweight. I learned that my internal organs were probably coated with a layer of fat long before those unsightly bulges of fat and cellulite began to appear around my face, my waist, my hips, thighs, ankles —you name it!

"And then one night I learned that a friend of mine had a food allergy. That beautiful woman is actually sitting here tonight." Diana pointed to Alison and asked her to stand up. "This is Alison Rifkin, the author of *Friendly Strangers* and two other best-selling novels." The audience strained to catch a glimpse of the well-known popular novelist as Diana continued her speech. "Alison is allergic to strawberries. She breaks out in welts if she eats them. She wouldn't think of putting one of those harmless little fruits past her lips. I watched her, fascinated by the willpower she exhibited. She said it didn't take much willpower to resist something that made her look ugly and feel sick. I was hit by a thought as strong as a lightning bolt. If you have ever had a moment of reality—an epiphany—then you will understand how clearly I saw my own life. I knew without a shred of doubt that I was as allergic to fat as Alison Rifkin was to strawberries. It took a few days for the import of my revelation to sink in, but I began to understand that even though I couldn't see an immediate reaction to fats—I didn't instantly break out in welts, as Alison did from strawberries—I did get long-term delayed reactions to fats, like lumpy thighs and a big belly, a double chin and shortness of breath, and most likely arteries clogged with plaque, which is the nice word doctors use for fat that builds up on the artery walls and leads to heart attacks. I eventually learned that if I continued to overeat fats I could wind up with breast cancer or even cancer of the colon.

"After that there was no stopping me. I began to see everything I ate as a potential agent for causing an allergic reaction if it had more than thirty percent fat in it. I only had to look at the offending foods and in my mind I saw fat. I saw it coating my insides; I saw it making me sick. I only had to hold a Mrs. Miniver's chocolate chip cookie and feel how greasy my hands were afterward to know that I couldn't eat this food and live to tell about it. I only had to see the oil oozing off a pepperoni pizza to know that if I wanted pizza, I would have to find another way to eat it.

"And I did. I love to eat. I used to love to eat hot dogs, pizza, sweets of all kinds. How was I to stay happy and stay healthy? It evolved slowly. Eventually I learned that I could eat many fun things as long as they were modified. For example, when I go to a ball game, I can have the bun and the onions and the relish and the mustard. I just tell them to hold the beef. Whereas before I would have thrown away the starchy bun and eaten the fatty meat, now I was doing the opposite and getting great results.

"And when it comes to pizza, I do the same thing. Where I used to eat the cheese and throw away the crust, I now take off the cheese and eat the delicious bottom. In fact, I find that many restaurants make the most scrumptious cheeseless pizzas now, with all sorts of other toppings that taste good—and are good for you.

" 'But how can I stay on this regimen when my friends aren't doing it?' you ask. To them you say, 'Hey, I'm allergic.' I've found no one gets on your case when you're allergic, although some people do go out of their way to cajole even their best friends out of staying on their diets. Try that response—'I'm allergic,' and then go find a low-fat substitute. They're all around you and I've compiled a list a mile long to prove it.

"So you see, it is possible to lose weight, to maintain your figure, and still to have fun eating without guilt. Nothing ruins a diet more than guilt. On my regimen, you never have to feel guilty if you wind up over-doing something. On my regimen you're always under control. When there is some candy you can eat, like Three Amigos, why would you even want to eat a same-sized Snickers, which contains three times more fat? I say, 'Hey, I'm allergic,' and stay far away from the fatty candy. For you the alternate choice may not be Three Amigos. It may be fat-free marshmallows, Red Vines, Mother's Fig Bars with only seventeen percent fat, non-fat frozen yogurt, or even crustless fresh peach pie coated with delicious Marie Callendar's peach pie glaze. There are lots of low-fat ways to satisfy that sweet tooth—without guilt."

Diana gathered up her notes, then said, "My regimen is the opposite of restrictive. It's creative. My regimen lets you travel anyplace in the world, eat at any restaurant, try all kinds of foods—the starchier the better. And all the while you will be losing the weight you need to lose. Your bodies will sculpt themselves as the excess fat melts off to reveal the real you.

"Does this sound like a miracle? Well, for me it has been. I am no longer a slave to the scale. I no longer eat and want to run into the bathroom to purge. I no longer wonder if I will ever be thin enough.

"A philosopher once said, 'It is better to build children than to repair men.' I have begun to think of all of us, whatever our ages, as naive children on the subject of diet and what is best for our bodies. We need to be shown the correct way to eat. We're all young enough to build for a healthier tomorrow. Why not start today?"

Even before the question-and-answer period had ended to a thunderous ovation, the girls and their mothers were lining up in droves to enroll in Diana's programs.

When at last the crowd had thinned and Diana began to put her materials together to prepare to leave, Alison approached her.

"What did you think?" Diana asked.

"I thought you were fantastic and I loved the allergic-to-fat concept. It's off the wall, but somehow it makes sense. In fact," Alison said, "I was thinking . . . would you consider writing a book?"

"Who needs another diet book?" Diana answered, as the two of them bade good night to the Gumbels, who had to stay for the reception on the veranda.

Alison helped carry Diana's visual aids to her car in the parking lot, all the while encouraging her to become an author. "But it wouldn't be just *another* diet book," she said. "Who in the entire world has ever written about being allergic to fat before?"

"No one," Diana admitted. She chuckled suddenly and said, "I think if Harvey saw my name in print with that title, he'd have me committed."

"Who cares what Harvey thinks!"

Diana paused, almost stunned by the realization that even now she still was in the habit of seeing the world through what she supposed Harvey's reaction would be. "You're right."

"Of course I'm right!" Alison said, "Let me call my editor tomorrow and pitch the book."

"Be my guest," Diana said. "I've got nothing to lose. If I've learned one thing in the past few months," she said—thinking of Stefan and Dierdre and even Fritzie, who had called her regularly during the first month she was home from Switzerland before he had finally given up on her—"it's to relax and let happen whatever is going to happen."

Chapter

18

Diana stood with a manila envelope tucked under her arm, waiting for an elevator to take her up thirty-two floors to the editorial offices of Beecham Press on Madison Avenue. Why had she ever let Alison talk her into flying to New York to deliver her book proposal in person?

What if she sounded stupid?

What if they laughed her and her proposal right out of the building?

What if they *liked* her outline and gave her money to *write?* That was the scariest possibility of all.

Only an hour ago she had called Alison in Los Angeles from her room at the Regency Hotel on Park Avenue, hoping her friend would agree that it was best simply to messenger the material over to Beecham and wait for a response before meeting the editor. Alison had scoffed at her sudden reticence. *You're* as important a marketing tool to them as your book, Alison had said passionately for the umpteenth time. *You're* what they're buying and banking on for the talk show circuit. Just go; don't worry so damned much, Alison had ordered and had hung up before Diana could even say one more "but."

The brass Art Deco elevator doors opened. Diana gulped nervously and was washed inside amid a surge of people. By the twenty-ninth floor, only Diana and two other women were left in the car. One carried a thick manuscript, the other two manuscript boxes. She wondered if they were writers or editors. Both women looked to be in their middle to late thirties, dressed casually, hair unstylish. She decided they were struggling writers. Misery loves company, Diana thought, suddenly feeling better. She smiled at them.

The doors parted and the three women emerged into a stark narrow foyer. There was a receptionist's station opposite the bank of elevators.

The two "would-be authors" passed the receptionist with authority and went through the frosted double doors at the far end of the hall. Diana realized they were editors. She would have to endure this ordeal alone. Her heart leapt up into her throat and stuck there like a chicken bone.

Her legs felt weak. She hesitantly approached the preoccupied receptionist who sat in front of the Beecham Press logo mounted in large brass letters across the entire wall. On another wall, Diana noticed a long shelf on which were displayed the company's latest best-sellers.

Feeling increasingly insignificant and foolish, Diana realized that to these people it would matter very little that she had taken great pains to dress for success in Carol's high-style Gianni Versace suit in a rich hunter green with matching hose and Carol's green crocodile pumps. How could she have been so superficial? So frivolous? For these bookish types, Diana saw clearly now, it's obviously what one *says* and *how* one says it that matters, not how much one spent on one's latest outfit! On the other hand, Diana thought, didn't Alison dress to kill in her expensive flash-and-trash clothes? Didn't Jackie Collins? On the other hand, what if she— Miss Diana Nobody—had overdone it and turned them against her? God, look how plainly they all dressed! Maybe she should have worn jeans? Or maybe a seersucker Brooks Brothers suit with a bow tie?

"Diana Lowe to see, uh, Guinivere Wineberg and Prescott Dickson," Diana said almost in a whisper.

The receptionist looked at her blankly, with exactly the stare Diana thought was befitting the nobody she was feeling like. "Oh. Just a minute," the woman replied in a nasal New York accent.

Diana paced the foyer, careful not to let Carol's eight hundred dollar shoes make too much noise on the parquet floor. She could feel the butterflies that plagued her stomach before any important event begin to take wing. She was glad she had decided to eat *after* her appointment.

The frosted glass doors parted without warning. "Diana?" a young woman with a pleasant, scrubbed look asked as she walked toward Diana.

Diana nodded and smiled, not trusting herself to speak.

"I'm Guinivere Wineberg. Alison's told me so much about you." She smiled and extended her hand.

Guinivere was dressed like the two other women in the elevator— haphazardly, as though clothes were the furthest thing from her mind. She reminded Diana of a female Ichabod Crane with two thousand dollars' worth of orthodonture. Diana was nearly blinded by her radiant smile, but it did put her at ease and she found her voice.

"And Alison's told me so much about *you*. She said she would never have achieved the success she's had without your help."

Guinivere beamed. "Come on in." She led the way through the double doors into the inner sanctum of Beecham Press.

The decor was unimpressive; in fact, it wasn't really decorated at all. The entire sprawling mess was nothing more than a bunch of glassed in offices, most of them so small they would have been crowded with more than two people sitting inside them.

As editor-in-chief, Guinivere nested in one of the larger offices. Hers had a desk, three chairs, a love seat, and a coffee table—all of which were littered with manuscripts. Apologizing, she cleared a space on the love seat for Diana.

"We'll be meeting with the publisher shortly," Guinivere said, sitting down behind desk on the only other chair not piled high with manuscripts.

Diana nodded. The *publisher*. The butterflies returned.

"Are you having a good stay so far?" Guinivere asked.

Diana was grateful for the small talk. "Oh, yes. I love New York. I've only been here twice before." When she was sixteen, Diana explained, she had traveled to Manhattan with her mother and father. She had been a self-conscious teenager, anxious to pretend that she was not with the gawking tourists who were her parents. The second trip had been with Harvey a few years after they were married. She didn't tell Guinivere, however, that although Harvey had promised to show her the time of her life, he had ruined the trip with his constant complaining, his favorite comment about New York City being one he had stolen from the comedian Morey Amsterdam: "I went out for dinner with my wife last night and had to sell my car to pay for the meal!" Now she was here on her own —with no one to embarrass her, no one to answer to. "I can't believe the energy in this town. No one ever seems to sleep."

"That's why I live in the suburbs," Guinivere replied with another blinding smile. "The time commuting on the train gives me an opportunity to read all this stuff you see around you," she said, pointing to the manuscripts and bound galleys. "Is that your outline and proposal?"

Guinivere asked, indicating the manila envelope that seemed to have been sewn to Diana's armpit, she had held it there for so long.

"Yes. Here."

Another surge of nervousness, like a rising river in a storm, flooded Diana as she watched Guinivere open the little metal clasp of the envelope and remove the cover letter and ten-page proposal. Suddenly Diana realized how much she wanted this opportunity to tell the world about her low-fat regimen. She almost volunteered to read the pages aloud for the editor so all the inflections and meanings wouldn't be lost in the translation, but she bit her lip and forced herself to keep quiet. Even Diana knew better than to assume that Guinivere, with her Ivy League smile, wouldn't understand the subtle shadings and nuances of the English language on her own.

"Well," Guinivere said after two seconds of scanning Diana's proposal, "it looks interesting. I'll have to read it more carefully later, of course."

"Of course." Diana felt sick. Her empty stomach heaved.

Guinivere asked Diana to tell her a little bit about the evolution of her Allergic-to-Fat Diet.

What does she mean by that? Diana wondered as she began a hesitant explanation of her diet. But as always happened whenever she got onto a soapbox to talk about her favorite subject, she loosened up. All the self-conscious stiffness that threatened to undo her now fled her body—and her words—and before Diana knew it, fifteen minutes had flown by and Prescott Dickson was walking into Guinivere's lair.

Alison had not prepared Diana for Prescott Dickson. From the grand sound of his name, she had assumed he would be tall, with broad shoulders encased in fine English tweed; she expected him to have a full head of hair—any color would do—that fell casually over his high forehead, the way William Buckley's did when he spoke; she had assumed that he would talk in studied, hesitant but brilliant *paragraphs* and cross his legs so she could see his brown suede Churchill shoes.

What walked in instead could only be described as a gnome. Prescott Dickson was no more than five feet five with narrow Woody Allen shoulders and a fringe of mousy brown hair that made the rest of his bald head look like a hard-boiled egg. He spoke in a staccato manner as though his mouth were a gun filled with bulletlike thoughts that he shot out in rapidfire succession.

"Glad to meet you, Diana," he said, his small brown eyes darting a look at her. He smiled briefly as though a smile were a waste of important energy. "Have you looked over the proposal?" he asked Guinivere, who seemed oblivious to her boss's curt manner.

She nodded and handed the second copy to him. He glanced at it briefly. "Good, good," he said, another little flicker of friendliness crossing his face.

Diana decided he couldn't be more than thirty-five or forty. Noting the disinterested manner in which he took her proposal in hand, she also decided that he hated her idea and had agreed to meet her only to please his star writer, Alison Rifkin.

"Have to get to another appointment," he said. "It was nice meeting you." Almost like a puff of smoke, he was there and then he wasn't.

"Don't mind him," Guinivere said with a laugh in response to Diana's look of dismay. "I've never seen Prescott sit down for more than two minutes in all the years I've been here. He liked you."

Still looking stunned despite that assurance, Diana eyed Guinivere. "How could you tell?"

"Oh, I just could," Guinivere said offhandedly. "Want to see how this place works?"

She took Diana on a tour of the other floors of the publishing house, all of them like the first.

An hour later Diana was back out on Madison Avenue with Guinivere's noncommittal "We'll call you" ringing like a death knell in her ears. She elected to walk to her hotel despite the chill in the afternoon air, thinking she was too depressed to go back to her room just yet. As she walked, she thought fleetingly that if she only knew which way was east, she might consider drowning herself in the East River. Fortunately she didn't, and after another few blocks her spirits lifted as the hum of the city made her feel good to be alive.

She decided she didn't really care that her career as a diet book author would never happen, for she was certain by the way Guinivere had said good-bye that she meant good-bye *forever*. The experience had been interesting anyway. Different. How many housewives from Encino, or anywhere else, ever got to "do" a meeting in the Big Apple with the editor-in-chief and publisher of one of the most prestigious publishing houses in the world? It sure beat an afternoon at Bloomingdale's. Well, maybe not.

She hailed a taxi so as not to waste even one more minute, and had the driver drop her off at the fashionable department store. Diana stopped in almost every department, buying little gifts for her kids and friends to be mailed back to Los Angeles. Eternities later she emerged into rush-hour foot traffic.

Pushing her way through a sea of humanity—maybe it was a sea of inhumanity—Diana walked the few blocks to her hotel.

The lobby of the Regency Hotel was small yet elegant. It was stately, though sparsely furnished, with understated colors and marble floors. Everything about the lobby oozed money and power, including the people who traversed it. Here one might rub shoulders with a financial wizard in town to complete a leveraged buy-out; art collectors from all over the world there to attend an auction at Sotheby's or Christie's; or even a movie star like Harrison Ford, who happened to be checking in as Diana approached the front desk to see if she had any messages.

"Why, yes. Several," the desk clerk said, retrieving a slew of phone messages from her mailbox.

After taking one last furtive glance at Harrison Ford—who she could have sworn had been eyeing her approvingly as she stood not two feet from him—she decided to go through her messages over a drink in the Regency bar.

Alison had called her five times. Carol had called to say "break a leg." Her mother had phoned twice. Even Jessica had called from Berkeley to wish her good luck at her meeting. Guinivere Wineberg had called, too. Diana checked the time of the call to see if she had phoned before or after their meeting. She had called two hours *after*, while Diana was frittering away the afternoon at Bloomingdale's.

When the waiter brought Diana her Tanqueray and tonic over ice, she asked for an extra twist of lime and a telephone.

He returned in a few minutes with both. He plugged the phone into an outlet behind the leather banquette where she sat, and she placed a call to Guinivere Wineberg at Beecham Press.

The receptionist transferred the call to Guinivere's extension. No one answered.

"She must have gone home already," the receptionist said in a bored voice. "It's almost six."

"Could you put me through to Prescott Dickson's office, then?" Diana was still green enough in the business world to naively assume that if she wanted to find out something she could go directly to the top.

Dickson's secretary came on the line. After hearing what Diana wanted, she abruptly told her she would have to get back to her in a few minutes.

Diana nursed her drink and waited, anxiously snapping pretzels in half. At last Dickson's secretary called back. She told Diana that he and Ms. Wineberg wanted to set a breakfast meeting with her in the hotel dining room at the end of the week.

Diana smiled. Alison and Carol had told her all about power break-fasts at the Regency. In fact, Diana had witnessed several of them with her own eyes and ears only that morning when she had come down for a cup of coffee. Busy-looking men and women, dressed in conservative suits, carrying slick briefcases, were "doing" deals in hushed tones over poached eggs and dry toast.

"I'll be there," she told Dickson's secretary, happy to extend her stay in New York. " 'If I can make it here, I can make it anywhere . . .' " she hummed.

A power breakfast at the Regency! Diana nearly laughed aloud. If Harrison Ford had walked by, she would have pulled him over to her table to tell him she was about to have a power breakfast with a publisher and an editor. Who was his PB going to be with in the morning? Nobody? Pity.

Diana Lowe, power breakfaster. Sounded impressive. Maybe wearing Carol's outrageously expensive suit hadn't been such a bad idea after all.

A power breakfast . . . that was *definitely* a promising sign.

Wasn't it?

The minute the plane's seat belt light turned off, Diana loosened her belt and retrieved her briefcase from under the seat. Her *new* briefcase. Her lizard-skin briefcase. The briefcase exactly like Alison's. The briefcase she had promised to buy for herself if Beecham Press offered her a con-tract.

Diana snapped open the shiny gold clasps. She saw out of the corner of her eye the man next to her glancing at the briefcase.

He should only know what's inside it, Diana thought gleefully.

A book contract. Diana Lowe, author. And power breakfaster.

She opened the case and peeked inside. Yep, the document was still there, all fifteen legal pages of it.

"That's a great-looking briefcase," the man said.

She reluctantly closed it, letting her fingers glide slowly over the expensive textured leather, and turned to look at him. She hadn't noticed before how handsome he was. She smiled brightly and said, "Thanks. It's new."

"It looks it," he replied, adjusting his small round tortoiseshell glasses on his straight patrician nose. He had exactly the kind of hair she had expected Dickson to have—dark brown, straight, with a boyish shock falling over his forehead.

She quickly assessed the rest of him. With his conservative pin-striped suit, tightly knotted club tie, and highly polished wingtip shoes,

Diana decided he looked like a Wall Street stockbroker or attorney. Probably lived in Rye, New York, and swam at the Yale Club in Manhattan. "I promised myself if this, uh, this deal I was working on came through, I would buy it for myself. That and a first class airline ticket." She laughed and patted the arm of the large first-class seat she occupied now.

He seemed amused and tried to make more direct eye contact.

"Does that make me sound spoiled?" she said.

"No, not at all," he replied sincerely. Diana noticed he had deep-set blue eyes and a nice face—strong without trying too hard to be manly. "I like people who aren't afraid to indulge themselves. Are you from New York?"

"No. I'm going home. To L.A. Encino, really. Do you know the San Fernando Valley?"

"Not very well. I'm from Montana, but I live in Santa Barbara now."

Diana looked out the window, then reopened her briefcase and took out a notepad. She started to make a list of things she had to do when she got back to Los Angeles.

Her mind wandered back to the PB that morning at the Regency. She had been too nervous to eat at first. But after Dickson handed Diana the contract, she had devoured her entire meal. Guinivere and Dickson had been impressed by the amount of food she could pack away in her svelte frame. She jokingly told them that her entire life used to revolve around her meals. Now, however, she promised them, her work always came before eating! They were relieved to know that she was a workaholic, for they were as anxious as she was to make a huge success out of her book. They had spoken of time as though it were the enemy, extracting a promise from her to finish the first draft of her manuscript and have it in their hands in three months.

Although she would have signed the contract on the spot, Dickson had urged Diana to have it looked at by an attorney back home, since she had come to them unrepresented by an agent.

She took the contract out of her briefcase and perused the impossible-to-understand language, murmuring several of the sentences under her breath. Sometimes when she read legal verbiage aloud, the words made more sense to her.

The man sitting next to her, who seemed engrossed in the *Wall Street Journal*, looked over at Diana and said, "Do you need some help with that?"

"Are you an attorney, by any chance?"

"I am, and I'm not," he said, folding the newspaper and stuffing it into the pocket of the seat in front of him. "That is, I don't practice law any longer. I'm in real estate now."

"Please tell me you used to be a literary attorney." She laughed. "Here I am a writer, and I can't understand half of what I'm reading!"

"A writer?" He sounded intrigued.

"Almost. Once this contract's signed."

"Fiction or nonfiction?"

"Nonfiction. I'm doing a diet book. Well, it's a *non-diet* diet book," she explained. "It's different. A new concept."

"I'd like to hear about it," he said, leaning toward her.

Diana got a whiff of his after-shave cologne. A woody scent. She liked it. In fact, the more he spoke, the more she liked him, this man from Montana. A cowboy with class. She was dying to see if he was wearing a wedding ring.

"By the way, I'm Rodney Carter."

"And I'm Diana Lowe," she replied, glancing at his hand—he wasn't wearing a ring. She smiled broadly at him and launched into a lengthy monologue that took them right through a movie that neither of them watched.

Afterward Rodney Carter took a cursory look at Diana's contract and offered to put her in touch with a friend of his who was an entertainment lawyer at a prestigious law firm in Los Angeles.

"Remember, now," she said with a cute smile, "my advance is modest, so I really can't afford someone too prestigious!"

They talked awhile longer, mostly friendly banter. At last, Rodney Carter gave Diana his card and on the back jotted down the name and number of his lawyer friend.

When they neared Los Angeles, he said he really had to study a few documents since he was meeting with some investors the minute he deplaned.

Diana was glad for the silence, too; she wanted to finish her list of things to do. She wrote down a reminder to follow up on Guinivere Wineberg's exciting suggestion—seconded without hesitation by Dickson —to bring in the Beecham marketing department right away. Guinivere wanted them to forge an alliance between Diana's diet book and Jupiter Candy Company, the family-owned company that manufactured Three Amigos bars. Guinivere had suggested at breakfast that Diana send the marketing people at Beecham Press every article and piece of information she had amassed on the subject of sugar versus fat. If Beecham planned to use Three Amigos as the hook to get people to buy her book, Diana was all for it. In fact, she was delighted her publishers had understood how revolutionary her whole concept was and were already planning ways to capitalize on it.

With her hand resting on the yellow legal pad, Diana was washed into a fantasy. She saw herself on the Johnny Carson show, holding up her book and charming the pants off the irreverent emcee. Then Oprah Winfrey was telling her millions of viewers that Diana Lowe had saved her life with her sensible eating plan. Diana saw herself becoming a worldwide sensation, her book staying on the best-seller list for years and causing all the other diet books to fall by the wayside. She saw herself rolling in money—zillions of dollars. She saw high-powered movers and shakers like Fritz Konenberg falling over one another to woo her, to please her, and to win her favor, and as the plane made its final descent into LAX, Diana plunged into the best fantasy of them all: she was wearing her wedding dress—taken in two whole sizes—and thumbing her nose at Harvey who was now down and out and begging for her forgiveness.

Chapter

19

"I don't see any reason for you to delay signing this contract," Sarah Good, attorney at law, said to Diana. Sarah was a junior partner in the Century City law firm of Marley, O'Brien, and Cohen. Despite her youthful appearance and diminutive size, Sarah headed the firm's high-powered entertainment law section and, according to Rodney Carter, wielded an iron fist over those who worked for her. Diana found her to be a pleasing mix of femininity in dress and demeanor spiced up with a hard, aggressive edge in her voice.

"That's what I wanted to hear," Diana said enthusiastically, relieved that the process had taken only a few days to complete. She was glad she had taken Rodney Carter's advice on the plane and called Sarah Good.

"It's a standard contract, nothing out of the ordinary in it at all." Sarah pushed the document across the lacquered ebony conference table. Her private office was modern in decor, while the reception area, her partners' offices, and the enormous glassed-in conference room looked like a movie art director's vision of a conservative Beacon Hill law firm.

After inching forward in the steel-framed black chair to reach the papers, Diana signed her name on several dotted lines. As she wrote her signature with a curly flourish, she thought back to the first time she had

gone to an attorney's office on her own. It had been only a few months ago
—her first visit to Peter Webb. Then she had been a meek, mewling,
rightfully frightened housewife, wondering how she would survive without
her husband's support.

"That should do it," Diana announced, pushing the papers toward
Sarah. "It's official."

"Congratulations!" Sarah said with a genuine smile.

"I still pinch myself to make sure all this good fortune isn't merely a
dream," Diana said. "A book contract. I feel as if I've won the lottery."

"Winning the lottery is pure chance, Diana. What you've done is the
result of hard work. From what you've told me, you've earned your success."

"Things do seem to be falling into place," Diana admitted. "Even
my estranged husband will have to take the pressure off me now that I can
defray some of my own expenses. I no longer have to think of selling my
house and being uprooted. Still, I sometimes feel as though someone up
there must be looking after me. Like meeting Rodney Carter—two complete strangers seated next to each other on an airplane. And the next
thing I know, here I am with you."

"Now *that's* fate! He hardly ever travels on commercial flights. His
private jet's out of commission while it's being redecorated."

"You mean he has his own plane?"

Sarah laughed. "His very own. You really don't know who Mr. Rod
ney Carter is, do you?"

Diana looked at Sarah with a sheepish grin. "I guess not. Who is he,
exactly?"

"I guess you could call him the largest landlord of commercial
properties on the West Coast. I fully expect him to be President of the
United States one day—but for now Rodney Carter is keeping a low
profile."

"God! He led me to believe he was just a moderately successful guy
from Montana who lives in Santa Barbara now."

"And London, New York, and—let's see—the south of France, too!
It's funny. From the way he's been calling here every five minutes to make
sure our firm's handling your contract properly, I assumed you were old
friends."

"He has?" Diana was shocked. She hadn't talked to Rodney at all
since she had come home. She glanced out Sarah's window twenty-six
stories above Century City. Beyond the steel and glass high-rises and past
the new pink granite Fox Plaza where former President Reagan now had
offices, Diana could see the Twentieth Century-Fox Studios. Backdrops

and fake cityscapes were fully visible among the sound stages. And here in the midst of it all, her own life seemed to be playing out like a Hollywood script.

"I guess I shouldn't be surprised that he'd take an avid interest in a complete stranger," Sarah said. "Rodney Carter's famous for doing the unexpected."

"Like what? Tell me more about him," Diana implored.

Sarah sat back in her chair and rubbed her chin, thinking. Suddenly she pointed out the window. "See that hotel?"

Diana couldn't miss it—the Century Plaza Hotel and Towers dominated Century City.

"Well, our firm was in the middle of negotiating for Rod to buy the whole damn thing when he decided it was more important to go to Washington, D.C., and march for women's right to an abortion."

"He did that? I can't picture him . . . I mean, he looks so conservative." She recalled Rodney's pin-striped suit, the starched white collar of his shirt, his round tortoiseshell glasses, the smattering of gray in the hair around his temples. The only thing missing was the meerschaum pipe.

"Just another quirk. Keeps people off guard, you know. So he marched and lost out on the hotel deal to a group out of Chicago." Sarah emitted a sigh; Diana thought she must be thinking about all those lost dollars to the firm. "But he couldn't have cared less. He told me there was always another hotel just around the corner. He's amazing." She paused, then said, "Then there was the time he—"

The buzzer on her intercom interrupted her. She answered it and said, "Yes, send him in." She eyed Diana with a new expression. Was it awe? Diana wondered briefly before Sarah said, "Speaking of Mr. Unpredictable, Rodney Carter's here now!"

Diana's heart fluttered. "What a coincidence," she exclaimed, hoping it wasn't.

Seconds later Rodney Carter burst into the office like a whirlwind, brandishing a bottle of Dom Pérignon, which he opened with great fanfare, endearing himself to Diana even further when he said that since he was one of the first to see her contract, he wanted to be one of the first to see it signed.

His voice was deeper and more sonorous than she had recalled, and although everything about him was authoritative, the overall effect of his potentially overbearing personality was tempered by an attractive boyish enthusiasm.

When they finished their champagne, Rodney apologized for having to drink and run, but he had a meeting downtown in less than an hour and then another one later in the day at the airport.

Diana gathered up her things and suggested that since her business with Sarah was completed, she would ride down to the subterranean parking garage with him.

In the elevator, Rodney whispered, "You're lovelier than I remembered."

Diana thanked him, then tried to think of something witty to say. Before she could get her mind in gear, however, Rodney Carter said, "I have one more present for you, Diana."

She eyed him with an amused expression, not knowing what to expect next from her unpredictable new friend.

He promptly produced a Three Amigos bar from the breast pocket of his tweed sport coat.

Diana laughed and took it from him. She noticed immediately that the candy wasn't in its usual wrapper. Rather, it was factory-sealed in bright gold foil. While the logo was the same, a few words had been added: "New. Fifteen percent more chocolate!"

"Where did you get this?" she asked.

"I'll never tell," he responded with a smile. "Unless," he added, "you say you'll have dinner with me tonight."

Diana playfully retorted, "What choice do I have—what time?"

Rodney laughed, but looked pleased. "I bought it at the newsstand on the first floor of this building," he confessed.

Diana turned over the bar and quickly scanned the nutritional breakdown. She frowned.

"Something wrong?" he asked, responding to her look of concern.

"Nothing." Diana forced herself to squelch a sudden fear about what the data on this new bar might mean. "I just haven't seen this gold version before."

Rodney's black Ferrari Testarossa was parked at the attendant's kiosk waiting for him, and when he offered to wait until Diana's car was brought up from the bowels of the building, she told him to go ahead so he wouldn't be late for his meeting. Before he drove off, however, he said he would call her late in the afternoon to let her know what time he'd pick her up. He told her to dress up, since he planned to take her someplace extraordinary to celebrate the signing of her contract.

She smiled until he was out of sight, then gave in to a fit of anxiety about this new candy bar. She told the attendant to hold her car aside, and she made a beeline for the first-floor news and candy stand. She had to see if they also sold bags of the miniature Three Amigos in this new gold wrapping. The stand only had the larger, individual bars—one box of gold and one box of the original.

"What does this mean?" Diana asked, holding one of each.

"I don't know," the vendor replied. "I take whatever they send me."

"I see." Actually, Diana didn't see anything at all except trouble. She took out her calculator and found that the new bar with fifteen percent more chocolate had over thirty percent fat.

Diana raced to the nearest market to find out if Jupiter planned to take the old candy bar off the market. She found the bags of miniatures came in both gold and the original white wrappers. "What does this mean?" she asked the store manager.

"Heck if I know," he replied.

"Well, does it mean they're not going to sell the old ones anymore? Or does it mean they're going to market both?" She was starting to sound slightly hysterical, for she had computed that with the addition of only one gram of fat, and without changing the total number of calories, the new miniature snack-sized bars had thirty-four percent fat whereas the old ones contained only twenty-two and a half!

"Heck if I know," he said.

"Thanks," she said glumly. "Does anybody know?"

"Heck if I know."

She drove to the Valley and went to her neighborhood Gelson's. They didn't have any of the new gold-wrapped Three Amigos. She asked the manager about them. He didn't know what she was talking about and seemed totally unconcerned. Feeling relieved, Diana impulsively hugged him, then drove home thinking only about her date with the suave, exciting, powerful—and very rich—Rodney Carter.

Todd was waiting for her. "I have great news, Mom," he said. To Diana's astonishment, her son—the very boy who had been embarrassed by her only months ago—now announced that he had volunteered her to lecture to his football team. His coach was "into health and stuff" and wanted her "to teach the guys how to eat right." Apparently Coach Rogers had read an article in the newspaper about the Washington Huskies football team, whose members had gotten lean and mean on a low-fat regimen, but their program wasn't fun like hers.

"Todd, I'm flabbergasted by this!"

"You're not mad at me, are you?"

"Mad? Are you kidding? I'm flattered beyond belief! To think that you would want me to stand up there in front of all your friends and tell them how to eat . . . it's amazing."

"I'm proud of you, Mom." Todd's eyes filled with tears suddenly. He blinked them back and looked away for a few seconds. Suddenly he laughed and pulled Diana into a gruff embrace. She hugged back with all her might, her own eyes filling with tears. "None of the other guys have mothers like you. I mean, all they do is complain that their moms only go out for lunch or shop all day."

So her son was proud of her. She sat down at the table and gazed at him, a smile lighting up her entire face.

"You will do it, Mom, won't you?"

"I don't know if your team can afford me," she said playfully, with a laugh, waving a copy of her signed book contract in front of his face. "Or if I'll be able to fit you guys in between Oprah and Johnny and Geraldo."

"Thanks," he said, ignoring her gibes. "I knew you'd do it."

"I may not be able to buy you tennis shoes every other day at a hundred dollars a pop, but I can give you and your buddies all the advice you'll ever want about food."

Todd bent down and kissed Diana on the top of her head. "I guess I don't need so many pairs of shoes anyway." He stood up, looking proud of himself, and said, "Gotta go to Bryan's now. We're studying for a trig test tomorrow."

"Okay. Have fun."

"Yeah, right." He grimaced as he lumbered out of the kitchen. "I won't be home for dinner," he yelled over the sound of the back door slamming.

"Neither will I," Diana sang out gaily.

An hour later, however, Rodney Carter called Diana to say he was going to be tied up in his meeting until well into the evening and he would have to reschedule their date for another night. He said he was coming back into town at the end of the week for a classical music concert at the Hollywood Bowl. He would be honored if she would go with him. He had a box, and they could picnic under the stars.

"I'd love that," she said, volunteering to bring the dinner.

"Not necessary," he answered. "I always play chef."

I'm in love, Diana thought. A cowboy with class—who cooks. Diana was walking on air until Carol called later that night. Had Diana heard? she wanted to know, then rushed on about how her market in Malibu was out of the bags of the original little Three Amigos and only had the new gold ones. Furthermore, Carol said, the manager of the store had informed her that they would not be receiving any more shipments of the old candy.

* * *

Why is Jupiter doing this to me? Diana wondered as she lay in bed at four in the morning unable to sleep. She didn't know which was worse—not having the candy to eat anymore or having Beecham Press find out that they couldn't use the candy as the hook for promoting the diet, and tearing her contract into a million little pieces.

At five, in a frenzy, she decided to call the candy company. But where was it located? She ran downstairs to her freezer, took out a bag of candy, and read the label. The corporate headquarters for Jupiter Candy Company was in Portland, Maine. With the three-hour time difference, she realized they might even be open now.

She got Maine Information, then placed the call. No one answered. She walked slowly upstairs and took two Excedrin. She could feel a roaring tension headache coming on as she paced her bedroom watching the clock.

By five-thirty she was back downstairs, sitting bleary-eyed at her kitchen table, drinking a cup of coffee and dialing the number for Jupiter again and again, until at the stroke of six she was almost taken by surprise when someone answered.

Her call was put through to the consumer affairs department.

Diana felt like a crackpot as she explained to the woman on the other end of the line that Jupiter was ruining her life. Did they plan to take the original Three Amigos off the market for good? she wanted to know, a desperate, pleading note in her voice.

The consumer affairs lady said yes.

"Why?" Diana nearly shrieked.

The woman calmly explained that after a great deal of market research and taste testing, the company had decided that tastes change, that the consumer wanted a new product, and that it was time for a new look and a new taste—after all, the candy bar had been on the market since 1932.

"But they can't!" Diana wailed. "Don't they realize that by adding fifteen percent more chocolate, they've added more fat, too?"

"I'm sure our brands researchers have thought of everything," the woman answered, sounding like a recorded message.

After that call, Diana behaved like a woman possessed. She threw on a warm-up suit without even showering. Then she drove to market after market, drugstore after drugstore, determined to buy up whatever supply remained of the old candy. Some places already had replenished their supply of Three Amigos with the new ones. The rest of the stores were selling off what they had left of the original recipe, and when it was gone, that would be it for anyone wanting this chocolate bar—the only one Diana had found with a fat content under thirty percent.

Even though the back of her station wagon was filled with over three hundred bags of her favorite chocolate bars, Diana still drove home feeling as though someone were trying to cut out her heart.

How could Jupiter do this to her? she thought again and again as she filled the freezer in her garage with candy, then stuffed the remaining bags into every unoccupied niche in the kitchen freezer. She heard the service porch door open and close. "Todd, am I glad you're home," she yelled.

Suddenly a man's hands were covering her eyes. Her body went rigid. In the midst of her panic, the man rasped, "Guess who!"

Before she could scream or even catch her breath, he spun her toward him, then let his hands rest on her shoulders.

"Chris!" Diana exclaimed, dropping the candy.

Chris engulfed her in a huge hug and said, "Christ, where's the rest of you?" He stepped back from her to get a better look. It was his turn to feel shock. "I'm speechless!" he said, continuing to stare.

"Chris, stop looking at me that way. You're embarrassing me." Despite what she said, Diana loved every second of Chris's unabashed ogling —until she remembered that she had been up all night and had run out of the house without a stitch of makeup after barely brushing her hair—in fact, after barely brushing her teeth! She thought of all the fantasies she could have conjured up for seeing Chris again; this scenario was not among them. "I'm a wreck," she sputtered, her hands flying to her hair to try to straighten it.

"If that's what a wreck looks like, then don't ever do anything more to yourself." He smiled. "Billy told me you looked great. He was right. I still can't believe it's you."

Laughing, Diana replied, "Well, it is. But I can't believe it's you. When did you get home?"

"About an hour ago," he said, watching Diana stoop to pick up the bags she had dropped when he first surprised her. He bent down to help her. "What's all this candy for?" he asked. "Certainly not for you."

"This and more," she said. "C'mon, I'll show you."

She led him out to the garage and opened her freezer.

"Christ." He whistled. "What's this—a shrine to Three Amigos?"

Diana laughed. "I guess it is, in a way."

"You're not going to tell me you lost half a person by eating those?"

"It's a long story. How many hours do you have?"

"As many as you need," he said.

It was dusk by the time Diana had filled Chris in on the odd twists and turns of her life since they had last spoken months ago. He said he was incredibly proud of her new career and especially excited about her book contract. In fact, he teased her about becoming a successful author before he could even get back to the first part of his great American novel.

"A diet book's hardly in the same class as your writing," she said. "And anyway, if I don't find a solution to this candy bar fiasco that's brewing, I may have had the shortest career as an author in the history of publishing!"

"Now, don't fret," he said. "We'll put our lovely heads together and come up with something brilliant."

"But how could Jupiter do this?" she moaned. "Don't they know what a gold mine they've got? When every food company in the country is reformulating to cut fats *out* of their products, Jupiter is going totally against the popular trend and has put more fat *in!*"

"Then you've got to let them know."

"I've already done that. I talked to their consumer affairs person this morning and she couldn't have cared less."

"Then you've got to get to someone higher."

"But how?"

"That's what we've got to figure out."

Somehow two bottles of fumé blanc consumed on her patio under the stars on a balmy September night interfered with their plans to figure out a plan.

Somewhere between the first and second bottle of wine, Diana stopped feeling self-conscious or caring that she still had not changed clothes, put on makeup, or brushed her hair. Chris certainly didn't seem to mind.

Later, after he had gone home, Diana lay in bed reliving the sound of Chris's voice and the affection in his gaze when he looked at her.

And she felt confused.

They *were* just friends, weren't they?

She thought of JoJo Jenkins and the steamy kiss she had witnessed that night driving past his house. She remembered the hungry look in Barbie Mallory's eyes in that picture of her and Chris in *People* magazine.

Diana could never have him.

She willed herself to put Chris out of her mind. That was easier said than done. Then Rodney Carter came galloping into her thoughts: Rodney whisking her onto his jet plane for a night on the town—in New York; Rodney inviting her to dine—at the White House; Rodney and Diana on the beach—in Tahiti; Diana and Rodney dancing under the stars—everywhere.

Still, she thought just before she finally fell into a sound sleep, Chris's gray eyes were bigger than Rodney's; his face was more expressive when he talked; his jokes were more brilliant; his—everything was more. But she could never have him.

Chapter

20

Harvey sat at the desk in his private office staring into space and balling his fists as he thought of his new dental assistant. He had to bite his lip to keep the rage he felt from erupting again. In fact, he thought, if his hair hadn't cost so damn much to implant, he would probably be pulling it out this minute. An oral surgeon with his stellar reputation could not afford to have an assistant who made errors of gross negligence; he could have been ruined professionally if he hadn't caught the mistake she had made at the start of surgery that morning.

This morning his assistant had rushed in late, and in her haste to clean off the tray in the surgery room while Harvey had stepped out for a minute, she had dislodged the valve setting on the patient's I.V. Valium drip. Harvey had returned to find his patient hyperventilating. If he hadn't been so quick to discover that the dial on the apparatus was not set where he had left it, the patient could have died. Harvey had gone berserk and had fired the woman on the spot.

Now he sat thinking how much he missed Laurie. As much as he had mistrusted her intentions toward him personally, he had never had any misgivings about her devotion to her work. As an assistant she had been more than perfect—flawless with detail, intelligent, and aware of what he

needed almost before he was. She would never have made such an error.
He wished now he had not let her go so easily.

Harvey let out a loud sigh. What was happening to him? he wondered. He wasn't sure of any of his decisions lately.

"So we'll never get married?" Laurie had asked him over brunch in
his tiny kitchen one sunny Sunday morning two weeks earlier.

"I didn't say never," he had replied, but his voice had sounded tinny
to him, as cheap as the words themselves. He knew in his heart that he
couldn't marry Laurie—not now, not ever. As much as he cared for her,
something basic was missing from their relationship. She had been right to
read between the lines of his promises. Whenever he thought of being
with her for the rest of his days on earth, he became so depressed he
almost couldn't function for hours afterward. As he peeked around the
corners of his life with her, he knew that they had begun on the wrong
footing, that what she wanted from him had dollar signs hanging all over
it. No matter what she said, some action always spoke louder than all her
words to undermine his sense of worth with her.

"I can't go on with this uncertainty," she told him.

He appreciated her animal instincts; he admired her ability to per-
ceive that he was merely paying lip service to a long-term relationship. But
even when she impressed him, even when she seemed to be madly in love
with him, even then something stopped him from wanting to marry her.

"What is this, Laurie? An ultimatum?"

Sipping his coffee, he had eyed her, waiting for her next chess move.
For that was how he saw her actions, he realized. She was on a cleverly
planned route to checkmate, and he was the king she was out to capture—
only he was a better player than she would ever be, he thought.

"I guess I am making an ultimatum, pet," Laurie had said in her
most kittenish voice, tears welling up in her eyes. "I want a husband. I
want a baby."

"A baby!" he had shouted. "Now you want a baby, too!" Diamonds
and pearls he was willing to pop for, but a baby? He already had his kids.

"I can't talk to you when you start to scream at me," she shrieked,
standing up. Her robe had fallen open and Harvey had glimpsed her naked
torso underneath. He made himself remain impassive. A few months earlier, he would not have been able to control his desire for her. Once the
mere sight of her made him rush to her and fall at her feet.

"Are you trying to force me to leave you?" she had asked.

He hadn't thought of that before. Was he? Perhaps. "Uh . . ."

"Don't play dumb with me, Harvey. Remember, I'm the other
woman. I know how your mind works."

"Oh, do you? What makes you such a genius suddenly? Huh?"

"I don't have to be a genius to see through you," she had said with such dignity it shocked him into speechlessness.

She had walked to the archway between the kitchen and the living room and stood there, her robe fully open. "I'm leaving you unless you make some move, some comment, that will prove to me that you really love me," she said dully, as though all emotion had been drained out of her.

Harvey realized that they had been having little warm-up arguments about marriage for the past couple of months as a prelude to this big one. The tension had taken its toll on her. He knew now he was an emotional wreck, too. Still, he had forced himself to remain impassive and watch her turn and leave. He continued to sit like a stone as she showered, dressed, and packed her things.

Although he insisted on helping her carry her suitcases to her car, he did not acknowledge the silent tears that streaked down her cheeks. He knew if he made one move to wipe them away—if he felt for even one second the softness of her skin—he would lose his control. And as confused as he was about Laurie and how she really felt about him, he knew with crystal-clear certainty that she had a physical hold on him that was going to be hard to get over. So he made sure that the only thing of hers he touched was her Louis Vuitton luggage.

Then Laurie was gone.

At first Harvey had felt a sense of relief that was almost cosmic in its intensity. Like the Ancient Mariner, however, he found that getting rid of the albatross provided only temporary respite from discontent. The silence, the very aloneness of being alone had finally taken its toll. Now he endured a new kind of purgatory. At the nadir of his existence, he had called Laurie one night, toying with the idea of asking her to come back to him. But she had remained adamant about commitment, about marriage, about children, and finally he had ended the conversation by asking her only if she would consider coming back to work for him. "Never," she had said with such conviction that he was nearly bowled over.

And now this new assistant—the latest of Laurie's replacements—had turned out to be the most lethal one yet. Again, he contemplated calling Laurie, then decided against it, for he knew that she would demand a pound of flesh from him in payment—marriage.

It was all too much for him, he decided, as he left his office earlier than usual and drove to his quiet, orderly condominium in Century City. He was grateful he was having dinner with Todd tonight; he didn't relish spending another evening alone.

Suddenly he had a great idea. Todd usually drove into town for their weekly dinner, but tonight Harvey felt a need to pick his son up at home in Encino. How long had it been since he'd been back? Not since Diana had changed the locks to keep him out. Almost a year! Yet even now he could draw from memory every nook and cranny in the entire 7,000-square-foot house. He wanted to drive up that long driveway again, see his oak trees, be greeted by his dogs, maybe even see his wife. He called Todd from his car phone.

"Dad, glad you called," Todd said. "I just missed you at the office. I forgot to tell you I can't make it tonight."

"Why?" Harvey asked, feeling a sense of overwhelming fatigue.

"Mom's going to speak to my football team about diet and fitness tonight. I forgot to tell you yesterday."

"Oh." He had difficulty getting the word out of his mouth.

"Dad, you okay?" Todd asked.

"Sure. A little tired, that's all. A few problems at the office."

"Oh. Anyway, I'll see you next week."

"Could you make it sooner? What about Sunday?"

"Can't. Mom's teaching a new holiday series for her cooking classes."

"So?" He was getting irritated now.

"Well, she needs to try out a few of her latest recipes, so she's making a special low-fat Thanksgiving dinner. A couple of my friends are coming over. We're gonna be her guinea pigs."

Harvey forced himself to say, "Sounds like fun." As he turned onto his street, he could almost smell the delicious aromas that Diana had filled *his* house with every year at Thanksgiving.

He opened the door to his condominium and let himself in, feeling as if he were entering a hotel room. It struck him as he hung up his jacket in his bedroom closet that nothing about this condo felt like home to him. He traversed the living room, noting now the white-on-white sterility of it, passed into the kitchen, and stopped in front of the refrigerator. He took out a beer. Even the refrigerator was like the ones in so many hotel rooms, except they were better stocked than his.

Sitting in front of the television, watching but not really listening to the evening news, Harvey was overcome by emotion. He started to cry; great sobs suddenly racked his body. The wailing was as surprising to him as a snowstorm in Los Angeles.

He got up and wandered into the bathroom. Everything was orderly and neat, no hairs in the sink, no signs of life other than his own. He looked at himself in the mirror and was shocked to see how tired and drained he appeared. What the hell was going on? he wondered as he splashed cold water on his face.

Without knowing exactly what he was going to do, Harvey sat down on his bed and picked up the phone. He found himself calling Jessica. As he waited for her roommate to fetch her from another room down the hall, Harvey made his plan. It was still early enough to fly up to Berkeley tonight and take Jessica out for dinner in San Francisco.

"Can't go with you, Dad," she said, when he excitedly told her what he wanted. "I have a ten-page English paper due in two days."

"Well, that's okay, sugar," he said. "I have some journals to read tonight myself. Just thought—"

"Hey, Dad," Jessica interrupted, "have you heard about Mom?"

"Now what?" he said, hoping irrationally that he was going to hear that Diana was fat and miserable again.

"She's going to be an author!"

"A what!"

"You heard right, Dad. She just signed a contract to write a diet book. Isn't that great?"

"For money?"

"Oh, Daddy. Is that all you think about?"

"Somebody has to in this family," he replied.

"She's getting a lot of money, I think."

After Jessica hung up, Harvey sat back against the padded headboard of his bed, staring into space. Nothing in his life seemed familiar anymore. What was happening to him?

He tried to picture Diana as an author. How could anybody think she was an expert on any subject, let alone dieting? How much money was a lot?

He laughed suddenly, a sound only somewhat less surprising to him than his sobs had been. Only Diana could hoodwink somebody into believing in her; he'd give her that much credit. She had a way with words, with people, with food.

Maybe he should call her. Just to talk. Didn't they say that writing was a lonely job? She was probably as lonely as he was.

Chapter

. . . .

21

Diana could feel blisters forming on the balls of her bare feet from the wet sand rubbing against them as she ran. She tried to concentrate on her breathing, but that was too difficult; she was beginning to make little wheezing sounds deep in her throat where her air passages were supposed to be.

She looked over at Chris, who was oblivious to the pain she was enduring in her quest to keep pace with him.

"I don't do windows, floors—or run," she had protested when he suggested she skip her stationary bicycle ride that morning and run along the Santa Monica beach with him instead.

He had ignored her jokes and hustled her into his Jeep. The next thing she knew she was trotting alongside him like an obedient Chihuahua trying to keep up with a Great Dane.

The day was typical for September—fog hung over the ocean like a thick pewter shield. Once in a while streaks of sunlight threatened to break through but couldn't. Diana was grateful for the cool weather even though the fog blurred the distinctions between water, sky, and sand, turning them all a monochromatic gray.

"Hawaii's never like this," Chris sang out, turning his head briefly away from the view of the ocean to glance at Diana, who had lagged farther and farther behind him. "Every day's bright blue and white."

"What?" she gasped, trying to wipe a thread of spittle off her cheek before he saw it.

Chris slowed down; Diana sped up, and when she was at his side he said, "The Big Island. The weather is never like this. Even when it's storming it seems bright. That's why I bought that ranch in the hills above the ocean. As far as the eye can see, it's all mine. Wide beaches, turquoise water, lava, and red earth. Trees. Zillions of flowers. On my ranch the horses graze on orchids. I love it there, Diana."

Diana grunted something like "That's great."

"If you talk while you run, you'll do better," he suggested, tugging gently at her arm to keep her at his side.

She felt as though her legs were beginning to sink into the sand. "I'm trying," she gasped.

"Thought you were in good shape," he laughed. "Miles on that silly bike in your bedroom."

"I thought so . . . too," she managed.

"But you look good in those slinky pants and that top," he said admiringly.

"But I feel . . . like shit!" she exclaimed. She was wearing her Susan St. John special spandex workout costume. It was one of several Susan had given Diana to thank her for helping her exercise studio begin to turn a profit. "It's the least she could do!" Carol had said sarcastically when Diana had told Carol about the gift.

"Then I'll talk," Chris said, slowing the pace even more. He regaled Diana—who was now certain she was suffering total oxygen deprivation— with more stories about his daughters. They had given him months of heartache about living in Honolulu, but then he had bought the ranch on the Big Island, Hawaii, and the girls loved it so much they had refused to come back to Los Angeles with him. Luckily he had found a private school for them, which they also loved, and he was a hairbreadth away from selling his Encino house and moving there full-time.

Diana's heart lurched. Chris was leaving forever? She tried to breathe faster and found that what was left of the air passage in her throat had constricted even more. She felt as though someone had wedged a cork into her windpipe. "Maybe I'm allergic to running," she squeaked, then came to a sudden halt and sat down in the wet sand.

Chris continued on a few paces, then turned and came back. He dropped down next to her. "Are you okay?"

"Haven't you been listening to me gasping beside you?"

"Everybody sounds like that at first," Chris said with a shrug. "Come on, get up. You'll be fine in a minute."

"Are you a sadist?" She laughed, but she stood up, inhaled deeply a few times, then began to trot beside him again.

After another hundred yards or so, Diana had had it. She plopped down and told Chris she was going to wait right there like a lox until he was finished abusing his body.

He waved and went on down the beach, getting smaller and smaller until he disappeared from view altogether.

Did Rodney Carter look as terrific in running shorts? Diana wondered briefly.

She found some flat stones in the sand, stood up, and threw them across the water, watching them skip over the glassy surface, then sink out of sight.

She didn't hear Chris return until he was upon her.

"God, why do you do this to yourself?" she exclaimed when she heard his rasping breath and saw his face beet red with sweat pouring down from his hairline to the tip of his chin, where it accumulated and dripped onto his chest.

"So I can be as beautiful as you." He pulled his tank top up to wipe his face.

Diana couldn't help but note how well defined his stomach muscles were. She had almost forgotten what a sexy body he had. Since he had come home he'd taken to wearing baggy cotton pants and oversized aloha shirts with blinding prints of hibiscuses and other tropical flowers on them —the kind of shirts Harvey made fun of whenever he saw "hicks" wearing them.

"Tell you what," Chris said. "If you beat me back to the car, I'll let you buy me brunch."

She limped after him, not trying to win this bet, barely able to put pressure on her feet, for her blisters were bigger than ever.

When she at last reached the Jeep, Chris gallantly agreed to treat her to a huge meal. She said the running had taken away her appetite.

"I like cheap dates," he assured her, throwing a ratty sweat shirt on.

Over breakfast at an outdoor café in Venice where they could watch the roller skaters on the boardwalk, Chris insisted Diana would save him an extra trip to the Valley if she would come with him to Desilu Studios in Hollywood to view a two-part segment he had filmed for his series. They'd had to redo some of the scenes, he explained, and the editing was finally done.

"A movie studio? You've got to be kidding! I can't be seen like this."

"Of course you can," he insisted. "We'll buy you some perfume and a brush and you'll be as good as new," he replied, loudly sniffing his own armpits. "Of course, I don't need anything! Anyway," he confessed, "it's not what you're thinking. I've rented a run-down screening room on the back lot. We'll sneak in, and anyway, nobody's going to be there but us and the projectionist."

"Well," she said, torn between the need to soak her blistered feet and a desire to be with Chris.

"I really would like you to see this segment, Diana," Chris said. "It's the most serious thing I've ever written or directed."

"You really want my opinion?"

"What you think means a lot to me," he said.

"Then how can I refuse?"

Chris smiled. "You can't."

Diana relaxed the minute she saw that Chris hadn't been kidding her —the screening room was located, as he had promised, on the second floor of a brown stucco building in a backwater section of the Desilu Studio complex.

They parked next to the fire escape-type stairway, and just as they entered the hallway, the projectionist greeted them.

"Everything's set, Mr. Berry," he said.

He was a rotund middle-aged man with a scraggly beard. He treated Chris deferentially, as though Louie B. Mayer himself had just walked through the door. Diana began to sense the kind of prestige Chris had, despite the offhand, humble manner in which he talked about his work and his position in the television community.

"Thank you, Jimbo," Chris replied. "Meet my friend and most important critic, Diana Lowe."

Jimbo nodded a hello, then said to Chris, "From what I overheard the studio execs saying this morning, there won't be nothing to criticize."

Chris seemed pleased. "Well, then. Let's see it."

They walked toward the heavy metal doors that separated the screening room from the bustle of the hallway. Jimbo told Chris that one or two cast members had called to say they might drop in to see this cut of the two-part story. Chris nodded absently and pushed open the door to let Diana enter ahead of him.

She expected to see *Hollywood*—padded walls, banks of telephones, plush seats with high backs, cigar butts.

Instead, the room was drab muddy brown, and the seats were mostly metal folding chairs, except for a couple of rows of the upholstered VIP seats that Diana had expected. And instead of stale cigar remnants on the control table, there was a Styrofoam container with the last of a pastrami on rye getting hard in it.

"Sit here," Chris said, "next to me. I have to be near the lights and the phone," he explained. "Unless you need it to call Carol to chat."

She eyed him, uncertain if he was being silly or serious.

She sank into the seat next to his. It squeaked when she rocked in it.

Chris made a couple of calls to the studio. Diana listened, but didn't really follow what he was saying.

An air-conditioning duct blew frigid air down on her bare shoulders. She began to shiver and suddenly wished she hadn't worn the spandex outfit.

Chris noticed the goose bumps and apologized, saying there wasn't anything he could do about the cold. When they turned down the air conditioning, it always shut off completely; then the room got so hot that they all thought they were going through menopause.

"Why don't you wear this?" he suggested, pulling his faded Rutgers sweat shirt off and handing it to her.

"Then you'll be cold," she said, pushing it away.

"I'm never cold," he promised her. "Wear it."

She put it on. It was baggy and smelled like Chris, but she didn't mind the sweaty odor. And it did stop the chattering that was threatening to take over her teeth. Content, she relaxed against the back of the velour seat.

"Can we start now?" he said, an amused expression in his eyes as he glanced at Diana. She nodded. "You look like a little kid." He smiled at her as he picked up the phone again. He pushed two buttons.

"We're ready, Jimbo," he said.

Diana felt a surge of excitement. In seconds the lights dimmed and the screen came alive with Chris's show. She had never been to a private screening before; there was a sense of incredible power, she realized, in being able to order a film to roll at the exact moment you wanted to see it.

Be critical, she told herself while the credits flashed onto the screen. He wants you to be brilliant, insightful.

But within the first five minutes, Diana was lost in the emotional story of a Red Cross "doughnut dollie" who worked in the same military base in Vietnam as the Barbie Mallory character. The relationship between the women was lovingly drawn. Their growth as individuals was intelligently portrayed. There was humor and pathos—and tragedy: Mallory's buddy was murdered one night in her bed by a deranged soldier just back from the front lines.

The tragedy was so well written and so well acted by all the principal characters that Diana even forgot to find fault with Barbie Mallory, whom she had subconsciously resented since the night she had seen that picture of her and Chris together.

Diana became so engrossed she didn't even notice that Chris had gotten up twice to walk nervously around the perimeter of the screening room or that he had called someone and whispered into the phone for several minutes. She didn't even notice the door to the screening room open soon after the story began to unfold, nor did she see a redheaded young woman sneak in and sit down at the far end of the last row of seats.

In fact, two hours flew by like two minutes, and when the lights went on, Diana was an emotional wreck, sitting in her seat sobbing.

"Does that mean you liked it?" Chris asked hesitantly, handing her a tissue from a box on the lighting console next to him.

She laughed through her tears. "You're going to win another Emmy," she exclaimed, then loudly blew her nose.

"I think it's pretty powerful stuff myself," Chris admitted. "Just a few more cuts—"

"Any more cuts and I quit the show!" a familiar voice bellowed. "It's perfect the way it is!"

Diana turned to see who was contradicting Chris. She was shocked to see Barbie Mallory, looking as wild as her unruly mass of flaming red hair, sitting behind them.

Barbie stood up and glided toward them in a slinky leather outfit. Everything she had on was white and tight. She's a *star*, Diana thought, even more exquisitely put together in person than on the screen.

Diana's heart sank. She had an urge to run and find a mirror to see how awful she must look in comparison—eyes red from crying, hair pulled back haphazardly in a stretch band showing up every flaw on her face, and wearing Chris's gargantuan sweat shirt, which made her look flat-chested. She eyed Chris to see if he had noticed how she paled in comparison to Barbie.

He didn't seem as impressed with Barbie as Diana was. In fact, he looked at her angrily and bellowed, "I thought I told you to stay away during the editing process."

Barbie, hands on tiny hips, challenged Chris with a furious look of her own.

They both stood stubbornly, neither one saying anything.

"And let you ruin my best work?" Barbie finally said after Diana thought both of them had been struck mute.

"You have no best work, as you call it, without me, babe," he sneered. "Don't you ever forget that."

Barbie turned with a loud harrumph and fled the screening room, letting the heavy metal door bang against the outside wall when she flung it open.

"And by the way," Chris said jokingly to the gust of wind that was left in Barbie's wake, "this is Diana Lowe." He turned to eye Diana. "Sorry you had to see that," he apologized.

I'm not, Diana thought gleefully. He hates her guts. "She's beautiful," Diana said.

"And a bitch!" He shrugged. "So tell me, what didn't you like about the show?"

"After what you said to Barbie, I'm afraid to tell you," she said, grinning. "But the heat you two generated in this room makes this unnecessary," she said, taking off his sweat shirt and handing it to him.

"I really do apologize." He waved up to the projectionist's booth to Jimbo, whom Diana could see had been looking down on the spat between Chris and Barbie.

Diana wondered briefly, as she followed Chris out into the day which had cleared of fog and was quite sunny now, how many juicy stories Jimbo could tell about the famous people who had sat in that room.

Diana had trouble walking down the stairs and could barely maneuver her body into the passenger seat of Chris's car. Not only were her blisters killing her but her calves had begun to ache, and her thigh muscles no longer seemed attached to the rest of her body. "I'm a total physical wreck, thanks to you," she kidded Chris.

"What you need is a good soak in my Jacuzzi," Chris said.

Diana saw that it was already after four. Rodney Carter was picking her up at six. "I can't," she said, "although I admit it sounds like a great idea."

"My pool heater has a special feature. I can get the water heated up in fifteen minutes," he said. "I really do want to discuss the show with you."

"I told you I have a date tonight. He's picking me up at six. I really can't."

"I haven't seen you in months. I come home and find the girl of my dreams lives in my own backyard, and you dump me for some guy you picked up on an airplane," Chris said. "So he has a few billion dollars. But does he have a wardrobe of aloha shirts like mine?"

"You've got a point there," Diana said, laughing. "But I'll have to take a rain check on that Jacuzzi anyway."

Chris looked crestfallen. "By the way," he said distantly after a long silence, "did I tell you I have to go back to Hawaii for a few days?"

Diana eyed Chris. "No. You didn't. When did this come up?"

"Today," he said.

"When are you leaving?"

"Tomorrow morning. First thing."

"When are you coming back?"

"It depends . . ." Chris's voice trailed off.

She almost asked, "Depends on what?" but something held her back. They drove up her driveway in silence. She opened the door to get out, then turned to look at Chris.

Impulsively, he pulled Diana toward him. He kissed her on the lips briefly, paused a second, then leaned forward and kissed her again—a long lingering kiss. "Have fun tonight," he said, then let her go.

Diana was unsettled as she made her way into her house. We're just friends, aren't we? she thought again. The first brush of his lips against hers had said yes, just friends. But the second kiss . . .

"Mom, that guy you're going out with tonight called," Todd said as she walked in a thoughtful haze past the kitchen.

"Huh? What?"

"That guy," Todd said with exasperation. "You know."

Diana snapped out of the spell Chris had put on her. "Well, what did he want?" she asked.

"I don't know. Here's his number. He said it was important."

He was probably going to break the date, Diana thought as she punched in his phone number. She wasn't sure she cared.

"I'm looking forward to tonight," Rodney said when he heard her voice. "But I wanted to let you know the weather report calls for fog. Dress warmly."

Diana was touched by his thoughtfulness and told him so. Only her parents had ever worried about such things, she confessed, adding that she had thought his call had been to break yet another date.

"Not this time," Rodney said. He told Diana that he had traveled through four time zones to get back in time for tonight. "I don't want to let you slip out of my life."

He's perfect, Diana thought as she slowly mounted the stairs to her room, her legs aching more with each passing moment. He's never said one wrong thing since I met him. Then why don't I feel more excited about tonight? she wondered. Somehow Chris seemed to pop up as a very good answer. But when she saw the French tulips that Todd had placed on her dresser for her—two dozen yellow ones—and read the romantic note from Rodney Carter saying how much he was looking forward to their date, Diana forced herself to push Chris out of her thoughts.

She ransacked her closet looking for an outfit that would impress Rodney, then opted instead for something practical and warm: wool slacks with matching turtleneck sweater and a multicolored shawl to throw over her shoulders if it really did get as bone chillingly damp as Rodney had predicted it might.

When Rodney pulled up to her door in his Rolls-Royce Corniche convertible, Todd's eyes grew as round as saucers. "A Rolls," he whispered.

"He's got a Ferrari, too," Diana replied, awed herself as she walked to the front door to let Rodney in.

"Wait till I tell Dad!" Todd exclaimed.

Ignoring her son's comment, Diana greeted Rodney, who was all smiles and enthusiasm for their evening at the Bowl.

Although he had told her he wanted to leave no later than six, he spent a few extra minutes wooing Todd. And he was good at it. Nothing about him seemed forced. He knew exactly what to say to make a favorable impression on her hard-to-please son.

Diana commented on his easy way with kids once they were settled in the car and on their way to the freeway. "You know," she laughed, "I don't even know if you've been married. Do you have kids?"

He told Diana that he had been married to a law school sweetheart for ten years and divorced for fifteen. "We had one child," he added after a pause. "But she died when she was four."

"Oh, how sad," Diana said.

"She had spinal meningitis. My wife and I grew apart after that. It happens sometimes. Finally we split."

They drove for a time, both thoughtfully silent. She kept thinking about Rodney's public image, that of a powerful deal maker, and how it contrasted with this man who had hesitantly allowed her to glimpse some of the emotional pain he had endured when he was younger.

"You have a daughter, too, don't you?" he said, breaking into her thoughts as they neared the freeway off-ramp for the Hollywood Bowl and joined an increasingly long line of cars. The summer concert season at the world-renowned amphitheater carved out of the Hollywood Hills always brought out throngs of people who dined before the concert under balmy skies in their boxes—if they could afford the premier seats close to the stage—or at picnic tables located all around the outside perimeter of the clamshell-shaped white arena.

"Yes, I do," Diana said. "Jessica's almost nineteen."

"I can't believe someone as young-looking as you can have a daughter that age," Rodney exclaimed.

"Flattery will get you everywhere, Mr. Carter," Diana said lightly.

"I don't hand out compliments very easily," he said.

"Are you saying you're a hard man to please?"

"Oh, I am. But so far, Diana, you're batting a thousand."

"You're just impressed because I live in the Valley," she kidded.

"I'm impressed with everything about you, Diana. You're like a breath of fresh air to me. You're open and funny. In control of your life. Keeping that house up, working full-time, having a great kid like Todd. Even writing a book." He paused, then chuckled. "You're like a diversified portfolio."

Diana told Rodney that perhaps her days as an author were numbered, explaining how his gift of a candy bar had been the beginning of the end of Three Amigos bars as she used to know them. She told him she had even called the company only to learn that there were no plans to bring back the original bar. Sympathetic, Rodney agreed to do some sleuthing for Diana. Although he personally didn't know anyone at the top of the family-owned company, he would think about it and perhaps he could come up with someone who knew someone who did.

They continued their conversation as they drove to the valet parking section of the Bowl where an attendant, who knew Rodney by name, helped unload from the trunk an array of picnic baskets, a Lucite cooking panel, and insulated wine carriers. Laden down, Rodney and Diana made their way to his front row center box.

He seemed in his element, setting up the Lucite panel which spanned the width of a box big enough to hold six people comfortably. When Diana asked if others would be joining them, he said no, he wanted her all to himself. He then instructed her to sit back and enjoy the "show," for that was what his preparations turned out to be.

He took off his suede bomber jacket and rolled up his shirtsleeves. Then he put on a chef's apron and followed that with what could only be termed a ceremonial lighting of the burner, which fit perfectly into a cutout at one end of the Lucite panel.

"Why don't you light the candles and put these flowers into the vases?" he said to Diana, who was enjoying being the center of this lavish experience.

She lit the two white tapers which were already mounted in crystal holders, then carefully arranged mauve roses and baby's breath into two Baccarat vases.

People sitting near their box stared at Rodney's elaborate setup, and a few even commented to him directly. He responded in his usual polite manner, even going so far as to offer those closest to them a taste of the first course, lobster sautéed in wine and saffron, which immediately infused the air with an aroma that had noses perking up and heads turning in their direction throughout the loge seating area.

As if on cue, an Asian waiter appeared, and Rodney looked up, smiled at him, and said, "Diana, meet Kim Suc. Kim, Mrs. Lowe."

Kim bowed slightly and said, "Pleased to meet you."

"Kim Suc is my houseman," Rodney said casually as he chopped and sautéed.

Without further fanfare, Kim uncorked a bottle of pouilly-fuissé and poured two glasses, handing one to Diana and leaving one on the Lucite panel for his employer.

Rodney finished his work, sat down, and let Kim serve him and Diana the appetizer.

While they enjoyed the first course, Kim discreetly stood some distance away near the stage.

As they dined, Diana became aware that Rodney was directing the conversation, almost as though he were interviewing her. She eventually succeeded in turning the conversation in his direction, however, and showed how adept she was at getting people to open up. The more he told her, the more interesting and complex he turned out to be—this business tycoon who could gourmet-cook even Diana under the table.

"And here I thought you were a cowboy," she said when he confessed that although he had been born in Butte, Montana, and had enjoyed all his summers on the family ranch, he was reared a city boy. His father had been a judge; his mother was from a Boston Brahmin family that valued education and culture above ranches and horses. She had insisted her only child go to Andover and Harvard as had her father, grandfather, and great-grandfather.

"But I rebelled," Rodney explained. "I went to Yale."

Diana listened and decided that on a scale of one to ten, this man had to be a twenty! Then why wasn't her heart doing a tap dance in her chest?

During the preparation of the second course—scallops sautéed with shallots, capers, and lemon—Kim reappeared and tossed the salad.

"Where did you learn to cook with such flair?" Diana asked Rodney.

"I make all my chefs teach me their trade secrets. Several years ago I even went so far as to bring over a Cordon Bleu instructor to live in my house and hone my culinary skills. I rarely have time to cook, but when I do something, Diana, I do it completely."

He took her hand and kissed her palm, looking meaningfully into her eyes. She returned his gaze, thinking bemusedly that this night was like living in a dream world.

Even his apricot sorbet was perfect.

Kim whisked away all the dishes and utensils moments before the Los Angeles Philharmonic began its performance, playing a Mozart concerto and two short works by Franz Liszt.

During the first half of the concert the weather turned predictably damp; a cool offshore breeze had blown in to cover them with a misty fog. Diana could feel her legs stiffening even more than the rest of her body, and she not only needed the shawl she had brought, but was grateful when Rodney suggested they snuggle under his cashmere blanket. As the music wound its way through her uncorralled thoughts, she tried again to make sense of Rodney's unmistakable verbal overtures to her. Did he actually want a relationship with her, or was he only interested in a fling? She couldn't tell. She wasn't sure she cared to know where this night would lead. Suddenly thoughts of Chris intruded. The way he had looked earlier that day running down the beach in his shorts. He was leaving again. Suddenly. Still, she had no hold over him, no right to be angry. Then why did she feel so shitty? Why did Chris's face, conjured up in the middle of a crescendo of music, make her want to get up and leave? She should thank God for dropping too-good-to-be-true Rodney Carter into her life, whatever he wanted of her.

Even his espresso was perfect.

During the intermission, Rodney produced a special coffee maker, and pressed a strong espresso, which he served garnished with curls of lemon rind in Limoges demitasse cups. The coffee and the persistent romantic fire in Rodney's eyes warmed her up completely, and she sat huddled under the blanket close to him to enjoy the traditional conclusion to this summer concert at the Hollywood Bowl—the 1812 Overture by Tchaikovsky, which ended with crashing cymbals and fireworks the likes of which Diana had never seen before. For ten minutes, the misty sky above them was filled with an array of brilliant colors, as though someone had opened a trunkful of jewels and flung them up, up, up, only to have them descend in a shower of sparkling profusion.

They drove home with the top up, Diana feeling cozy and more at ease with Rodney now, although she still wanted to pinch herself to make sure this night was real as she listened to the pleasant drone of his voice suggesting all sorts of future plans for the two of them.

"I'm a busy man," he reminded her again just before she opened her front door, "but I plan to find time to fit you into my life." He took her in his arms and kissed her.

" 'Night," she said, then watched him drive off before shutting the door.

She felt like a giddy teenager for the first time in years. She had to fight down an urge to call Carol and giggle with her like a sixteen-year-old over the import of every word Rodney had said to her during their date. Something held her back, though. It was almost as if she feared just talking about the future would ensure that it would never happen.

Todd was in the den watching television. Slouched at one end of the couch, he looked exactly like his father.

"Did you like that guy?" he asked, turning down the sound on the television.

"He's nice," she said, coming into the room.

"And obviously rich!" Todd replied.

"How much money a man has doesn't make him anything but rich."

"I know, Mom." Todd looked at her with an exasperated expression.

Diana stood eyeing Todd, wondering briefly if she should say anything more. She didn't want to tamper with this era of good feelings between them. Still, she was a mother, and she couldn't hold back her fears as she blurted, "I worry about you, that's all."

"Why?"

"I don't want you to become too focused on material things. It's important to me that you have good values." She considered pointing out that his father's values were in the toilet, but she didn't.

Annoyed, Todd responded, "So this guy, Rodney with the Ferrari and the Rolls-Royce, is he filled up with good values?"

"I don't know," Diana said.

"But you're going to see him again?"

"I hope so. Does that bother you?"

Todd hesitated. "I guess not. But I wouldn't want to see you get dumped on."

Diana smiled and jokingly replied, "Thanks for having so much confidence in your old mom. Have faith, you little creep. I'll have you know he talked about dates with me into the next century!"

"That's great, Mom!" Todd said. "I mean it. I just worry about you, that's all."

Diana couldn't believe her ears. Not only was Todd proud of her career, but now he was worrying about her, sounding less like a son and more like a concerned father, watching out for her in a heartwarming, protective fashion.

Todd turned back to the horror movie he'd been watching. Diana was dismissed. She wanted to go on talking, to go on communicating, to go on finding out more about the way her son was developing. But she knew he was through with her for the evening. She couldn't force it.

Diana walked over and bent down to kiss the top of his head. He didn't stir, accepting her affection without having to acknowledge it.

"See you in the morning," she whispered. He nodded absently, his eyes riveted once more to the screen.

The phone started to ring just as she entered her bedroom. She glanced at the clock. It was after midnight. A little flicker of alarm rushed through her.

"Who is it?" she asked.

"Me."

"Rodney, where are you?"

"I'm in my car. I missed the sound of your voice. Have breakfast with me."

She had planned to start working on her book first thing in the morning. It could wait a couple of hours. It wasn't every day a man straight out of the pages of *Fortune* missed the sound of her voice.

He would pick her up at nine—sharp.

Chapter
....
22

Rodney Carter's assistant called and canceled breakfast with Diana—
something about an urgent meeting he had to attend in London.

Two days later Rodney phoned Diana from New York. He had arranged an unlimited credit line for her at a number of Rodeo Drive
boutiques. "Buy everything you need," he said, explaining that he wanted
to take her to a gala three-day event. The controversial Wall Street finan-
cier, Jordan Hoch IV, was throwing himself a birthday party on his private
Caribbean island the following week. The Who's Who in American business and society would be there bejeweled and dressed to the hilt. He
wanted Diana to "feel comfortable," and therefore he couldn't ask her to
spend her own funds even though she protested, saying she could afford to
buy her own clothes.

"He almost made it sound like a business investment," Diana told
Carol later that day, adding that she was still contemplating turning his
offer down.

"You're crazy," Carol replied.

"Maybe. But if I sleep with him I want it to be my decision. Just
because he's clothed my body, I don't want him to think he owns it, too."

"Has he put any pressure on you so far?"

"No."

"Then stop agonizing. Cross that bridge when you come to it."

"Maybe you're right."

"Of course I'm right. Go for it!"

Go for it she did. A few days later Diana was cutting twenty-five thousand dollars' worth of price tags off a whole new wardrobe of party, daytime, and evening clothes, purses, wraps . . .

Rodney sent his luxurious jet for her. She flew to New York alone, pampered by Kim Suc and entertained for part of the way by the copilot who came to sit with her in the lounge, which was equipped with a stereo system and hundreds of CDs, a library including all the latest best-sellers, and a VCR with dozens of videotapes.

After their chat, the copilot handed her a note and departed. It was from Rodney. It read: "Hope you're enjoying the flight. Sorry I couldn't be there with you. There's enough Dom Pérignon in the fridge to drown a regiment of thirsty soldiers. And I've put a tape in the VCR that should get you in a relaxed mood for our weekend."

She turned on the television and pressed the button for the VCR. Soon she was watching Playboy's *The Art of Sensual Massage*. Somehow when she and Stefan had been doing it, she had felt special; watching that tape made her feel cheap. She wondered if all Rodney's women were treated to new clothes from Rodeo Drive salons and soft-core porno tapes at thirty-five thousand feet in the air.

Rodney met her at the airport. "Did you watch the movie?" he asked after kissing her hello.

"For a few minutes. I got bored. I prefer the real thing."

"And so do I," he cooed, pulling her into another embrace. "It just saves some time, that's all," he murmured into her ear.

I should have guessed, she thought, recoiling ever so slightly. She felt a sinking sensation in the pit of her stomach. Was he so busy that he expected her to start their sexual foreplay alone?

"You're going to be the belle of the ball," he told her when they encountered several of the other guests assembling at the private hangar from which many private jets and two charters were to leave for Hoch's party.

He told her in quiet tones who everyone was. Most of the names were familiar, as were many of the faces.

Once they all arrived and settled in at Hoch's island paradise, the talk changed from who everyone was to how much their host had spent. It was rumored that Hoch had dished out at least five million dollars on this affair.

He had brought over the Cirque de Soleil. Yachts of varying sizes were available for pleasure-cruising as well as for fishing. Every water sport imaginable was offered to the guests. Hoch's private eighteen-hole golf course was in constant demand, as were his seven tennis courts.

At night festivities ranged from jazzy disco parties to white tie affairs, and in Arabian-style tents the food, drink, and entertainment were in such unending supply and of such variety that they would have made Henry VIII's head spin.

No one seemed to sleep.

As an outsider on the arm of an insider, Diana had a bird's-eye view of how discontented and bratty many of the rich and famous turned out to be. As lavish and as well thought out as everything was, the guests were exposed to this type of self-indulgence too often. It was almost as though the more Hoch gave them the more they expected. Diana looked into their eyes and saw bottomless wells of expectation.

Rodney was effervescent and charming at all times, like a politician out to win votes. In fact, Diana decided, that was exactly what he was doing. During a long chat with the mayor of a midwestern city, Rodney admitted he was taking up some social issues that could be used as a springboard for any political aspirations he might have "down the line."

"Is that how you felt about your pro-choice march?" she asked him later.

"Sure," he replied.

He dipped down another notch in her estimation.

On the rare occasion when there was a break in the action, Rodney seemed edgy. Diana wondered if he didn't know what to do with himself when he couldn't be near a phone or looking over the documents that were faxed to him daily.

Sex with Rodney was yet another performance—like his cooking. Setting the scene was as important to him as the act itself. He made the right moves the same way he used the correct utensils in preparing his favorite foods.

He had to control the environment and tenor of their lovemaking down to the last detail. Diana wanted spontaneity, and the lack of it caused him to dip yet another notch in her estimation.

She was aroused as much from her own response to the surf, the sun, and the heady presence of so many powerful people as she was by Rodney himself. She wanted him to take her, to love her, right in the middle of their crammed afternoon schedule. But Rodney put her off—kindly, of course—making it clear that they would make love later that night, as he had planned.

And, oh, he was adept. A well-schooled lover. Rodney knew just how to use his fingers. How to use his mouth on her mouth, on her breasts. He knew just how long to taunt her to make certain she was wet and ready for him.

Even his cunnilingus was perfect.

But he was not wild; he was not carefree.

"Fun" was not a word that ever entered Diana's mind whenever Rodney entered her body.

As the weekend drew to an end, Diana was glad to be leaving. Nothing seemed right about their being together, although Rodney didn't seem to notice that.

"I'm not going to see him anymore," Diana told Carol after arriving back home. "We're too different."

Again Carol told her she was crazy to back out of a budding and very exciting relationship with such a brilliant and wealthy man.

"Even the sex wasn't that great."

"Give it time," Carol told her. Let it develop slowly; maybe Diana could change him.

Maybe Carol was right.

Then again, maybe Diana was right for once. Maybe she should trust her own instincts?

"I'm crazy about you," Rodney said, calling Diana from his plane en route to São Paolo late that night. "You were wonderful this weekend. I know these affairs aren't easy. I know I'm not easy."

He always said the right thing.

She wavered.

Maybe Carol was right. What harm was there in giving their relationship a chance?

"Mom, it's not fair. I'm sick of constantly having to sleep over with friends. It's embarrassing getting farmed out every time you go off with that guy."

Diana sat slumped at the kitchen table peering into a cup of muddy brown coffee. Her travels with Rodney were becoming very complicated. Having to pick up and go at a moment's notice was harder than anyone could imagine. In the four weeks they had been seeing each other, she had been to New York twice, London, Paris, Monaco, Rome, and Deer Valley, Utah, in addition to Hoch's Caribbean island. She didn't know what time zone she was in half the time. She was developing perpetual dark circles under her eyes. And now this crazy relationship was starting to drive a wedge between her and Todd. Not only did she rarely see her son, but he was more than hinting that his mother was becoming an embarrassment to him.

"I'll just tell him I can't go to Acapulco with him, that's all," she said. "It's only for two days anyway."

"Will Rod be mad?"

"It doesn't matter. You come first, Todd. He knows that. *I* just forgot."

Todd looked relieved. He brushed his mother's cheek with an affectionate kiss and hugged her, then rushed out the door.

Diana phoned Rodney and left a message with his assistant that she was canceling their plans.

Rodney phoned her back almost immediately. "What is this about Todd?"

"He's been shuffled around too much lately, Rodney. I can't go with you to Mexico."

Rodney was silent on the other end of the line.

"Say something," Diana pleaded.

"Buy him a baby-sitter."

"Don't be absurd."

"I didn't mean it. I'm just disappointed. I love you, Diana. I need you with me."

He had told her he loved her many times in the past few weeks. She believed him. She also believed that he wanted everything on his terms.

"If you loved me, you'd want to be with me," Rodney insisted.

She wanted to love him, but she wasn't sure of the depth of her feelings yet. "I care about you a great deal," she said. "But I also have a son. Todd doesn't ask for much. He needs me now. I can't let him down."

"So it's final? You're not going to be with me when I need you?"

"It's not fair of you to put it that way. Can't you postpone your meeting and stay in L.A.? Spend time with me and Todd."

"I can't do that," Rodney said coldly.

"But you expect me to drop everything."

"I don't want to fight with you," he said forcefully.

"No fights. No communication. No relationship."

"Is that your decision?"

"I guess it is."

The phone went dead. Diana sat holding the receiver for several seconds. Suddenly she panicked, thinking she had done something really foolish. She called him back.

They agreed she would fly with him to Acapulco for the afternoon and have the pilot ferry her back late that evening. That way she could placate both Rodney and Todd.

But Todd wasn't placated. "You're only coming back because you have to," he said, "not because you want to."

"That's not true."

"You make me feel like I don't belong anywhere anymore. Not at Dad's. Now not even in my own house."

"That's not true either," she protested.

"Well, it's how I feel," he cried and stormed out.

She had never questioned why her son had come home to her from Harvey's. Now she saw that he was comfortable here. This was his home, not some unfamiliar stopping place. Like any kid, he wanted his own bed, his own things, a mom, and a refrigerator full of food. She was threatening all that again with this new man. Her life was turning upside down. On top of everything with Todd, she hadn't even written one complete chapter of her manuscript since Rodney had charged in and taken over.

"If it weren't for the weight of the clothes you're wearing," Diana seethed, eyeing Rodney in his linen pants and striped pastel sport shirt, "you wouldn't know if it was summer or winter, or if your meeting was in a boardroom in Alaska or this living room in Acapulco! Can't you ever stop working long enough to smell the roses?"

Rodney glanced up from his sheaf of papers, took off his glasses, and said, "Huh?"

"This view," she pointed out angrily. "You dragged me here supposedly because you wanted me to be with you, to savor everything with you, but I'm sick and tired of watching beautiful sunsets all over the world alone."

Rodney got up and walked over to Diana. "Relax," he said soothingly, reaching for her, "don't get so upset. I have a deadline. Certainly you can understand that."

Diana thought about her own manuscript deadline, which was in jeopardy because Rodney insisted that she *not* bring her work with her on their trips together. He wanted her to be ready for him at a moment's notice and not preoccupied with her own thoughts.

Diana backed angrily out of his reach. She walked out onto the veranda of their posh accommodation overlooking the ocean in the exclusive Las Brisas section of Acapulco. She leaned against the wrought-iron railing and heard Rodney sigh audibly as he followed her outside. "It is beautiful," he admitted. "If you could have stayed with me for a few days, we might have been able to enjoy more of it."

Diana stormed past him back into the living room. He stood at the sliding glass door, the last remaining streaks of orange casting light that illuminated his beautiful hair. "Now what?" he asked tiredly.

"You're so self-absorbed. You want me to give up everything for you. My career. My son. You want all my attention, but you give me none of yours. I'll never be a big enough part of your life. Yet you want to be the entirety of mine."

Rodney started to defend himself, but Diana interrupted him.

"Wait, let me finish," she said, her face taut and strained. "When we first met you complimented me and said—to put it in your own words—I was like a diversified portfolio. You also said I was like a breath of fresh air, but I feel stale now, Rodney. You said I was in control of my life, but the reality of it is, you want to control every part of my existence. You liked it that I worked, that I was writing a book. But when I try to stay home and work, you want me to be with you, and when I was so crass as to bring my work with me, you insisted it upset you to have me preoccupied. You loved me because of my commitment to my son, but in fact you're making me push him away."

"Anything else?" Rodney said icily.

"I can't give you what you want, Rodney."

"And what is that?" he asked.

"Everything."

Diana returned past midnight to find Todd barricaded in his bedroom, refusing to come out to talk to her; she felt too tired to press the issue. She didn't even have the energy to tell him that she wasn't going to see Rodney anymore.

No sooner had she reached her room and undressed than the phone began to ring. She was used to Rodney's calls at all hours of the night. Tonight she didn't want to listen to him beg her to kiss and make up long-distance.

"Hello," she said irritably into the phone.

"Hi," a cheerful voice greeted her.

"My God, Chris! Where are you?"

"At home . . . down the street."

"So you're back." Diana's heart skipped an excited beat. "It's late. Are you okay?" she said.

"I just saw you being chauffeured up the street in a pretty impressive limo." He paused. Diana said nothing. "So. How was your date?"

"You called to ask me about a date at this hour?" she said with a laugh.

"I was worried about you. Beware of men bearing gifts in limos. . . . Oh, and I thought maybe your legs were still aching from that run on the beach."

"May I remind you that was eons ago?"

"Oh, yeah. How about that Jacuzzi now?"

"It's midnight. I'm beat."

"I've heard midnight is the very best time for soaking in a Jacuzzi. Don't fink out on me again."

"I really can't." She didn't sound very convincing even to herself.

"Sure you can. Just give me one really good reason and I'll hang up." Diana said, "Uh, well."

Chris laughed. "See. You can't think of one reason not to sit under the stars in my backyard with me."

"There aren't any stars. It's too overcast tonight."

"Okay," he said, sounding like a little boy. "If you don't want to . . ."

"I didn't say *that*," Diana protested.

"Good. I already turned up the heat. See you in, say, five minutes?"

"Okay," she said and hung up, then rushed to put on a kelly green one-piece bathing suit with a low back, plunging front, and legs cut up to her waist, one of the more revealing items she had bought for Hoch's Caribbean extravaganza. She took one last look at herself in the mirror and almost changed into a less sexy black one, then decided to throw caution to the wind. She put on a terry-cloth robe and hurried out of her room.

Todd was in the kitchen making a late night snack, so she had to tell him where she was going. Embarrassed, Diana was careful not to make eye contact with him. She didn't especially care to see his approving or disapproving—or even questioning—look, for she had no answers herself.

"So what's with you and Richie Rich?" Chris asked soon after they had settled into the Jacuzzi. "Is it serious?"

Steam rose from the water and filled the damp air around them, hanging suspended and seeming thick enough to grab.

"Actually, it's over," she replied after a long pause.

"Should I be sorry for you?"

"No."

"Good."

They sat and sipped cognac out of snifters, staring at each other.

"This feels terrific," Chris said. "Relaxing. How're your feet and legs doing?"

"Something always aches," she said languidly. "I guess it's called getting old."

"Here, let me rub them," Chris said, putting down his drink. He glided through the water, stood in front of Diana, and gently took hold of her feet, which forced her to lean back against the wall of the tub.

"Does this feel good?" Chris asked, intently working on the balls of her feet.

She sipped her drink and stared at him, saying nothing. She felt a warm sensation begin between her legs and a sense of the rest of humanity fading away, leaving only her and Chris in the world.

"You have beautiful feet," he murmured, lifting one to his mouth and kissing the arch. A memory of the torrid scenes between her and Stefan exploded into Diana's consciousness, then receded. Chris was her focus now as he leaned forward, taking the glass out of her hand and placing it on the pool ledge behind her. "Diana." He murmured her name like a caress, his face only inches from hers now. "I've missed you like crazy."

The misty air sparked with their intersecting currents.

He pulled her to him, and the buoyancy of the water made her body float into his, her legs naturally intertwining with Chris's.

They kissed. Softly at first, then more aggressively, with an urgency to their embrace.

Perhaps not since her first time with Harvey, and never with Rodney, had Diana felt such a rush of emotion connected with passion.

He nudged her swimsuit straps down. It was so natural that there was no question of whether she would protest.

Suddenly the phone began to ring. "Forget it," Chris said huskily, looking into Diana's eyes with such longing that she wanted to freeze the expression in time.

They kissed passionately, mouths fully open now, tongues meeting.

The phone rang again.

"Shit," he said. "I better get it. Maybe it's one of the twins. It's earlier in Hawaii."

She floated out of his embrace. "You're right."

It was Todd. A neighbor of his grandmother's in Palm Desert had just called to say that Betty had been rushed to Eisenhower Medical Center.

"My God!" Diana said, the rosy hue from the hot water and her passion completely draining from her face. "She was fine when I spoke to her yesterday."

She pulled up her straps, quickly got out of the water and threw on her robe.

"Wait," he said, grabbing her arm.

"I have to go!" she cried.

"To the desert?"

Diana nodded, looking ashen and grim. She shuddered as much from fear as from the cold night air. She wrapped her robe more tightly around her and stepped into her sandals.

"Diana." Chris took her in his arms and held her tightly. "I'm going with you."

"You don't have to," she replied, her face pressed against his chest.

"I know," he said simply.

Chapter

. . . .

23

They arrived at the Eisenhower Medical Center shortly after four in the morning. Diana jumped out of the Jeep almost before Chris had parked it. A blast of frigid autumn air chilled her as she rushed ahead of Chris toward the entrance to the central hospital building.

The double glass doors were locked. "Now what?" she said, on the verge of hysteria. Diana had never been to this hospital before and had no idea how to find her mother.

"Well—" Chris started to say when a voice from the intercom on the wall interrupted him.

"State your business," the voice said. "I can see you from the camera above the doors."

Both Chris and Diana glanced up to see a surveillance camera directed right at them.

"My mother's in Emergency," Diana said quickly. "I have to see her."

"State your name and your mother's name, please," the voice said impersonally.

A security guard patrolled the main quad area. He stopped near a central fountain that had been turned off for the night and stared at Chris

and Diana as if this was the first interesting moment in an otherwise
monotonous shift.

Chris nodded at the guard, who nodded back solemnly.

"Diana Lowe. My mother's Betty Miller," Diana said into the intercom.

"Spell that last name, please."

Diana felt so frustrated by this delay that she wanted to bash in the
camera. "M-i-l-l-e-r," she said angrily.

"Thank you. Just one minute."

Chris put his arm around Diana's shoulder, pulling her protectively
close to him. "Try to keep calm," he whispered. "Your mother needs to
see you strong."

Diana replied, "I know. It's just—"

A buzzer sounded and the voice said, "Enter now and take the elevator down to the basement."

The harsh glare of the fluorescent lights in the emergency ward made
Diana squint and gave her an uneasy sense that everything happening here
was surreal: an accident victim covered in blood, the sounds of pain and
choking, the odor of antiseptics and the faint sour smell of illness and
human wastes.

Chris found the emergency admitting room. Diana followed him in
and approached the desk. "Is Betty Miller still here?" she asked a tired-
looking receptionist who sat swigging a Diet Coke.

The woman looked up at Diana. "Miller? When she come in,
honey?"

Diana eyed Chris. She was so distraught now that she drew a blank.

"At least two hours ago. Probably longer," Chris answered for her.
"They brought her in by ambulance."

"I'll check." The receptionist pushed her overweight body up out of
her chair. She waddled on stubby legs to a pile of folders and selected one
to scan with a chubby finger. Diana noted her frosted orange nails were
like a parrot's claws, long and curved downward. The woman glanced up,
wiped a strand of hair off her face, then said finally, "*Betty* Miller?"

Diana and Chris nodded.

"She's been transferred to the ICU. Says here she had a stroke."

"Oh, God! Chris . . ."

Chris gazed at Diana sympathetically. "Let's not jump to conclusions
before we know everything," he said quietly.

"Where's the ICU?" Diana demanded of the receptionist.

"First floor. Go past the oil painting of Mamie and the President and turn right. Then follow that corridor to the end. You can't miss it. Ring the bell and . . ."

Diana was out the door before the woman could finish her instructions. Chris stayed to hear the woman out, then sped after Diana, but he missed the elevator she had gotten into.

Diana stopped in the main floor lobby to orient herself. There was nothing hospital-like about it: the floors carpeted in desert beige; colorful southwestern paintings lined two of the walls; the information booth was open and nonthreatening, as innocuous as a concierge's desk in a posh hotel; large bronze plaques covered the other walls, appearing weighty and important. She knew the list of names included local and international celebrities, all benefactors of this medical oasis in the desert. The only eyesore in this otherwise dignified and serene lobby was a pair of clear glass spherical chandeliers suspended like monstrous sea urchins with long lighted spiny projections, reminding Diana as she raced to her mother's side of the garish, tasteless decor of a Las Vegas casino.

When Diana reached the Intensive Care Unit she pressed the bell and waited for an answer. "I'm here to see Betty Miller," she responded to a woman's voice coming through a mesh intercom speaker in the wall next to the bell.

"Just a minute," the voice said.

Diana stood shifting her weight, feeling numb and edgy at the same time, wondering where Chris was. As she looked down the corridor, she noted that once she had left the lobby, the rest of the building looked just like any other hospital, with that same stale twenty-four-hour feeling that always depressed her so.

"What's happening?" Chris asked, striding quickly toward Diana.

"Someone's coming out."

"Good."

He stood leaning against the beige wall, his hands stuffed into his jeans pockets. Chris appeared calm and in control, the opposite of the way she imagined she must look now. Diana was grateful he was with her, even if he could do nothing but hand-holding. She couldn't even fathom what Rodney might have done in this situation—if he had enough time to be there with her.

Thoughts of Harvey filled her mind. She knew exactly how he would have acted. He would have made a dozen calls before they even left the house in Encino; he would have insisted on talking to Betty's doctors, would have demanded to be informed and apprised of every aspect of her mother's case. Harvey's need to take over had always been a kind of luxurious crutch for Diana; part of her longed even now for that comforting sort of caretaking despite all the downside consequences for her self-esteem that had come along with it.

One of the heavy double doors to the ICU swung open a crack, and a young nurse stood between them, only her curly blond head poking out. Diana glanced past her to see if she could spot Betty. She couldn't.

"Your mother is resting comfortably," the nurse said in a sweet voice. "What is your name?"

"Diana. D-Diana Lowe," she stuttered, starting to shiver.

The nurse smiled at Chris. "Another family member?" she asked.

"Uh." Diana glanced questioningly at Chris, then back at the nurse. She noted the woman had a patch of moles near her left eyebrow, detracting from her otherwise flawless complexion and pretty face. "Would it make a difference?" Diana asked. She wanted Chris to go in with her to see Betty; he had told her in the car on the agonizing ride down to the desert that he felt very close to her mother.

"We do only allow immediate family," she answered, stepping outside the doors into the corridor and letting them close silently behind her. She took a pamphlet from a plastic sleeve on the wall next to the intercom and handed it to Diana. "Read this. It will be helpful."

Diana took the white folded paper from the nurse like an obedient child and held it in her hand without looking at it. "He's her nephew," Diana lied, glancing at Chris who stood looking as innocent as a lamb.

The nurse eyed Chris, then Diana. She smiled knowingly. "Of course. Would both of you like to come in for a few minutes to see Betty?"

Diana nodded. Chris stepped forward, taking Diana's hand. His hand was cold, like hers. She realized he was as scared and nervous as she was.

They followed the nurse into the ICU. She explained that the machines Betty was hooked up to might seem a bit scary. They made noises that sometimes frightened visitors into thinking the patient was in distress. In fact, she said, the opposite was true; the blips and gurgles and whirs and hums were all telling the nursing station how the patient was faring. The sounds were good signs, not bad.

Every bed in the ICU was filled. Most of the patients were asleep; some stirred and moaned. All were hooked up to the machines the nurse had warned them about. Diana wanted to cover her eyes. Trying to make herself blind to all the suffering, she looked straight ahead, focusing inward.

"Here she is," the nurse announced.

Betty was draped with a sheet. Diana took one look at her mother and felt her legs collapse under her. Betty looked ghastly. And none of the soothing explanations the nurse had given had prepared Diana for the sight of her mother unconscious and with her face contorted, hooked up to I.V. drips and to a slew of machines, including one that was breathing for her.

Chris caught Diana under the elbow and steadied her until she recovered sufficiently to remain upright on her own.

"She looks so . . . so twisted!" Diana cried. "What would make her look like that?"

"Edema, perhaps. Paralysis, perhaps."

"Oh, God! Oh, God," Diana murmured.

"She's had a rough night," the nurse said sympathetically. "But she's doing better now. Much more stable than when they brought her up from Emergency."

"Has she been unconscious all this time?" Chris asked in a near whisper.

The nurse nodded at him. He continued to look grimly at Betty. She explained, "Betty's in a coma. When the doctor returns he'll be able to give you more information."

"Call him," Diana ordered, feeling she had to play Harvey's role now that he wasn't here.

"It's four-thirty," the nurse said. "There's no emergency. I really can't bother the doctor. He'll be back in a few hours."

Diana didn't have the emotional fortitude to start a fight with this understanding, kind nurse even though she knew Harvey would have stood his ground until he got his way. "I'll be outside that door waiting for him," she said, tears stinging her eyes suddenly.

The nurse noticed the tears welling up in Diana's eyes and patted her arm. "I understand how frightening this is for you. Please trust me, though. Will you do that?"

Diana nodded reluctantly.

"Go home and get some rest. Come back in a few hours. Stroke patients in a coma need to hear your voice and sense your presence. When you read that pamphlet you'll see it's important for you to sound fresh and optimistic, not sad and scared."

"We'd better do as she says," Chris said, taking Diana by the arm and gently leading her out of the brightly lit ICU.

Once they were out in the corridor, Diana said forcefully, "I can't leave her alone even for one minute. You go to her condo and get some rest." She started fumbling through her purse. "I'm going to sit right by this door until she wakes up."

"But—"

"I can't leave." Diana unhooked her mother's condo key from her chain and handed it to Chris. "I just can't."

"Okay." He turned, then stopped. "This is stupid," he said, pressing the key back into Diana's hand. "I can't leave you here alone. Not even for one minute."

For the next thirty hours, Diana and Chris made the hospital corridor their home. They found a couple of uncomfortable chairs in the coronary surgery waiting room and pushed them out into the hall for their own use. It was better than sitting on the floor, they both decided, after having tried that for several hours the first morning.

Except for the very real physical discomfort Diana was enduring, nothing seemed real about the time she was spending in this hospital. She lived for those five-minute visits with Betty every hour. Then, as Diana stood at her bedside watching the machine push air into her mother's lungs, studying the unmoving face of the woman who had always been there for her no matter what, Diana wondered what she would do if her mother never again opened her eyes. The mere thought overwhelmed Diana with a sadness that had no form, a sense of exasperation that made her want to scream and kick.

Only Chris's calming presence kept her from totally losing control over her emotions.

He sat patiently, her intelligent but unobtrusive sounding board, as she went over and over the phrases the doctor had used: blocked carotid artery leading to the brain, ischemic episodes, showers of clots, brain damage, cardiac arrest. He had asked Diana whether she wanted any heroic life-saving measures. . . .

Chris and Diana spent hours telling stories about their family lives. His had been so different from Diana's—parents rarely home even before their divorce, servants to cater to his every whim. He'd been lonely growing up that way; his only sister had been ten years older and long gone from the house before he could develop a relationship with her. Diana, on the other hand, had been raised in a home with both parents always there for her. It had been a home filled with laughter and love. Her father had been a manufacturer of costume jewelry, and although he had traveled extensively, Diana's memories were of her father and her mother always there. They had spoiled their only child, Diana admitted to Chris, and sheltered her, too. In fact, she said to him, her growing-up years had been so uneventful that they seemed boring compared to his life.

"That's the kind of boring I wanted for my girls," he told her.

"I don't know what I'd have done without you here," she told him.

"I am a pretty indispensable guy," he joked, using humor sparingly but with impeccable timing to perk her up whenever she seemed to be winding down to another low point.

"Harvey always made it easy for me, you know. Taking over at times like these."

"What a guy!" Chris said sarcastically. She seemed somewhat taken aback by the forcefulness of his remark. "I'm sorry. You probably miss him."

She paused thoughtfully, then said, "Not anymore."

Chris got up from his chair and came to sit on the wooden arm of Diana's. Several other people lined the corridor now waiting to hear about their loved ones. They all looked up when Chris changed his place, for any movement was of interest in an otherwise agonizing and boring wait.

He kneaded Diana's shoulders and she sighed. "That feels good," she said softly. "You always know just what I need."

"That's my specialty," he said, finishing his one-minute massage, then standing up to stretch.

They had been in that same corridor, or in the nearby coronary care waiting room, seemingly forever.

She looked at her watch and saw that it was five o'clock. "Is it day or night?" Diana asked.

"Beats me," Chris said. "Let's go outside and find out. You can't go in again for an hour anyway."

As they ambled past the dancing waters of the central fountain and saw the bustle of activity in the hospital parking lot, they concluded it must be five in the evening.

They walked past boxed oleander trees, their pastel pink blossoms in full bloom, toward a lagoon where white wrought-iron benches had been placed under purple-flowered jacaranda trees. They settled on a bench near a bridge that connected a satellite building to the main one.

Neither of them spoke for several minutes.

"A penny for your thoughts," Chris said at last.

"I was thinking how busy we all are with our little dramas, how important we make so many unimportant things." She paused and stared at Chris. "Then something catastrophic happens to jolt us, and it puts our lives into perspective." Chris put his arm around Diana. She said, "You know, I haven't even thought of Three Amigos in almost two days."

"I recall when I was at Rutgers," Chris said solemnly, "I was worrying about midterms. I mean neurotically worrying about them. Then John Kennedy was assassinated. My own crisis paled in comparison to that cosmic tragedy. Since then I've tried to keep the events in my life in perspective."

"How did you do on your exams?" Diana asked.

"I flunked them all," he said with a twinkle in his eyes, "but I didn't care."

Diana laughed and said, "We'd better get back inside. It's almost time for the next visit with Mom."

When they stood up, a pure white crane fluttered out of the water to perch gracefully atop a fountain jet that had been turned off in the lagoon. The bird seemed to be looking straight at Diana. Was that an omen of good things? she wondered.

Betty's attending physician was coming out of the ICU just as Chris and Diana returned to their chairs in the corridor.

"Oh, Diana," he said, his eyes shaded by bushy blond eyebrows. "I'm glad to see you. I don't want to get your hopes up too high, but while I was checking Betty a few minutes ago, her eyes fluttered open."

"That's great!" Chris exclaimed.

"Does that mean she's alert?" Diana asked.

"Not necessarily. She was not responsive to my commands. But it could mean that whatever swelling she had in the area of the clot is subsiding."

"Yes . . . ?" Diana said.

"Well, that could mean she might regain consciousness. The brain damage question is still up in the air."

"Can I go in now?" Diana asked him.

"Certainly," the doctor answered. "I want you to talk to her. As you know, the sound of a familiar voice can help."

Diana rushed into the ICU and hurried to her mother's bedside, thinking of the majestic crane staring at her. Maybe the impossible was possible.

"Mom," Diana said cheerily, "it's Diana." She had said this same sentence a hundred times in the last hours. Now she said it with new conviction. "I know you opened your eyes a few minutes ago. Would you open them for me now? I want to see if yours are greener than mine," Diana said. Nothing happened. She took her mother's sere hand in hers, squeezed it, hoping to feel some response. Nothing happened. Her spirits sagged. "Come on, Mom. I know you want to hear all about Todd and Jessica. About my book." She kept talking, aware of the five minutes ticking by, aware that Betty seemed as lifeless as ever.

At the end of five minutes, Diana reluctantly laid her mother's hand at her side on top of the sheet. Suddenly she thought she saw Betty's hand twitch. She stared at it and waited. Nothing more happened. Overwhelmingly distraught, Diana felt her eyes fill with tears. She wished the doctor had not given her such hope. She felt tricked. Frustrated. "Hope" was becoming a dirty word in her mind.

Then Betty's fingers moved again.

"Mom?" Diana whispered, bending close to her mother's face. "Mom? I love you, Mom."

She stood up and saw her mother's eyes open. They appeared unfocused, watery almost. Lifeless.

"Mom, it's me. Diana."

Betty closed her eyes. Diana felt that something very precious was slipping away from her. She wanted to grab her mother, shake her, make her come back into her body.

A nurse approached. "Diana," she said gently, "time's up for now."

Diana whirled around and cried, "I can't leave now! She opened her eyes."

The nurse's expression changed to one of avid interest. "Really?" She walked over to Betty's side and flicked her arm with her thumb and index finger, saying at the same time, "Betty, open your eyes."

Diana watched. She waited, praying without even knowing it.

Betty's eyes opened again. This time there was something akin to life in them. She was focusing them.

The nurse smiled at Diana. "You're right. I think she may be coming out of the coma."

"Oh, dear God! Thank God. Mom!"

Betty blinked, then opened her eyes wide. She focused only on Diana.

"Mom, you're going to be okay," Diana said, standing next to Betty again, looking intently into her mother's eyes. "I love you."

Betty blinked and one lone tear appeared in the corner of her eye and rolled down her cheek. Diana bent down and kissed it away. "I'm here now. You're going to get well," she whispered, almost too overwhelmed with happiness to keep her own tears in check.

"Would you like to have her nephew come in to see her, too?" the nurse asked Diana.

Diana appeared baffled for a second. Then she smiled. "Oh, Chris. Please, would you get him?"

Chris and Diana stood for another five minutes, watching Betty's awakening like proud parents standing over their firstborn's crib.

The next ordeal was the removal of Betty's breathing tube and the anxious wait to see if she could breathe on her own. When Betty had passed through that trial with flying colors, she was moved from the crowded ICU into a private room.

By the time the doctor and every nurse on Betty's floor convinced Diana that she could leave her mother in their very capable hands, it was almost nine o'clock in the evening.

Feeling stale and smelly in the same clothes in which they had arrived, Diana and Chris decided to shower at Betty's condo in Palm Desert before inflicting themselves on the general public.

Although ravenous by now—neither one of them had eaten more than coffee and fruit since arriving in Palm Desert—Diana wanted to call her kids and tell them the good news about their grandmother before going out to dinner. Jessica wanted to fly right down, but Diana talked her out of that. Todd started to cry when he heard Betty was out of the woods. After a few speechless moments he recovered enough to tell his mother she had a couple of important messages. Harvey had called, and when he learned of Betty's stroke he insisted Todd tell Diana he was available if she needed him. "Rodney Carter called a dozen times, too," Todd told her. He said he was going out of the country on business for a few days, but he had gotten the name and phone number of the marketing director at Jupiter Candy Company, and he wanted her to have it right away. "He also wanted to know if you liked the roses," Todd added.

"What roses?" she asked.

"The ones that are all over this house," Todd said with a mild tone of teenage disgust at such a blatant show of affection.

She knew the Three Amigos ploy was Rodney's way of trying to woo her back into his clutches. It wouldn't work. "It's okay, Todd. Just keep water in the vases. I can't believe him—roses in every room of the house!" Diana exclaimed.

Chris grabbed the phone away from Diana. "Throw the damned things out," he told Todd with a laugh, then handed the phone back to Diana. "I can compete with a Rolls-Royce," he said to Diana, "but I can't compete with a guy who's going to put his florist at the top of the *Fortune* Five Hundred."

By ten-thirty Chris and Diana had finished spreading the good news about Betty to their children and just about every one of their friends.

In a mood for celebration, they set out to find a café that served noninstitutional meals, preferably a place without bright fluorescent lights. Diana directed Chris to the El Paseo section of Palm Desert, the ritzy avenue that had replaced in allure Palm Canyon Drive, the famous main drag in Palm Springs.

Chris couldn't believe what had sprung up in the few years since he had last been down there. The buildings were all desert chic—part Egyptian, part Greco-Roman, part southwestern terra-cotta and rough-hewn beams; and every prominent designer seemed to have a shop of his own in which to display his wares.

They found a trattoria that was still serving dinner; they sat on the patio under an inky black sky dusted with brilliant stars. They ate pasta and drank Pinot Grigio to the strains of George Gershwin tunes coming through speakers attached to the lattice trellis above them. They toasted Betty's recovery and all good things for everyone in the world they had ever known or might know.

In this generous, expansive, and tipsy mood, they strolled along El Paseo for a short while after dinner, then drove back to Betty's condo.

They found half a bottle of wine in the refrigerator. Diana filled two glasses and suggested they sit outside for a while. After calling the hospital once again to check Betty's condition, they stretched out on two chaises and chatted about everything, about nothing. Easy talk. Comforting company.

Diana yawned and fell silent. Chris continued to talk to her, then stopped when he realized she was sound asleep, the glass tipping and almost out of her hand.

He removed the glass and put it on the wrought-iron table with his.

Chris picked her up and murmured, "You're as light as a feather."

Diana's eyes fluttered open. She smiled languidly, then closed her eyes. Her head fell gently against Chris's neck as he carried her into Betty's room and laid her on the bed.

After staring at Diana for a long time, he walked to the door to leave.

He turned and stared at her again, hesitating. He walked back, took off his clothes, and lay down next to her. He shut off the table lamp and lay there, staring into the darkness until Diana inched her way closer to him. Then he closed his eyes, snuggling into the curve of her back.

He fell asleep, his own breathing tuning itself to the rhythm of hers.

Diana awoke with a start a couple of hours after Chris had settled her on her mother's bed. She was surprised to see Chris lying beside her, nearly naked.

The bedroom had become chilly. She got up, careful not to awaken Chris who was in a deep sleep, and tiptoed across the room to turn on the heat. Then she took off her jeans, socks, and T-shirt, leaving on her underwear.

She slipped back into bed and lay with a space between her and

Chris. She thought about him. Disjointed thoughts, middle-of-the-night thoughts: how much he meant to her as a friend, how she didn't want to become just another one of his conquests but wanted to remain special to him, how physically attracted she was to him.

She dozed, falling slowly back to sleep. Suddenly in her half-twilight state, she was aware of Chris's body next to hers, of his hands almost absently caressing her.

She felt him push against her groin, his erection complete. Fully awake and aware now, she took off her bra, slipped out of her panties, and pressed her body into his, facing him.

"Chris," she whispered.

He opened his eyes. "I love you so much," he murmured sleepily.

She covered his face with kisses. She brazenly tugged his underwear down, and he slid into her.

He rolled onto his back, pulling her along with him until she was astride his beautiful body. Just the thought of his strong stomach muscles excited her. Just the feel of his hair and his arms made her delirious. Just the look of love in his eyes, as he fixed them on her while his own pleasure grew, made her feel blessed. And when he finally let go and ground her into him with each thrust and caress of his hands on her buttocks, they reached a simultaneous climax that had both of them laughing and crying at the same time.

They awoke in each other's arms a few hours later.

"I can't believe I'm in love with my best friend," Chris said as he soaped Diana's body in the shower.

"Now, that's a miracle," she kidded him, returning the sensual favor.

"See what you do to me," he laughed, pushing his erection into her soapy hand.

"Me and a few hundred other women," she said, one wet eyebrow arched.

"C'mere," he said, sitting down and pulling her on top of him. "There's nobody for me but you."

They made wet and wild love with the water crashing down upon them.

Diana had never felt so happy.

"Would you have loved me if I had stayed fat?" she asked as they drove back to the hospital to visit Betty.

Chris took a long time to answer. He eyed Diana with his most serious expression and said, "I think I have loved you for a long time. Fat was your obstacle, not mine. It was you who kept me away."

"Well, I was happily married, or so I thought."

"No, even after you and Harvey split up, you gave me some sort of hands-off message."

"I've had a lot of growing up to do in this past year," She sat contemplatively, then said, "You know, Chris, maybe now that there's less of me, I have more to give."

Chris smiled and suddenly swerved the car off the road, pulling to a stop on the soft shoulder of Country Club Drive. "I love you, Diana Lowe!" he shouted, then pulled her into his arms and kissed her passionately for several breathless minutes.

"Doesn't everything look more beautiful today?" she said a few minutes later when they were walking toward the hospital building. "Isn't the white on the buildings whiter? The green grass greener? I'm so happy I feel like a kid. I'm so happy I'm seeing everything through rose-colored glasses."

"Don't mention roses," he warned with a laugh, grabbing her hand at the same time.

Hand in hand, they practically skipped up the steps into the quiet lobby. He nuzzled Diana's neck on the ride up to Betty's floor, drawing furtive glances and some outright smiles from the other passengers. "She loves me," Chris said to the people as he and Diana left the elevator and walked down the corridor.

"You are so silly," she admonished him with a little pat on the fanny.

"So are you," he answered, pinching her butt.

Diana was stunned for a minute by his remark. Harvey had hated her silliness, her "stupid" jokes, as he had called them. Chris appreciated her. "I love you," she whispered to him at the door to Betty's room.

The private-duty nurse looked up from a magazine she was reading in a chair across the room from Betty's bed. She nodded. Diana and Chris, still all smiles, nodded back.

Betty lay still, her eyes closed.

"How's she doing now?" Diana asked. She had phoned again earlier in the morning and had learned that Betty was still resting comfortably.

"Same as before," the nurse said. She was a dark-skinned woman, tall and angular. She looked as if she might be part Indian.

Diana nodded and approached her mother's bedside. "Hi, Mom," she said gaily. "I'm here to see you."

Betty opened her eyes. They seemed wavery again, but she didn't close them. After a few minutes, they seemed to focus on Diana and Chris, who now also stood at Betty's side.

"Mom, I want to tell you something wonderful," Diana said, blushing. "Chris and I—"

"We're in love," Chris finished for Diana. His voice sounded sure and confident.

Betty blinked.

"I hope you understand," Diana said.

The nurse chimed in, "She might. Then again . . ."

Chris turned to wait for her to finish her sentence, but she was already looking down at her magazine.

He shrugged and winked at Diana. "Betty, I need some of those cookies you made for me at Diana's. My pixilated princess won't put any fat in them for me now."

They went on chatting with Betty for some time as though she were actually participating in the conversation.

As happy as she was, Diana felt a drain of energy as she pretended her mother was responding.

At last even Chris tired of the charade and they both sat down and just stared at each other.

"I don't think she knows us," Diana admitted sadly.

"Don't be so sure," the nurse responded. She asked them to watch over Betty while she went to get a glass of juice.

The nurse had been gone for no more than a few seconds when Betty began to make sounds.

Diana jumped up and rushed across the room to her mother's bedside, followed by Chris.

Betty's eyes were moving wildly now and she seemed agitated. Even her once inert fingers were clenching and unclenching. Diana grabbed her mother's hand and held it tightly.

"Mom, it's me!" Diana cried. "You're going to be okay."

Betty was trying to move her mouth now.

"She's aware, Chris."

Chris nodded. "Maybe I'd better get the nurse anyhow." Before Diana could reply, Chris had darted out the door and disappeared.

"Do you know how much I love you?" Diana said. "How I need you to get better, Mom?"

Betty's eyes moved. She tried to move her lips as well; nothing but gurgling sounds came out. Then Diana felt the tiniest sensation of her mother's hand squeezing hers.

Chris returned with the nurse to find Diana in tears.

"What's wrong?" he asked as the nurse raced over to Betty.

Diana looked up at Chris. "Nothing. She knows I love her. She squeezed my hand."

An hour later the nurse asked Diana and Chris to take a walk while she bathed Betty.

They went to their favorite area under the jacaranda trees next to the lagoon. They sat on the grass watching the ducks and the crane in the water.

" 'God's in his heaven, all's right with the world,' " Diana said to Chris as they made their way slowly back to the hospital building. "That's how I feel today," she sighed. "Do you know who said that? For the life of me, I can't recall."

"Robert Browning," Chris replied instantly. "Everybody knows that," he kidded her, then planted a wet kiss on the tip of her nose.

They rode the elevator up, kidding each other about who knew more lines of poetry by heart, vowing to have a contest in the car on the way back to Los Angeles.

As they rounded the corner to Betty's corridor, they both stopped talking. There was controlled pandemonium outside Betty's room.

Diana broke into a run. Chris followed. Both of them were stopped outside the door by a burly orderly who blocked the entrance.

"What's going on?" Diana said, feeling a ring of ice form around her heart.

The orderly eyed Betty's private nurse. "Your mother's had a cardiac arrest," the nurse said in a quiet, dull monotone. "Please cooperate. You can't go in there now."

"When?" Diana cried. Had it been just at the moment she was believing there was a God and he was looking down on her? "When?" she shouted.

Chris pulled her away from the door so another group of doctors and technicians could get into the room.

"Diana . . ." He held her, saying nothing more for many tense moments.

She knew instantly from the looks of defeat on the faces of the people coming out of her mother's room that they had not saved her.

Still, they made Diana wait until they "cleaned her up" before letting her go in to sit with death. "I have to be alone with her," she explained to Chris.

Betty looked peaceful. Diana was struck by the thought that this was the last time she would be with her mother; she knew Betty wouldn't want an open casket at her funeral.

"Mom, what am I going to do without you?" she whispered, tears coursing down her cheeks.

She reached down and touched her mother's lifeless hand. She bent over and kissed her cold cheek. She thought for a minute Betty was going to tell her—as she always had whenever Diana had a bad dream—not to be afraid.

I'm nobody's child now, Diana thought, as she finally broke away and walked out of the room.

Chapter

· ·

24

It was not the right sort of day for a funeral, Harvey thought as he parked his Porsche at the curb next to the cemetery chapel. The sun shone too brightly, the weather was too mild, the breeze too gentle; thunder, lightning, and torrential downpours were more appropriate for mourning.

At least fifty cars already were parked in orderly lines ready for the procession to the grave site after the service. Harvey was surprised; he had expected a smaller turnout for a woman who had lived out of town for so many years.

He straightened his black and gray tie, checked to make sure his French cuffs were just peeking out from under the sleeves of his charcoal Giorgio Armani suit, then walked through a milling group of older people with deep desert suntans, nodding to them as he passed through into the Forest Lawn chapel in Glendale with the authoritative air of someone who belonged.

In reality, Harvey was nervous as hell. He had talked to Diana once since Betty's death; she had still been in Palm Desert. Diana had shocked him when she suggested he think long and hard about coming to the funeral, considering all the horrible things he had said about her mother only last year.

"People say a lot of things they don't really mean when they're upset," he had replied in his defense.

"Oh, do they?" she had answered. "I see."

He had been so taken aback by her attack that he was not nearly
forceful enough when he offered to come and arrange for the return of
Betty's body to Los Angeles. She had thanked him coolly but declined his
help, and he had been unable to get her to change her mind.

Diana had done a good job, he decided, seeing the pewter casket
covered with sprays of white flowers on a bier at the front of the small
chapel. Elegant choice, he thought.

He stood at the back of the room, which was fast filling up with
mourners, looking for familiar faces. He spotted Betty's brothers and sis-
ters and their spouses huddled together in the front near the casket. Old
friends wandered over to them to say hello, to pat them on the back, to
hug. Harvey made his way down the center aisle and approached them,
too. The way they greeted him—openly, with affection—made him think
that Betty had not told them much about his leaving Diana. He was
relieved.

Standing in the front of the tiny chapel now, he turned and noticed a
covey of his and Diana's friends. He nodded toward some of them, many
whom he had not seen in almost a year. Others, like Billy and Carol
Benton, got up and walked over to speak to him.

"I'm glad you decided to come after all," Billy said to Harvey.

Harvey nodded, looking properly solemn. He brushed Carol's cheek
with a kiss. "Have you seen Diana?" she asked him.

Harvey looked around for his wife and children. "No. But I plan to
sit with them," he explained.

Carol's expression registered surprise. "Does Diana know that?" she
asked.

"I haven't spoken to her," he answered, "since that first day. But I've
talked it over with the kids. They agree that it would be appropriate."

Carol eyed Billy. "This should be interesting," she mumbled under
her breath, then excused herself to return to her pew.

"How's the back?" Harvey asked Billy, who looked uncomfortable
now.

"Back? Oh, getting better. Best thing I ever did was listen to you and
change doctors."

"Thanks," Harvey said, beaming. He noticed a striking woman out of
the corner of his eye and turned to see her better. "That's Alison Rifkin!"
he said to Billy. "What's she doing here?"

Billy turned to see where Harvey was pointing. "I was wondering who she was," Billy said. "A real looker. I hear from Carol she's the one who helped get Diana the book contract."

Mark Rifkin suddenly walked down the aisle, spotted Harvey, and nodded, then went to sit with his wife without coming over to say hello.

Harvey was both irate and puzzled by this odd turn of events. How in the world had Diana become friends with *his* friends, especially since he and Mark were arch rivals now?

A mortuary assistant walked out of a side door, a signal that the service might begin soon.

"I'd better go find Diana and the kids," he said to Billy.

Billy nodded, punched Harvey lightly on the arm, then went to rejoin his wife.

Harvey went up to the funeral assistant, a somber middle-aged man whose gray hair, face, and suit all blended together, and asked him for directions to the family pews. He took Harvey outside and left him at the private entrance to the mourners' partitioned area. "In there," the man said, his voice a low, modulated drone, which he must have been trained to think was soothing; it grated on Harvey.

Harvey opened the door and saw Chris Berry standing next to a slender woman in black. Her back was to him, but he could tell that she had a flair for clothes, dressed as she was in a designer suit with a narrow, straight skirt that was slit to expose beautiful, shapely calves, and a jacket whose peplum flared out, accentuating her tiny waist. Covering her curly hair was a wide-brimmed black hat. He decided she was either Chris's girlfriend—one of his young honeys, probably—or a young relative of Diana's whom he had never met.

Harvey shut the door behind him. He wondered briefly if Diana had stepped out for a minute.

"Dad," Todd said, standing up to greet his father.

Chris Berry stopped talking and the woman turned around.

"Harvey," Diana said quietly, stepping toward him.

"Diana?" he said, unable to keep the stunned questioning tone out of his response.

Jessica somehow was at his side now. "Daddy! It is Mom. We told you she'd changed."

Harvey eyed his daughter, then glanced at his son. Both of their faces registered such pride when they gazed at their mother that Harvey felt somehow diminished. Suddenly his face felt hot; he suspected he was bright red.

"Diana," he said again. Impulsively, he took her hand and pulled her into an embrace. "I'm sorry about Mom," he whispered.

Diana pulled away from him, carefully rearranging her hat, which had been dislodged during his impromptu hug. "You remember Chris Berry," she said.

"Saw your new show," Harvey told Chris. "Liked it."

"Thanks," Chris answered. "We've gotten good reviews. Guess that means I'll be working for a few more months." He eyed Diana. She smiled at him, an intimate smile. Harvey turned his head, feeling jealous that she was eyeing some other man the way she used to look at him.

Harvey's discomfort was alleviated when the minister entered the partitioned family mourning area and said solemnly, "Are the grandchildren still planning to speak?"

Diana nodded.

"Then we're ready to begin," the minister said, leading the way into the chapel.

Another awkward moment swept over them when Diana sat down and motioned to Chris to sit next to her in the pew just as Harvey walked over to do the same thing.

Jessica and Todd looked stricken. Diana looked embarrassed and enraged at the same time.

"You know," Chris said quickly, "I think it would be better if I sat with your friends." He stood up, squeezed Diana's hand, smiled at Todd and Jessica, who looked grateful, and departed before Harvey knew what had hit him.

Feeling smug now, Harvey took his seat next to Diana. In some ways he was grateful to his mother-in-law; her death had allowed him the opportunity to be with his beautiful wife and children—where he belonged.

"My grandmother Betty was a special woman," Jessica began when it was her turn to speak. "She was generous and giving; she was sweet and understanding." Harvey only half listened; he was thinking about Diana. He still couldn't believe she was the same woman he had left. He would have been willing to bet his dental practice that Diana couldn't lose fifteen pounds successfully, let alone fifty—and keep the weight off. Harvey would not have recognized her if he'd run into her on the street. She was even more beautiful today than she had been when he had fallen in love with her in college.

"And so, dear Grandma," Jessica was concluding, "you will be missed."

Then it was Todd's turn. He seemed more nervous than Jessica, less willing to lay his feelings out in the open. Harvey ached for his son, feeling more responsive to the boy's emotions than he had ever felt toward Jessica's. That's the way it is with fathers and sons, Harvey had often thought in the past. He forced himself to pay attention.

"My, uh, grandmother was very special to me," Todd said haltingly, glancing over toward Diana in the sectioned-off pew. "Like Jessica said, she was a rare lady. Capable of making me feel like one in a million. My grandmother loved our family unconditionally, without reservations. . . ."

Todd was really becoming a man, Harvey thought with great pride. When had it happened? Harvey felt jealous again; Diana had been luckier than he had been during this past year.

"Like my mother," Todd said, grabbing Harvey's wandering attention, "my grandmother loved me even when I wasn't very lovable. She had the patience to wait for me to learn that family is everything. Grandma, you may be gone in body, but your spirit lives on in me, and in Jessica and Mom."

Harvey felt proud as a peacock as he observed his son. Without being able to see the other guests, he was sure there wasn't a dry eye in the place. Diana was crying quietly, too, and he took her hand in his.

"I feel as though the kids were talking to me," he whispered to her during a pause in the minister's closing remarks. "Family *is* all there is in the end."

Diana extracted her hand from his, but quietly. He was grateful she was not out to embarrass him. As he observed Diana, Harvey felt an intense desire to make love to her.

Harvey was relieved to see that his house was as he had remembered it—bright, cheerful, filled with flowers and wonderful smells.

Diana hadn't taken down their family portrait from its spot over the fireplace or removed any of the framed photographs from the lid of their baby grand piano.

He removed his suit jacket, donned a bartender's apron, and made himself comfortable behind the bar he had designed. He had specifically wanted it sunken so as not to obstruct the view of the garden. Everyone from the funeral, as well as a dozen or more who hadn't been able to attend the service, stopped by to express their condolences to Diana and her children, and by extension to Harvey.

Harvey hadn't felt so contented in months.

If only Chris Berry would dry up and blow away, everything would be perfect. Who did that prick think he was, anyway, horning in on this important day when Diana needed Harvey?

When Todd took over tending the bar for him for a while, Harvey planted himself at Diana's side. Only then did Chris Berry wander off to speak to others. Harvey didn't even care that Diana seemed peeved by his intrusion. He wanted her to know that he cared about her again.

People kept arriving all day, well past the dinner hour. Diana's cooking class students had made dozens of her recipes and had brought them over. Delicious aromas wafted out of the kitchen and the dining room where the chrome and glass table and fossil-stone buffet were laden with gourmet low-fat and traditional foods for their company. Harvey even sampled the students' cuisine and had to admit to Jessica, who stood by watching her father's reaction, that Diana had hit the jackpot with her diet.

"Her students love her," Jessica said to her father.

"That's because she's lovable," Harvey admitted.

"Oh, Daddy. That's the nicest thing you've ever said," Jessica exclaimed, throwing her arms around Harvey.

He was pleased to see that his daughter obviously wanted her mother and father to reunite.

Reunite!

Was that what he was thinking, too? Perhaps. It was an enticing thought suddenly.

Chris Berry had resumed his place next to Diana by the time Harvey had finished eating and talking to Jessica. Seeing no way to intervene again without seeming too much like a rival suitor, Harvey wandered from room to room, talking to guests like a bona fide host.

When he saw Diana wearily mounting the steps to the second floor, he excused himself from some of her relatives and started to follow her. He stopped when he saw that Chris had beaten him.

He felt angry. Who did this guy think he was, invading his territory as soon as Diana started looking good? He marched up the stairs, but some of his resolve had ebbed by the time he reached his bedroom door.

He hesitated at the entrance, thinking realistically for the first time since he'd seen Diana looking like a vision of loveliness at the chapel. *She doesn't belong to me anymore.*

His competitive spirit rising up nevertheless, Harvey purposefully pushed open the door and walked in. All the lights in the bedroom were off except two small recessed ones in the ceiling that spotlit a large contemporary oil painting, the last piece of art they had bought before their separation.

He could hear sounds of Diana's crying coming from the dressing room.

Harvey found Diana in Chris's arms, sobbing. He held her as ten-

derly as Harvey ever had. It made him sick to see the way Chris smoothed
her hair with his huge paw, murmuring soothing words of comfort and
love.

Harvey wanted to murder him. He clenched and unclenched his fists.
He cleared his throat.

Startled, Chris looked toward the sound.

Harvey saw Diana stiffen in Chris's arms. She pulled back and turned
her tear-streaked face to stare at Harvey.

"Why are you doing this to me?" she asked him.

He looked stumped. "Why, uh."

"Can't you see what you're doing to her by being here?" Chris said.

Harvey cleared his throat again. "The last time I looked, this was my
house, too," he seethed. "Diana, are you telling me I'm not welcome here
at a time like this?"

Diana eyed Chris, then Harvey. She appeared to sag wearily into
Chris as she said, "No. I'm grateful for your support. It's just such a
strain."

Harvey looked triumphantly at Chris. "I guess that settles that."

He turned without another word and left them standing there, two
forlorn figures, watching him walk out the door.

As the crowd thinned out, however, and it became clear that Chris
Berry was not about to abandon Diana until she was too tired to keep her
eyes open, Harvey wearied of the tactical sparring. He told Diana and his
kids that he had early surgery in the morning and he had to get going.

He asked Diana to walk to the door with him. "I think we need to
get together and talk," he said.

"We do?" Diana replied, seemingly surprised.

"We have a lot of decisions to make."

"I don't know, Harvey." She hesitated. "I really can't think clearly at
a time like this."

"I understand," he said sincerely. "Diana, I want you to know that
I'm here for you. Really."

She nodded, saying nothing.

"You look beautiful, honey," he blurted suddenly. "I'm proud of all
you've done for yourself. I mean that."

Diana smiled faintly, tears filling her eyes. "Thanks. Somehow I still
care what you think of me," she said, then turned and walked back to
Chris.

Chapter

. . . .

25

For the first few hours after Betty died, Diana had been too stunned to respond with any real emotion, and before her numbness ebbed, she was thrown into the planning of the funeral, which had kept her too busy to fall apart. After the funeral, her children, friends, and visiting relatives had surrounded her; they behaved as though they were on a mission to protect Diana and distract her from her grief.

By the end of the week, however, the world had beckoned them. When she was finally alone, the utter desolation that her mother's death had caused came crashing down upon her.

She stopped taking calls, sat morosely in her bedroom reading her favorite poetry over and over, refusing to eat despite the frightened look on Todd's face when he saw her in the morning before school and again in the evening in a dark and depressing house. She wouldn't even see Chris, although she knew she was hurting him by shutting him out of her life; even knowing he was leaving soon for Hawaii couldn't rouse her out of her lethargy.

On the third day of her isolation, Chris stole into the house after Todd had left for school.

He found Diana wandering between the kitchen and the small study

off the entry hall, muttering something that sounded very much like a
T. S. Eliot poem to herself, looking wild-eyed and disheveled in a nightshirt and furry slippers.

"Oh, baby," he said, "you can't do this to yourself." He stopped her
and pulled her into his arms. She struggled to break free, but he held her
tightly. "Go ahead, get it out. Cry!"

As she looked into his eyes, the dam broke. She began to sob. "I feel
so unmoored. No father. Now no mother. Every last tie to my past is
gone."

He walked her into the study and sat down on the couch, holding her
close, his arm around her shoulders. He sat quietly, letting her speak
between her sobs.

"I keep thinking about how my mother and I grew apart during this
past year. It kills me to remember the hurt look in her eyes when I got
mad at her for eating too much, for not being able to change. . . . How
could I have been so selfish? She was there for me whenever I needed her.
And now she's gone. Just like that. I'll never have her to talk to again.
Chris," she wailed, "did she know how much I loved her?"

"She knew, sweetheart. She knew."

"I miss her so already. Little things keep popping into my mind. The
way she looked with flour on her face when she baked. Her laugh. The
sound of it. She was so much fun. She would have had the best time this
week," Diana said with a teary laugh suddenly. "She loved parties so
much."

"She gave you her love of life," Chris said thoughtfully. "She passed
on to you the best parts of herself. As Todd said, Betty's body may be
gone, but her spirit lives on. She lives on in you. Whenever you need the
right answer, look inward. Your mother will be there to help you see which
way to turn."

They sat in pensive silence. Diana was grateful for his patient presence, as always.

"I'm such an emotional mess," Diana finally admitted. She moved
out from under Chris's arm. "How do you put up with me?"

"You think you're weak; I just think you're human." He pulled her to
him and kissed her lightly. "Everyone I've ever met and gotten to know
past the first hello has turned out to be an emotional mess to some degree;
some of us just hide it better than you can in your vulnerable state."

"Vulnerable is right. Speaking of that, how did you get in here?" she
asked. "All the doors are locked."

"I broke in," he replied smugly.

"How?" she asked, looking frightened.

Chris looked at her face and quickly said, "I'm kidding. Todd gave me his key when he left for school. We plotted this whole thing yesterday. He was worried you might become suicidal."

"He asked you to come over and talk to me?"

Chris nodded. "That kid really loves you. Lots and lots. You're a lucky woman, Diana. I think you've got to pull yourself together for Todd, if for no one else. Your mother would understand if you got on with your life."

"I kept hearing this line of poetry go around and around in my head the past few days. It's by Edna St. Vincent Millay. It's about a woman whose husband has died. The next morning she says to her children, 'Anne, eat your breakfast; Dan, take your medicine. Life must go on; I forget just why.' "

Chris hugged Diana. He looked deep into her eyes and said softly, "Sometimes just enduring, going on with the mundane part of life, is all we can do."

"That's what I keep telling myself. Just keep breathing and maybe the pain will lessen." She tried to smile, but she couldn't. She stood up and faced the window looking out on her rose garden. "Rodney Carter called last night," Diana said, her back to Chris.

"Oh?"

Diana turned finally. Chris sat with his arms folded across his chest, one leg slung casually over the arm of the couch, a half-amused, half-questioning look in his eyes. She started to walk out of the room as she said, "He was on his jet bound for Madrid. He wanted to know how I was faring with my Three Amigos crusade."

"And?" Chris asked, following Diana up the stairs into her bathroom.

"I told him about Mother. He was quite solicitous. Said all the right things. He's good at that."

"Oh?" Chris replied, watching Diana take off her nightshirt and turn on the shower jets.

She eyed him ogling her and a faint trace of a playful smile entered her red-rimmed eyes. "He wants desperately to see me when he gets back."

"And what did you tell him?" Chris asked, yanking his T-shirt over his head, hastily stepping out of his faded jeans, and kicking off his red Topsiders.

"I told him I couldn't wait," Diana said coyly, disappearing into the steam of the shower, leaving the glass door open a crack.

"Oh, did you, now?" Chris said, coming up behind Diana and pressing his body into her back. He planted an open-mouthed kiss on the nape of her neck. "And did he tell you he wanted to do this to you, too?" Chris asked, turning Diana around to face him, then bending down to kiss her breasts. "Or this?" he murmured, planting little kisses down her midriff, then kissing her belly. "Or this?" he said, looking up at her for a second before burying his tongue between her thighs.

Diana called the marketing director of the Jupiter Candy Company the next morning. He was in a meeting, but when she mentioned Rodney Carter's name, his assistant said Mr. Binghamton had been expecting her call and would get back to her right away.

Binghamton finally called her late in the afternoon.

"Stan Binghamton here," he said, his tone formal. "I understand you have an interest in the future of Three Amigos."

Diana chuckled. "I suppose you might put it that way." She explained who she was, what she had discovered about the candy, and how she had incorporated it into a low-fat regimen that had set her neck of the woods on fire. Finally she told him that her publisher wanted to use their little candy bar as a hook to entice the reader.

Stan Binghamton said he was interested but added the caveat, "We're swamped with projects right now, and you should know that our company has never jumped into niche marketing before."

Diana felt a giant jolt of apprehension. "Niche marketing!"

"You know," Binghamton intoned, "targeting one consumer group over another. In this case, those who want a low-fat candy."

"But, Mr. Binghamton, losing weight has become a multibillion-dollar business. And my diet is the only one that advocates eating chocolate candy—your candy—as part of the regimen. Surely you must realize what a financial windfall that could be for your company."

Binghamton paused. She waited. "Well, you have a good point," he said at last. "But we have spent many millions of dollars reformulating after serious market testing."

"I know that, sir," she said, sounding a little more impatient with this bureaucrat than she intended. "But why couldn't you reintroduce the original candy bar and keep the new one, too?"

"I follow you, Mrs. Lowe. Really I do," Stan Binghamton replied. "And I promise you that your idea will get the full scrutiny of our entire department. You must understand, however, we are really swamped with other projects."

Diana hung up, unable to get his last sentence out of her mind, or the tone Stan Binghamton had used when he said it. He left her with a sinking feeling that he was going to file her request in his wastebasket because it was too problematic, coming so close on the heels of the successful introduction of the new Three Amigos bar into the marketplace.

"I'll give him ten days," she told Alison Rifkin, whom she called immediately afterward.

"Why don't you just call Beecham?" Alison replied. "I bet you've misunderstood their intent."

"No, I haven't, Alison," Diana answered. "Guinivere made it perfectly clear what they wanted. She kept talking about *The Eight Week Cholesterol Cure* and how oat bran is doing for its sales what she expects Three Amigos to do for my book."

"Couldn't your allergic-to-fat concept serve the same purpose? *I* love it."

"Oh, I don't know anymore. The Beecham people don't seem as excited about that as they are about the candy."

"I still think you should call Guinivere and find out for sure."

"I'm actually afraid to call. They'll want their money back if the candy connection is cut. I know it."

"Do you want me to snoop for you?" Alison offered.

"Maybe that would work," Diana said contemplatively.

"Just keep a good thought," Alison replied. "And remember, Diana, I'm here for you. If you want to talk. Anything."

No matter what Alison found out from the Beecham Press people, Diana resolved as she planned dinner for Todd and Chris, then met with one of her private clients for an hour, come hell or high water she was going to win the fight for that low-fat candy or go down in flames trying.

But when Alison called back awhile later with the depressing news that in her nosing around she did learn from Guinivere that Beecham was expecting to market the book with Three Amigos as a come-on, Diana's mood tumbled into darkness.

When Chris returned from a meeting with his agent, he found Diana morose again, whimpering about the book, crying about missing her mother. He offered to take Todd out for the evening, but she insisted that if they left her she would feel like an even greater failure.

She roused herself, washed her face, put on fresh makeup, and by eight o'clock had a passable meal on the table for the three of them.

During dessert, Diana announced, "I've been thinking it over. I don't want to lose that book contract."

"That's more like it, Mom," Todd exclaimed, looking at Chris.

"So it's a fight, is it?" Chris added.

"To the finish!" Diana retorted, looking more like her old self than she had in days.

Chris suggested it would be good therapy for her to begin writing the first chapters immediately and worry about Jupiter later.

She started late that night, long after Chris had gone home, long after Todd lay snoring lightly in his room.

When Todd came down for breakfast the next morning, he found Diana asleep at her desk in the study, the light still illuminated, the pencil still in her hand, the yellow legal pad on which she had been writing on the floor at her feet.

He gently extricated the pencil from Diana's hand, but she woke up anyway. "Oh, God, I ache everywhere," she moaned when she realized she had been sitting with her head bent over at an awkward angle for several hours.

"Whew," Todd said, handing his mother the legal pad. "You wrote almost twenty pages in one night!"

"I have a lot to say," she said. She picked up the tablet and scanned the pages quickly. "It's awful," she groaned, ripping half of them off and throwing them into the wastebasket. Then she laughed. "I've always wanted to do that. Like a real writer."

She bent over and retrieved the crumpled pages.

"Now what're you doing, Mom?" Todd asked, looking bewildered.

Diana smoothed the sheets of paper and laid them down on the desk. "I was just kidding. I actually think it's not too bad. Come on, I'll make you breakfast."

"Oh, you don't have to. Just keep writing. I'll make my own."

Diana stood staring at Todd. "You don't need me anymore!" she said. "My life's over."

Todd checked Diana's face to make sure she was kidding, then said jokingly, "Mom, I think your life is just beginning."

"Well, it can begin in half an hour, after you've left for school. Today I'm going to make you breakfast whether you like it or not! Is that clear, young man?"

Todd laughed. So did Diana. They walked arm and arm into the kitchen.

Harvey phoned soon after Todd left. He sounded depressed, and Diana's mood plummeted instantly.

"How's it going?" he asked. He had been calling her daily since the funeral, always asking the same question.

"Oh, okay," Diana said, as she did every time.

"That's good." He always said that, too. Then, as always, he launched into a short recap of his previous day's activities, and as always, Diana patiently listened. When he neared the end, she expected him to say he would call tomorrow to see how she was doing, but today he said, "I think it's time for us to get together. As I said last week, we have a lot to talk about."

Diana was wary. She hesitated.

"Don't you want to see me, Diana?" he asked.

He sounded so melancholy that Diana said, "Sure I do, Harvey. It's just that we've dealt with each other through attorneys until now, and I don't know why you suddenly want to change."

"I've been doing a lot of thinking."

"Oh," Diana said, remembering how she had felt the day she saw Harvey's smiling face next to Laurie's staring out at her from her son's skiing vacation pictures. "How's Laurie?" she asked icily.

"We're through. Finis. Kaput. Good riddance to bad rubbish."

"Is that what you told Laurie about me when you left me?" Diana lashed out.

Harvey sounded chastened. "Touché, Diana. I deserved that. That's why we have to talk. There's a lot of explaining I want to do. Face to face."

"I'll think about it," she said noncommittally.

"That's all I ask," he said happily.

When she and Chris walked to Ventura Boulevard for lunch at the Gold Grill, she recounted her conversation with Harvey.

"What should I do?" she asked Chris.

"That's not fair, sweetheart. You can't ask me to decide what a husband and a wife should do."

"Oh, Chris. Come on. Help me."

Chris held her hand as they walked silently for a long time. "Okay," he said just before they got to the restaurant, "let's put the shoe on the other foot. What if I told you Marylou wanted to meet with me to have a heart-to-heart talk? Would you want me to go?"

"First I'd swear I'd kill you if you did. Then I guess I'd insist you go."

"There's your answer."

"So you're telling me I have to meet with him," she said glumly as they sat down at their favorite table on the patio next to the babbling brook with its mossy, flowered banks.

He nodded, looking just as glum.

"Aren't you even going to fight for me—a little?" she said, picking at the thick slice of sourdough bread; she had lost her appetite.

"Maybe he only wants to talk about finances," Chris said, begging the question.

Diana squinted thoughtfully. "Maybe you're right."

"And if you put him off, make him angry, he could become vindictive. I've seen it happen."

Diana looked sick. "Harvey is capable of that. He really is."

"Then meet with him. Give him the benefit of the doubt."

"He wants to take me out for my birthday," Diana confessed. "Are you sure you can't stay in Encino another week?"

"Come to Hawaii for your birthday. I'll make a little nest for you to write at my house. We'll make love behind the cameras on the set between takes."

Diana sighed. "We're both too busy. I can't leave yet. There's Todd . . ."

Chris leaned over and kissed Diana, then sat back and stared lovingly at her. "Yeah, I understand."

"I know," she said with a smile.

Chapter

26

It was drizzling intermittently by the time Chris and Diana reached the Century City Mall, a sprawling outdoor complex on the north edge of the business community and adjacent to Twentieth Century-Fox studios. Chris had put off, until this last day in Los Angeles, attending to his daughters' shopping list of items they insisted could be found only in this particular center.

There was a bittersweet feeling between Chris and Diana as they walked arm in arm through the mall. They huddled in their thick parkas, as much to keep warm on this bitingly damp afternoon as to be physically close to each other during these last hours before parting again.

Chris made his purchases quickly, wasting no time in any of the stores. When they passed a funky new shop that specialized in cosmetics and hair ornaments, Diana persuaded him to go in with her so she could buy his girls an assortment of trinkets. Chris was visibly moved by her gesture. "Their mother should only be so thoughtful!" he said with a hard edge in his voice.

Diana eyed him, but said nothing. He didn't much like talking about Marylou and was reticent whenever Diana broached the subject of his pending divorce. But today, when they sat down for a cappuccino at

Boulangerie, a croissant shop in the mall, Chris spoke without prompting about his estranged wife and how angry he was that his daughters didn't have a positive female role model in their lives.

Diana listened as Chris ranted bitterly about his failed marriage. "Every time I look at my girls, I think how much they have been hurt by Marylou and me not being able to make a go of it."

"Would you take her back?" Diana asked, holding her breath until Chris said a vehement no.

"It's over. Dead as a doornail between us. We were two kids of the sixties. I grew up. She didn't. She may have traded in her love beads and leather sandals for healing crystals, channeling, and grizzlies, but 'a rose by any other name is still a rose.' "

"It sounds like she just won't accept responsibility."

"Exactly," Chris replied. "She's as much a child as my kids. More so. Totally egocentric. She was pampered by her parents, especially her father. He gave her everything, including an enormous trust fund. She has enough fuck-you money to finance all the whims she could ever dream up in a lifetime. But she doesn't have the slightest desire to be a parent. That's what hurts the most." Chris paused, then frowned. Diana gently caressed his hand. He smiled gratefully at her, then said, "It's ironic. The very things I find so repulsive now in Marylou are the same things that originally attracted me to her."

"Have you two talked about this?" Diana asked hesitantly.

"Talked? We've yelled and fought about it for years. Nothing will change her. She likes being the way she is. She thinks I'm the jerk. The ones who suffer are our kids."

"I know," Diana murmured.

"Hey," Chris said suddenly, popping the last of his croissant into his mouth, "let's not get ourselves down."

Diana agreed.

They sat chatting about other less painful things, and drank a second then a third cup of cappuccino. Diana could tell that while Chris was trying to push the frustrations and anger he felt about his family situation out of his mind, their conversation about his failed marriage had in fact put a damper on a day that already wasn't easy for either of them.

"We're the unhappiest happy couple I know," she finally said to him after a long lull in their conversation where he sat staring gloomily out of the window of the bakery.

"Shit! I'm ruining your day, too," he admitted. "C'mon, let's walk around and buy something really silly."

They left the Boulangerie. As they wended their way through the mall, they passed the popular Fourteen Cineplex theaters.

"How about a movie?" Chris said impulsively.

"In the middle of the afternoon?"

"Sure. Why not?" Chris asked.

Seeing the twinkle enter his eyes again, Diana acquiesced.

Lugging all their packages, they bought two tickets and made it to their seats just in time to see the opening credits roll.

Once their eyes were adjusted to the dark, Diana expressed her surprise to see the theater half filled in the middle of the afternoon.

Chris sat with his arm casually around Diana's shoulders. She settled in and crossed her legs, eventually draping one of them over his lap.

As the movie unfolded, Chris almost absently pushed down her tennis sock and began to caress Diana's ankle and bare leg below the hem of her jeans. "That feels good," she murmured, not expecting Chris to unlace her shoe and take it off. When he let it drop onto the cement floor with a thud, Diana looked around to see if the noise had disturbed anyone near them. It hadn't. Then, as he had so often done when they were alone, Chris began to sensually massage her arch, first with her sock on, then with it off.

Diana turned slightly, playfully maneuvered her bare toes into his crotch and began to knead him into arousal.

It seemed to Diana that they didn't need the hilarity of a comedy to lift their spirits. She and Chris seemed to be doing fine on their own.

As if taking up her silent challenge, Chris slipped the hand that was around her shoulder inside her blouse and unhooked her bra. Diana was shocked, but not nearly as much as when he started to play with her nipples.

She felt like a naughty teenager on a hot date as she furtively looked around again to see that while no one was sitting directly on either side of them, there were at least two people several seats to Diana's right, several more two rows behind them, and a couple in front of them. No one seemed to notice their actions.

Feeling more daring now, Diana unbuckled Chris's belt, then undid the buttons on his pants. He turned his head slightly, eyed her silently, and smiled knowingly. She stifled a giggle as she slowly inched her hand inside his jeans.

Chris took his parka from the seat next to him and put it over his lap as Diana maneuvered her hand inside his underwear.

After spreading the jacket across Diana's lap, too, Chris became even bolder. He unzipped her jeans. The sound was muffled under the jacket, but Diana darted yet another self-conscious look to her right, although at this point she was too aroused to care if anyone had noticed what they were doing.

Sitting upright now, pretending to concentrate on the movie, she was really zeroing in on Chris's long fingers toying with her. In. Out. Around. In. Out.

"You'd better stop," she whispered breathlessly, "or I'm going to have an orgasm right in the middle of this theater!"

"That's the idea," he whispered into her ear.

She squirmed ever so slightly, and as her excitement mounted, she let go of his penis, hard and huge in her hand.

She began to shudder, then contract against his fingers. Her feet pressed against the cold floor; her hands gripped the velour armrests; her back almost arched. Christ almighty! she thought, as she began to pulsate uncontrollably from his touch.

When the movie ended soon after, Diana hastily threw her jacket on without bothering to hook her bra, and Chris willed his own erection down so they could walk out of the theater giggling but without letting anyone know what they had been up to.

Still titillated, Diana melded into Chris's form on the escalator ride to the subterranean garage. She could feel him spring to life again as she pressed herself against him.

They had planned to dress up and go to the very chic, romantic French restaurant, L'Orangerie, that night, and if they remained on schedule, Chris would have to hurry to get Diana home in time to change. But after the foreplay in the movie theater, Chris broke all speed limits despite the now torrential downpour to get back home, not to watch her get dressed but to get her undressed.

He cut the engine in his driveway and wordlessly pulled her onto his lap. They kissed passionately.

"Oh, shit!" Chris suddenly exclaimed. "Consuelo's still here cleaning. And I have to have you now."

Diana laughed. "Todd's home, so we can't go to my house, either. We'll have to go park somewhere to be alone. Or we could always go to another movie."

"How about right here?" he suggested, pulling her closer into him.

Shrouded by the driving, pelting rain against the windows of the car, they struggled out of their pants, their hot breath fogging the glass. Chris leaned back against the passenger seat, with Diana straddling him. He groaned, spreading her wide with his hands, putting himself into her. Slowly, slowly, she slid down on him until he filled her completely. He hungrily gripped her ass, moving her in a friction-filled rhythm that brought them both to a wild climax.

"What an interesting day," Diana said, her face still flushed with passion, as they made their disheveled way into the house awhile later.

"And I feel much better," Chris said happily, buttoning up his fly.

"I should go home and change for dinner," Diana said.

"If you leave me I'll get depressed again," Chris said lightly.

"We're like those two old people in that joke . . . he's walking across the room with his wife hanging onto his leg . . ."

"And the caption says, 'I'm only going to the bathroom, dear!' " Chris finished the punchline for her.

"What are we going to do?" Diana asked.

"How long does it take you to get dressed, anyway?"

"Only ten minutes to throw on my clothes. But I have to take a bath and wash my hair."

"The ten minutes apart I can stand," he said with a grin, "but you can take your bath and wash your hair here. Go upstairs and start the water while I pay Consuelo and get rid of her."

Chris's bathroom was Diana's favorite room in the rustic ranch house. It was more than a bathroom: it had a wood-paneled alcove filled with floor-to-ceiling bookshelves, a space for Chris to write at a window that overlooked his oak tree-shaded backyard, and a specially constructed stone fireplace that looked like one in a hunting lodge. The toilet and bidet were separated from the main part of the bathroom where the sinks and the large Jacuzzi tub were set into a bleached wood floor covered by a tan and white hide rug.

Diana lit a couple of imported scented candles encased in glass and silver holders. Instantly their perfume infused the air.

She turned on the water full force because the over-sized tub would take a while to fill. Diana poured droplets of oil into the water, adding to the fragrant aromas enveloping her.

She disrobed and went to get a towel to wrap around herself. As she took it from the shelf, she eyed herself in the mirror. Her body wasn't perfect, but with Chris she always felt like the most beautiful woman in the world. He had added to her heightened sense of being desirable and sexy, which had begun to flower in Switzerland. It still amazed her that a mere year ago she had felt emotionally and sexually dead. Now, she exulted, she believed she was the luckiest woman in the world. She had the love and respect of a man she loved and respected. Their afternoon delights in the movie theater and the car were a revelation of sorts for Diana —never in a million years would she have felt confident enough to be that daring, that bold, that lustful, with anyone but Chris. He allowed her most sensual side to emerge. What they shared was an admixture of so many things—together they were playful and mature, silly and serious, erotic and adoring.

Together they were perfect.

Chris joined Diana a few minutes later. Taking her in his arms, he kissed her passionately again. "I can't get enough of you."

"Nor I of you," she purred as she watched him undress, then light the logs in the fireplace. The orange flames cast wonderful shadows across his handsome face and his nude body.

They sank into the swirling oiled bathwater. Reclining into the curve of Chris's body, Diana felt more relaxed and content than she had in years. They talked intermittently, punctuating their thoughts with kisses and expressions of their growing closeness and how sad they both felt that they would be separated by thousands of miles again so soon. Then they just sat entwined, silently enjoying the sensuality of the warm water, their bodies and the vision of the dancing flames and glowing embers.

Going out to dinner was the last thing either of them wanted to do now.

"How about if I make something for us here?" she offered.

Wearing Chris's shirt, which hung down to her knees, Diana padded downstairs. Clad only in his partly buttoned jeans, Chris followed her.

Diana made herself right at home in his kitchen and began whipping up omelets.

Chris watched her dice and chop and whip and stir.

"You amaze me," he said proudly. "Want a gin and tonic? I can make that, at least."

"Sounds great," she said, her eyes looking greener than ever, her skin rosy and glowing.

Chris took two bar glasses out of his cupboard and filled them with ice. He disappeared into the den and returned moments later. Kissing her lightly, he handed Diana her drink. He took a swallow of his and put an ice cube into his mouth. "Look at this," he said, sticking out his tongue. His new ice maker made cubes with holes in the middle and he had stuck his tongue through one.

When Diana turned to see what was so funny, he playfully grabbed her and kissed her, slipping his tongue and the ice cube into her mouth and then sucking it sensually back into his own mouth.

"That was interesting," Diana said with a sultry laugh.

"Oh, you like that kinky stuff," he kidded, unbuttoning her shirt and, with his tongue, tracing a slow, icy path down her chest, around her bare breasts, across her nipples, and down to her belly.

She responded to the cold, laughing and shivering and calling him a sex maniac.

"You just keep cooking and don't pay any attention to me," he instructed, turning her around so she faced the chopping block again. He took another ice cube into his mouth and traced a path down her back. When he reached her buttocks, he slipped his cold tongue between her cheeks. The ice melted, leaving little rivulets to cascade down her inner thighs.

"We're definitely perverted—don't stop," she cooed, enjoying every minute of his lusty explorations.

On his knees now, Chris prodded her legs farther apart and cooled her cunt with the ice.

He had gotten her so aroused she couldn't concentrate on anything but the pleasure he was giving her.

"Turn around," he ordered huskily.

She did and he continued to taste her. When Diana was nearly perched above his face, he took another ice cube in his mouth, and this time put it entirely inside her. The cold made her contract, and when he began to pull at her clitoris with his lips, she had successive piercing orgasms. When she caught her breath at last, she pulled Chris upright against her, then with her tongue traced her own path down his muscular torso, taking him finally into her mouth, where she teased him, oh, so slowly. . . .

After dinner, they made languid, cozy love—for dessert—this time in his bed. Spent at last, but still entwined in each other's arms, they fell into a stuporous sleep.

Diana awoke an hour later and lay in bed listening to Chris's even breathing. He even slept calmly, she thought, feeling wondrously in love with this man who had become an island of pleasure and serenity for her.

Chris stirred. Diana crept into the crook of his body. He seemed to sigh with contentment. They slept that way until the morning sun streaking through the windows nudged them awake.

"If I go to the airport it'll be bad luck," Diana said fearfully over a cup of coffee before Chris went back upstairs to dress and finish packing.

"Nothing's ever going to come between us," he said, kissing her fears away.

"Don't say it that way—so confidently. It'll give us bad luck."

"You're the most daft woman I've ever loved," he said, leaving her at the kitchen table.

"Okay, I'll drive," she announced when he came downstairs later with an army duffel bag—his casual excuse for a suitcase—slung over his shoulder.

"Not so fast," he replied. "I've been thinking over what you said. Now you've got me superstitious. I'll take a cab. Or will that be bad luck, too?"

Diana rushed over and threw herself into Chris's arms. He was so much taller that he lifted her off the floor and spun her around. She fought back tears, but without much success.

Chris kissed the salty drops at the corners of her eyes, then set her down and stepped back to take all of her in one last time. "Aloha," he whispered. "That means good-bye and hello. We'll be together again."

Diana glanced back over her shoulder as she went out the door. Chris's sandy hair was still darkly wet. His large gray eyes were misted over with emotion. His arms hung loosely at his sides as though he didn't know what to do with them now that he didn't have her to hold.

Chapter

27

"As soon as I saw you at the . . . at your mother's funeral," Harvey said to Diana, "I knew we had to come here for your birthday."

They stood on the stone patio outside the Bel Air Hotel dining room where Harvey had made dinner reservations.

The mood was romantic. In front of them, a pond with swans gliding across its mirrored surface was softly illuminated by strategically placed garden lights that also cast interesting shadows upward among the dense tropical foliage.

Diana looked at Harvey in his trendy European-style suit and said, "I don't understand."

He reached over and took her hand. She wanted to pull away, but didn't. He looked with his puppy dog eyes into hers. She noticed his hair had thinned out in the front, revealing several of the implant scars; even his carefully brushed curls couldn't hide them. She felt bad for him.

"Diana, this hotel has always held a special place in my heart. I made love to the girl who would become my wife here," he said softly, caressing her hand.

Diana's stomach cramped. She extricated her hand from his.

"And now she's come back to me," he added, sounding as wildly in love as he had when he first proposed to her.

Diana stared at him aghast. "Harvey, what are you talking about?"

"Well, uh . . ." he paused, as though searching for just the right words.

Diana waited, not inclined to help him at all.

"You look like you used to. Better, even."

"So?"

"So, uh. You became a different person when you were fat. Emotionally different, too. Now you're you again," he finished in a rush.

"I see." She hesitated. "Harvey, what if I told you I don't think I was different when you knew me thin or fat?"

"Well, then. We'd disagree. I know what I'm talking about, Diana."

"And that's that?" she bristled. "You're the authority on what's going on inside *me?*"

He looked almost angry for a split second as he stared past her at a duck squawking at another one on the bank. "I have insights." He turned to gaze into her eyes. He smiled, but his eyes were sad. "I don't want to fight. It was just a statement. That's all. It's your birthday."

"At least we can agree about that!"

Harvey laughed. "Let's get a drink inside, shall we?"

Diana needed one. Somehow being with him was feeling like a huge mistake. She felt off-balance, unsure of what he might say next.

They entered a richly paneled lounge that resembled the library of a grand estate; they sat down on a green velvet love seat facing a fireplace filled with glowing embers. Diana furtively placed one of the tapestry throw pillows between herself and Harvey.

"That's a smashing outfit," he said, helping her out of her Escada jacket. "I love the plaid lining," he added.

She nodded, thinking how ironic it was that she was finally wearing the infamous three thousand dollar purchase for a date with her husband —taken in three sizes since she bought it—only now it didn't matter.

"Do you still drink wine spritzers?" he asked, moving the throw pillow to his other side and inching closer to her. Harvey summoned a waiter.

"No," she answered. "I'll have a Tanqueray and tonic."

"Graduated to gin, huh?" Harvey said after the waiter departed.

"I'm a grown-up now, Harvey," she retorted pointedly.

"So I've observed," he said admiringly. "You have a certain sexiness about you now." He paused. "Have I told you how much I like that yellow eye shadow?"

Diana laughed, spontaneously this time. "You are the only straight man I know who would notice such a thing!"

"That's why you love me," he answered with a boyish grin, the smile she would have sold her soul to see a year ago when he looked at her.

"*Used* to love you," she said quietly, looking down at her skirt.

The waiter returned with their drinks. They both sat without speaking until he had departed.

Harvey picked his drink up and clinked his glass against Diana's. "To my Diana."

Her stomach cramped more tightly. "How's your condo?" she inquired.

Harvey told her he hated it.

The conversation came to an abrupt halt then. They sat drinking in silence for a few minutes. He never took his eyes off her. She looked everywhere but at him.

"Hungry yet?" he asked.

"Oh, yes," she lied, feeling that at least if they were seated at the dinner table they could talk about something impersonal and safe like the menu selections.

"I have a surprise for your birthday," he confessed the minute they were seated in the elegant peach and celadon room. Their table was in an alcove with French windows that looked out on the flower-filled patio where they had stood earlier.

"I don't think I want any surprises," she said. "I'm too old."

"You look young to me," he said, leaning across the table to pat her hand. "And very beautiful."

They studied their menus, talking about every item as though they were debating important world events. Still, Diana preferred this to the more precarious waters in which they had been wading earlier.

She relaxed finally, letting down her guard, chattering like a magpie about her cooking classes, her Fernberg seminars, and her private sessions with dieters. Harvey said he was incredibly impressed with Diana's successes, especially after he heard who some of her students and clients were.

"A Who's Who of Valley and west side society," he interjected several times. Had he always been this pretentious? she wondered briefly, feeling embarrassed for him.

When the waiter brought Harvey's first course—oysters Rockefeller —he glanced at his watch, then toward the entrance to the restaurant.

"In a hurry?" Diana asked.

Harvey eyed her with a delighted look. "No. Not at all."

She sipped her drink and watched him eat. Always so fastidious, precise, poised. Serious. In control. She had admired those things about him once. She ached for one small joke; how she missed Chris right now.

Harvey glanced at his watch again as the waiter took away his plate, then returned with their salads.

"Be right back," Harvey said. Without any explanation, he left her with a perplexed look on her face, her chilled fork poised in midair.

When Harvey returned, looking pleased, he ordered gaily, "Go ahead, begin. You shouldn't have waited for me."

He ate his Caesar salad with gusto while she toyed with her wilted spinach.

"Diana," he said over their main courses, "I want to apologize to you for my insane behavior last year."

She dropped her fork; it made a loud clanging sound against the china dinner plate before it tumbled to the floor and came to rest at her feet. She saw Harvey wince but try to keep the smile on his face at the same time; it was almost comical.

She slowly retrieved the fork, wiped it clean, then laid it on the plate. "You had to do what would make you happy, Harvey," she said at last.

"You were smart to take it like that. Some women would be bitter."

"Bitter?" she blurted. It came out almost like a hiss. She held her breath, then managed to say, "I've gotten over how you humiliated me, I'm doing very well with my life now. Why should I be bitter?"

He seemed unaware of the bubbling-up of her rage. "You have every right to be. I was selfish. I behaved like a bastard."

He was undercutting her at every turn. She wanted to poke the tines of her fork into his face, but he was giving her no reason to.

"Oh."

"Look at you. You haven't eaten a thing," he said. He laughed suddenly. "I guess I'm not used to the new you." He looked proud that she had no appetite.

"There's a lot more to the new me than meets the eye, Harvey. I'm not sure you would like her."

"I like everything about you *now*, Diana."

He looked toward the entrance yet again, but this time he smiled and waved. "Here comes your surprise," he said.

Diana turned her head and saw Todd walking their way. He looked uncomfortable in a new sports coat and slacks that were obviously Harvey's doing; she had never seen these clothes before. And even more surprising was the sight of her daughter, Jessica, emerging from behind her brother; she had flown down from Berkeley for this auspicious occasion.

Both of them were grinning from ear to ear.

Diana smiled in spite of herself. And when Harvey jumped up to greet his children, hugging them both tightly and kissing even Todd, she felt her cheeks grow hot and tears fill her eyes.

The conversation at the table picked up. Everybody turned chatty and excited. The Family was together again. Diana felt the camaraderie, the wonderment of four people connected by blood and genes and shared experience.

She even indulged in a chocolate soufflé, which they voted to have instead of birthday cake. Harvey whispered elaborate instructions to the waiter, who returned twenty minutes later with candles in two of the servings, for Todd's birthday was the following day.

Harvey then ordered after-dinner drinks for himself and Diana, and as soon as they were delivered to the table he tapped his brandy snifter with a teaspoon and said, "I have another special surprise for Mother."

Todd and Jessica beamed and looked first at Harvey, then at Diana in anticipation. She reflected their happiness with shining eyes of her own. Harvey had indeed found the one thing that could still connect them happily—their children.

He took a small box out of his jacket pocket and handed it to Diana. She hesitated. "Take it, Mother," Jessica said, pushing her mother's hand toward Harvey's.

He placed the box in Diana's palm. "I love you," he said.

Diana felt some of her salmon rise up. She noticed how anxious Todd had become. She forced herself to look at Harvey and smile.

"Open it, Mom," Todd urged.

She untied the white ribbon, then removed the foil paper. The box was from Tiffany's.

She thought of the vitrines filled with jewels she couldn't afford in the lobby of the Palace Hotel in Saint Moritz; she thought of Chris making love to her and telling her they would meet again. She felt as though her neck were in a noose and it had tightened suddenly, and her whole life was passing before her.

Shaking off the urge to gag, she opened the box and took out a lovely diamond and emerald ring. A simple band of baguettes, it was tasteful and expensive—and serious—like everything else about Harvey.

A little card accompanied it.

"Read it out loud, Diana," Harvey prompted.

She glanced down and in a choked voice said, " 'I want to come home. Will you have me? Harvey.' "

She saw the pleading look on Jessica's face. Even Todd, who she knew adored Chris, wore the half-fearful, half-hopeful stare of someone who is afraid his mother will let him down at the most important moment of his life.

And Harvey. He looked positively radiant; he looked downright young again, like the man who had taught her to love that night so many years ago in this very hotel.

She broke into tears. Then she laughed. Then she excused herself from the table, ran to the ladies' room, and threw up.

Composing herself, she shakily made her way back to her family and told them she was so taken by surprise that she didn't know what to think right now. She needed time. Too much had happened to just say yes.

Thankfully, Harvey agreed.

But Todd and Jessica became terribly subdued, and Diana felt intense pressure to come through for them.

It must be midnight, Diana thought as she heard the faint sound of church bells ringing in the distance. When it was very still, as it was tonight, she could hear them sometimes even though the church was over a mile away.

She was doomed, of that she was certain. If she went back to Harvey she could only envision herself becoming one of the walking dead; if she ran away, she would be condemned by her children.

She loved her son and daughter more than anything else in this world, even more than herself.

They wanted this reconciliation. She had seen it clearly in their beaming faces at dinner. Even now she could hear their whispering voices coming from Jessica's room across the hall. She didn't have to be clairvoyant to know what they were talking about.

Diana nervously paced the length of her bedroom, still fully clothed although Harvey had dropped her off more than an hour ago.

There would be no sleep tonight. Maybe not ever again.

She sat down on the edge of her bed and picked up the phone. Carol and Billy were in Puerto Vallarta. She had to talk to Carol. But realistically what could Carol advise her to do? She was Diana's best friend, but Diana knew in her heart of hearts that Carol wouldn't want to be thrust into the middle of this decision. Diana cradled the receiver.

If only her mother were alive. Diana felt the intense loss of her mother's understanding eyes and loving arms at this moment. As she paced the room again like a caged animal, she tried to look inward as Chris had told her to do, but when she tried to dredge up her mother's infinite wisdom, all she could hear was Betty telling her that Harvey wasn't such a bad husband, and he was the father of her children. Think of the children.

Diana sank back against the headboard of her bed now, feeling drained and empty.

She stared straight ahead, her temples throbbing.

Jessica and Todd.

What about Diana and Chris?

What about Harvey? He had confessed his sins—his affair, his need to sow his middle-aged oats—and he had learned that family was everything.

Jessica and Todd.

Again she thought how she loved her son and daughter more than anything in the world, even more than herself. She ached for Chris—the sillinesses they shared, the way he looked at her when they made love, the smell and feel of him.

Diana picked up the phone again. She hesitated, then placed a call to Chris's ranch in Kona.

His daughter Meg answered and seemed genuinely happy to hear Diana's voice. Diana's heart spilled over with sadness—how could she even be thinking of ruining her own children's happiness? "Is your dad home?" Diana asked.

"He's in Oahu tonight," Meg said, explaining that Chris had to attend a dinner party for a general at Schofield Barracks, where Chris's series was filmed, and he wouldn't be back until the next morning. "But I have the number where he can be reached," she offered.

"Oh, no. I don't want to bother him there," Diana said. "Well . . . maybe I'll take the number anyway."

Meg rattled off the number almost faster than Diana could jot it down on the pad on her nightstand.

She hung up and sat staring at the number. It was only nine o'clock in Hawaii, certainly early enough to call Chris.

There was a timid knock on her bedroom door.

"Come in," she said.

Todd and Jessica, both in what they called their sleeping clothes—old ratty cutoff sweats and T-shirts—stood shyly at the entrance to her room. "Can we come in for just a minute?" Jessica asked.

Diana marveled at how much Jessica looked like her now. Their eye color and even the shape of their faces were identical. She had worried about Jessica's tendency to gain weight, but realized now that she had stopped thinking about it when she licked her own weight struggle. Diana sensed that when Jessica was ready, she, too, would adopt Diana's diet.

Todd looked frightened as he walked over to Diana's bedside and stood there with his hands dangling at his sides. "Mom," he said seriously, "me and Jessica have been talking."

"I know," Diana replied, too drained to correct her son's grammar.

"And we want you to know, Mother," Jessica added, walking to stand next to her brother, who for the first time in their lives now towered over his sister. "As much as we want you and Dad to get back together, no matter what you decide we'll still love you."

Diana was too choked up to speak. She held out her arms and both her children rushed into them. The three of them sat hugging.

"One more thing, though," said Todd, the first to break out of their three-way embrace. He stood up and stepped back a pace, putting a greater distance between himself and his mother. "I really hope you decide to go back with Dad. He's very unhappy without you. And I miss him."

Todd turned and left before Diana could reply. Jessica stood, too, kissed Diana, and the started to cry. She said she also hoped Diana would forgive Harvey and let him come home.

Diana forced herself to get up and undress. She washed off her makeup and eyed herself critically in the mirror. She thought she saw a selfish woman reflected there. Was that what she had become in the past year? Self-centered, self-involved? As bad as Harvey? Thinking only of her own pleasure?

Wasn't family everything?

She stepped into her nightgown and slipped into bed. She lay on her side with the light on, staring at the paper with Chris's phone number on it.

She began to shiver as she placed the call. A woman with a strong southern accent answered the phone. "Y'all hold on, now, I'll go and fetch him right away." Diana held the receiver as though it were the enemy, suddenly feeling very insecure. She had never asked Chris how he spent his free hours in Hawaii all last year; it hadn't seemed important a few weeks ago. What if he had a date? She saw with acute clarity that his life was going to go on, with her or without her. She had no right to do this to him. . . .

"Diana?" Chris said, concerned. "Is everything okay?"

Just the sound of his voice caused the sobs to rise, making her chest

heave. She couldn't speak; she couldn't catch her breath. "I . . . can't
. . . talk."

"Try to calm down, honey," Chris said soothingly.

"I'm . . . trying."

"Good. I'll hold on as long as you need me to. Take your time."

She continued to cry; she could hear him breathing calmly. Finally
she regained control over her emotions long enough to tell him what had
occurred at the Bel Air Hotel that night.

"Whew!" was all he managed to say.

"Chris," she whimpered, "what am I going to do? I love you . . . so
much." The sobs came again, racking her body until her chest ached.

Chris continued to talk to her, soothing her with words of love.

She calmed down again. "I'm so conflicted," she said. "I want to do
what's right for my kids. You can understand that."

"Of course," he said.

"But what about us?"

"That's something you have to decide yourself, Diana," Chris said
sadly. "I can't do it for you."

"But I want you so much. You said yourself we're best friends."

"What are you trying to say? Try to think this through clearly, Diana."

"I don't know. I'm so confused."

"Diana, why?"

"Well . . ."

"Don't you see, Diana, that if you're confused there must be something in you that really wants to try to make a go of your marriage. It's
what you've wanted since the day he walked out."

Chris's words were like ice water thrown into her face. What he was
saying made her understand clearly for the first time since Harvey cor-
nered her in front of Todd and Jessica why she was having such angst.

She was her mother's daughter after all. She believed in marriage and
family. It was what made her tick. It had always been her raison d'être.
She was mad for Chris, but to give up the love of her family for him would
be to admit that her life had meant nothing.

"Can we still be best friends?" she asked hopefully.

"I couldn't stand seeing you with him, Diana." Chris paused. She
could tell he was trying to hold his own emotions in check now. "Have a
great life," he said sadly, then quickly hung up.

Chapter

28

Another piece of Diana died when she drove by Chris's house and saw a real estate agent pounding a For Sale sign into his front lawn on the day Harvey moved home.

She snapped at Todd for things she had been overlooking for months. She was short-tempered with her new housekeeper, only half listened to her five private clients, and even forgot several key ingredients in two of her cooking class recipes.

Harvey at first seemed oblivious to her foul mood, complimenting her on the dinner she cooked and making small talk with Todd in such a congenial way that Diana began to feel like the Wicked Witch of the West in comparison.

But when he came up behind her in their dressing room and grabbed her ass and she flew out of his grasp as though he were a leper, he finally commented that she seemed a little tense.

A little tense! she wanted to scream. She was jumping out of her skin.

"This is hard on me," she said, standing away from him. "I keep feeling angry, Harvey."

"Oh? You'll get over it."

"Maybe," she said.

"Of course you will."

"But I've suffered through so much."

"Now it's over," he said with absolute certainty. End of discussion.

He undressed, put on a new pair of pajamas, brushed his hair, flossed his teeth, then got into bed with a thick oral surgery journal. Diana lingered in the bathroom.

When she finally came into the bedroom, he was fast asleep. Thank God, she thought. She had been worried he might ask her to make love.

She awoke early the next morning to the feel of Harvey's manicured hands between her legs, stroking her. He was nude and aroused already. He went through his routine—she knew every sexual move he was going to make seconds before he made it—and then climbed onto her and pushed into her.

She felt him pump, and she heard him groan. Some part of her tried to be generous, loving, even enthusiastic. But the desire wasn't there. Every intimate sound and murmur he emitted only made her feel sadness —and rage—for what could never be again. Every thrust of his pelvis only made her feel more numb, as though her sexual parts had died, too, the day the moving van brought back his things. She wasn't even aware when the first tears began to glide down her face, but by the time he grunted with his final spurt of satisfaction, she knew this reconciliation was not going to be easy.

"That was great!" he murmured, getting up immediately to take a shower.

Diana was almost repelled now by how fastidious he was about sex and its messy aftermath. She lay on his side of the bed, feeling like a naughty child as she deliberately left her legs spread apart, letting his semen drip, drip, drip out of her onto the sheets. She half hoped they were ruined; they were his favorite sheets, the last pair they had, and the manufacturer had stopped producing them.

How could she be so horrid? Her husband loved her; he wanted to make love to her in the morning before she brushed her teeth!

She got up and wandered into the bathroom. "Come in the shower with me," Harvey sang out when he saw her.

That would be too painful, she decided, recalling the passion she and Chris had shared that way. "Got to get to work on the book," she said.

"Make my favorite breakfast first?" he asked.

"Sure," she answered apathetically.

She watched him eat and couldn't wait until she was alone in the house.

"You okay, Mom?" Todd asked quietly after Harvey had gone and again just before he left for school.

She eyed her son. He sees through me, she thought. "Of course I'm fine," she protested with forced gaiety, daring him to question her sincerity.

"Good," Todd said, accepting her at her word. He then darted out of the kitchen in his usual rush to beat the tardy bell.

Carol stopped by for a quick cup of coffee on her way to the office. Diana was abrupt with her, saying she was in a rush to get to one of her cooking classes and after that to a seminar at Fernberg's office.

"It's not working, is it?" Carol asked as Diana walked her out to the car.

"It's okay," Diana replied dejectedly, avoiding Carol's eyes. "I plan to make this marriage work. It'll take time, that's all."

"I hope you convince yourself better than you're convincing me," Carol said sympathetically, then drove off.

After a hectic afternoon, Diana returned home to find an important message on her machine. Mr. Binghamton from Jupiter Candy Company was finally getting back to her. She glanced at the clock; it was already eight on the East Coast. She would have to wait until morning to reach him.

Harvey phoned then to tell her he'd be late for dinner. Diana reacted viscerally to his words; she realized that however innocent his activities were now, she didn't trust him. Resentment rose up in her like bile.

The intensity of her feelings made her agitated. She poured herself a glass of wine and went into the family room. She turned on the television news and sat staring at it. People were suffering all over the world.

The phone rang again. It was Rodney Carter. He missed her. He wanted to know how she was recovering from her mother's death. He wanted to cheer her up, to make her laugh, to see her again.

"I have an invitation to a formal dinner party this week," he said, "and you're the only one I want to take." He rushed on before she could get a word in edgewise, "I've got a breakfast meeting, but I'll send a car and driver for you at eleven, and we'll meet at my airplane. We could be in D.C. by eight. We wouldn't even be too late for President Bush's reception line."

"Dinner at the White House?" Diana murmured.

"I can be away only for the night. Or if you prefer, we could fly back and sleep on my plane," Rodney said. "That way, Todd won't even miss you. I'm going to try to reform my ways for you—"

"Rodney, stop," Diana nearly shouted. She told him she couldn't see him again. "I've reconciled with my husband." The words nearly stuck in her throat.

He was hugely disappointed, but he gamely said he admired her for her gumption to give "the lucky guy" another chance.

She had drunk a second and a third glass of wine by the time Harvey came home.

He stood in the kitchen watching her try to navigate while tipsy, and he remained astonishingly patient with her even though she ruined the entire dinner and angrily threw it into the garbage.

It was Todd who sent her up to her room in tears when he sauntered in during the worst of her tirade and exclaimed, "Mom, what's *wrong* with you lately?"

She barricaded herself in her bathroom until Harvey gave up trying to reason with her. Then she climbed into bed and buried her face in her pillow to muffle her sobs. She cried herself to sleep and didn't hear Harvey slip into bed next to her.

"Diana?" he whispered several times until she awoke.

She deliriously thought it was Chris for a moment, then realized it was her husband. "Huh?" she answered.

"You're going to be all right," he said in a strained voice.

"I'm not so sure, Harvey," she whimpered.

He turned away from her then. Grateful to be left alone, she rolled onto her other side. They fell asleep, hugging the opposite edges of the bed.

"I have a terrible headache," Diana mumbled when Harvey reached for her early the next morning.

"That's because you're tense," he murmured. "You have knots in your neck and shoulders," he announced.

"Ouch!" She winced when he tried to caress her. "Please stop."

He let go of her and disappeared into the bathroom.

She lay on her stomach, face pressed into her pillow, trying to will the pulsating pain away. Her head felt as if it might explode.

"Don't bother to make me breakfast this morning," Harvey said, leaning over to brush the top of her head with a kiss before leaving for work. "You just get rid of that headache."

"Thanks for being so understanding," she murmured.

"If you're sick, you're sick," he said unemotionally, then left.

Todd came in and kissed her gingerly. "It was the wine," he said as he walked out.

She wished he were right. Cut out wine, get rid of the headache. But she didn't believe the wine had caused this much pain; she knew without being able to frame the thought that she was like a pressure cooker right now, filled with conflicting emotions, and it was going to take all the control she had to keep them all inside.

She fell back to sleep and awoke at ten. Not only did she have a late afternoon cooking class to prepare for, but she had wanted to call Binghamton first thing in the morning. Now it was one o'clock in Maine, and who knew where he would be?

She dragged herself out of bed, took a long shower, letting the spray of water hit her face full force. The pain in her head began to ebb.

She dressed and went downstairs. She made coffee, then called Jupiter. "Mr. Binghamton, please," she said. "Diana Lowe returning his call."

She was put through immediately to the same assistant with whom she had spoken almost ten days before. "He's at lunch," the young man told her.

"I'll be home for another two hours," she explained. "Then he can reach me at this number." She gave the man the number of the Gold Grill.

She spent an hour trying to write the third chapter of her book. She couldn't concentrate and put it away. She recalled how Chris had wandered around the neighborhood on those days when his creative juices temporarily dried up. His house hadn't sold yet; knowing that perked up her spirits.

She arrived early at the Gold Grill and set up her demonstration table on the patio, her mind on the phone call that hadn't come through yet.

Students trickled in, finding seats, going over the photocopies of Thanksgiving recipes they would be learning today. The mood, as always in Diana's classes, was festive. She managed to keep her personal problems and the pain they had caused her hidden for the two hours of her classes. Except for the time right after her mother's death when she became tearful while teaching, Diana presented an image of a happy person in control of her life.

Binghamton's phone call came in the middle of Diana's preparation of the nonfat crustless pumpkin pie.

Binghamton sounded aloof as he told Diana that although her idea had merit, at this time the Jupiter Candy Company was not prepared to change back to the old recipe. He was uncommunicative when she asked him if he had taken her idea all the way up through the company's structure to the top. There was little Diana could say to counter him; it was clear to her that his mind was made up.

She returned to her students and tried to resume the cooking lesson, but she couldn't hide from them this time her acute feeling of defeat. She surveyed the group before her, all people who counted on her to show them the way to a healthy low-fat life that would also make them look better. All of them had taken her advice about candy—about Three Amigos—and she had failed them. Suddenly she couldn't go on.

She took a deep breath, then explained in detail what she had been going through in the past few weeks since she found out about the change in Three Amigos. She also told her students she feared her diet book contract would be canceled as a result of her failure to convince Jupiter Candy Company of the marketability of their candy as a low-fat alternative.

One of the students, Ben Peters, raised his hand. He usually attended the early morning class, but today he was making up one he had missed.

"I've got an idea," Ben said. "Why don't we help you?" Diana eyed him questioningly. "I'm a press secretary," he explained. "For Supervisor Dealey. I work in the political arena, but I don't see why we couldn't use some political tactics here."

"What do you mean?" Diana asked.

"Grass roots stuff—the way the public convinced Coca-Cola to bring back Coke Classic. We could circulate petitions. Things like that."

Nancy Gumbel, Diana's most avid fan, was also in the class. She said, "I love the petition idea. Diana, we could get all your students involved. We could get the exercisers involved. Why, we could even get the girls at Stony Ridge, who adore you, involved. We could—"

"We can get the whole county involved!" one woman shouted enthusiastically.

"How about the whole *country?*" another woman blurted with a little accompanying twitter.

Nancy Gumbel said, "Why don't we form a committee this minute? Who wants to start a petition with me?"

Several hands went up.

"Good," Nancy said. "Yesterday Coca-Cola, tomorrow Three Amigos!" she shouted.

Diana overheard one lady up front stage-whisper sarcastically to her friend, "Nancy must have been a cheerleader in high school."

After the cooking lesson, the self-created Petition Committee stayed on to plan strategy with Diana. The students would set up shop in front of all the local supermarkets, using Diana's cooking class students, her Fernberg seminar students, and her girls from Stony Ridge. They would also try to enlist Todd's football team and all the other athletes at his high school.

Diana brought them back to her house to continue their meeting when they were forced to leave the restaurant to make room for the evening rush.

Harvey came home awhile later to find his study filled with strangers. The committee was hard at work, and Diana had completely forgotten about dinner. With great enthusiasm, she explained the situation and asked Harvey if he would take Todd out to eat.

"No more headache?" Harvey asked coolly.

"All gone," Diana replied brightly.

"You look all recovered," he said. "Your eyes have some of that sparkle in them again. But don't do anything foolish," he warned as he left with Todd.

Diana rejoined the group, unable to shake off Harvey's final words and the tone of his voice. It was astonishing to her that in one short sentence, he could still undermine her, still make her feel insecure, still make her doubt herself, still make her feel stupid and silly.

But sometimes a crusade—even a silly one—transcends the one who started it and it takes on a life of its own.

Chapter

29

" 'Housewife Goes to War with Jupiter!' " This is astonishing, Diana thought, muttering the headline of the *Los Angeles Times* story about her. By the time she finished reading the View section's two-page lead article, she was finally becoming convinced that the media coverage of her petition drive might lead to a victory over the candy company.

When Ben Peters had called Diana to say he had written a press release that had been picked up by the wire services for transmission to all the news planners in the county, Diana had had no idea what that really meant. She had expected no response at all. In fact, Ben had created a wonderful monster, for that first day of the petition drive had been a slow news day, and just about every local television station and at least three newspaper reporters had shown up to interview Diana at Gelson's Market in Encino where she had stationed herself to collect signatures.

Once the shoppers saw television cameras, they became intensely interested in the petition. People were falling all over themselves to sign the sheets of paper that would be sent to the Jupiter Candy Company to demand that the confectionery company bring back the low-fat chocolate bar.

One local television station and two radio stations carried the story on their five, six, and ten o'clock newscasts. All treated the report with some levity, and some of them began to refer to Diana Lowe as the Candy Bar Lady.

That weekend Diana's warriors collected five thousand signatures at markets, health clubs, and movie theaters all over town.

During the succeeding week, Todd's football team and other athletes from his school, Nancy Gumbel and her cooking class contingent, and even Sean Gumbel and her friends from Stony Ridge collected ten thousand more signatures.

Ben Peters put out another news release. More cameras and reporters showed up to cover this "most interesting phenomenon."

Reuters picked up the story, as did Associated Press. Tom Brokaw closed his nightly newscast with a wry comment about the suburban housewife crusader in Los Angeles, the Candy Bar Lady, who had gone to war with Jupiter over the fat content in the new Three Amigos. "It's nothing to Snickers over," he said just before signing off.

Harvey was not amused.

The next night he stormed into the house. As usual, dinner was not on the table; it wasn't even in the first stages of preparation. Diana was on the phone talking to a reporter from Lompoc, and Todd was poring over a slew of petitions.

"Get off the phone," Harvey demanded.

Diana looked at him impatiently. She put her hand over the mouthpiece of the phone and said, "Ssh! One minute."

Harvey stood with his hands stuffed into his pants pockets, glaring alternately at Diana and Todd. Todd kept his head bent over, looking intently at the papers on his lap.

At last Diana finished her interview and cradled the receiver. "What's the matter now?" she asked in a tired tone.

"You're the matter!" he bellowed. "Do you know what you're doing to me with this . . . with this publicity stunt?"

Diana eyed him blankly.

"Well, answer me, dammit!" he said.

"What does my petition have to do with you?" she finally replied, her voice a near whisper. She was certain if she spoke up she would begin screaming at him.

"You're my wife. If you act like a deranged lunatic and take on a billion-dollar company over *candy*, it reflects on me."

Diana looked aghast and couldn't reply. She noticed Todd eyeing her, waiting to see what she would do.

"That billion-dollar company *makes* candy," she said at last, her voice rising a few decibels as she became more agitated. "What else would I be taking them on about?" Harvey started to answer, but she interrupted him. "And as for being your wife," she said, beginning almost to pant, "I can do something to solve *that* problem."

"Mom," Todd interjected, his face draining of color, "don't say that."

"Shut up, Todd!" Harvey spat. "We're finally getting to the bottom of this. So, Diana, you're feeling pumped up, huh? So sure of yourself. You make me sick. Jesus! Don't you know what kind of a buffoon you really are?" He paused, rocking forward then back on his heels. He sneered and spat, "Well, I'll tell you."

"Don't shout at me," Diana warned.

"Dad!" Todd pleaded.

Harvey turned his fury on his son, standing over him menacingly, his fists clenched. "If I have to tell you to shut up one more time—"

"Harvey, control yourself," Diana pleaded, getting to her feet.

"How can I when I'm married to a buffoon? People have been coming up to me snickering, laughing at *my wife* and her ridiculous crusade over fucking candy bars. 'How's the Candy Bar Lady?' they ask with a wink. Do you know how that makes me feel? Do you? Do you!"

Diana stood speechless now.

"It makes me feel humiliated. Yes! Humiliated. And now you've gotten our son—*my* son—involved in your lunacy."

"It was my choice," Todd said bravely. "I wanted to be the head of my school's petition drive."

"You see what you've done, Diana?" Harvey said, a spray of saliva flying out of his mouth and landing on the front of her blouse.

They both looked at the wet spot; neither said anything.

Diana thought he would have hit her if she had done that to his shirt.

"You see what you've turned that boy into?" he continued, working himself into a lather. "A lunatic like you. He actually thinks that what he's doing is a good thing. That this action is worthy of his time. He should be studying his math, not standing on street corners like a kook!"

"But, Dad—"

Harvey spun and glared at Todd. "Well, as of today, as of this minute, you are *forbidden* from being part of your mother's insane crusade. And if I ever find out you've disobeyed me, I'll take away your car. Forever."

Todd's eyes filled with tears. He put the petitions down on the floor at his feet and got up from the easy chair. Physically he towered over his father now, but his psyche was much smaller. He didn't have Harvey's acerbic eloquence, and he was powerless in the face of his father's verbal attack. He stood, not knowing what to do, where to turn. He eyed Diana for some sign.

"Harvey, you can't do this to your son," she said.

Harvey glared at Diana triumphantly and spat, "Looks like I just have."

"I want a divorce," Diana said.

"So you can go back to that slob Chris Berry? Is that it, Diana?"

"Leave him out of this, Harvey." Diana's face paled, her hands shook, her voice trembled as she said, "I'll probably never see him again. It's you I can't go on with another minute. You're a despicable, unpleasant, ungenerous man. I won't be bullied by you another second. And I will never let you treat our children with such disrespect again."

"Mom, it's okay," Todd said. "I don't need to be involved." He ran from the room.

"You've done it now, Diana," Harvey said.

"Don't turn this argument upside down on me. I won't let you get away with that tactic again."

"You'd better think about what you're saying. If you continue making me look like a fool in front of my colleagues, my patients, even my own children, I will never forgive you."

He stormed out of the study and left the house. She heard his car screech down the long driveway. As distraught as she was for herself, as angry as she felt about the injustice of Harvey's attack, she still thought of Todd first.

She found him lying on his bed crying, his face blotchy. She sat down next to him and rubbed his back without saying anything. He stopped crying, but refused to look at her.

Diana looked around his room. He was still such a mixture of little boy and maturing young man. On the floor was a collection of toy soldiers he had started collecting when he was six years old. He still played with them from time to time, when he wasn't busy with his Nintendo games. Next to the toy soldiers was his new tennis racket. On his desk was a jar full of rubber dinosaurs, and tacked up behind it was a centerfold from *Penthouse* magazine. Above his bed was a framed poster of a red Lamborghini.

"Honey," she said softly. "We have to talk."

Todd shook his head, but he turned to look at his mother.

"We have to," she insisted.

"I don't want to be the cause of you and Dad getting divorced," he said sullenly.

"You could never be the cause of something like that."

"But you were fighting over me."

"You and a million other things all at once. Todd, I don't understand your father. Maybe I never have."

Todd sat up and said, "We're not a happy family. I always thought we were."

She had to reach up to put her arm around his shoulders. He leaned against her.

"I'm real sad," he said. "Like something's cracking inside me."

"Me, too. I so wanted your dad and me to work. I don't know now."

"Is he coming back? I heard him drive off."

"Don't know." Diana sighed. "But I have to get back to writing and talking to my committee people. Want some dinner first?"

She stood up and gazed with sad eyes down at Todd. He shook his head and lay down again.

"Not hungry," he mumbled, closing his eyes.

"Well, when you are, just tell me. I'll be in the study."

She sequestered herself behind closed doors, but she did hear Harvey come home. She heard Todd race down the stairs to greet him. She heard their muffled voices in the kitchen. She kept on working.

"Coming up to bed?" Harvey asked at midnight.

He was in his pajamas and his face was freshly scrubbed. She supposed he had already flossed, too. He looked as if he wanted to be friends again.

She didn't have the energy even to try. "Nothing's different," she said to him. "This marriage is dead."

"I see," he replied. "I don't plan to leave again," he said as he turned to go upstairs.

Despondent, lonely, aching for Chris, whom she felt she had no right to call, Diana turned back to her work. It was the only thing that seemed to distract her from her troubles now.

She slept in her clothes on the couch in the study. She wasn't certain, but she thought she saw the first light of day force its way through the shutters just as she closed her eyes.

She dreamed she was in her rose garden in the backyard. Her gardener was with her and they were admiring a white sac that hung suspended from the largest oak tree on her property. The sac was brightly painted, like a Chinese lantern, in vibrant reds and yellows and greens. Suddenly the bottom of the sac began to pulsate; it opened and a huge hairy spider crawled out. Diana jumped back and stuffed her hand in her mouth to keep from screaming. "Don't worry. It's a harmless spider even though it looks scary and poisonous," the gardener told her. "But I hate seeing it," Diana replied. "What if it touches me?" He told her it wouldn't, but then a second spider emerged, much bigger than the first and began to crawl even closer to Diana. "Oh, please, kill them," she begged the gardener. "Not necessary," he said in a soothing voice. "If you want to get rid of them, just tell them to crawl back into the sac; they will listen to you." "They will?" she said, amazed that spiders would listen. Then she was overcome with fear again. "But the sac has been ripped open by their emergence," she said to the gardener. "How can I be sure they'll stay in?" He explained, like a teacher to a slow learner, that all she had to do was tie the jagged opening with string to seal it closed, like a sutured incision. "Oh," she said, relieved. She immediately willed the spiders back into the lovely sac and closed it up as the gardener had instructed. She was standing admiring the sac, marveling at how something so beautiful could have such scary, ugly things in it when a bell began to ring—

Diana's eyes opened. It was the phone ringing on the table next to her head. The content of her dream flashed disturbingly across her mind. She wondered what it meant as she glanced at her watch and saw that it was seven in the morning.

She sat up, rubbed her eyes, smearing mascara around them. She looked like a raccoon. "Hello?" she said.

"Diana Lowe, please. Guinivere Wineburg speaking."

"Guinivere?" Diana replied. "It's me."

"Hope it's not too early to call," Guinivere said. "It's rather important."

"Oh, what can I do to help you?"

Guinivere sounded troubled as she said, "I saw you on the news. Tom Brokaw."

Diana felt her face grow hot. "That was rather a shock." She laughed.

"I'll say," Guinivere replied. "Why haven't you told us what's been going on with your book?"

"Well, I, uh." She paused and started again. "You see, I didn't want to bother you with this until it was settled. I guess things have mushroomed way beyond what I ever expected."

"And *is* anything settled?" Guinivere asked.

Only my marriage, Diana thought, the full force of last night's encounter with Harvey hitting her again. "Not with Jupiter," Diana admitted. "The jury's still out."

"Diana, Beecham Press is still behind you. But if the jury comes back with a negative verdict, I'm afraid we'll have to pull out. I'm sure you understand."

"I was afraid of that," Diana mumbled. She was glad she had not spent the first installment of her advance. "If Jupiter doesn't put the low-fat candy bar back on the market, couldn't we stress the allergic-to-fat aspect of my book? I mean, it's as important, if not more important, than the candy bar."

"True, true," Guinivere said, sounding as curt and as impatient as Prescott Dickson. "But it just doesn't have the same hold for our people here. It just doesn't *sing* for us, if you know what I mean."

"Just keep writing," Alison Rifkin counseled when Diana called her to pass on the news that Beecham wasn't so excited about her diet book anymore. "Put them out of your mind until you know for sure what Jupiter is going to do."

"I think Harvey and I are through," Diana said before she hung up.

"You sure?"

"As sure as I've ever been about anything. But he won't leave the house. He's already told me that. My life is becoming a pile of manure."

"That's even more reason to keep your nose to the grindstone," Alison said.

Diana called Carol next. "That bastard!" Carol exclaimed. "He really won't leave?"

"That's what he says. At least last night."

"Tell him you want him out," Carol suggested. "Be forceful."

Diana found Harvey in the kitchen making his own breakfast. Todd sat across from him, scowling into a bowl of cereal. When he looked up at Diana, she could see that his eyes were still red-rimmed. He looked subdued and miserable.

"'Morning," she said to both of them.

They grunted.

"Harvey, we have to get the house situation settled."

He took a gulp of his coffee, made a face, and poured it down the drain. "It already is settled," he said. "I'm not leaving my house again. Ever."

Diana exhaled loudly. Todd eyed her, looking intensely interested now in what she might say or do.

"Then I'll have to leave, is that it?"

"As you wish," Harvey answered matter-of-factly.

"I will do it," Diana said.

"Where will you go, Mom?" Todd asked. He looked frightened now.

"Someplace where I can feel loved. Respected. Happy."

"Can't you feel that way with me?" Todd asked.

"Of course!" Diana exclaimed. "You can come with me."

"He goes with the house," Harvey bellowed. "You walk out, you walk out on him, too."

"We'll work this out," Diana promised her son, but he left for school in tears anyway.

Harvey canceled his morning patients; apparently he wanted to stand guard over his things as Diana, with grim-faced determination, packed a few suitcases, mostly with her clothes and mounds of papers connected with her work. When she tried to put the clock radio in her suitcase, he grabbed it out of her hand.

"That stays," he insisted. "It goes with the house."

"Like our son?" she answered.

"I won't dignify that comment with a response," he said with a smirk.

She lugged the heavy valises to her car. Harvey stood watching her from the window of their bedroom.

She hugged her dogs, who licked her face as though nothing were wrong. "I'm going to miss you guys," she whispered. Then she went back inside to get her purse.

"Leave the house keys on the entry table," Harvey said icily.

"Harvey, don't be like this."

"Like what?" he asked innocently.

"Vindictive," Diana replied tiredly.

"Just leave the keys," he said, then turned and walked into his study.

"Tell Todd I'll call him tonight," Diana said to his retreating back. He didn't acknowledge her.

With shaky hands, she removed her house key and left it on the table near the front door.

As she left her street, then her neighborhood, then the city, then the county, the enormity of what she had done began to dawn on Diana. By the time she was halfway to Palm Desert and her mother's condominium, the break she had made with Harvey and possibly with her children hit her with such force that she had to pull off the road because she was trembling so hard.

She realized that she didn't want to go on to Palm Desert; her mother's home would be too painful a reminder of the last really happy days she'd had with Chris before her mother died.

She didn't want to go back to Harvey. The thought of him made her feel physically ill.

But she didn't know what else to do. And there was Todd to think about.

And that was all she did for the next hour as she drove back toward Los Angeles—she thought about Todd. Would he really be happier with both parents in the house even if they hated each other? And what about Jessica? Would she be happy returning for the holidays to a loveless, tension-filled home?

Would any of them be happier expending all their energy keeping the rage between her and Harvey in check, or would they be better off accepting the failure and getting on with their lives?

She suddenly knew what her dream the night before had meant. Wasn't it better to leave open the brightly painted sac and allow the spidery ugliness, the anger, the bitterness, out once and for all instead of stuffing it back inside and trying to pretend it was filled with feelings as beautiful as the outside?

She couldn't go back. Ever.

"Of course you can stay with us, doll," Carol Benton said when Diana called her at her office from a pay phone in Pomona. "As long as you like. The guest house is all yours."

Carol's guest house was located behind their pool at the back end of their property. It was an unimposing structure, unlike their forty-year-old house, which they had completely remodeled several years back. They had left the guest house in its original state: rustic. While there was a certain charm about it—the walls were all thick knotty pine, the fireplace in one of the two bedrooms was basket-weave used brick with a raised hearth, and the red tile floors were partially covered with large multi-colored rag area rugs—there was no heat or air conditioning, the kitchen was barely large enough for one, and the bathroom was even smaller.

Beggars can't be choosers, Diana thought, as she put her suitcases in the bedroom where the Bentons had stored their patio furniture for the winter.

She sat on the couch that would be her bed at night and stared out the window. Carol's housekeeper was tending the garden. The pool man was busy emptying leaves out of the filter, a constant problem for Encino pools because of all the messy oak trees. As he worked, the sun glistened off his sweaty shirtless back. It was going to be a hot day, for the Santa Anas had come up in the night, blown away the smog, and left clear air and balmy weather.

Carol came out of the back door, looking anxious. She disturbed the quiet pace of her workers as she raced around the pool and took the brick path to the front door of the guest house.

She hugged Diana, who stood up feeling awkward suddenly. "Everything's going to be okay," she purred.

Diana clung to her friend. She choked back tears. She couldn't speak. She crumpled into a chair. Carol sat next to her, paused, then said, "Diana, you're upset now. Come into the house. We'll have a glass of wine. Talk over what you have to do next."

"Next?" Diana replied.

"You have to call Webb. Start the divorce all over again. See if you can get Harvey out of the house."

Diana felt too tired to move. "I think I'll sleep for a while," she said.

"Sure. That's a good idea," Carol said softly.

It was hotter when Diana awoke late in the afternoon. The dry, hot wind had increased in intensity. She changed her clothes and walked across the lawn to the main house.

The Benton kids were creating a racket. One was on the phone. Another was screaming at the housekeeper about a pair of missing shorts. The third was making cookies with two friends. Carol was on another phone reprimanding an airline representative. Billy was in and out of the room, asking everyone to quiet down.

Diana took all the happy tumult in and began to cry. Before Carol could get off the phone, Diana had turned and run out of the house.

"Let's walk," Carol said, intercepting Diana at the door to the guest house.

"Leave me alone," Diana begged. "There's nothing you can do. Nothing anybody can do."

Carol retreated, looking crestfallen.

Diana sat sweltering inside the stifling guest house as darkness descended. Still, she made no move to get up. She heard sirens in the distance. She could smell smoke. Tomorrow there would probably be ashes on her car. The Santa Ana winds brought out the firebugs this time of year. The dry brush of the Valley foothills was always a prime target. The hotter it got, the more beautiful the sky became, the more likely it was that someone would sneak out with a match and set whole mountain ranges on fire.

Everything good brought with it something bad, she thought morosely.

Diana fell asleep, then was startled awake by her own thoughts in the middle of the night. If everything good and beautiful brought with it something bad and ugly, couldn't the converse be as true? " 'In poison there is physic,' " she murmured over and over again until she fell back to sleep.

In the morning she called Peter Webb and told him to expect to hear from Harvey's lawyer. She asked Webb if Harvey could stay in the house if she had been there all along.

"It's his house, also," he replied. "You could stay there, too. Both of you could dig in and fight it out."

"Forget that," Diana said wearily. "I'm not going to get embroiled in an acrimonious fight. He can have the house. I don't need it," she said with bravado.

As she got dressed in the tiny bedroom, she thought about her conversation with her attorney; she realized she hadn't been lying to him.

"I don't need a house to be happy," Diana told Carol awhile later.

"Of course you don't," Carol said in a placating tone of voice.

"I mean it!" Diana protested. "Houses don't make you happy. It's what's in them. The people. The love."

"Todd called last night," Carol said quietly. "He wouldn't let us disturb you. He just wanted to know you were okay."

"He's an amazing boy. I better meet him at school and talk to him. I better call Jessica, too."

Carol told Diana she liked seeing the fire in her eyes again. She had been worried about her rambling discourse and her odd state of mind the day before.

"I'm like one of those clowns you fill up with air. You punch them and they fall down, but they always bounce back."

"I'm glad to hear that," Carol said happily. "Because you also got a call from Binghamton at Jupiter, and his message wasn't that great."

"Tell me!" Diana insisted.

Carol handed her the piece of paper on which she had written the note. Diana scanned it.

"So that's that," she said. "At least they've told me the bad news first before making their public statement."

"You gave it your best shot, doll. They're a huge company. It would have been a miracle if they had bowed to your pressure."

"I know," Diana said. "I just hoped . . ."

"You've still got your classes. Students galore. Money coming in. And your book."

"The book deal is out the window now," Diana said. "I better call Guinivere and tell her before she hears it on the nightly news again."

How many times can a blow-up clown get knocked down before the air goes out of him completely? Diana wondered, feeling almost too deflated to move when she had finished with the depressing task of informing the Beecham Press people that she had failed with Three Amigos.

She canceled her private clients' sessions and drove to intercept Todd before he went to football practice.

They had a warm, tearful reunion in her car. She promised to find a place to live quickly, and if he wanted he could move in with her.

"I'd like that," he said quietly.

"I know," she replied.

"I spoke to Jessica, Mom. She said you called when she was out. I told her about you and Dad."

"I'll call her again later. How is she?"

"Sad. Like me."

"And me," Diana said.

"Dad's just angry."

So what else is new? Diana thought. "He'll get over it."

"Maybe."

"I lost my book contract," Diana said as Todd was getting out of her car.

"Oh, Mom. I'm so sorry." He leaned back in and rubbed her shoulder. Then he was gone.

She sat in the car, watching him for a time as he and his teammates practiced in full football gear. In less than a year he'd be out of high school and in college. She suspected he would want to go someplace far away from home. She didn't blame him.

She would have liked to be someplace far away, too. She thought of Chris suddenly.

"Do you think I should get in touch with him?" she asked Carol that evening after dinner.

"Of course I do, doll!"

"After what I did to him?"

"You had to try to make your marriage work. Didn't he say so himself?"

"Still."

"Still nothing! That man loves you. I wouldn't even call him, Diana. Some things have to be addressed in person. And this is definitely one of them."

"Just pick up and go?"

"Yes. Yesyesyesyes. You deserve some happiness."

Diana smiled at Carol. "I do deserve some happiness."

"That's what I want to hear," Carol said with a grin. "There's a plane leaving at nine tomorrow morning. L.A. to Kona—nonstop!"

"With the airline strike, do you think it'll be all booked?"

"I know of a good travel agent who—for a price—might be able to get you a seat."

Chapter

30

Chris was right, Diana thought as she traversed the tarmac to the outdoor baggage claim area of KeAhole Airport—the air in Hawaii was sweeter; the sky was bluer; the clouds were whiter.

She didn't even mind the gusts of hot, sultry wind that swirled around her. It actually felt good after being in the stale atmosphere of an airplane for five and a half hours.

She took out her baggage ticket, then glanced at the piece of paper on which she had written Chris's address. At this moment it was her only link to him, for although she had wrestled with the notion of forgoing a surprise, in the end she and Carol had decided it would be best for her to show up on Chris's doorstep unannounced.

Because the plane had been booked to capacity as a result of the airline strike, throngs of impatient travelers were standing three deep, jostling to be the first in line to claim their baggage from the outdoor carousels at this airline terminal covered only by a thatched roof.

As Diana waited, her nostrils were assailed by the sweet and pungent aroma of all sorts of fragrant tropical fruits and flowers. Several vending stalls near her had orchid leis for sale. Other outlets hawked pineapples.

To add to the generally bustling atmosphere, there were porters and hotel limousine drivers rushing between curb and carousels to locate their fares.

After a brief delay, Diana's suitcase came down the chute; she half dragged, half bumped it against her thigh the short distance to a waiting taxi.

Her driver was a big-bellied Hawaiian who wore a turquoise and orange aloha shirt very similar to one Diana had seen on Chris. Suddenly the reality of what she was doing hit her; she became even more excited than she had been during the flight.

Diana settled against the cracked vinyl backseat of the taxi, enjoying the warm humid wind that blew through the open windows as the driver sped away from the airport onto Highway 19.

The highway paralleled the Kona Coast and cut through a rolling lava-bed landscape. On the ocean side, the hardened lava flows undulated into the sea, where the black color contrasted startlingly with the bluest of blue water.

"It's awhile longer," her driver said, pointing out the exclusive resorts that dotted the coastline.

At last they turned inland and began the ascent up the mountain to Chris's ranch.

"Must be close to the Kohala and Parker ranches," her driver said.

"I think I've heard of Parker," Diana replied.

"Everybody knows Parker. Over 255,000 acres!" he informed her. "Second largest cattle ranch in the world."

"Somehow I can't picture cowboys in Hawaii."

"We've had cowboys—paniolos—and ranches for six generations," he said proudly. "It's true West—only Hawaiian style," he added. "Rodeos and branding irons. No place else is as beautiful. You will see."

Indeed, Diana was beginning to understand why her driver bragged about this ranch land that seemed like some wonderful secret kept from most of the travelers who came to the Big Island. They drove through rolling green pastures, through terrain that included forests of eucalyptus and pine trees.

"I always thought of the Big Island as the home of volcanoes and orchids," Diana admitted when he explained that there were two distinctly different coastal areas to the island—one marked by boulder-strewn deserts and ranch lands with snowcapped mountains where wild boar abounded, the other a rainy, lush, and dense area suited for growing anthuriums, orchids, and sugarcane.

"We're close now," he said suddenly.

Diana's heart began to race. She could feel her blood pulsating against her temples as she took out her brush and ran it through her hair.

The entrance to Chris's ranch was up a narrow gravel road shared by Chris and three other owners. The properties were separated from one another by whitewashed split-rail fences.

Atop the main gate into Chris's ranch was a logo: crossed pitchforks with the name Twin Forks Ranch written above them.

God, he's silly! Diana thought, her face breaking into a smile; she felt her whole body relax.

She got out of the taxi and pressed the button on an electric gate speaker. A man with an accent asked who was there. Diana identified herself as Chris's friend from Los Angeles, and when the gate swung open she hopped back into the car.

They approached the main house on a road bordered by towering eucalyptus trees. Their strong, fresh scent permeated the air.

A Hawaiian houseman, looking perplexed by Diana's unexpected arrival, stood on the charcoal granite steps at the entrance.

She paid the taxi driver, who sped off.

"I'm Diana Lowe," she explained. "Mr. Berry isn't expecting me. I'm sort of a surprise," she added with a shy laugh.

"Oh, I see," he said, smiling now. "I'm Sami."

Diana noticed Sami had a gold-capped front tooth that shone brightly when he smiled. He had friendly eyes and appeared to be in his fifties. He wore a white aloha shirt, white trousers, and jute thongs.

He walked briskly down the stairs and took Diana's suitcase from her. "Let me," he insisted. "Too heavy." Diana gratefully released her grip. "Come in, please," he said warmly.

From the exterior, Diana thought the house appeared more like a Hawaiian fantasy than a ranch house. It was a combination of white plaster and highly polished teak, with wide overhanging eaves.

Inside, Diana's heels clicked on the slate floors of the gallery entry. She was impressed by the dramatic two-story space, which opened onto a skylit domed atrium filled with delicate orchids, dwarf palms, bromeliads, and stocks of ginger.

Straight ahead and down two steps was a living room with one entire wall of glass panels, which were open, giving the sense of living both indoors and out. There was a spectacular 180-degree view; Diana could see lime green grasslands interrupted by stands of dark green trees and, beyond them, the glittering ocean.

What little furniture there was in the living room was built in and contemporary with overstuffed Haitian cotton cushions. Sisal mats partially covered the slate flooring.

"You sit here," Sami ordered, bowing. "I take luggage to Meg's room."

Diana almost told him to take her suitcase to Chris's bedroom, but she decided she and Chris could rectify that minor detail later.

"When will Mr. Berry be back?" Diana asked when Sami returned.

"Soon," Sami said. "He riding. No working this afternoon."

"And the girls?" Diana asked, wondering if Chris was out with his daughters.

"At school. They live there now. Come home next weekend."

"Ah, I see," Diana said.

"Tea or juice, missus?" Sami asked, backing away. "You like to try Mr. Berry's passion fruit special? We make from trees outside."

"That sounds perfect," she said.

Just moments later Diana sat nursing her drink, which Sami had served in a tall, frosty glass, fantasizing about living with Chris in this idyllic setting.

She got up and strolled out of the living room and through the open glass wall to the veranda. Down three steps was a natural rock swimming pool.

Diana kicked off her heels and walked along the perimeter of the pool, skimming the air-warmed water occasionally with her toes, feeling whimsical and free.

An errant rain cloud blew overhead, and a shadow fell across Diana and the water, turning everything darker suddenly. She stood watching the sky as the cloud partially emptied itself on her, the rain on her skin like a gentle tickle; then it passed, leaving her squinting as the radiant sun reappeared.

It had been almost an hour since she had arrived. She meandered back into the house and refilled her glass from a pitcher Sami had left for her. She sat down on the couch. The walls were bare, there were unopened packing boxes everywhere, and the two bookcases at the far end of the room near the fireplace were only partly filled. Chris's personality really hadn't affected this house yet; most of him still existed back on Live Oak Lane.

Diana heard the front door open and shut. Sami was greeting someone. Yes. That was Chris's voice. After a moment of trepidation when her stomach knotted, she put down her drink and bolted excitedly toward the entry hall, calling out his name.

"Diana?" Chris said, hesitating at the top of the steps that led down to her.

Diana stopped when she saw an ominous look enter his eyes. She said, "I know this is a surprise, but—" Diana interrupted herself mid-sentence. She was thunderstruck by the sight of JoJo Jenkins bounding through the entry seconds behind Chris.

"Well, well," JoJo drawled, an almost haughty look entering her eyes as she linked her arm through Chris's in a proprietary way.

JoJo was as beautiful a woman as Diana had ever seen, even when her hair was flyaway and wild-looking from a hard ride. In fact, she looked energized. Her alert eyes were the color of violets, and her famous full lips were parted in an easy, cocky smile. Diana thought that JoJo's pointed chin jutted out now in a faintly defiant manner as she appeared to assess the situation. She leaned in toward Chris, her large breasts, which threatened to burst the confines of an indecently tight T-shirt, brushing his arm.

Diana's breath caught in her throat. She tried to appear lighthearted, but she knew she must look as stunned as she was. *She* wasn't the actress among them.

Chris cleared his throat nervously, looked quickly at Diana, then at JoJo, and said, "JoJo, you remember the woman I was telling you about— uh, my neighbor." He paused awkwardly. "My, uh, friend. Diana Lowe."

Diana wished the floor would open up and swallow her. Only minutes ago she had considered herself the love of Chris's life. Now she had been reduced to "neighbor" and "friend"!

If she was fazed by Chris's discomfort, JoJo didn't show it. In fact she pushed her arm farther through his and she even seemed ingenuously unaware of the bright blush that crept up Chris's neck as he saw Diana's eyes following the enticing movement of JoJo's talented chest against his body.

"Why, Chris, honey, you didn't tell me your neighbor was in town for a visit," JoJo crooned. "Nice to meet you at last. Chrissy's told me so much about y'all," she added with her world-class-beauty smile, the one where just the tantalizing tip of her tongue peeked through her moistened lips.

Diana felt nauseated. What had she walked into? "Maybe I, uh . . ." She laughed nervously. "Maybe I ought to go."

"No! Stay. Stay, Diana," Chris said, his voice sounding unnatural. "You must stay—for a drink at least."

"At least," JoJo sang out, looking more protective of her territory by the minute.

"No, I can't stay," Diana protested.

"Well, I see you've already been served. Isn't Sami wonderful?" JoJo chirped, finally letting go of Chris and sauntering down the stone steps, her dusty riding boots looking perfect on her.

"Yes, he is," Diana replied softly, her mouth going dry on her sud denly. She had never felt more uncomfortable in her life or more mortified, humiliated, and stupid.

Suddenly Chris was standing next to her. "Where's Harvey?"

Diana stepped back. "There is no Harvey, Chris," she said in a near whisper. She sounded anguished as she added, "I've left him."

"I don't know what to say," Chris muttered.

"Well," JoJo said with forced gaiety, "isn't this an interesting development?"

"JoJo!" Chris said. "Shut up. Please."

"I've lost my book contract."

Chris looked stricken now. "I'm so sorry," he finally said. He looked as though he might reach out and pull her to him. Then he changed his mind and let his hands drop awkwardly to his sides. "So sorry. About everything."

"I think I need a drink. A real one," JoJo said. "How about you, Chris? Diana? Scotch? Gin? Cyanide?"

"JoJo!" Chris exclaimed.

"I really have to be going," Diana said and started to walk up the stairs.

Suddenly Chris was mobilized; he intercepted Diana at the top of the steps. "Wait," he begged. "Will you at least talk to me for a minute alone?"

"What's there to say?" she asked.

"We were history, Diana. You went back with your husband." He watched her turn and walk away from him. "What did you want me to do?" he called out lamely.

Diana stopped and turned back toward him again. "At least you could have waited until the body was cold," she said bitterly.

Chris seemed stunned; he stood there saying nothing.

At last Diana broke the tense silence. "Where can I find Sami?"

"In the kitchen. What do you need?"

"My suitcase," Diana said meekly, feeling even more ridiculous and mortified now that Chris knew for certain she had come to stay with him. "He put it in Meg's room."

Chris eyed Diana with compassion, then flew into frenzied action, retrieving her bag himself. "Please stay," he said again.

"I'll need a taxi," she replied icily.

"Where are you going?"

"To a hotel. I guess."

"I'll drive you," Chris insisted.

"No," Diana said with finality.

"I insist," he said stubbornly. "I want to drive you, dammit."

"And I want to take a cab. There's nothing more to say, Chris."

"It takes forever to get a cab up here. Why don't you at least let Sami drive you."

"I don't want anything from you."

"Don't be like this. Let Sami take you. Please."

She relented then, and sat quietly in the passenger seat of Chris's Jeep. As Sami drove out of the gated estate, Diana felt as despondent as she had on the day her mother died.

"Where to, missus?" Sami asked her when they reached the highway.

Diana shook her head. Where did she want to go? She spotted a big lava boulder and thought she might like to crawl under it and die. "Is there a hotel in town?"

"Oh, yes. I take you to town."

The main drag in Kona looked honky-tonk and vaguely sleazy to Diana, but she thanked Sami for the ride and went to the desk in the hotel, where he thought she could get a room for the night.

It was booked.

Part of her was relieved. She realized she didn't want to be here another minute, let alone a whole night.

She hailed a cab, and twenty minutes later she was standing before a ticket agent at KeAhole Airport asking to be booked on the next flight back to L.A.

"Next flight's in two hours," the agent informed her, immediately checking her computer. "Oops! Sold out."

"It can't be," Diana moaned.

"The strike. You know how it is."

"Can I fly through Honolulu?" Diana asked.

That way was out, too. So were all the connecting flights through the other outer islands. "I have one first-class seat available tomorrow," the agent told her.

"I'll take it," Diana said. At any price, she needed to get as far away from paradise as possible.

Diana paid for her ticket and went to the phone booth. She called the Mauna Kea Beach Hotel and found that she could get a room there for the night.

She hailed yet another cab and spent the entire ride in the backseat with her eyes closed, trying to calm down, but she was unable to get the mortifying image out of her mind of Chris and JoJo Jenkins arm in arm, looking like lovers.

"We're here, lady," her driver announced, pulling up at the entrance to the Mauna Kea.

A porter took her valise and she walked slowly into the main lobby. She and Harvey had brought the kids here for Christmas many years before, and the hotel was just as she remembered it: South Seas plantation elegant, with rooms built around a central atrium filled with graceful palms and other tropical greenery flourishing amid waterfalls and ponds stocked with koi.

As she waited her turn to check in, she felt overwhelmed by the happy chattering of hotel guests around her. Being surrounded by happiness right now only made her feel worse. She couldn't stay here another minute. She couldn't stay at any hotel.

Diana stepped out of line and found a porter, who took her suitcase back out to the portico. Soon she was inside another taxi.

"Where to?" the driver asked.

"Anywhere," she said, feeling frenzied and looking wilted. "I'll tell you when to stop."

"Okay, lady. I got the time, if you got the dime."

"At least talk to me," JoJo whined.

It had been hours since Diana rushed out, and Chris hadn't said one word to JoJo in that time. They sat on the veranda at a rattan and glass table, their dinner getting cold. Neither of them had touched the delicious food Sami and his wife had prepared and served to them by candlelight.

Chris eyed her, remaining mute.

"Dammit!" JoJo said, standing up and dramatically throwing her cloth napkin across the table into his face. "What the hell did I do to deserve this treatment?"

Chris laid the napkin on the table. He sat staring at JoJo, then said sullenly, "You're here. That's what you did."

She came to stand in front of him, her legs spread defiantly, her hands on her hips. "Have you forgotten that *you* called *me*? That *you* sent *me* a first-class ticket—one way—and asked me to come and make the hurt all better?"

Chris stood up and strode into the living room, where he settled glumly on the couch.

JoJo stormed in after him. "What did you want me to do?" she said, her violet eyes welling with tears. "*Leave?*"

He eyed her sadly and said nothing.

"Don't do this, Chris. I don't deserve to be treated like a hooker. Every time one of your loves walks out on you, I get the call. 'I need you, JoJo. Come hold me. Make love to me.' And I come runnin'. Do you know why, Chris?"

He eyed her blankly.

"Because, you dummy, I love you," JoJo said, the tears spilling onto her cheeks. "That's why."

Chris looked sick.

"But you don't love me, do you? You only want me when you need me. You make me love you more and more. Then your wife comes back. Then she leaves again. Then you fall madly in love with your *neighbor!* Then *she* leaves you. And I wait like a dumb jerk in the wings for your call. And I come to you every time. Every time, Chris." She began to sob.

Chris pulled JoJo onto his lap. He cradled her, feeling like a heel because all he could think about was Diana.

"Make love to me, honey," JoJo purred.

"It wouldn't change anything," Chris said, releasing her from his embrace. He got up and eyed her sadly. "You're wrong, JoJo. *I'm* the jerk. I had no right to take advantage of you that way. I know that. But I guess I'm a pretty selfish guy sometimes. I know I am."

"You really do love her, don't you?"

Chris nodded. "I didn't know how much until I saw her standing in this room."

JoJo walked toward the hallway that led to Chris's bedroom. "It's gettin' late, honey bun. If you're gonna stop that gal, you better go after her now."

"She'll never talk to me again after this," he said in a self-pitying tone.

"If you think that, Christopher Berry, then you don't know the first thing about that woman."

"What're you going to do?"

"Don't worry. I won't interfere with you and Diana again."

"Thanks," Chris said. "Thanks for everything. I mean it," he said as he charged off to find Sami.

Sami told Chris he had dropped Diana off in the heart of Kona Village at the Kona Lagoon Hotel.

Feeling ebullient now, Chris tore out of the house and drove into town. He went straight to the Kona Lagoon, but Diana wasn't registered.

Dejected but not defeated, Chris stopped to regroup at the hotel's bar, asking the bartender for the names of all the hotels in the area. Fortified with the bartender's list and a potent mai tai, Chris set out to find Diana.

He returned to his ranch at dawn, alone. Diana had disappeared.

"Where's JoJo?" he asked Sami, who looked as if he hadn't gotten much sleep either.

"She gone, Mr. Chris." Sami handed Chris an envelope.

Chris ripped it open and read JoJo's note: "Gone back to Los Angeles. Somehow the idea of smog and traffic and men who are crazy about me sounds pretty good right now. I'll always love you, Chris. But do me one favor—if Diana leaves you again, DON'T CALL ME. JoJo."

"When did she go?" Chris asked.

"Very early. Before sun come up."

Feeling depressed, Chris said, "I'm going to bed."

Diana felt someone shaking her shoulder. Her head snapped back and she opened her eyes. She realized she must have fallen asleep. After still another aimless taxi ride, she had spent half the night like a waif in this uncomfortable chair at the airport.

"JoJo?" Diana said, rubbing her eyes.

"The one and only." JoJo loomed above Diana, looking like a beautiful apparition.

Diana straightened herself in the chair. Her neck ached; so did her back and head. "What're you doing here?" she asked.

"Better yet, honey, what're *you* doin' here?" JoJo replied. "Chris should have found you hours ago."

"What are you talking about?"

JoJo dropped her travel bag onto a chair opposite Diana, then sat down next to her. "Chris and I had it out last night. He can't give me what I want." She laughed, a hollow sound, her face looking sad.

Diana eyed JoJo with a questioning look.

"Love, honey. He can't give me *love*, 'cause he's given it all to you! I know it; he knows it. I guess you're the only one who still doesn't know it."

"But—"

"But nothin'!" JoJo said. "If he's too stupid to find you, then you go to him."

"But I'm leaving on the next flight."

"Y'all actually have a ticket?" JoJo exclaimed.

"The last seat, so I'm told."

"Honey, you're not gonna need it now—but *I* am." Taking a checkbook out of her bag, JoJo asked, "How much do I owe you?"

"No, I owe you! This one's on me." Diana jumped up, handed JoJo the airline ticket, and raced out to the taxi stand.

Chris stirred. "JoJo?" he murmured groggily. "You back?" He opened his eyes.

"No, it's me," Diana said softly. "Sami told me you'd been up all night, so I didn't want to disturb you."

"You didn't go?" Chris said, sounding astonished.

"It's a long story," Diana purred, snuggling her naked body against his. "Do you want to hear it?"

"Later," he said, covering her lips with his.

Chris acted as if he couldn't get close enough to her, nor could she to him. It was as if they had to be inside each other, not just in a sexual sense but actually inside each other's skin. It was almost a crime, Diana thought fleetingly before her senses took over completely, that there were only physical acts of communion they could perform to express the spiritual and emotional bonds they were forging.

They partially came down to earth two days later. Chris had to go back to work in Honolulu. He insisted Diana accompany him to the sets at Schofield Barracks, where they were filming again. She didn't want to interfere, but he couldn't bear to spend his days without her. She was treated like a queen by the cast and crew, including Barbie Mallory, who was now madly in love with Chris's associate producer and who had learned to listen meekly to Chris since the series had debuted to sterling reviews, all of which said that without Christopher Berry's deft touch with difficult concepts, stories, and *people*, there would have been no hit series.

When they returned to Twin Forks to spend the weekend with Meg and Missy, there was a message waiting for Diana. Dierdre Nieuwirth had tracked her down there and needed to talk to her immediately.

Diana called Dierdre at her daughter's home in Dallas. Apparently Dierdre had seen Diana and her candy bar crusaders on television and had followed the story to its unsuccessful conclusion. "I may be able to assist you, my dear," Dierdre warbled. "I have an association with a Swiss candy manufacturer. Maybe you've heard of it—Noedle Haus."

"Noedle Haus!" Diana exclaimed. "As far as I'm concerned, it's only the best chocolate in the world!"

"Well, I agree." Dierdre laughed. "I own a few shares in the company. I'm Swiss at heart, you know. Anyway, I've called Karl Noedle, and the dear man wants to meet with you straightaway. He has an interesting proposition."

"I've gotten used to the idea of you being a lady of leisure," Chris said later that night at dinner as they talked about Dierdre's proposal. "You'd have to leave me again," he added, sulking.

"I know. But I can't stay on here indefinitely anyway. There's Todd. I have my clients, my classes. Even if I don't have the book contract."

"Well, you might even have that again if this Swiss candy company comes through for you. I think you should write it. You could submit it to other publishers through my agent."

Diana smiled at Chris. He had pouted at first, but the more he talked about her career, the more excited he sounded. She pointed this out to him.

He smiled sheepishly. "I know how much it means to you, that's why," he admitted.

"Dierdre needs to meet with me before she goes back to Europe next week."

"I won't stop loving you if you leave," he said. "I promise I won't even call JoJo!"

Diana laughed. "JoJo's the sexiest woman I've ever seen. Now that she's out of your life, I'll admit it. She must have been something in bed!"

"Let's just say sex is sex . . . and then there's Diana."

"How can I leave when you flatter me like that?"

The next morning while Diana lay naked in bed, Chris came out of his dressing room, sat down beside her, and ceremoniously hung a string around her neck with a key attached to it. "This is the key to my house in Encino," Chris said solemnly. "I called and took it off the market. You can live there. Consider it yours. You'll be close to Todd. And that way I'll always know where to find you," he added, attacking her lustily one more time before she hit the road.

Epilogue

five years later

    The pilot's voice came over the cabin speaker, startling Diana, who had been deeply engrossed in a sheaf of papers on the small worktable in front of her.

    "Better buckle up," he cautioned. "We're headed for some turbulence."

    Diana immediately fastened her seat belt. Her chief pilot knew his air pockets; he was the best in the business, and she had been lucky to hire him to fly her around the country in her new Gulfstream II. After Rodney Carter had been forced to let him go because of severe business reversals —something about the junk bonds used to finance his real estate deals plummeting—his former pilot had been inundated with offers, but he had chosen to work for Diana.

    Closing her eyes, Diana settled in for some uncomfortable moments. Still, she mused, occasional trepidation in stormy weather seemed to be about the only turbulence she had encountered since her book, *Allergic to Fat,* had hit the racks four years ago. It had been followed soon after by a cookbook, and Diana's rise in popularity had been like an exhilarating ride on thermals in a glider, soaring higher and higher until she now headed

the eighth fastest growing company in the United States, Allergic to Fat
Industries.

Diana, who had founded the company, oversaw the franchising of
weight and counseling centers throughout the country, with two more
soon to open in Europe. She loved the challenge. In fact, she was now
devoting a hefty portion of her time to workout apparel and frozen food
divisions. Happily, Jessica had recently come aboard; she was now working
for her mother in the marketing and publicity department.

And God bless Carol Benton and her creative travel ideas. She had
put together the lucrative ATF Travel Club for those who wanted to see
the world and not gain weight.

Just the other day Diana had spoken to Todd on the phone. "We've
come a long way since those early days standing at markets getting signatures on petitions," she had reminisced with her son, a mature young man
who was now on the threshold of a three-year commitment to Stanford
Law School.

Todd had responded with mirth, finally able to laugh about those
awful months before Harvey and Diana had separated for good. "Remember how Dad threatened to take away my car if I continued to be involved
in your lunacy?" he asked Diana. How well she did, she had replied. They
spoke without anger about those days, both glad they were long past.
"Now look at you, Mother," Todd had added. "You're a conglomerate and
a celebrity!"

And she was.

If only her mother had lived to share in the excitement of it all.
Would she approve of the new me? Diana wondered.

Not that she was all that different. Thin, yes. Happy, yes. Autono-
mous, yes. When interviewed, she liked to say her life was like a delicious
cake—low-fat, of course—and that the icing on it was Chris.

Ah, Chris. Never intimidated by her extraordinary successes, he had
stayed quietly in the background, busy with his own important projects.
Still, he was always available to give Diana moral support, to encourage
her, and in his quiet yet light manner, to spur her on to become everything she could ever dream of being.

As the jet made its bumpy way down through black clouds toward
the airport, Diana suddenly thought of Harvey. Landings often brought
his image to mind. She didn't know why.

She wondered if she would ever forget him. She doubted it. You can
take the woman out of the marriage, but you can't take the marriage
completely out of the woman. She would always be attached to him just a

little. Always care about him just a little. Always be angry with him just a little . . .

No. Success had freed her, actually. She could be magnanimous toward Harvey at last. He was, after all, the father of her children, she thought as her plane touched safely down on the tarmac. And she wished him well.

Harvey browsed through his closet until he found the jeans he wanted to wear. He yanked them off the hanger, his temper flaring when he saw they had been hung in the wrong section of his casual pants. "Carlos and Sophia will have to go!" he yelled.

Carlos and Sophia were the third live-in couple he and Laurie had hired in the past few months. Harvey insisted they were as inefficient as the other two couples had been.

"What?" Laurie yelled back from the bedroom. She had been ordered to bed five weeks ago by her doctor, and Harvey had bought her one of those sixty-inch television sets to pass the time. It blared now.

"Shut the damn TV off for a second, will ya?" Harvey replied. Although he was trying to be understanding, calm, even patient with his wife of four months, the constant noise of the television on his days off drove him crazy.

Harvey and Laurie had married not long after she had confronted him about his on-again, off-again desire to be with her on a permanent basis and, with admirable dignity and bravery, declared that even if he refused to marry her, she was going to have the babies anyway.

Harvey zipped up his jeans. They felt tight. He had put on a few pounds himself lately, but he knew he could take the weight off any time he wanted. Right now he didn't feel like thinking about it.

He threw on a shirt and walked into the bedroom. Laurie lay on her back, her head propped up by huge throw pillows, her legs elevated slightly by another pillow, to keep the edema in her ankles down. She reminded him of the proverbial beached whale. Her face was so bloated that her eyes were more like little slits than round sockets; her fingers were too swollen to wear the diamond engagement ring he'd given her; her feet wouldn't fit into shoes; and her implanted breasts had mushroomed to frightening proportions.

Being six months pregnant with twins was hard on Laurie's body, but it was hard on Harvey, too. He could barely *look* at her, she was so grotesque.

"What did you say?" she asked, pushing the remote-control mute button.

Harvey stood with his back to the television and vaguely eyed his wife. "I said, our maid and her do-nothing husband are worthless."

"What did Sophia do now?" Laurie groaned, pushing her unbrushed mass of permed curls back off her forehead.

"Hung up my blue jeans with my white pants. Can you believe it? How many times have you told her—"

"At least five," Laurie commiserated, having become as rigid and finicky as her husband about such matters. She flipped through the channels, keeping the sound off. "Oh, look," she said. "It's time for the Daniella Devereaux show. She's doing a week-long thing on diets."

Harvey turned absently toward the screen. "Turn up the sound," he ordered suddenly as the television camera panned the audience and he thought he spotted his son and daughter in the front row.

Laurie instantly responded to his barked command. She tried to adjust her position and grimaced, with an accompanying groan.

"Ssh!" Harvey turned to glare at her for a second. "I thought I saw Todd and Jessica," he said, looking at the screen again.

"Well, it could have been. Their mother's the featured guest on the show today," Laurie said knowingly. "Jessica called the other day to tell me to be sure to watch."

"And you didn't even tell me?"

"Of course I didn't," Laurie replied indignantly. "Look at you. You get crazy every time you see that woman's face."

"That's not true," Harvey protested.

He didn't see Laurie mocking him, since he was now intent on Daniella Devereaux's introduction of his former wife.

"Welcome to our show on diet: The One That Works," Daniella intoned in her silky voice, going on to extol Diana's accomplishments since her first brief appearance on the show as the best-selling author of the book, *Allergic to Fat*. In addition to being founder and CEO of Allergic to Fat Industries, she was presently the chairwoman of the President's Council on Fitness and Diet and spokeswoman for Noedle Haus, the Swiss candy company that manufactured and distributed Sweet Sensations, the delicious low-fat chocolate bar.

The camera moved in for a close-up of Diana. She had never looked more beautiful, Harvey thought grudgingly. She was wearing a simple ecru cashmere sweater and skirt, and she moved with the grace of a gazelle across the stage to sit next to Daniella. Her hair was still vaguely wavy with a silky caramel-colored sheen to it. And when she flung her hair back behind her ears, Harvey noticed she wore simple new earrings and a necklace—large, perfectly shaped South Sea pearls. Her dusky tan showed off her green eyes. Living part of the year in Hawaii obviously agreed with her. Even after all this time, however, Harvey couldn't admit that Chris Berry's constant presence in her life might have a little bit to do with the glow that she radiated.

"She looks older, don't you think?" Laurie commented.

"I guess so," Harvey replied tiredly. Seeing Diana so successful—looking like the hundred million bucks she was now reported to be worth —always sucked the energy right out of him.

"Sophia's bringing me up some salt-free broth. Should I call down and have her bring some up for you, too?" Laurie asked.

"Okay," Harvey said dully, climbing onto the king-size bed next to his wife to watch the rest of Daniella's talk show.

"Yours is the only regimen that has ever worked for me—and I've tried them all," the newly svelte talk show hostess told Diana and the audience after a commercial break. "As you know, we've been discussing those other diets all week—the ones that take your money but don't give lasting results."

"Mine seems to work, Daniella, because it really isn't a diet. Diets are regimens people go on for a short period of time. They lose weight, then go off. Old eating habits rise up, and before you know it—bam! You're fat again."

Diana smiled into the camera's harsh lens, and her sincerity shone right out into Harvey's bedroom—into the bedroom where he had told Diana years before that he needed to get on with his life and find something better out there.

Harvey glanced at Laurie, who was busy filing her nails and only half listening to Diana.

"But why candy?" Daniella was asking Diana after a station break.

"It was important to make my regimen different from all the others. No one ever thought it was possible to eat real chocolate candy and still lose weight. But I proved it *was* possible."

She sure did, Harvey thought; he had to give Diana that much credit.

"I know it's impossible to stay on most diets forever because they're restrictive about the things that people who get fat love to eat. I set out to find low-fat foods that fat people like me could eat and get satisfaction from, and still lose weight and be healthy, too."

"Noedle Haus and you have a new bar out now, isn't that correct?" Daniella queried.

Diana nodded and held up the third new product that Noedle Haus had recently introduced. The camera dollied in for a close-up of the brightly packaged Sweet Sensations chocolate crunch bar that was only twenty percent fat.

"When I was desperate to find the right candy bar several years back, a friend came to my rescue. She's here today. Dierdre Nieuwirth."

The camera located Dierdre in the audience, sitting next to Todd and Jessica, and the stunning woman stood up briefly.

Harvey had heard about Dierdre from his children; seeing her now, he was fascinated in spite of himself. Totally engrossed, he didn't hear the maid enter the bedroom. She tended to walk quietly, being a rather timid woman who instinctively shrank from her new employer's unpredictable outbursts.

"Dierdre has a financial interest in Noedle Haus, and she was the one who introduced me to the president," Diana explained. "It just so happened they wanted to break into the American confectionery market in a big way, and they decided to use a new low-fat chocolate bar as their entrée. As you know, our 'marriage' has been enormously successful."

"Meester, you want soup and crackers now?" Sophia asked in her timid broken English.

Obviously irritated, Harvey rudely barked, "Huh?"

"It's your soup, dear," Laurie said patronizingly.

Harvey took the proffered tray, then flicked his hand, dismissing Sophia. He took one taste, then ignored his food, turning his entire attention back to the second part of the Daniella Devereaux show: "Women Who Diet and the Men Who Love Them."

Harvey chuckled. "This should be interesting. They probably won't have anyone to interview!"

"Oh, Harvey. Really," Laurie said, slurping her soup.

Harvey eyed her disdainfully. "How many times have I told you it makes me sick to hear you eat? I need a mute button for *you*," he snapped.

"Are you trying to upset me?" Laurie asked.

Was he? He really didn't know why he felt so irritated by everything she did today. He shook his head and rubbed his hand across her abdomen. He felt little rippling movements under his fingers. One of his fetal daughters was energetic right now. A rush of affection filled his conflicted heart.

Daniella had two other women and their husbands join Diana on stage. Both women gave testimony about how supportive their spouses had been once they had gone on Diana's regimen.

Then with great fanfare Daniella surprised Diana by bringing out the Emmy-winning writer, producer, director—and heartthrob—Christopher

Berry. Chris had made it back from a trip to the Orient just in time to be on the show.

"What right does *he* have to be up there?" Harvey exclaimed.

"He's Diana's husband, Harvey. When will you accept that she's gotten on with her life?"

Laurie had a point. When was he going to get on with his own life instead of merely sleepwalking through it, going through the motions of living?

"As my own boyfriend has said," Daniella intoned, "he loved me when I was fat, but he admits that thin is better. How do you feel about that, Chris?"

Harvey winced as he watched Chris gaze lovingly at Diana. The chemistry between them was undeniable.

"Before I answer that question, Daniella," Chris said, a playful look entering his eyes, "I have another surprise for my wife."

Diana eyed Chris curiously.

"Diana thinks I've been in the Orient doing research for the screenplay I'm writing. Well, I have been working, but not on my script." He glanced at Diana and smiled like the cat that ate the canary. "This trip was all for her."

"Oh, my word!" Diana exclaimed. "You haven't!"

Chris nodded, looking ever more pleased with himself. He promptly stuck his hand into his jacket pocket and retrieved a miniature calculator on a cord. He ceremoniously put it around Diana's neck. "For you, darling," he said in an intimate voice. "Your very first Allergic-to-Fat Meter."

He turned toward Daniella and said, "This model was made especially for Diana, but our other calculators will be in the stores by Christmas."

Diana's eyes filled with pride as she inspected the dedicated-function calculator. To determine the fat content of a food, she merely had to enter the number of calories and grams of fat and then press one more little button; the instrument would then do the computations. Diana fiddled with it, then began to laugh.

"Let us in on the joke," Daniella Devereaux implored.

"Oh, this calculator is no joke," Diana replied. "It actually will make my regimen as easy as one-two-three. I'm laughing because my husband has taken my idea and added his creativity and unique brand of humor to it."

Diana took the calculator from around her neck and showed it to Daniella and the audience. Chris had had the meter designed to look like a face. The calories and the grams of fat were the eyes, the number pad

was the nose, and the mouth was the percentage of fat. If the fat content
was below thirty percent, the mouth smiled. If the food product exceeded
thirty percent fat, the mouth formed a frown.

"I don't know how Chris does it," Diana said lovingly, "but he manages to turn every endeavor into fun."

Chris took his wife's hand and caressed it gently. "She's much too
modest," he said, building Diana up, as he always did. "She likes to pretend she couldn't have accomplished anything on her own. But I know
the real Diana," he said softly. "She's tough and resilient. She has the
uncanny capacity to turn adversity into profit. And she's an indefatigable
worker. Life's funny that way. Success seems to come by accident to those
who work the hardest to achieve it."

"You can say that again!" Daniella agreed, to resounding applause
from the audience.

"To get back to your question, Daniella," Chris said when the audience quieted down, "I loved Diana when she was overweight. I adore her
equally now. What has always attracted me to her the most is her warmth,
her generosity of spirit, her easy sense of humor. Those traits were as
evident to me in her fat body as they are in her thin body.

"I guess what I'm trying to get across, Daniella, is that it really
doesn't matter to some men if the women they love are fat or thin. To
some men, beauty of that kind is only skin deep. I've known that kind of
beauty. I'm surrounded by it in my business. And I guess that has made
me acutely aware of what is really important in a relationship."

Harvey smirked as he listened to Chris speak in superlatives about
Diana. That prick's a bald-faced liar, he thought gleefully. Someday he'll
make Diana miserable. Someday he'll go gaga over one of those beauty-is-skin-deep honeys, sue Diana for half of her millions, then leave her in that
harsh Hawaiian sun to shrivel up and grow old alone.

Harvey sighed and shut his eyes. He didn't have to hear another
word. The thought of Diana failing at something calmed him. Suddenly
the walls didn't feel as though they were closing in on him anymore.

There was justice in this life after all.